Introducing
# Aita Ighodaro,
## author of
# Sin Tropez

Aita Ighodaro read modern
languages at Oxford
University. While studying
for her degree, she
supported herself by
working as a fashion model
in Europe, where she
attended shoots in
St Tropez and Cannes.
As her own experiences
of life with the rich,
the beautiful and the
jet-set became ever
more extraordinary,
Aita began collecting
the stories that
would work
their way into
her fiction.

*Sin Tropez* is
her first novel.

# Sin Tropez

## AITA IGHODARO

CORVUS

This paperback edition first published in 2011 by Corvus.

First published in Great Britain in 2010 by Corvus,
an imprint of Atlantic Books Ltd.

9 8 7 6 5 4 3 2 1

A CIP catalogue record for this book is available from the British
Library.

ISBN: 978-0-85789-663-7

Printed in Great Britain by CPI Bookmarque, Croydon

Corvus
An imprint of Atlantic Books Ltd
Ormond House
26-27 Boswell Street
London WC1N 3JZ

www.corvus-books.co.uk

*For my sisters, Enida and Natasha, with love*

# Part One

# Chapter 1

*RE: St Tropez!*
*Please email me all your details and a picture if possible*
*as we are starting to arrange our summer in the sun.*
*Let me know what passport you have and if you need a*
*visa for France. Yeah, yeah, yeah, summer is on its way!*

Tara Wittstanley read the message aloud to her best friend, Abena Ankrah.

'Ah donnt belive eet!' Abena thundered with a wildly exaggerated Ghanaian accent – a departure from what was actually her cut-glass English one, which always cracked Tara up. 'A picture?'

'Sweetheart,' Tara replied, 'this *is* Reza we're talking about. Absolutely nothing would surprise me. I'm just astounded his assistant hasn't asked for our cup sizes and sexual preferences too. This, darling, is what you'd call a mind-bogglingly rich, spoilt and depraved little man.' But her eyes were flashing fire and her heart was beating hard and fast.

Tara had been introduced to Reza months earlier through the gorgeous Domenico, who she'd met in Milan during fashion week.

In order to get the time off university so close to her final examinations, she'd told her old tutor at Oxford that she was having 'Women's Problems'. Those two simple words were enough to put terror into his bespectacled eyes and, rather than have to delve any deeper into the nature of said 'Problems', he advised her to take a week off her studies with immediate effect. And so Tara spent her entire student loan that term on a trip to Milan for a week of fashion parties and hobnobbing with editors, designers, models and photographers. She went mainly because she felt like it, but also with a vague secondary interest in securing contacts for a job in fashion after she graduated. That hadn't worked, but she *had* met Domenico.

Domenico was well dressed, in that flamboyant way she pretended to hate, incredibly good looking and, at just twenty-seven, was already running an unusually successful men's clothing retail company. The 'Women's Problems' quickly developed into a full-on 'Woman's Crisis' and the pair embarked on a passionate but doomed fling. They spent Tara's second week off uni at Domenico's spanking new penthouse on the seafront in Monte Carlo, where Tara fell completely, unashamedly and far too quickly for everything she'd always felt was so wrong with the Riviera. She was seduced by the way he deftly handled his red Lamborghini while stroking her thigh, which glistened in the Mediterranean heat. She was seduced by the feel of the wind blowing through her long, sun-bleached hair and floaty cotton dress (worn without undies) as she thought to herself how glamorous they must look, speeding down the empty road in their open-topped love machine.

On their first evening in Monaco he took her to Jimmy'z nightclub, where even a glass of water cost more than her budget airline flight to Milan. They danced all night on tables outside, relishing the fresh sea air, the starlit sky and the music that blared so cockily loudly. Like they owned the whole world and didn't care who heard. They had no plan whatsoever, only to dance and dance and dance. With the wild, frenzied movements of their long limbs they kept knocking over full bottles of expensive champagne. But it didn't matter because there was always more. There, dancing on a table under the stars with this man, nothing mattered. She was far away from her parents and Willowborough Hall, with all its history and unspoken demands and expectations, far from the relentless social whirl of London and far, far away from her dreary Oxford don. She knew it was love.

Domenico declared he couldn't live without her, so they rushed back to his apartment and in a state of post-coital and drunken euphoria logged on to the internet where Domenico booked a flight to London for the first weekend after Tara's finals and then every weekend for the rest of the summer. He wanted to book in every weekend for the rest of his life but Tara stopped him, saying she'd come and visit him in Italy and Monte Carlo too.

On her flight home she was called aside by immigration officers and questioned as to why her passport had been defaced with hearts and kisses and possibly, therefore, invalidated. She had talked her way out of that one, luckily – if the situation had escalated she'd have had trouble convincing everyone at Oxford that a trip to Monaco was the best cure for Women's Problems. All awkward questions deflected, she sent word to Domenico that she was safely back home. He kept his promise and flew to London weeks later, and that's when she first met Reza.

It turned out Domenico knew a lot of people in London already.

He invited Tara along as his date to a series of lavish parties hosted by his profligate friends, where the finest wines, champagnes and available girls flowed in abundance. Once there, however, he all but ignored Tara, making constant suggestive comments to other women and basically enjoying catching up with people she neither knew nor particularly liked, and many of whom she found trashy.

The parties culminated in the much older Reza's fiftieth birthday extravaganza. This began with various dinners and luncheons held at Nobu Berkeley and the original Nobu, and at China Tang and Cipriani. Restaurants where babies are conceived in cupboards, where all the American Express cards are black and unlimited, and all the women eye-wateringly hot. To crown the celebrations, Reza hosted a party for four hundred guests at his Mayfair mansion. For the occasion Reza had commissioned a life-sized sculpture of himself and had it positioned in the triple-height hallway on the spot where a replica of Michelangelo's David usually stood. On arrival, all guests were given an iPod packaged in an ornate platinum case. It came ready loaded with pictures of Reza throughout his fifty years, many of which Tara suspected had undergone a healthy amount of Photoshopping. Reza's favourite music was also on there, along with a tribute song recorded by a variety of well known personalities, including someone who sounded suspiciously like the Pope.

Tara was astounded when the smooth black floor of one of the five main reception areas suddenly turned transparent, revealing the indoor pool below. A troupe of topless female swimmers in diamond- and ruby-encrusted thongs began performing a synchronized routine to a recording by the recently deceased musical genius Cantonelli. Reza caught and enjoyed her gasp of surprise

4

and strutted over, running a deeply tanned hand over his thinning hair, dyed brown to disguise the grey. Without bothering to introduce himself to Tara or ask her name, he stood beside her and gazed down through the glass at one of the swimmers below. She was face down in the rippled water and her muscled legs were now parted in a rather undignified split. It looked painful, and even more so with a row of priceless gems wedged between her buttocks.

'Infuriating that Cantonelli died just days before he could perform here. I had him scheduled to play in person. I would have been the very first person to have Cantonelli perform at home. If he'd only died just a week later, I'd have been the only man ever.'

Tara didn't quite know what to say to that so Reza continued talking, eyes still glued to the girl in the pool. He licked his lips. Tara thought he was sweating a little. He hadn't looked at her once since he'd come over and that in itself was annoying her. She was in her purple velvet off-the-shoulder vintage mini-dress, which revealed acres of leg. Her grandmother's diamond-and-pearl earrings shimmered at her earlobes and her newest sample-sale find – super-high, nude patent ankle boots from Christian Louboutin – finished off the outfit. She had teamed this with minimal make-up and artfully messed-up hair falling out of a loose knot on top of her head. Was Reza ever going to tear his pervy eyes from that girl's bum?

'I'm getting nervous about those gems,' Reza declared. 'But at least I've had my team of specialists develop special chemicals to make sure the water doesn't diminish their sparkle. Of course the chemicals are not great for the girls, but …' With that he finally looked up and met her eye. In heels she was far taller than him and had a clear view of the bald patch he'd attempted to cover up. 'Why are you here?' he asked.

'Oh, I, er, well, I came with your friend, my boyfriend Domenico.' Tara was taken aback by the abruptness of Reza's question and looked around anxiously for Domenico. She needed him to come and bridge the gap between them. Where on earth was he?

Suddenly Reza turned purple with fury. 'Domenico you great big Italian idiot, get the hell out of my pool!' Tara looked down and was crushed to find a drunken Domenico flailing around in the pool, looking like a mischievous child caught with his hand in the candy jar.

That was the end of their summer affair. Having had the opportunity to scrutinize Domenico away from the slyly deceiving Riviera sun, Tara came to see him as the sleaze that he really was and found she didn't miss him. She was, however, intrigued by the crazy opulence of his set. She was used to moving among the fashionable and the Old Money of English society – she'd grown up with many of them – but very few had the show-stopping wealth of the international super-rich. Wealth that ran into the billions, not millions; that could commission whole teams of scientists to design its own chemicals just so that a girl could wear diamonds underwater. So when she bumped into Reza again weeks later, at a showbiz restaurant opening to which she and Abena had both wangled an invitation, she was secretly delighted that he recognized her.

He asked for her and Abena's numbers so that he could invite them to what he called a 'humble gathering' he was planning for the New Year. This turned out to be a spectacular concert at the Royal Albert Hall, which he'd hired out for the evening, followed by a huge firework display in Hyde Park. With the world's most eminent classical performers assembled in one room, Reza's guests listened, enraptured, for the first twenty minutes. Then they gossiped, flirted, competed, and scoffed handmade chocolate truffles and champagne for the remaining hour. The gathering was about as humble as the Palace of Versailles, and immense fun. With so much going on and so many people around, Tara and Abena barely needed to speak to Reza at all and had themselves a great time instead.

Fast-forward a few months and his assistant was including the young girlfriends on Reza's summer guest list.

In their flat in a dodgy street in Ladbroke Grove, conveniently close to the more upmarket areas of Notting Hill, Abena and Tara were preparing for a browse around the vintage shops and boutiques of Portobello Market. Abena picked up her keys, her head still shaking with amusement at the cheekiness of hideous Reza's requesting a photograph, as though choosing an escort from a website, and asked Tara whether she was ready to go. She dropped her keys into her roomy, soft, brown leather tote, newly purchased online at a discount. They were immediately lost among the mess of make-up, fashion magazines, her digital camera, a dog-eared copy of Wordsworth's poems and several men's business cards. Really, she seemed to collect these cards in the most random of places and could never remember who anyone was. Once she'd got so confused that she called up a homosexual masseur, Sam T, to arrange a hot date, thinking he was Sam C who she'd met at a party. She thought it was odd that he worked at a spa but had just assumed he was on the business side there. Meanwhile a dribbling medic who'd told her she looked like Naomi Campbell's petite younger sister and whose card she'd only taken out of politeness thought Christmas had come early when she asked him, instead of Sam T, over to hers for a full-body massage. Well, she was in a hurry and the damned card said something about chiropractic!

Moments later, the young women were strutting side by side through the stalls of Portobello, watching all the fashionable girls pick up edgy trinkets and garments, and secretly enjoying, but pretending not to notice, the admiring glances of all the boys. Even among the experimental fashionistas at the market the pair stood out. Abena wore a retro blazer over an ex-boyfriend's oversized wife-beater vest knotted at the hip. Skinny blue jeans and towering wedge heels gave her some much appreciated extra inches. Tara had dressed quickly in a black corset which, in her own inimitable way she had thrown on top of a thin silk Meadham Kirchhoff blouse. She too wore jeans but hers were ripped and wonderfully ancient and were tucked into flat, slouchy, even more ancient fringed boots.

'Hon, this would look incredible on you,' Abena commented as she pulled out a fuchsia silk dress and held it up in front of her friend.

'Mmmn, that's stunning,' Tara agreed, stroking the silky lining before casually checking the price tag. Her face reddened. 'It *is* a bit mumsy though,' she muttered in a change of heart, and placed it reluctantly back on the rack.

Tara wasn't conventionally beautiful. She was bony and pale, with bad skin, thin and lifeless blonde hair and a smallish mouth so crammed with large teeth that she'd been described as 'horsey' in the past. Yet there was something about her. She knew how to turn her tall, pale skinniness into a fashion statement that people aspired to, and her skin problems she covered expertly with high-end concealers and foundations. The lankness of her light blonde hair fitted with the slightly grungy look championed by Kate, Agyness and the other top British models – ultra-groomed, big, bouffant hair was for pop star wannabes and footballers' wives.

They continued to browse the various collectors' stands, quietly despairing at some of the prices, until Tara stopped suddenly and turned. Mischief danced in her wide blue eyes.

'Abbi, we *deserve* a break! Why don't we take Reza up on his offer and go with them to St Tropez? You know what he's like; it's all for show. When has he ever seriously tried anything on? I mean, I'd be surprised if he can actually get his feeble little dick up any more … And if by some sick twist it turns out that he can, well, I'm sure one of the 'models' will be more than happy to oblige. Come on, a smart holiday – what's the worst that could happen?'

Abena contemplated this for a moment and hooted with laughter. The way Tara had put it made it seem downright silly to turn the invitation down. She was single, apparently attractive, twenty-two, and this was her time. She had sailed through school and secured a good degree at Oxford, despite her incessant partying. Now she needed to make a life for herself and fulfil the potential she knew she had – that everybody has, even if some people are lazy about jumping on opportunities. Why not enjoy a break in the sun with her girlfriend? Who knew, she might meet the love of her life there. She'd set her sights considerably higher than the chinless types of Notting Hill. Neither were the faux bohemians any better – no matter how grubby your clothes look, or however many hours of alternative yoga you do, if you can afford the rents

9

in Notting Hill then you ain't the bohemian free-spirit you fancy yourself to be.

Abena was becoming dismally disillusioned by a seemingly endless string of disastrous dates and disappointing boyfriends. Sod any misgivings. Why not see what was out there? Give herself up entirely to whatever the summer might bring.

She so desperately wanted to fall in love.

'OK, let's do it.'The pair exchanged guilty grins.'Reza and his crew know that neither you nor I are"that sort"anyway.'

'Exactly,' Tara affirmed, a touch more strongly than was necessary.

'Shall we ask a couple of the others – safety in numbers? Perhaps Sarah will want to come along too?' Abena added as an afterthought.


'He said WHAT?'exclaimed Sarah on the phone, wrinkling up her button nose.'That is obscene!'The wholesome, jolly-hockey-sticks side to Sarah left her unamused by the invitation.'There is absolutely no way I am letting a fifty-something Syrian Lothario fly me out to the South of France and put me up on his yacht for the weekend, and definitely not on the basis of a photograph!'

'Darling, relax,' soothed Abena, 'you're making me feel seedy.' Then she saw Tara yawning dramatically at Sarah's response and, stifling a giggle, felt better.

Although Abena was immensely fond of her friend Sarah, Tara had always thought her terribly bourgeois and so was not at all surprised to see her putting on a show of middle-class righteousness at the mere idea of decadence and glamour.

'God, hon,'Tara wailed,'purlease let Sarah stay at home with

10

her miserable excuse of a boyfriend and her earnest endeavours at the local paper. You and I'll have much more fun on the trip as a double act and anyway you've never been to the French Riviera have you? Peasant! We can lose Reza and his lot and get into all sorts of compromising scrapes with rock stars and eccentric aristos,' she laughed.

'Yeah, well then they'd better be of the moneyed kind, not the impoverished stock you're from,' Abena hit back. 'Little Miss Worldly, one of my exes has an apartment in Monaco. It might do you good to remember that while you were pissing around with Domenico, I was even further away, having a wild time in Lagos watching Kunle play polo for his father's team. Harrumph.' Abena grinned.

'True,' Tara replied. 'Sadly neither of us was back at Oxford where we should have been.'

'Well, all's well that ends well – we got our degrees didn't we? And the real fun starts here.' Abena bopped up and down on the spot then planted a big kiss on Tara's cheek. This was going to be one hell of a holiday.

\*\*\*\*

The biggest bruise stretched across her ribs, forming an ugly red blotch under her heart.

Natalya stood naked in front of the mirror and surveyed the damage before turning and climbing into the marble bath. She lay back, closed her eyes, and let Mozart transport her to a kinder world. She lay dreaming for some time while the water soothed her young body, still aching from the previous night. Had the beeping of her mobile not jolted her back to reality, she would have lain longer, enjoying its gentleness. Drying herself with a fluffy white towel and wandering through to the bedroom, she reached for her BlackBerry. The message made her gasp:

> *RE: St Tropez!*
> *Please email me all your details and a picture if possible*
> *as we are starting to arrange our summer in the sun.*
> *Let me know what passport you have and if you need a*
> *visa for France. Yeah, yeah, yeah, summer is on its way!*

Natalya trembled. Though it was only April, Reza was already thinking about jetting out to St Tropez, and this breezy message from his young assistant, Henry – permanently bronzed and waxed like Reza himself, except that Henry was blond and gay and Reza was dark and very straight – confirmed what Natalya had been hoping for. That she would be accompanying Reza and his set on some of their weekend jaunts to the French Riviera. She would be flown from one glamorous location to another in Reza's private plane. She would stay on the 120-foot yacht, moored far enough from the shore to distance the privileged party from any less fortunate onlookers, but certainly close enough to ensure that all could admire the splendour and opulence of the vessel, and the glamour and beauty of the girls aboard it. She might get a shopping trip thrown in – a new Cartier watch, perhaps. Most importantly, though, here was a chance to escape Gregory's brutal and unsophisticated clutches and seek out a gentler, more malleable man. Perhaps he'd be even older; less libidinous, more giving … appreciative of the beauty of youth.

Natalya skipped across the room to her walk-in wardrobe. Pushing aside rack after rack of designer gowns, jeans and fitted sweatshirts, she burrowed her way to the summer section at the back and emerged with an armful of cut-out swimsuits, bikini briefs and tops. Starting with the bejewelled two-piece, she worked her way carefully through each bikini outfit – adding a beach skirt here or a kaftan there – until she'd tried on her entire collection. At long last she studied her reflection for the final time. Standing hand on hip in a pink tasselled Dior two-piece, a wide-brimmed straw hat, giant dark shades and five-inch Cavalli heels, she groaned before throwing herself back on to the magnificent four-poster bed. No, she decided, I look hot as hell and I know where that always gets me.

What she needed was a change of strategy. No more nubile and eager Riviera dolly – that made her *far* too desirable to men, which, ultimately, would work against her. Men, the simple creatures, could never reconcile themselves to the fact that a girl can be both sensationally sexy and devoted and homely at the same time. If she was to snare the oligarch she wanted for good – and not just for good times – it was essential that she dress the part. Out with the ostentatious tasselled Dior and in with the subtle sexiness of a white Chanel one-piece, set off against her cocoa tan and freshly highlighted choppy layers. To that she would add a couple of flirty dresses in pastel shades, but nothing too clingy. Only elegant or cutesy would achieve the desired effect. She'd make men fall off their yachts in their haste to protect her and keep her in the lifestyle she so desperately wanted in these uncertain times.

Natalya had intended to avoid Gregory for a while after his

especially rough handling last night, but she needed to be taken shopping. And since her last modelling job had been another 'hugely prestigious editorial', which would secure her great exposure but no pay cheque, she was left with no other choice than to make amends. Reluctantly, she picked up her mobile and dialled Gregory's number. He answered immediately, his heavy breathing perceptible even before the phone had reached his mistress's ear.

'Baby is that you? Why didn't you return my calls? Did you get my messages?'

She rolled her eyes. As she purred into the phone, a sexy Latvian twang could be detected in her accent. 'I hef been missing you bébé …' she breathed. 'Come over to Knightsbridge. I want cock.'

# Chapter 2

In a tiny, run-down flat on the outskirts of Latvia's capital city, Daina's weary face cracked into a smile of motherly pride. She ran a bony finger across the page ripped from the latest edition of *Harper's Bazaar*. Natalya's chiselled features, golden hair and smooth, honey skin seemed to jump out at her like a ray of light in the darkness of her surroundings. Her brave darling must be doing so very well now, she prayed.

Natalya was the eldest of her six children. Six years ago she'd been spotted by a scout from London's Moda Nova Models while the family were in St Petersburg, on a rare trip across the border. Ever since, Daina had spent many hours anguishing that she had been wrong to let Natalya go and live abroad at just fifteen years of age. The world of modelling seemed a weird world indeed. Such strange people and strange practices and strange preoccupations. Would they take advantage of her child? Would she earn enough to survive? London sounded unbelievably expensive. She hoped Natalya had finally found somewhere, in amongst all the Japanese fish and French cuisine she wrote home about, to buy good, simple Latvian rye bread. She didn't seem to eat much bread at all nowadays, no wonder she was still so thin! Oh how she missed making Natalya's favourite *pîrâgi* with her, like they'd used to as a special treat when they'd saved enough for meat. She closed her eyes and pictured them sitting together and watching the soft buns rising around the crispy bacon, filling the place with warmth and delicious smells. She could almost taste the buns now. Their family was poor and she had had to juggle three jobs to feed her brood, but at least they'd had each other, and that must surely count for something.

Shuddering, she let her mind flick briefly back to when she herself had been just fifteen. A sheltered fifteen-year-old who, until that horrific year, had known nothing of the deviousness of the male psyche. Over the years, Daina had learnt not to think about what *he* had done to her. She had learnt not to let her thoughts revisit that painful period because she needed to be strong. For her children. Especially Natalya. She needed to forget, or at least not think about her hatred any more, because she did not want to hate the father of her firstborn. She owed it to Natalya.

And she owed it to Natalya to protect her. Yet she had let her go. Just like that. Look what good her own 'protected' upbringing had done anyway! But Daina *had* tried to protect her baby daughter, all those years ago. If Natalya could have known the whole truth about the Englishman. About Stan. Well, this was the life that God intended for her. There must be a reason for her suffering and, in Natalya, Daina knew that the purpose of all her pain was being realized.

As Daina always knew she would, Natalya had become a huge success in London and made a good living for herself. She must now be very wealthy indeed, Daina mused once more. After all, she had been working non-stop since the very beginning, and now, at the age of twenty-one, she had a luxurious apartment in one of London's best neighbourhoods. For three years she had been sending her mother money and prints from fashion shoots. Although it saddened Daina that her daughter was seldom able to return home and visit her, she had been putting the extra money to good use and all five remaining children could now be clothed, fed and sent to decent local schools.

The children's education was the most important thing for Daina, as it had been for Janis, her late husband and the father of her five youngest offspring. Despite their poverty, the children had led culturally rich lives from the moment they were born, and that very trip to St Petersburg, during which Natalya had been scouted, had been the result of years of saving. Seeing the Philharmonic Orchestra perform there at the splendid Mussorgsky Opera House had been a more magical experience for them than any fairy tale. All six children were bright, and for Daina the choice between spending Natalya's contributions on more pleasant surroundings and living conditions or educating the children as richly as she could was an easy one to make. But, looking at yet another captivating set of pictures of her little light, perhaps she would soon be able to move to a flat closer to central Riga, one with another room, so that they would not all need to share.

What Daina did not know was that, despite being represented by one of London's top agencies, Natalya was yet to make any real money. Natalya had indeed been enjoying a comfortable lifestyle, but the price of this was greater than her beloved mother needed to know.

\*\*\*\*

17

The Hon. Tara Wittstanley had more in common with girls like Natalya than she cared to acknowledge. Both girls had what could be described as regal looks, and though in Tara's case her fine patrician features clearly did reflect a noble ancestry, her family's current situation was far from financially secure. No longer able to compete in this era of industrial tycoons, global speculators and City high-rollers, Tara's family were on a downwardly mobile track to refined poverty. Tara wished desperately to reverse this trend and, like Natalya, she wanted more than she had.

The family did at least still own Willowborough Hall, a Regency pile in Gloucestershire with six hundred acres of land. Like generations of Wittstanleys before her, Tara had grown up there. Unlike most of her ancestors, though, Tara didn't have a trust fund to see her through adulthood. An artistic and whimsical family, the Wittstanleys had not made the most of their considerable acres and over the years had squandered substantial wealth through ill-fated investments and unwise marriages. By the time Tara's father, Hugo, had been born, all that was left was the family home and the right to the title Lord Bridges, of Bridges in Gloucestershire.

When the time came for Hugo and his two younger brothers to make their final career choices – a day job outside the running of the estate now being, irritatingly for them, a necessity – his brothers swallowed their pride and jumped head first into the world of commerce and City banking. Hugo, however, stubbornly decided to pursue his artistic leanings and attempt to make a living by dealing antiques and doing equestrian paintings for friends. He travelled the world in search of sights and horses to paint, visiting some of the former colonies in Africa and Asia and, with some help from high-powered friends in the government, even venturing into hostile territories such as the closed USSR. Life had been exciting but not lucrative, and he had failed to make good money from his art and antiques.

Tara often found herself musing over how her family had evolved over the years. If only they hadn't been such suckers for aesthetics. Maybe then her father would have made a more sensible career choice. Perhaps there would have been some sensible marriages. A strategic coupling with a rich heiress would have restored the wealth her grandfather had gambled away. Instead, both her grandfather and her father had married ambitious young beauties with no wealth or name to speak of.

Her own dear mother, Tina, was in fact often a source of embarrassment to Tara. Twenty years younger than Hugo, Tina had met and seduced him on a flight to India on which she'd been working as an air-hostess.

In those days hostesses were employed above all for their alluring looks. For Tina, who was eighteen at the time and had never left Liverpool, the job was a dream come true. She enjoyed the travelling and loved meeting the smartly dressed, upscale passengers even more. She was awed by the women in their elegant twin-sets, with their well-behaved children who didn't trouble her. And the men were all so dapper, never without blazers. She liked to study the passenger list before they arrived and was excited to see that there was a lord on her first ever flight to India.'Can I offer you a drink, my Lord?' she asked him when he embarked looking bored, tired and unremarkable. She wondered whether she ought to curtsey. She poured him a Martini at his seat and then turned to offer a drink to the gentleman on the other side of the aisle. She leaned over so that her round little bottom pushed against the taut material of her navy-blue pencil skirt. Then, out of the corner of her eye, she saw his lordship lean forward as if to get up.

'Oh, toilets at the rear,' giggled Tina.

'The only rear I'm interested in is this one,' his lordship murmured, letting his signet-ringed hand slide across her buttock as he glided ever so slowly past her. 'Splendid little filly aren't you,' he whispered in her ear. His breath was hot on the side of her face, the faint aroma of alcohol filling her nose with its intoxicating promise of champagne, ponies and high tea with the Queen. Men were expected to be chauvinists and molesters in those days, but women were certainly not allowed to show it when they enjoyed it.

'Oh, my Lord!' she tittered, feigning shocked offence.

But she still took her time demonstrating the safety procedures in front of him, lingering over the one about the overhead luggage compartments as she knew that with her arms up above her head her breasts were at their most uplifted and must look fantastic straining against her tight shirt.

She was sad when the flight landed in Bombay. 'Can I do anything else for you my Lord, you know, to ease your trip?'

'Yes,' he replied. 'Come with me.' So she followed him to his hotel in India and cleverly remained chaste during their stay, although she relented a little when he asked her to put her uniform back on and point out the emergency exits for him while he pleasured himself. Then, at the moment of climax he liked her to assume the brace position.

Afterwards they returned to Willowborough Hall, where he painted her on horseback. That painting remains, to this day, Lord Bridges' most well-received piece. Critics hail the extraordinary look on the rider's face as an artistic coup: she appears unsure yet deliriously happy, beautiful but wretched; with an impenetrable smile like that of the Mona Lisa.

With her family's approval Hugo asked for Tina's hand in marriage. Despite their backgrounds being worlds apart, Tina was so impressed by his title, confidence and family home that she ignored his paunch, his condescension and his drinking habits and jumped at the chance. Likewise he, hopelessly excited by her young and nubile body and her naive devotion to him, did his best to forget that she'd had a strong Liverpudlian accent when they met, had not been educated at a 'decent' school, and could not tell the difference between a Mondrian and a Modigliani. In this way the couple had limped along for twenty-three years. But for some time now, the cracks had been beginning to show.

Luckily, given the Wittstanleys' financial situation, Tara had managed to secure scholarships to her expensive boarding schools, where she excelled effortlessly. Her haughty looks and her witty, if also bitchy, tongue ensured that the other girls admired her; a few also feared her. In her adolescence she grew prone to extremes of feeling and behaviour. Or, as her detractors put it, she could be a complete drama queen. By the age of twenty-two she had already checked herself in and out of different rehabilitation centres and a psychiatric hospital for a range of modern conditions from exhaustion to body dysmorphic disorder. At heart, though, she was a kind person whose prickliness masked a deep-rooted feeling of unlovableness and inadequacy, brought about by her overbearing yet needy, neglectful and self-absorbed parents. To the few people Tara deemed interesting and glamorous enough, she was a loyal friend. One of those was her dear friend Abena, whom she'd met at Oxford.

Initially Tara had had no interest in getting to know other girls and concentrated on stalking the Bullingdon boys in search of a privileged sponsor for her rampant partying. The Bullingdon was the university's most exclusive gentlemen's drinking society, whose members rollicked around Oxfordshire starting food fights and smashing up smart establishments so that they would have something to spend their inheritances on when the repair bill arrived. It seemed this was excellent training for going on to run the country. But, having slept her way through almost the entire society, Tara came to the sorry conclusion that the Bullingdon boys were pitifully overrated in virtually every way imaginable. Disillusioned with anything the students had to offer, she turned to the celebrity speakers who regularly descend on Oxford to address the Union, the university's historic debating society.

One evening, determined to leave with the handsome deputy prime minister of a small Balkan state, Tara had dressed up in her best 'political wife' outfit of a plain and decent-length fitted black dress, a cashmere cardigan and a string of fake pearls. Sitting primly in the front row of the Union's grand main hall, she gazed up at her target just as Abena's dark, feline eyes bore down on the speaker from the balcony above. At the end of the discourse, the room emptied until the only participants left were Abena, Tara, the dashing speaker himself, and Giles, the gangling Oxford Union president who slept with a postcard of William Hague under his pillow to inspire him to greater heights. Tara could see it was going to be tough to shake off the other two. Giles grandly led the way into the Union bar and the speaker turned to insist that she and Abena join them to further discuss the 'exciting' political issues he'd been talking about. Abena, with her sexily slanting eyes, unnaturally long, wavy black hair, perfectly smooth dark skin and full seductive mouth was starting to irritate Tara. As was her toned and tiny five-foot-three frame, which, from the look on the speaker and the Union president's faces, rendered her irresistibly cutesy and adorable to boys – something that Tara, in all her elegant cool, had never managed.

Abena winked at Tara and ordered a magnum of Moët from the bar. She then made a point of continuously filling the glass of the Union president, who didn't notice how fast he was drinking, being so engrossed in his own rants about cash for peerages in the Labour party, and 'sexing-up' various political dossiers that were not sexy and never would be. Because drinking was fairly new to him, his stringy body was unable to take the quantities Abena smilingly pressed upon him and he was soon face down on the bar muttering something incoherent about poll tax.

With Giles out of the picture, it was a stand-off between the two girls. Tara peeled off her demure cardigan to expose the exceptionally low front of her dress, while Abena leaned forward and, pressing the deputy prime minister's leg, gently asked how it felt to be one of the most powerful men in the world. The politician, growing increasingly excitable with the abundance of champagne and gorgeous young flesh beside him, seemed at a genuine loss as to whether he was more turned on by the Western threat, baring its breast in front of him, or by the dark and mysterious excitement of Africa to his left.

And so it was that the two girls spent their first drunken evening together. As it progressed into the early hours of the morning, each recognized in the other a far more feisty and fun proposition than the deputy prime minister, who was now dribbling in the corner of his chauffeur-driven limousine. It was unclear whose idea it had been to risk scuppering the poor man's chances of ever making it to the Top Job, but in the morning he was found by his concerned driver, slumped in the corner of the vehicle and dressed in nothing but his socks, with his navy tie tied neatly around his cock. Neither girl was anywhere to be seen.

Three years later, Tara and Abena, now relocated to the bright lights of London and determined to make their mark on the city, were the best of friends and still as mischievous as ever.

****

Having accepted the invitation to the South of France, Abena and Tara were growing more and more excited about the impending excess that awaited them there. Finally, at the start of the first May bank holiday, it was time to set off. Scrambling into the black chauffeur-driven Mercedes that Reza had sent to the apartment, Abena asked for her Nikki Beach CD to be pumped up as they headed off to Farnborough, the private airport where Reza's plane awaited them.

Pulling up at Farnborough, she tried not to gawp at the scene unfolding before them. Stepping out of an assortment of vehicles, each of which alone might have cost more than her rented apartment, was an array of some of the most breathtaking beauties she had ever seen. She glanced at Tara, who was looking stonily ahead at the surreal sight. They had both been among the bigger fish in the small ponds of school and even university, but this was a different league altogether. These girls were supermodel standard. Moreover, observed Abena, one or two of them actually *were* bona-fide supermodels. She watched a six-foot Slavic blonde she recognized from the pages of *Vogue* wait in a shimmering black Ferrari with alligator-skin seats until its driver had raced around to her side and opened the door for her. Nervous excitement and exhilaration swelled in the pit of her stomach. She looked at Tara again, wanting her to share in her thrill but her face was set in a rigid expression Abena knew all too well.

Nobody liked being outshone or made to feel insignificant, but Abena knew that unless she could shake Tara out of this mood, she'd be haughty, rude and unsociable to cover her insecurity. Or worse, she'd make a beeline for the nearest narcotic and get absolutely off her head, leaving her vulnerable to the wolfish men who were surveying the women appreciatively.

These men were themselves outdone by some even more predatory females, who matched their looks fiercely, eating them greedily with hungry eyes framed by painstakingly threaded arched eyebrows, some concealed under big dark glasses. Their figures were gym honed and Atkins dieted to an alien-like perfection. Clothes were smart-casual but perilously body conscious and very, very expensive. Abena noticed lots of cashmere that didn't really know what to do with itself. There was a sweater vying for attention but it couldn't possibly be worn because, well, why cover up such a generous bosom? So instead it was draped over a pair of lean shoulders clad in a skimpy, low-cut, crocheted white vest top. The cashmere sweater offender was a smiley brunette and was also in tight white jeans, a Fendi belt and high-heeled Jimmy Choo sandals. She was apparently called Tatiana and had a gorgeous face. Her eyes were wonderful and shockingly bright, and her blow-dry was so voluminous that her hair was big and silky, almost reaching the small of her back. It was ever so seductive, the perfect *digestif* to wash down an immense visual feast.

'She's just got too much of everything hasn't she?' Abena quipped. 'It's like God got a bit sleepy creating her and forgot that he'd already done her boobs and eyes and hair and ended up giving her a double portion of it all. Do you think the breasts are natural?'

Tara snorted. 'She looks like she's just stepped out of a budget issue of *Nuts* magazine. And tight white on tight white? That combination should be made illegal outside of Essex. Sweater on shoulders? Should be banned full stop.'

'I'm sure I've seen you pulling a white on white before – I certainly have, not to mention double denim, a sequin catsuit and loads of leopardskin.'

'Yeah, but hon, when we do it, we do it with integrity, you know, fashion integrity … aware of the context and the surrounds in which we're inflicting a certain look on the world.' Tara broke off with a grin when she realized how ridiculous she sounded. 'But OK, OK, the girl she's talking to, even *I* can't deny that she is truly breathtaking – but then you can tell she's a complete bitch.'

'Takes one to know one it seems.' Abena tickled Tara's bare underarm and was pleased to see her crack another smile then give a throaty laugh before scrabbling in her bag and adding a shiny slick of lip gloss. Good. Tara was back in the game.

As Abena and Tara gossiped, Natalya made half-hearted small talk with Tatiana but she wasn't really listening. She ran her eyes across the selection of men. Who would be her oligarch? Sure as hell not the one in the pale blue silk shirt, currently undressing her with his eyes. Despite his mahogany tan – a useful factor in

26

calculating a man's net worth – he had only undone two of the top buttons on his shirt, not the three that would indicate he was a true member of the exclusive club known as the super-rich, membership of which she'd long been angling for. She checked his watch, which only confirmed her prior observation. His Patek was last year's model. She'd wager he was worth something pretty pitiful, twenty mill, perhaps, on a good day. In the current climate, Forbes would halve that. Not that he'd come anywhere near making their list. The next man's customized new Rolex had the opposite problem – so big and flash on his wrist, Natalya wondered how he could even fit his hand into his pocket to reach for his wallet. It was too … obvious; he was clearly trying too hard, a pretender. Even Gregory could buy his overweight arse, so that ruled him out. She turned to the guy he was chatting to and perked up – a hundred mill at a guess and he's just bought himself a new watch, a new car and a new woman (the supermodel waiting by his black Ferrari had been dating an actor last month) so must have had a good year; his stock was on the up. Finally she spotted Reza. Two billion and rising.

Unlike Heathrow, at Farnborough one only needed to arrive fifteen minutes before take-off, which cut short the girls' sizing up of the men and each other. Before Abena and Tara had a chance to panic, or change their minds altogether, they were swooped upon by a grinning Reza in his customary leisure ensemble of blue jeans, brown loafers, crocodile-skin belt, and tight white shirt stretched over his hairless orangey-brown chest. He made a big show of kissing each one of them on both corners of the mouth, which, he seemed to feel, counted legitimately as part of the cheek. Then, taking both girls' hands in his, he lifted them high above his head so that their short summer dresses rose up dangerously, and proceeded to do a peculiar jig. Gyrating his pelvis from side to side as his surprisingly pert bottom strained against the scant material of his jeans, he threw his triumphant face upward towards the heavens and roared 'Where the fuck is St Tropez? Come on baby – all aboard the jet.'

Seconds later Reza's assistant, Henry, whom both girls had come to adore, shimmied over with his boyfriend, Anders, a young Dutch singer with a new rock-band. Abena ran to hug him as he led them to the aircraft. The plane was streamlined and compact, in dark teal with a red-and-white stripe across its side. From the outside it was surprisingly understated and quite beautiful. 'Not as flamboyant as you'd expect from the big man is it? But then my boss is shrewd enough not to let pleasure get in the way of business. He parties like there's no tomorrow but he also needs to be taken seriously when doing deals and if he happens to want investment from an abstaining tycoon whose wife wears a burqa, then it doesn't look great to have a crystal replica of a naked woman embellishing the wing of his PJ,' explained Henry, ushering them in after Reza. Abena was surprised at how few seats there were, each surrounded by acres of space.

'Oh, so sad,' whispered Tara, 'there'll be no room on the PJ for Ms Vogue and the rest of her posse.' Henry, having followed her envious gaze towards the other girls, confirmed that they'd be flying with Eric, the tall Swedish financier she'd glimpsed earlier. The two groups would reconvene once they reached France.

Just as she thought they were in the clear and that there were to be no models joining them, Tara saw with irritation that the very slender, young-looking blonde with choppy layers and an angelic face was tottering towards the plane. Doubtless an evil old witch, she thought bitchily. 'Here comes Slutlana,' she muttered to herself.

'Aah Natalya, how are you sweetheart, meet Abena and Tara,' said Henry, introducing the girls to each other. Directed to a seat beside the newcomer, Abena was unsure which was lovelier to look at: Natalya herself or the sleek, beige and dark brown interior of the plane. The leather upholstered chairs were vast and butter-soft and could be reclined right back to become a bed. Each place was ready stocked with a selection of current newspapers and magazines, and there were bottles of Evian and tall crystal glasses by the arm rests. Reza hadn't been able to resist a little personalization here, so there was a gold company crest embedded in each glass. The uniformed captain introduced himself, pointing out the fully stocked mini-bar and the freshly baked cakes, snacks and savoury treats ranging from cucumber sandwiches to sushi and caviar, which Reza always had specially sourced.

Tara had been staring surreptitiously at Natalya, who was, in turn, staring out of the window looking bored. 'Abbi,' she whispered, 'look at her neck.'

'Oh my God!' Abena gasped. A patch of skin on the side of Natalya's neck that should have been covered by her hair was exposed with the twist of her head to reveal an angry red welt.

A few more people filed into the aircraft and eventually the last arrival was seated. The male passengers were mostly either employed by Reza or were potential business clients. As well as Henry and Anders there was a silver-haired Englishman called Piers and Reza's two right-hand men, Darren and Fadi. Burly Darren was his minder and Fadi was the money man, which meant that he literally followed Reza around with a fortified brief-case filled with the £50 notes that Reza needed to pay for things on a day-to-day basis. The female passengers were all attractive. Besides Tara, Abena and Natalya there were two Italian girls who appeared to be about seventeen and barely spoke English, and two older, ultra-groomed brunettes in daringly, if not commendably, skimpy outfits who looked with disapproval at the 'mere children' around them.

'Mutton-dressed-as lamb alert,' Tara whispered. 'Next thing you know my mother will be out here.'

Abena digested the first woman's look: a small Prada bra top with high-waisted short-shorts – ropey enough on the anorexic-looking teenagers who exhibited it on the runway, let alone unleashed here. The second woman was also falling out of one of those looks that should never, ever be allowed to leave the catwalk. 'Hmmn, certainly a clever time-saving trick – put your beachwear on *before* you reach your holiday destination. I'm quite tickled by it,' she murmured.

Reza looked over the inhabitants of his shiny teal toy as a king might survey his kingdom. He thought of his childhood, of growing up with his Syrian father and Belgian mother, living first in Syria and then in different Middle Eastern countries, so that he and his brother were constantly being dragged around and pulled out of new schools. Somehow his brother had always managed to adjust. He'd done well and been happy everywhere, while he, Reza, had been the misfit. But that was then. He leaned back, letting his lips curl into an awful smile. If the kids who'd picked on him at school could only see him now. But then, they could, couldn't they, he smirked, glancing at his picture in the business pages of *The Times*.

Reza recalled the strange dream he'd had the previous night, still mildly aroused by it. He'd dreamt he lived in a mythical land where he had the gift of unlimited ejaculations. But as he came, all his produce morphed into a torrent of £50 notes so profuse that he filled entire seas with money. And then the girls appeared like mermaids, bikini-clad and swimming around in the notes in ecstasy. Mmmn, marvellous young girls. There was Lilith, who he'd asked out as a spotty adolescent and who'd laughed cruelly in his face. Well she wasn't laughing here. Then Farah appeared. She'd agreed to one date with him because his mother had paid her – and then nipped to the loo during lunch and never returned. All the young beauties he'd ever wanted, who he still seethed at now for spurning him, were present, thrashing around in his seas of passion. They chased after the notes and whenever they got hold of one were amazed to find that it was no longer Her Majesty the Queen's face emblazoned upon it, but Reza's own, complete with dazzling tan and glinting white teeth.

Now, as his plane roared down the runway and sailed into the sky, a frisson of excitement rippled through the cabin. Reza reached into the mini-bar by his seat and pulled out a bottle of champagne. 'Doooooooooom,' he chanted at Fadi, Henry and Darren, who immediately sang back in unison 'Pé, Pé, Pérignooooooooon.' Then he shook the bottle hard, popped the cork and unleashed his fizz all over the shrieking passengers, spraying them and the immaculate interior.

'Open up, Ciara,' he ordered, leaning forward to pour the champagne directly into the pretty teenager's ready and willing mouth as she thrust out her chest and threw her head back, damp hair falling wantonly everywhere.

Henry opened another bottle and poured Reza a glass before helping him off with his loafers.

'It's showtime!' Reza roared.

# Chapter 3

With the plane a few hundred feet in the air, its passengers could glance down and smile a satisfied goodbye to southern England, now just a series of concrete clusters divided by swathes of green fields. Hidden somewhere among the buildings of central London stood the office blocks where both Abena and Tara worked, and the girls considered their careers from this new vantage point.

Tara had been employed for only three weeks the previous month. She'd fallen into temping after leaving university because she was reluctant to commit to any of the careers on offer. She'd rather wander homeless through the streets of London than confine her lifestyle to a rigid and mundane routine. Not for her the daily grind of taking a ghastly bus to a drab office every morning, then sitting in front of a computer with a bunch of people she would never normally have chosen as her friends, before trudging home with just enough time for some supper before bed. She *knew* that somewhere there was a more glamorous life waiting for her. In the meantime she would temp, accepting only the bare minimum of work. This usually meant three weeks of secretarial work a month in order to cover her half of the rent.

She found it wasn't necessary to spend much to maintain a

hectic social life, having discovered soon after her move to London that if one is invited to the right parties, a diet consisting almost solely of canapés is more than substantial. Besides, she was regularly invited on dinner dates, where, despite being a modern woman, she never had any intention, or need, to open her ostrich-skin purse when the bill came. Cars to ferry her around from restaurant to bar to nightclub or party were normally taken care of by either the date for that evening or a friend, be it the owner of the restaurant or the PR person for the venue. Tara had soon learnt that being fashionable and connected is not just agreeable, it's lucrative.

The only thing she sometimes felt she ought to accept more work for was high-end clothing. A connoisseur of fashion, Tara flatly refused to buy clothing on the High Street. Instead, she made do with a wardrobe of beautifully cut vintage hand-me-downs from her grandmother, mixed with goodie-bag freebies from the shows in Paris and London, sample-sale finds, and a considerable collection of designer gifts from wealthier friends and a couple of ex-boyfriends. This arrangement would have to suffice until she found herself an eligible man because the only occupations that could possibly hold her attention were in fashion PR and fashion journalism, neither of which would enable her to afford a cutting-edge Preen wardrobe.

Abena, too, was struggling to achieve job satisfaction. Hugely ambitious, she was determined to make something of her sharp mind and friendly nature. Exotic good looks inherited from her Ghanaian parents might have helped her charm her way through life, but she wanted to use her 'interpersonal skills' to get ahead. She enjoyed surprising people, whether with her cut-glass English accent or Oxford degree, and what could be better than a career in the media, where she could surprise people by engaging them in issues they might not have been interested in. She wanted to show disillusioned young people that the world doesn't have to be a closed place and that they can carve out their own path. She wanted to tell tales of far away, and show people new places. And so it was with the zeal of a romantic youth who has sailed through life that Abena had pressed the 'send' button on her job application to Mallinder Films five months earlier.

Mallinder Films turned out to be a bitter disappointment. She loathed the tedium of her office routine. Plonked in the accounts department on her first day, she had soon become aware of some irksome facts about business. Firstly, that even if the product to be sold is an electrifying film, the accounts still need to be tracked daily on a spreadsheet; and Mallinder Films was fond of spreadsheets. It was fond of targets. And it absolutely loved 'performance indicators' for all of its employees. Tracking the number of calls that the tubby head of sales had made last Tuesday was about as far removed from Abena's vision of inspirational creativity as a position stacking shelves at Somerfield.

By the same token, although she'd been thrilled to be given her own assistant, the sweet but dowdy Wendy, she was by now bored rigid of hearing about the woman's home life. No, she did not wish to see another photograph of Wendy in the garden with her big, black dog Bruno. Or one of Wendy on holiday – with Bruno. Or a group shot showing Wendy's sister with her husband, Wendy's brother with his wife, and Wendy herself with, well, Bruno. It pained Abena to think of Wendy grinding away at Mallinder well into her middle age, getting progressively more bloated and pockmarked as she bought more dogs and cats. I need to get out now while I still can, she thought.

Mallinder Films was also excruciatingly tight with money. Abena already knew that most of the staff were paid barely enough to keep them in lovefilm subscriptions. But she hadn't realized quite how bad things were until a celebratory team meal was held not at the delicious Arbutus restaurant near their Soho offices but at Bangers and Beans, a greasy spoon two doors down. Olympia, the CEO, wasn't prepared to cough up for more. Mallinder Films was clearly far from being the powerful international player in the world of film that Olympia had implied at interview. In fact Abena quickly learnt that hardly anybody outside of Mallinder Films had heard of Mallinder Films.

But now she was on the plane and by the time the second bottle of champagne lay empty, all thoughts of work were forgotten. 'Cheers hon!' Abena raised a glass to Tara and helped herself to a praline, ignoring Natalya's disapproving look. She noticed Reza pulling faces and sticking his tongue out at a bewildered Ciara, who giggled uncertainly, sitting opposite him at the back of the plane with her wide-eyed young friend Francesca.

'If in doubt, just smile and giggle when it comes to the big boss,' advised Henry.

'But what if he's not joking? Or I'm not amused?' Abena asked. The faces Reza was pulling were beneath the dignity of a man in his fifties.

'Trust me, sweetheart, just smile and giggle. He doesn't do small talk. He mostly talks business and makes party plans, preferably with men. With girls, it's just smile and giggle at his jokes.'

Stubbornly, Abena turned to Reza, determined to engage him in normal conversation. When he looked over and caught her eye she leaned forward and raised her voice.

'Thank you so much for inviting me. This is incredible – so exciting. I don't even know where we're staying when we get there? Are we all on your boat?'

Reza looked blankly at her.

Feeling foolish, Abena smiled sheepishly and giggled. Immediately, Reza came alive.

'Abena, baby,' he boomed. 'Have some more Dom!' He waved at Henry to fill up her glass before turning back to Ciara and flirtatiously pushing a champagne cork down her vest top.

'See what I mean?' Henry raised an eyebrow at Abena before whistling as he reached for the culture section of the paper in front of him. 'Flaming Nora, I'm in love!' he swooned theatrically, fanning himself with a manicured hand. 'They could be right out of a Bruce Weber shoot.'

'What? Who?' Abena and Tara spluttered in unison, peering at the paper.

The headline read: 'ART WORLD LUMINARY TO PAINT PARTY BOY ADVERTISING HEIRS'. Under this heading was a photograph of two incredible-looking men. They clearly had not been amused to see the paparazzi but even their scowls could not detract from their amazing beauty. Reading on hungrily, Abena learnt that 'despite being publicity shy, brothers Alexander and Sebastian Spectre are known in fashionable circles for their good looks, fast living, rampant womanizing and their jaw-dropping wealth, but now they are making a new name for themselves with this unexpected collaboration ...'

'I had no idea they looked like that,' exclaimed a mooning Tara.

'I've never even heard of them. Where have they been all my life?' Abena said.

'I think the press have stung them a few times in the past, so you never see their pictures anywhere really,' said Henry. 'Last time I saw a photo of the kids was twenty years ago or so – I was ten, the elder Spectre boy was ten, and even then I was stirred. I think that was when I first knew …'

Seven bottles of champagne later, the plane touched down smoothly in the radiant French sunshine. Henry wiggled off to finalize logistics while the others disembarked at a leisurely pace. To his large villa by the beach next to Club 55, Reza brusquely dispatched Piers, Darren, Fadi and the two older women, who, it emerged, were best friends called Julia and Anna. They were both single and pushing forty and, though impeccably groomed, had that weather-beaten quality (possibly helped along by extensive plastic surgery) acquired from a very early start on the party circuit and far too many years of inebriated sleeping around with unsuitable men. They were quite unlike the yummy mummies and mega-rich divorcees of the Riviera who, though of a similar age, enjoyed an expensive and well-preserved beauty that lingered long into their forties. These women had benefited from a more restful period while married, and were now guaranteed future privilege due to hefty divorce settlements. The never-managed-to-marry-a-millionaire contingent, on the other hand, were by this age feeling the strain, and had to rely on the same freebie holidays they'd relied on in their youth, and these were becoming harder and harder to come by.

Reza's proposed sleeping arrangements put all the younger

girls with him on his boat – the winningly named *Deep Pleasure* – along with Henry and Anders, who, being homosexual, would have no intention of spoiling his fun.

'Oh no!' exclaimed Tara. 'That's such a shame as, er, *Deep Pleasure* sounds fantastic but I just cannot sleep on water. Never been able to – since I was a child. I get so horribly seasick. I'd be no fun whatsoever on the boat.' She sighed in anguish then pouted in that spoilt-child manner that certain men like. Abena, imagining the logistics of trying to escape Reza's advances when surrounded by deep water, added that she ought to stick with Tara. Julia and Anna then made it difficult for Reza to protest by immediately proffering their own services for the boat instead. Very tired services at that, Reza thought. He hadn't wanted to invite them but Henry had informed him that Piers liked a mature woman.

The teenagers tugged at their low-cut tops and pulled them down further to reveal more of their perky chests as they giggled. Anna and Julia might have been right when they'd huffed that seventeen was an optimistic estimate and that these girls could well be minors, mused Abena. Poor things, they seemed so young and out of their depth. 'Hi girls' Reza kept saying, to increasingly uneasy laughter.

'OK, listen up please everyone,' Henry called out. 'We're going to get you all in cars and after everybody has had a chance to settle in and freshen up we meet for dinner at Villa Romana, where we'll link up with Eric and his lot, and some more very lovely ladies who we've flown out on commercial flights. *Poooohee!*' He held his nose.

'Get on with it you miserable little fairy, I've got a conference call in ten minutes,' snapped Reza.

' And then after that I've organized the best table, a king-sized table, a *Reza*-sized table, in the VIP section at Les Caves. Yeah, yeah, yeah!'

Piers ushered the girls to the first waiting car and, beating the driver to it, held open the door for them. Abena noticed how much he resembled her old tutor at Oxford. 'He's got something of Professor Hughes about him hasn't he? A masterful quality …'

'Only *you*'d be able to see the good in that navel-gazing bore. I think my tutor was a eunuch,' laughed Tara.

'I just like men who I can learn from,' Abena protested.

Piers climbed into the passenger seat, a dimple forming in his cheek as he asked what outfits he would be dazzled with later. 'You girls had better start getting ready right away – it's almost five o'clock,' he teased. Although Piers was joking, the girls were already planning what to wear as they were driven towards Reza's villa in the uplifting sun, fully aware that London rules don't apply in St Tropez. Here, it was all-out glamour and sex-appeal. The adjectives 'tasteful' and 'understated' were obsolete in this part of the world and the girls knew that this was as much the resort's triumph as its failing. As they were transported past picturesque pastel-hued cottages and café-lined cobbled squares they felt nothing but love for the place.

The tall gates to Reza's villa were flanked by dense rows of palm trees. They opened to reveal a magnificent example of cutting-edge architecture set back in the gravelly grounds. The asymmetric front wall was painted a bold red and slanted dramatically from a single storey on the north side to three storeys on the south. It was breathtakingly audacious.

'Look at those windows!' Abena exclaimed, astounded by the glass shapes embedded into the wall. There were stars, moons and circles big enough to let in tons of light, but nothing resembling a standard rectangle.

An assortment of uniformed staff emerged and lined up on the front steps as the car approached. As soon as the driver braked they burst into a flurry of activity, unloading baggage and helping the girls and Piers out of the vehicle. A maid attempted to show Abena and Tara to their rooms but they sped past her in their haste to explore the villa, taking in the surprisingly minimal, spotless white spaces.

The sun went down but the evening remained warm and inviting. A butler brought a silver tray of Mojitos up to Abena's room, where the girls were getting ready together, and then, before they knew it, it was time for their driver to take them to dinner.

The Italian restaurant was furnished sumptuously, unapologetically overdone with gold-leaf furniture and mythical oil paintings adorning its walls. It hummed with the loud buzz of excited and exciting people. As the large group began congregating at the long corner table that overlooked the entire room, heads turned to stare at the unfolding spectacle.

Abena and Tara were the first of the girls to arrive, both clad in figure-hugging mini-dresses. Abena shimmered in a navy-blue skin-tight Roberto Cavalli number embellished with sequins that came right up to the neck at the front but was cut almost indecently low at the back to reveal an expanse of toned flesh. She had teamed this with a pair of flat gold gladiator sandals – the dress was foxy enough without heels, and besides, there were so many amazingly tall model types around that she figured she was better off going for the enchantingly petite and feminine effect, which made even the weediest of men feel as big and strong as Spartacus when she coquettishly looked up at them from under her curly dark lashes. Tara, however, had pulled out all the stops, and in five-inch heels was over six feet tall. She had opted for a black vintage Alaia bandeau dress. It needed no embellishment; she would let her whippet-like figure speak for itself. The men, with the exception of Reza, had arrived earlier, and now shot eager looks at the assembling delights. As Natalya and three tall Eastern European blondes strode across the room towards their table, all legs and big hair, Piers smirked. They had the attention of every single table in the restaurant and that was just as he liked it.

Pair by pair, women kept arriving to join the group. Striking women vastly outnumbered the men, who promptly set about making energetic displays of largesse, waving vigorously for rare bottles of champagne and enquiring after their favourite brands of cigar for after dinner. A place at the head of the table was reserved for Reza, but everybody else just pulled up a chair wherever there was a space. Piers grinned at Eric, a fellow financier, and winked in the direction of Tatiana, whose huge breasts threatened to tumble right out of her flimsy silk vest and knock over her Bellini each time she shook her long tresses from one shoulder to the other.

'So, I, er, think I made a mistake asking my latest "project" to come join us out in France tomorrow. There's already more than I can handle on this side of the Channel,' Piers told Eric, looking pointedly at Tatiana's chest as she ran her fingers slowly up and down her glass and pretended not to listen. 'Perhaps I can tell her I got called to a meeting and send her to Harvey Nicks with my credit card instead,' he mused. 'I haven't had time to look for another wife but I've always got a "project" on. As long as you keep them in holidays and watches and set them up with a nice convertible then they're happy.'

'Holy cow! Can *I* be a project?' cut in Tara, looking pained. Piers and Eric appeared momentarily surprised and then as Tara's face creased with laughter they joined her, guffawing a touch too loudly. Some of the other girls shot her irritated looks, annoyed that she'd managed to infiltrate the boys' talk and was threatening to rise above arm-candy status.

Natalya peered down from the other end of the table, where she sat in a strategically selected black silk dress that quietly skimmed her subtle curves. She'd been purposefully ignoring the men around her as this was always the most effective way of gaining attention from those not used to being disregarded. She stared enviously at Tara. All those flippant comments. Everything in her simple life could be neatly summed up, dealt with in a throwaway remark or a privileged laugh.

Finally Reza appeared, flanked by the two young Italians, Ciara and Francesca. Ciara, in a one-shouldered burgundy cocktail dress with her dark hair piled up high on her head and shimmering diamond drop earrings, looked like a sweet child who had raided her sexy elder sister's wardrobe. She took a seat squeezed in beside Reza and, pulling out a compact and lipstick, repainted her pouty mouth a brighter shade of red.

'Do my thighs look a little chunky in this dress?' Abena whispered to Tara, starting to regret having worn flats.

'No, no, you look great,' replied Tara without looking. Walking into the restaurant was a man in his late twenties or early thirties with swept-back ash-blond hair, finely chiselled cheekbones and a long Roman nose not dissimilar to her own. He was dressed in a pink shirt tucked into low-slung, pale blue jeans, with a chunky Rolex hanging loosely around his wrist.

As if reading Tara's mind, Henry winked and purred like a cat.

'Who is he meeting? Oh please God, don't let him have a girl-friend,' she muttered.

He sauntered through the restaurant and joined a dark-haired friend already seated with his back to the group. Abena had been studying him earlier, surprised that he was so casually dressed in shorts and a beat-up white T-shirt at this exclusive restaurant. He was enjoying a glass of chilled Sancerre, completely at ease waiting on his own, apparently oblivious to the female waitresses, each desperate to serve him. He rose to greet the blond newcomer and Abena found herself longing for him to turn round so that she could see the face above such promisingly broad shoulders. They were both tall and even from the back had that lazy air of youths who are used to easily having whatever they desire. Now they were laughing loudly over something, still standing. Over his shoulder the blond caught sight of the raucous corner table and ran his eyes briefly along it. He said something to his friend, who turned to glance at their table and, noticing the girls scrutinizing them with such intensity, directed a curious gaze at Abena. Jolted, she dropped her eyes hastily and studied her menu upside down.

'I'm sure I know them from somewhere,' she said.

As the bottles of vintage Bollinger gradually emptied and the night set in, the drunken group, buoyed up by the attention they'd been commanding, moved on to dance off their excited energy at Les Caves du Roy, the chicest and most exclusive nightclub in St Tropez. Reza, who was well known there, led the group past the queue of impossibly pretty young women and pushed his way to the entrance, stopping only to let Cameron Diaz enter before him. Once their table in the raised VIP area had been loaded with Grey Goose vodka and magnums of Cristal, Henry handed out glasses with a theatrical flourish. A few extra glasses of champagne were awarded to the hopeful hangers-on who were circling their prey like killer-heeled vultures. Swept away by the charged atmosphere, Tara and Abena started to dance on their seats, swaying crazily as they tried to emulate the sexy continental girls gyrating to the loud, catchy beats. 'Ooooooh Yeeeeaaahhh!' boomed the DJ with a phoney American accent. 'Welcome to Seeeaaaaiiint TRO PAY!'

Natalya stared at Tara and Abena, laughing and fooling around as they danced. The duo had amassed a fan club of men who were cheering them on from the floor below. Suddenly a gorgeous young Frenchman broke out from the crowd, vaulted over their table and landed behind them on the railing that separated the VIP area from the rest of the club. He hung upside down, swaying precariously in time to the music, trying to impress Abena. They seemed so happy and carefree. Natalya wondered what it would be like to have a close girlfriend with whom she could gossip about boys and go shopping. She felt pressure, constantly. Pressure to look after her mother and siblings. To secure a future for herself and to make sure she would never again know the kind of hardship she'd endured in Riga. Friendship was for other people. All the while a bright smile never left her face and her hips continued to wind in time with the music. She fixed her blue eyes on Reza and moved her body more slowly and sensually than before. Reza held her gaze, transfixed.

From her elevated position, Tara could see across the entire dance floor. Her heart skipped a beat as she noticed a pale, skinny man with peroxide blond hair flailing his arms and legs into a cluster of sycophantic clubbers. Surely that wasn't Dan Donahue of The Doctor, the hottest rock band of the moment and set to headline this year's Glastonbury festival? St Tropez didn't seem like his sort of place. Tara could imagine him holed up in some grungy New York studio getting high on heroin with his super-model girlfriend, but not here, bopping with the trillionaires. But, if her eyes were not deceiving her, the supermodel girlfriend was nowhere to be seen. That was definitely Dan Donahue, and what's more he was giving her the eye. Snaring a rock-star boyfriend was something Tara was not about to miss out on. She would just pop to the bathroom to perk herself up a little. And then he would be hers.

As she squeezed past Reza to head towards the bathroom, he grabbed her arm and shouted that he was going to move the party to his yacht in the next half hour or so. 'Sure', said Tara; all she could think of was the task at hand. Finally a cubicle in the female toilets came free and Tara pulled out a small ball of cling film filled with some of the cocaine that darling Henry had organized for her. Cutting up two fat lines with her credit card, and then adding another smaller one as an afterthought, she rolled up a fifty-euro note and snorted all three. That's better, she thought, as she grabbed her clutch bag and set it down in front of the mirror outside. She looked at herself critically. Her heart seemed to jump in her chest with every beat. Yes, she was stunning, she concluded. She was thin, well bred and well educated – she'd never felt more confident. She took out her concealer and dabbed some under her nostrils where they had gone red and tingly. Then she added a thick ring of kohl around each eye and shook her head violently to mess up her hair, scrunching it with her fingers. Now she looked like a young and gorgeous Courtney Love.

Striding into the middle of the dance floor, Tara pressed herself up against Dan, grinding in time to the music. He grabbed her hair with both hands and licked the side of her face as she lifted a willowy leg and coiled it around his thigh. 'Come on the boat', she shouted, struggling to make herself heard above the music. She grabbed his hand and pulled him on to the dimly lit street and through the central square towards the port, where Reza had already gathered a group. The pair kissed furiously all the way to the boat, then staggered up the gangplank, their passion only momentarily interrupted by one of the crew instructing them to remove their shoes so as not to ruin the pristine white interior. Tara was oblivious to everyone and everything as she pushed Dan into the first available cabin and locked the door. By the sultry light of the cabin he looked even paler than before, white, with burning black eyes like something out of *Twilight*. God he was sexy. So … dangerous-looking.

Dan threw her backwards on to the bed and leaned back against the wall, watching, leering. She reached into her bag and got out the rest of the cocaine. Not bothering to cut it this time, she put a little on her forefinger and sniffed it. She held some out for Dan to do the same. He grinned at her, baring his yellow teeth for the first time that evening, and greedily snorted the drug. Then in one quick movement he pulled off her skimpy dress and frantically undid his flies.

Tara was not wearing a bra; her pert, childlike breasts required no additional support. In their urgency to make it they didn't even think about foreplay. Pulling aside her lacy knickers, Dan rammed his cock inside her and thrust away for what seemed like ages. In awe of his rock-star status and desperate to impress, she found she was unable to relax and enjoy herself, and barely even noticed that he in turn was unable to climax, having probably taken too much coke that evening. Eventually, exhausted, the two lay sprawled on the bed in silence. Tara's mind was racing, imagining her future as a rocker's girlfriend. A hit song dedicated to her perhaps. Matching tattoos. A crazy life on the road in LA and a star on Hollywood Boulevard … Or maybe a shotgun wedding, her own rock-chick clothing range, and an entire issue of *W* magazine dedicated to Dan Donahue's English fashionista wife …

A loud hammering on the door interrupted her fantasizing.

'Hey, what's going on? I need to get to my cabin!'

Tara and Dan sat up, startled, as they heard a female voice calling from behind the door. Scrambling into her dress, Tara smoothed down her hair and emerged with Dan. She wasn't embarrassed, she was invincible now, she was with Dan Donahue.

Outside, the party was in full swing. 'Baby, let me get you a drink,' she cooed, turning to Dan.

'Shit,' he muttered, checking the time on his phone. He kissed Tara's forehead and stroked her cheek with the back of his hand. 'Listen Lara, I've gotta go. You're sweet.' And turning on his heel, he hurried down the gangplank and ran down the road back towards Les Caves.

# *Chapter 4*

Tara woke up shortly before midday the following morning. Remembering the mortifying details of the night before, she promptly buried her head back under the soft white covers and tried to erase him from her mind. Finding she couldn't go back to sleep, she put on a bikini, a kaftan, a wide-brimmed sunhat and a giant pair of fuck-off shades and made her way through the villa to the breakfast table on the patio, which overlooked the Jacuzzi and enormous infinity pool. One of the housekeepers had laid out a feast of warm croissants and pastries, coffee, tropical fruit, yogurt and freshly squeezed fruit smoothies. She poured herself a cup of black coffee and nibbled half-heartedly on some fruit salad. All ten places had been set, which was customary throughout the summer in case Reza sent any of his 'projects' over to the villa on a whim.

'Sooo ... Tell all!' boomed Abena, skipping happily outside to bask in the strong sun. Tara winced. For someone so small her friend's voice was pretty deep and powerful.

'Baby, it's far too early to be in such high spirits.'

Abena joined her pal at the table and plonked two pains au chocolat on her plate. The diet can start tomorrow, she thought to herself, a thought that occurred every single day.

'I can't believe you pulled Dan Donahue, what happened? Are you seeing him tonight? I looked for you everywhere at Les Caves and on the boat but I couldn't find you. Come on, cough up you little minx!'

'Aaargh, Abbi, it was soo WRONG!' Tara groaned, removing her shades to reveal swollen, bloodshot eyes. 'I really thought he was into me. He kept saying I was stunning and sexy and whatnot, and that he wanted to take me to his gigs back at home, and that he'd been staring at me dancing for ages before we spoke.'

'Mmmn, he couldn't take his hands off you in the club,' agreed Abena through a mouthful of pain au chocolat.

'Well anyway, I brought him along to the boat and well, you know, we kind of got carried away and ended up shagging. But, literally, as soon as it was over, and I mean, like, the second it was over, he said he had to leave and just walked out. And to add insult to injury, he didn't even remember my name! God I hate him!' Tara put her sunglasses back on so that Abena wouldn't see that she was crying.

'Ouch. Well, he might still call you today, he's probably just being rock and roll – how long is he in town for?'

'He didn't bother to get my number,' Tara sniffed, 'and he flies back to New York this afternoon.' She was careful to avoid any mention of cocaine, as she knew that Abena, who'd had what she thought was a mini heart attack the last time she'd done it, was now set against her taking the drug.

'Well why don't we get dressed up a bit and head down to Nikki Beach. I met a bunch of really sweet guys last night who are going down today and we can join them. It'll be good for you to take your mind off Dan.' And then, when Tara still wouldn't budge, 'If he's off today he's bound to go for a last round of partying at the beach before he leaves.'

'Alright, alright, let's go to Nikki Beach then,' conceded Tara, getting up and sliding into the pool for a few laps to work off her misery, then emerging twenty minutes later slightly cheered.

The girls took their time over the ritual of dressing for the beach, luxuriating in the fresh sea air and bright sunlight shining directly through the patio doors and into the villa.

'Oh fuck, what are you wearing, hon?' Abena asked, popping her head into Tara's room. This is more stressful than I imagined it'd be. It's been far too long since I've had everything on show like this.'

'Dunno, thought I might get into the swing of things and go for my cut-out one-piece, but I don't want to mess up my tan …'Tara replied. She had perked up considerably and was now dancing naked to dodgy music from a local radio station that she'd turned up as high as it could go.

'How about you? Surely you remember the advice we were given by the paragon of elegance and good taste that is Natalya?' Tara raised an arched eyebrow mockingly.

Abena thought back to what Natalya had said the night before about the importance of dressing for the beach and chuckled. As mercenary as Natalya had been, she'd kind of had a point when she'd claimed that 'it's at private beach clubs and pools that serious decisions are made'. By the bright light of day at Club 55, she had explained, the owners of the largest yachts can be seen descending on to the shore for lunch, giving anyone looking to sell – shares, businesses, homes, even their body and soul – access to dozens of potential business partners and clients. Across the champagne-saturated pool at Nikki Beach, a girl can be seen in all her glory as her bikini-clad body teeters on the brink of deep water, never quite entering. 'Anybody who has seen or been seen by day,' Natalya had said, 'will make an appearance at Les Caves or VIP by night, and at these clubs, on dance floors and at tables, the seduction takes place.'

Abena laughed at the memory. 'Natalya's cynicism is terrifying, but somehow I like her. She's amusing and very, very intriguing. I kind of feel sorry for her sometimes.'

'Intriguing? Or downright shady? She makes me uneasy.'

In the end, the girls both settled coincidentally on animal-print bikinis. Black-and-white zebra print for Tara. She wasn't yet tanned enough to wear the plain white one that made her feel like Ursula Andress emerging from the sea. Abena wore a leopard-print string bikini, an ostentatious choice considering she felt self-conscious next to skinny Tara. No matter how many times she told herself that Tara had the body of a peculiarly tall, prepubescent little girl whereas she had a trim, athletic, young woman's body, she always ended up feeling that her muscular thighs were too chunky. They threw on floaty chiffon mini-dresses in pastel colours and stepped into flat bejewelled sandals. The bikini-and-high-heels look was for the likes of Natalya.

Next came full faces of make-up, expertly applied to give the impression of flawless and bare summer skin. Hair slicked into chic top-knots and big sunglasses completed the seasoned jet-setter look. Abena picked up her phone to text the boys she'd met last night. *Just ask for my table at the entrance* came the immediate reply. God, these guys are all so arrogant! she thought. They expect everyone to simply know who they are. Struggling to focus through her hangover, she texted back: *My mother told me never to meet boys whose sirname I don't know.*

Beep beep and in came the smug reply: *And my mother told me never to associate with girls who can't spell "surname". Banio.*

Embarrassed, Abena was tempted to reply that seeing as neither of their mothers were likely to approve, they should just call it quits now. Instead she gritted her teeth and typed in a smiley face, followed by: *Ha, ha – you got me! Great, see you in a few minutes.*

When Abena picked up a book to bring along, Tara stared at it and guffawed loudly. 'Leo Tolstoy's *Anna Karenina*! It's a great book, hon, but I somehow don't see you getting round to reading that this morning.'

'Yep, sod that,' laughed Abena and grabbed a copy of *Vogue* instead. She was here to party; Tolstoy could wait till the plane.

When the girls arrived at Nikki Beach and were pointed in Stefano's direction, even consummate partier Tara paused to take in the scene. The place was not so much a beach as a large pool with a busy bar area painted brilliant white and surrounded by white sun loungers and beds. It was 2 p.m. and a DJ was already spinning dancey house music. The boys were lying on the loungers, drinking champagne. There were four of them although Abena only recognized Stefano Banio and somebody she vaguely remembered being introduced as Pietro, who'd been wearing his shades even inside the nightclub. None of the boys was especially handsome, yet there was something impressive and attractive about each one of them. Perhaps it was simply that they were a great deal younger than the majority of men the girls had met so far. Tara thought it was also their collective air of confidence. They had a uniform look, which oozed luxury, from the cut of their slim-fitting tailored shirts and colourful shorts to the self-assured way they were sprawled on their sun loungers. Even their floppy dark hair was silkier and shinier than any of her girlfriends' back in London. Their eyes and teeth shone with vitality and their deep tans and Mediterranean features hinted at lives as fast and flamboyant as Ferraris.

The boys rose and introduced themselves as Stefano, Alessandro, Gennaro and Pietro. They fussed over the girls, making sure that they were comfortable and had drinks, and commenting on how fantastic they looked. Tara in particular appreciated the boys' attentiveness in the light of Dan's humiliating treatment of her the night before. They were all from Rome but were studying for post-graduate degrees in London and spoke eloquently in English. They tended to spend every other summer weekend in St Tropez as some of their families had villas there.

A shower of cascading Dom Pérignon suddenly interrupted the group. This was accompanied by a squeal from a skinny blonde who had been the intended target of an orgy of champagne spraying taking place beside them. Looking again, Stefano let out a horrified groan. 'Oh no, Paris Hilton is here!'

By early evening, Nikki Beach was full of gorgeous people dancing under the romantic dusk sky. With its gleaming white decor, the place looked like a fashion shoot. Most people had been drinking since lunchtime and whatever problems anybody might have had were forgotten for the evening. Poseurs relaxed and insecurities melted away alongside sobriety. The atmosphere was delicious. Tara had been lifted up on to Alessandro's strong shoulders and was dancing in her bikini, all thoughts of Dan Donahue forgotten. Stefano made a similar grab for Abena but she squirmed away from him with an impish grin, dodging his attempts to throw her into the pool.

'What does everyone feel like doing for food?' called out Pietro from where he lay languidly on a sun lounger, one hand behind his head and the other idly massaging his chest. He had not once removed his dark glasses and Abena wouldn't have been surprised if he wore them to bed. Unbeknown to him, the girls had renamed him 'the Celebrity', which was causing them endless giggles.

'We should probably get going actually. We need to go back to our villa and change for dinner with the guys who invited us out here,' replied Abena. 'It'd be much more fun to go for dinner with you guys though …'

'Well why don't we?' cut in Tara. 'It's not like Reza will miss us. He probably won't be able to see past Tatiana's humongous boobs to notice that's there's nobody on the other side.'

'I just think it's too rude, hon,' Abena laughed. 'After all, it's because of Reza that we're here in the first place.'

'Whatever you say.' Tara jumped off Alessandro's shoulders, with his help, and Abena found herself wondering, as she often did, at her friend's willowy elegance.

They made plans for the boys to come and party on Reza's boat later, and were just about to put on their dresses and leave when Stefano waved over some friends who looked familiar.

Immediately, Tara added some lip gloss and did her best to seem uninterested. Strolling towards the group were the two incredible-looking guys they'd spotted last night at dinner. They were brothers. Stefano introduced the blond as Alex and his darker-haired sibling as Sebastian. Abena glanced at Tara, who got it immediately. They were the very same Alexander and Sebastian Spectre they'd read about on the flight over. No wonder they'd looked so familiar yesterday. Up close, the image of the two brothers standing side by side was so powerful that for a few beats neither Abena nor Tara could speak. With his bright green eyes and smooth skin, Alex, the older brother, had a soft, refined elegance that stopped just short of effeminacy. Sebastian, who seemed younger, had a harder handsomeness. His eyes were greeny-brown and his face was tanned and chiselled, with not an ounce of fat masking the striking structure of his high cheekbones; designer stubble framed his wide, sulky mouth and his coolly dishevelled brown hair was just the right side of long.

If the brothers recognized anybody from last night they didn't betray it.

'Hi,' Alex said to Tara, fixing her with a lingering stare.

She managed to extend her hand. 'I'm Tara,' she attempted, but it came out as a high-pitched squeak. Whipping out her mobile, she shot off as if to make a call, but really to stop herself from staring or gibbering inanely.

Meanwhile Sebastian smiled at Abena, enjoying both her discomfiture and her skimpy bikini. Forcing a smile, Abena reached out to meet his hand. She knew his type: always surrounded by doting girls; annoyingly good-looking, intolerably vain and narcissistic; flighty, unreliable and ultimately only concerned with themselves. She'd been suckered by that sort of man before, but since her last few boyfriends had all proved such painful disappointments she'd been weaning herself off them and was determined to meet a good old-fashioned man with intelligence, ambition and integrity, not a fashionable pretty-boy who spent his entire life at parties.

'I … I think I saw you at the restaurant last night,' Abena faltered, regretting it immediately.

'Did you?' Sebastian replied. 'I didn't see you. I'm sure I'd have remembered something that delicious.'

Abena felt intensely aware of how much flesh she was exposing under his hot, suggestive gaze, and she hated that he absolutely knew how handsome he was. She turned away from him to face Stefano as a catchy song that had been playing at Les Caves the night before came on. His face lit up with delighted recognition and he started to bounce along to the beat.

When Tara returned she was not amused to find Abena holding court, surrounded by the four Italians and the two new English recruits. She'd been telling a story and the guys were roaring with laughter as she went on to conclude '…and then when my mother patted her stomach and finally told me where babies really *did* come from, I refused to speak to her for a whole week because I thought she'd eaten me.'

Tara's display of uninterestedness had clearly not impressed Alex as she'd hoped. Wanting a piece of the action for herself she joined in the raucous laughter, clutching at Gennaro's arm with the hilarity of it all. When nobody looked her way, she turned to Sebastian and Stefano and asked how it was that they'd all met.

'Just a second,' Sebastian grinned, 'I want to hear this.' Once Abena had finished her jolly monologue, Sebastian replied, 'Oh, in space.'

'Oh right, in Ibiza?'

'No. In space. Our families were some of the first space tourists.

57

Long before all these companies sprang up and starting taking bookings to organize trips.'

'No way! Tara was astounded, and by now the rest of the group were also listening.

'It's true,' Stefano admitted, blushing sweetly. 'It's not something we normally tell people about.' He glared at Sebastian, who met his eyes unrepentantly.

'But wouldn't you have been all over the news?' Tara asked.

'There's nothing in this world that can't be paid for,' countered Sebastian, raising an eyebrow at his brother, who backed him up with a casual nod.

There was an awkward silence. 'Well, we'd better go,' said Abena, looking at Tara, unable to think up a good excuse to ditch their plans and hang out. They said their goodbyes and walked off arm in arm out of Nikki Beach. Aware that the brothers were likely to be watching their retreating backs, Tara couldn't take in Abena's keyed-up chatter, concentrating instead on wiggling a little but not too much, for their benefit. Only once they were out of eye-shot did she stop and release her barely contained excitement.

'Aaaargh!' Tara screamed, hopping from foot to foot like a lunatic.

Abena shook her head with a knowing grin. 'Alex is very you!'

Personally she'd been floored by Sebastian's infuriating magnetism, but Tara had been eyeing Alex and was clearly smitten.

'To be honest I wouldn't say no to either of them. They are divine. Abbi, is it wrong to feel this way? Am I a completely shallow, heartless thing to be so looks obsessed?'

'Of course not darling – what was it the Greeks said about beauty? About how it's an earthly reminder of a higher, better realm and therefore an incredibly important and far from shallow preoccupation? If Plato's cool with it then so am I.'

'I don't think Plato was thinking about you and me in string bikinis on Nikki Beach.'

'Honey, I'm throwing you a line – just take it.'

They made their way giddily back to Reza's, trying to find a Greek philosopher who'd allow Tara a guilt-free bitch about her mother.

# Chapter 5

Sarah didn't yet know it, but today was to be a special day. She had been working at the *Wimbledon Gazette* for just over three months. It was her first job since graduating the previous summer, and although they were only paying expenses, she enjoyed it. For as long as she could remember, she'd dreamed of being a journalist. Proper journalism. Perhaps she'd be a foreign correspondent reporting from war-torn parts of the world. None of this ridiculous fashion writing or presenting reality TV series, which would just be depressing. At least from a state of war things can only get better, but for the *Big Brother* wannabes of this world there is no hope. After leaving university Sarah had duly fired off a series of applications for the graduate schemes at *The Times, FT, Independent, Guardian, Observer* and *Telegraph*. It seemed that almost every other graduate in the country who could string a sentence together had had the same idea, and she had been devastated not to get an interview anywhere. Setting her sights lower, she'd then applied to small local papers and had still struggled to get her application taken seriously. Eventually Pam from the *Wimbledon Gazette*, which was close to her home, had offered her a four-month work experience placement to start early in February. She had thought hard over whether she could afford to accept an unpaid offer, but eventually decided that it was important for her to get a foot in the door. She would just have to delay moving out of her parents' house in leafy Wimbledon for a month or two.

It was now just a few weeks before her internship was supposed to come to an end and Sarah needed to start thinking of what she would go on to next. Pam had hinted that there might be a chance for her to stay on longer, but it wasn't clear whether that was a job offer or simply an extension of the internship. Still, there were only six people working on editorial for the *Gazette* and four of them were nearing retirement age so surely they must be looking for someone. Then perhaps she could apply for something more stretching in a year's time.

She let herself into the small office and was surprised to find the usually subdued team chatting heatedly.

'What's up?' she asked. 'Anything exciting happening in the ghettos of Wimbledon?'

'Well actually,' replied Tom, struggling to pick up a stapler that had fallen off a pile of papers on Sarah's desk, 'we do have an interesting assignment for you.' Tom, her youngest colleague at thirty-four, but with a chin for each year of his life, had been in love with Sarah since she'd first walked in, and she found his ardour very sweet. Not that she'd ever fall for it, she was very happy in her relationship with Simon Tamarand, her childhood sweetheart.

'As you might have heard,' continued Tom, 'Willy Eckhardt is moving to the UK from LA to make a fresh start, trying to resuscitate his pop career while setting up a series of business ventures in the entertainment sector. Anyhow, the place he has chosen for his new home is none other than our very own Wimbledon.'

'And,' cut in Pam, 'he's agreed to give us his first interview this evening.'

'Exactly,' said Tom. 'He's notorious for not giving much away, but as you can turn men into babies with your smile we thought we'd give you the assignment! We've booked the Wolseley for 9 p.m. this evening and you're to meet him and his publicist, Gloria, there for supper.'

'Oh gosh!' exclaimed Sarah. 'Well OK, yep, sure. Um. OK!' This was very out of the blue. She hadn't had any big pieces to do and suddenly they were giving her their biggest star all to herself. Willy was huge! Sure, a couple of things he'd done were verging on naff – that *Willy Make it in Hollywood?* documentary was truly dreadful – but in terms of exposure he was massive, everybody knew him. Good thing she hadn't changed her mind and gone on that free holiday with Abena; this was an amazing opportunity. She glanced back at the others, not quite believing it, and noticed that Tom was still gazing at her with a pained expression on his face. He reminded her of the rescued French Bulldog puppy she'd had when she was younger, which had looked at her in that way whenever she wasn't paying him any attention. Feeling sorry for him she asked Tom to accompany her to the theatre tomorrow as Si had to work late.

Sarah had an understated beauty that crept up on you. She was not a bombshell in a flashy, look-at-me kind of way. Instead there was a quiet loveliness about her. Nothing in her appearance stood out for its unusually gorgeous configuration, but every feature fitted in neatly with every other feature. Nothing was exaggerated and nothing was lacking. Sarah's mouth was not full and seductive, nor was it too thin. Her nose didn't draw attention to itself, because it was not extraordinary in any way. Her eyes were mid-brown, neither large nor small. Her skin, smooth and lightly tanned all year round, had no interesting quirks; no childlike freckles, no Cindy Crawford moles, just a clear complexion. And her thick hair was a natural dark brown and fell to her shoulders in a simple, straight cut. She looked like a healthy young woman who one day would bear a brood of gorgeous wholesome kids with their own set of perfect features. She was friendly and easygoing too, and almost every straight man fell for her in some way.

It was not that they merely *fancied* her. Women have never found it difficult to seduce men. What was exceptional about Sarah was that she made men want to marry her. They wanted not only her body but also everything she stood for. She was beautiful but not threatening. Her face and body welcomed and reassured them – had a maternal quality that made them feel as though they could bury their heads in her ample bosom and she would stroke away all the monsters. And yet she made men feel like men; she was so soft and womanly and kind to them that they wanted to be by her side and protect her always. Where they could only admire or objectify or lust over other women, men *loved* Sarah.

And so it was with full confidence in her ability to charm any skeletons out of Willy's closet that the *Wimbledon Gazette* dispatched her on this task. There was one minor problem. Because the whole thing had been announced at such short notice, she only had until six o'clock to memorize everything there was to know about Willy Eckhardt. She had promised Si that she'd have drinks with him at six-thirty and had no intention of cancelling. Since he'd started working at Atkins & Allison she barely saw him and they'd already had to miss 'snuggle Sunday' last weekend as he'd been paintballing at a team-bonding event.

\*\*\*\*

Sarah arrived at the Wolseley at nine o'clock precisely, dressed as she had been all day in a colourful, floaty knee-length skirt, a cream polo neck and ballet pumps. She was rarely late for anything and tonight was no exception.

'Hunter … booked for three,' murmured the elegant maître d', checking his list of table bookings. 'You're the first to arrive Madam, shall I show you to your table? Or there's also a table up on the gallery which has just come free?'

'Actually,' replied Sarah, 'I think I'll have a drink at the bar while I wait for the others, if that's OK?' As the bar was situated at the front of the sweeping central dining room, Sarah guessed she'd see Willy and his publicist as they arrived, and she hoped she'd blend in more in the crowded bar than if she waited alone at the table, where someone might spot that she didn't really belong in this sophisticated restaurant, that she was an impostor.

She ordered a small glass of house white, glad she'd stuck to water with Si. The clock above the bar showed that it was now five past nine. Sarah was grateful for more time to collect herself and prepare her questions. By the time she finished her wine, though, it was nine-thirty and she began to feel nervous, then a bit annoyed. If she were famous, not that she particularly wanted to be, she'd try even harder to be on time for everything, and to be lovely to everyone too, simply because it wasn't what people expected. She got out her mobile; perhaps she had missed a call from Willy's publicist. Nope. She ordered another glass from the attentive barman.

'Been stood up?' he grinned.

'I really, really, *really* hope not,' Sarah responded.

'Well he'd be an idiot to leave you in the lurch.'

'Thanks.' Sarah smiled shyly. Normally she was uninterested in appreciative comments from men but she was seriously nervous now and starting to regret not changing her outfit, so on this occasion the compliment was welcome.

Glancing at the entrance for the umpteenth time she was relieved to see Willy bounce into the restaurant, unaccompanied, and approach the maître d', cracking jokes and doing comedy impressions with everyone from the doorman to a departing diner on the way. He was casually dressed in blue jeans and a long-sleeved white T-shirt. At once her nerves disappeared and she jumped off her stool to greet him.

'Mr Eckhardt,' she breezed, 'I'm Sarah Hunter from the *Wimbledon Gazette*. Lovely to meet you. Welcome to London.'

'Nice to see you, to see you …' He made a rolling gesture with his hands and then pointed at Sarah with a dazzling, toothy grin, as though he was waiting for her to finish his sentence.

'Er … nice?' Sarah faltered, astonished he was up on nineties British television.

'You got it,' he cried in a broad American accent, pumping her small hand with his strong, neatly manicured one. 'So sorry to be late. And I'm afraid Gloria fell ill and is unable to be here.'

'Oh that's quite alright, I've been having a drink at the bar, I haven't waited long. Very sorry to hear about Gloria though, I hope she feels better soon. Now tell me, would you like to sit up on the gallery, or by the window?'

'Wherever's fine. I'm easy. Just put me where ya want me.'

Sarah was surprised at how open and friendly Willy was. She'd been expecting diva-like behaviour but he was charm personified. Physically, he was shorter than she'd imagined, but other than that he looked exactly as he did in photos. At forty, with sandy hair, even features and a slim, athletic build she supposed he was suavely handsome, but she'd been with Si for so long that she no longer looked at men in that way.

They both ordered quail eggs to start and these arrived quickly.

'Say, are you French?' Willy asked the waiter. 'You are? Oh la la! Fabulous place.' He put up a hand to high-five the bemused French man and Sarah was impressed to see Willy being chatty and interesting with the waiter. She mustn't be so prejudiced, she chastised herself; not all famous people are monsters.

'So, tell me about student life here. The lady at the *Gazette* told me you went to Oxford. Is it all homo-erotic high jinx, plummy accents and posh tomfoolery like in *Brideshead*?' Willy gave a hearty chuckle.

She laughed. 'Well, if that's what you go in for, Willy, I think we've got the beginnings of a very juicy interview already. This is far easier than I expected … But, actually, no, you can involve yourself in whatever scene takes your fancy. I got really into student journalism. Have you been to Oxford?'

'No, not yet,' replied Willy. 'I gotta. I've barely even had the chance to explore the sights of London – visited tons of times but all I ever get to see are the insides of airport lounges, offices and restaurants! It's a real shame, there's such a wealth of culture here.'

'Oh yes there is; in Oxford you must have a wander through

67

the colleges and go punting along the Cherwell. It's ravishing in spring, particularly with a group of friends or a partner ...' she trailed off, blushing.

Willy nodded vigorously. 'My wife and kids would just adore that.'

He looked thrilled, so Sarah started to list all the things she thought he might like about the city. 'Christ Church is marvellously old and beautiful and of course *Harry Potter* was filmed there, so your boys might like that,' she began.

It seemed like only a minute had passed since they'd sat down to dinner but already they were almost through their mains: sea bass for Willy and scallops with risotto nero for Sarah. Willy reached for the aged Gavi di Gavi, but it was already empty.

'Ooops, looks like we need another.'

'Whoops,' Sarah giggled. 'I thought LA people didn't drink anyway.'

'Actually I'm not a heavy drinker, but, hey, when in Rome! Anyway I'm not exactly an LA person.'

'Hey!', she laughed, remembering why she was there, 'you've managed to evade interrogation thus far, but we're here to talk about you! Come on – so what really made you give up singing so suddenly? It looked as though you were on a winning streak.'

'I'll tell you what,' Willy replied, 'I am happy to tell you anything you wanna know, but first, why don't we pay up in this posh joint and go get some dessert, or "pudding" as you guys would say, at a great place I know a block from here?'

'Sure.' Sarah signalled for the bill, curious to see what sort of place he would take her to.

A waiter placed the bill discreetly in front of Willy, at which point Sarah retorted that he should 'pass that over here right this minute'. She reached into her purse and placed her tatty debit card on the small silver tray. She'd claim it all back on expenses, she just hoped there was enough money in her account to cover all that they'd chomped away on so far.

Immediately, Willy removed her card.

'How many of you guys are there at the *Gazette*, huh? It's a small outfit isn't it? Please let me pay, it's the least I can do after such a delightful evening.'

Despite the possibility of an embarrassing scenario during which her dismal fiscal situation could be revealed, Sarah wouldn't hear of it.

'Listen, Mister, we're welcoming you to Wimbledon. The *Gazette* will take care of this no problem.'

They eventually settled on Willy paying at the Wolseley and the *Gazette* would cover pudding.

As Willy bundled her into the dark green chauffeur-driven Bentley he had waiting outside, Sarah realized that she hadn't had this much fun in ages. Si was always working late, and when she saw him they liked to cosy up together on the sofa. Of course Abena and some of her other friends were always out at places like this, but somehow whenever she met up with them it was for relaxed lunches or to go to the theatre. She supposed she fell into the 'boring married' bracket, and if a wild night were on the cards you'd call someone like Tara. Well she couldn't wait to tell Abena, and no doubt bitchy Tara would be in tow too, all about this evening.

The Bentley pulled up outside an innocuous-looking place in Soho called The French House. The spot was packed with arty types in eccentric outfits and had an unstuffy atmosphere. Sarah found herself warming to Willy even more for bringing her here: she wouldn't have thought he, in his chauffeur-driven car, would like this sort of thing. They walked inside and headed upstairs to the restaurant.

Sarah struggled to decide which of the five desserts to choose, so Willy beckoned the waitress and ordered all five.

'You know, I wanna apologize again for keeping you waiting earlier. I have a new team over here and my assistant's a great girl, but not a clue. She booked that big car and then sent it to the wrong place, which is why I was so late. She sent it to my house, but it's not ready yet as my design team and workmen went AWOL, so we're in a hotel until we can find out where to get new ones to finish the job.'

'Oh really, don't worry about it – I'd forgotten already. How are you planning to do up your new home?'

'Well my wife loves bright colours, I love big, open spaces and we both love contemporary art and furniture, but we gotta think about the kids too. Especially being over here when all my wife's interiors contacts are back home.'

'Hmmn … Vast, colourful, modern spaces for all the family … I might have a few ideas for you. Let me do some research and get back to you.' She made a note to send Willy the information along with her sightseeing suggestions for Oxford and London.

'So, now tell me about you, Willy. Why did you stop singing? You've always been very coy about that.'

Willy stared into his empty dessert wine glass, his eyes opaque and unreadable for the first time that evening.

'When you're a man and you have bulimia, you sometimes

70

don't want to shout it from the rooftops.'

Sarah said nothing.

'Nobody knows. Apart from my wife.' He looked up and shrugged his shoulders.

'Willy, that's a deeply personal thing and I'm not going to print that.' Sarah fought back compassionate tears. Her drunkenness wasn't helping.

'It was a very brief and strange thing – lasted just a few months. But it said something to me. That all the pressure was getting too much. I was just a kid from Minnesota and I'd achieved this cult status worldwide with one silly, gimmicky song. I couldn't handle it. I wasn't strong enough, my voice wasn't strong enough. And my body was trying to find a way to tell me that. But do, please do, print it. Because I think my story should be told. If I can help one other man out there then I've done a wonderful thing. And anyway that was twenty years ago. The key is I'm older, wiser, stronger now. In the interim I've grown up. I know about song-writing. I've written hundreds of songs for other artists and made a lot of money. I understand the entertainment industry and I know I can help nurture talent. Encourage young musicians in the way I was not. So that's what I'm going to try to do with the production of *Britain's Next Musical Megastar*. It'll be better than all those other TV talent shows already out there because I feel it in my heart, I've suffered for it and I believe in it.'

Wow, thought Sarah. *Gazette* mission well and truly accomplished. But all she wanted to do was reach out and hug the man. Checking the time, she gasped when she saw that it was nearly 1 a.m. Willy appeared to be thinking the same thing, but before they parted outside the restaurant, he put a hand on her shoulder

71

and said, 'You're too good for that place.'

'Thanks Willy, I'm actually job-hunting now anyhow.'

Politely refusing his offer of a ride home, Sarah climbed into a taxi and they headed to opposite ends of town.

# Chapter 6

Sunday was supposed to be everyone's last day in St Tropez but Tara and Abena had no intention of going anywhere. Tara, having got over the immediate hurt of being used for sex by Dan Donahue, was now feeling rather pleased with her conquest and couldn't wait to let everybody know she'd pulled him. Since then she'd been having a fabulous time hanging out with the Italians and had barely seen Reza at all. The Italians were flying home on Tuesday morning and she was desperate to stay one more night and try to seduce Alex, who she hadn't seen since they had been briefly introduced at Nikki Beach. Likewise, Abena was in no hurry to leave and felt it wouldn't be the end of the world if she called in sick tomorrow.

'Do you think Reza will stump up for our flights home if we stay an extra night?' Tara asked.

'Hmmn, I'm not sure – that might be pushing it. Let's see if he's on form.'

Reaching for her phone by the side of the villa pool, where the two were sitting dangling their feet in the warm water, Abena dialled Reza's number and waited. He still made her nervous.

'Reza, how are you? I've barely seen you in the last couple of days. Not fair! I want to be on the yacht with you!' she flirted, winking at Tara, who got up and moved away so that Reza wouldn't hear her hooting with laughter.

'So you've missed me have you?' Reza leered down the phone. 'I haven't been … playing with you, have I? I know you want some Reza time …' He was talking bizarrely loudly and Abena suspected he had company he was keen to impress. As if on cue she heard excited female shrieks in the background. 'Oh Reza', someone moaned.

'There's not enough of you to go round,' Abena sighed into the earpiece as Tara made a puking gesture at her.

'I wanna make it up to you girls. You can both see me now – I'm throwing a lunch at Club 55 on the beach. Talk to Henry. And look goooood.'

When the girls arrived at Club 55, Reza was already seated, on time for once. Beside him Ciara looked adorable in a short black chiffon dress over a black bikini. Natalya was on his other side and dressed surprisingly demurely, in a white shirt over a white Chanel swimsuit and white linen trousers. Also present were two blondes with dark roots who nobody seemed to know, and who looked as though they could be hookers picked up the previous night. They sat in silence throughout the meal, smiling thinly at Reza. Gradually the group swelled as more of Reza's business partners and clients arrived with their girlfriends. The seafood lunch was light and delicious and Abena decided to go and thank Reza as an excuse to strike up a conversation. She slid into Ciara's seat, which she'd vacated to go to the bathroom, and Reza nodded, putting a moist hand on her thigh as he shovelled a forkful of lobster into his mouth.

Abena was just trying to work out how to tell Reza that she would be staying on longer, when she felt scrabbling under the table by her feet. Suddenly Reza dropped his fork and moaned, much to the surprise of his lunch companions. Before he could explain, Ciara returned from the ladies and headed for the seat that Abena had usurped. Reza barked, 'Go and finish your food. I'll send a car for you later for the plane.'

'Well, that's the thing; Tara and I were thinking we might stay here one more night as a girlfriend of ours is arriving later.'

A flicker of irritation could be detected in Reza's eyes.

'OK. You got money?'

'Umm, er, yep, yeah sure,' Abena lied, and returned to her seat at the end of the table. She was heartened later, though, when she heard Reza instruct Henry to book flights for them from Nice the following afternoon.

Julia and Anna, who'd not been seen since the flight over, now appeared with a couple of short, fat, balding men. For such unattractive men, their arrival caused a big stir in the restaurant and Reza jumped up to ostentatiously welcome them to his table. Anna was ridiculously dolled up for lunch on the beach, in bright red lipstick and vertiginous heels. An intricate pendant nestled between her cosmetically enhanced breasts. Her forehead was too shiny, as if the skin had been stretched over her skull. She leaned over and whispered something in her man's ear, but he wasn't listening. He was staring at Tara, who was eyeing everything but him. Changing tack, the man mopped his sweating brow with a napkin and leaned across towards the more curvaceous of the two hookers. 'You having a good time?' he asked. She smiled and giggled.

Tara watched the exchange out of the corner of her eye and winced. Turning to Abena, she muttered, 'So painful to see past-it women desperately on the look-out for a rich husband, having to compete with nineteen-year-old models, and even prostitutes!'

'Come on it could happen to anyone,' said Abena. 'We can't just click our fingers and magic up a soulmate when we feel like it. I guess it just happens, and in the meantime, why not try to have fun?'

She broke off as the two men made as if to leave and Reza tapped one of the hookers on the arm.

'You two. Go with them,' he growled.

Wordlessly they followed the two men out of the restaurant, while Anna and Julia pretended to be deep in conversation, affecting indifference that yet another tycoon had slipped their ringless fingers.

As dusk set in and lunch had long since ended, it seemed to Natalya that she had only just arrived, and yet it was already time to leave. Truth be told, she was irritated that Reza had kept such a close eye on her throughout the weekend. It's not as though he wanted to date her himself. Everybody knew that Reza didn't do girlfriends; he was too busy making money. But he had still claimed her as an acquisition, a part of his empire, and as a result she had been unable to meet anyone. Married Gregory was small fry, she'd dated him on and off since she was sixteen and he bored her to tears. So what if he paid the rent for her apartment. She wanted someone who could buy her the bloody apartment. Make that the entire apartment block. That's the man she wanted to marry.

She thought about all the times she'd overheard people, so-called friends, calling her a cold bitch, a gold-digger. Well she didn't care. It was better than being a sucker. If she never let a man get close to her she would never get hurt. Others called her a 'Tomb Raider' for always being with older men. People thought she wanted a father-figure, but how could she want that when her own father was a monster? When her own father, Stan, had taken such horrible advantage of her naive young mother, who'd thought he just wanted to kiss her goodnight and hadn't known how to stop him going further. And to think he is still out there somewhere. Natalya wanted to kill him. She wanted to find out his full name and where he lived, and she wanted to hurt him as much as he'd hurt her mother. She sometimes felt that the only person she hated as much as him was herself. Over the years she had learnt to suppress these thoughts, but they were always there, burning below the surface. She closed her eyes and pushed them back down to the depths of her consciousness. She cleared her mind of the horrors of her mother's past and her own conception and returned to the present.

As she entered the lobby at the small private airport, a gleaming, hushed space that reeked of privilege, she glanced at herself in the mirror spanning the width of the room. She sometimes startled herself with her own exquisite looks. In St Tropez, or among some of the girls back home in Latvia, this didn't happen quite so often, but in the UK she was an exceptional beauty. No wonder her agency sent scouts out to Eastern Europe, Brazil and Scandinavia to recruit models. Of course there were exceptions in Britain – like that stuck-up society girl Tara, who had a certain something, even if it was in that weird, scruffy way that was all the rage with

London girls. Stealing one more look at herself she laughingly reflected that she'd become so brown she could almost be mistaken for Abena's half-sister, were it not for her now white-blonde hair and blue eyes.

'Yeees, you are very good,' sneered a soft, Swiss-accented voice behind her. Spinning round to dismiss whoever had the audacity to make fun of her, she found herself face to face with just the person she'd been waiting years for. Standing in front of her was a man in his mid-sixties. His face was pink, puffy and bloated and his thinning hair white-grey. Years of fine wines and sumptuous meals at top restaurants had played havoc with his waistline. His protruding belly fell over the top of his belt, threatening to burst the buttons of his silk shirt at any minute. A very limited edition Lange & Söhne watch that Natalya had read about with interest hung proudly around his wrist. It could change hue automatically according to the wearer's skin tone.

'Where are you flying to this fine evening?' he asked with a wink.

'London.'

'My plane is leaving in ten minutes, let me give you a ride.'

'No thenk you. My plane is leafing now.' And she turned away and wiggled purposefully off, but not so fast that he wouldn't be able to catch up with her.

'Please wait,' he called. 'W-w-what's your name? I am Claude. At least let me have some way of contacting you.'

'I am afraid that won't be possible,' Natalya replied, and tottered to catch up with Reza, pulling the Louis Vuitton trunk she had got for her birthday behind her. Before disappearing completely from Claude's view however, she was careful to drop her little pocket notebook on the floor as if by accident.

This time round, Reza had filled most of the plane with a group of British catalogue models in their late twenties over whom he had sprayed endless bottles of champagne at the Voile Rouge beach club. In compensation for, according to the models, ruining their designer bikinis, he had offered them a ride back home and a shopping trip once they got there. Henry ushered them oohing and aahing on to the plane. The prettiest one, with long, flaming ginger hair had whipped out her phone and was now yapping down it heatedly, 'Oh my God, Dave, you should see this plane – I'm actually on a private jet, it's amazing! Oh, oh yes, I forgot you were leaving tonight. OK have a good trip, Davey baby, love you.'

As they boarded the plane with much shrieking and animation, they gossiped and giggled amongst themselves. Natalya rolled her eyes and went to sit in the back, trying to tune out the ginger girl's conversation with Henry, who was braiding a lock of her hair.

'I'm a bit sad, Henry.'

'Oh, Angie my love, why ever are you sad?' Henry stopped playing with her hair and pulled a forlorn face.

'It's my boyfriend Dave, he's in the army and he's been called out to serve in the war in Afghanistan, I'd forgotten he's off today, and now I won't see him before he goes.'

'Sweet Jesus! You must be worried about him!' Henry exclaimed.

'Yes I am – he'll be so miserable out there, I mean all the poor thing will be able to think about is how many guys must be chatting me up back at home now that he's not around.'

Natalya smiled wryly, imagining this Dave character dodging bombs and bullets in Afghanistan but unable to give it his all because he was thinking of Angie being bought drinks at her local.

'Dave once told me, there'll always be war, but there'll never be another Angie ...'

'Er ... yeah,' Henry said, 'you're certainly very special.' He glanced at the back of the plane and caught Natalya's eye.

'I'm on my own now too,' Henry added. 'My boyfriend dumped me on our first night out here and now he's staying on an extra week with some fancy hotelier. Never mind, plenty more fish in the sea.'

Henry broke off when Reza clicked his fingers and beckoned him over. 'Sorry, important business to discuss!' he trilled, and grabbed his Filofax and BlackBerry ready for action.

Reza checked no one was listening before he spoke. 'We need to update our records for next time.'

'Oh yes,' cooed Henry. 'The girls have all been *very* happy to be here with you.'

'Tatiana is fun, very good. Invite her next time.' Reza's face broke into a smile and he shifted in his seat as he remembered the zeal with which she had given him head under the table at Club 55: he should drop his cutlery more often.

'I liked Liliana,' he continued. 'And Ciara is sexy. Sexy girl. But those two ... um ... Abara and Tena, they're no fun.'

'Tara and Abena?'

'Whatever.' He paused and thought for a moment. 'Actually, no, my investors liked the look of them. Maybe keep them on the list and see how things go.'

One by one he listed the girls they had partied with that weekend and decided, on the basis of his singular set of criteria, whether or not they were any fun and would therefore be invited back out. The rules were simple: had they, should they or would they sleep with him. Henry knew the answers to all three of those questions and made organized notes for his boss.

Initially, Reza had been reluctant to hire somebody like Henry as his main PA, finding homosexuality distasteful. After all, he ought to have a woman as his assistant. Men weren't born to serve, women were. But the problem with women was that if they were young enough to have all their marbles then they were young enough to be banged, and Reza needed to concentrate at work. Play was one thing, but in his office he was all about focus. So he'd decided on a homosexual: neither man nor woman. He then put an advert out on one of the less murky Boys Only dating sites, announcing his quest for the Ultimate Gay PA.

He asked them all to come to the interview in casual dress – he needed to make sure that whoever was chosen wouldn't turn up in a tutu to a football match where Reza was entertaining clients in his box. Henry had clearly done his research as he arrived in exactly the same leisure outfit that Reza always wore, right down to the brown crocodile-skin belt. As obvious as it was, Reza appreciated the flattery and decided that the boy's lack of subtlety marked him out as honest.

Henry had astounded Reza by surpassing even his exacting standards. From ordering him the most zealous tarts to scheduling his Botox appointments, Henry attended to Reza's every need and whim speedily, discreetly and willingly, and made his life a whole lot easier without getting in his hair. Moreover, Reza sensed a certain similarity between them, the foreigner and the fairy, in that they'd both had a rough ride at school. Over the years, Henry had become the only person in Reza's life for whom he felt genuine warmth and affection. He congratulated himself once again on such an inspired decision.

And the best thing of all was that Henry was proving wonderful with all his girls. He could ferry them around and organize them all without Reza ever worrying that he would try to steal any for himself. What's more, particularly with the very young ones, it made them feel safer, more comfortable. They could relax and get tipsy with fun-loving Henry, oblivious to the fact that the real reason Reza always arrived so late at his own parties was to give the saucy things time to get into a far more receptive mood.

****

While Reza's plane was heading north across the Channel, Tara and Abena were wandering through the port at St Tropez, hoping to bump into Alex. Out alone for the first time on the trip, they felt that buzzy excitement that comes from not knowing what a night will bring, but knowing that the possibilities are infinite. They sat down outside a loud, lively bar crammed with people, choosing seats that looked out directly on to the port. Ominously, there were no prices on the drinks menu.

'Good evening, ladies, can I 'elp you?' asked the friendly French waitress.

'Bonsoir, please could we get, er, actually, how much is a vodka tonic?' asked Abena.

'Is fourty euro,' smiled the waitress.

'Oh right, erm, what about a glass of house red?'

'Is fourty euro,' said the waitress, looking less impressed.

'A glass of water?' Tara cut in.

'Laidees, all drink is fourty euro.'

'OK, so it looks like it's one cocktail each and we're gonna have to make it last two hours, at least, until the clubs open,' Abena grinned. She felt as though she was poorer these days than when she'd been a student. At least then she'd had a student loan and could also justify scrounging off her parents from time to time, after all, to their minds anyway, she did have textbooks to buy. Since then, though, Mallinder Films' paltry offerings had been her only income.

Just as it seemed they couldn't nurse their Bellinis any longer, Tara noticed a small man bounding eagerly towards her. 'Why is it that even though I'm five foot nine I always seem to attract midgets?' she groaned. 'And the less interest I show, the keener they get!'

'Maybe they've got some dominatrix fetish.' Abena caught sight of the subject of Tara's disapproval and chuckled. 'They probably get off on fantasies of being stamped on by the spiked stiletto of a towering goddess.'

'Oh God, just don't look at it and maybe it will go away,' whispered Tara, shuddering as he reached their table.

'Hey girls!' he boomed, 'I'm Larry. I gotta couple friends who wanna meet you real bad. We've been watching you for an hour now, and I gotta say, you twos are really som'in'.' He grinned goofily at Tara. She stared at him in amazement, unable to say what she was really thinking, which was 'look at you, look at us; I don't think so honey!'.

Abena wondered whether they wanted a second drink desperately enough to invite him and his friends over to join their table. Eventually she decided that she'd at least take a peek at his side-kicks before making up her mind.

'Where are your friends?'

'Oh we're just up on the yacht,' said Larry breezily, and pointed to the largest boat in the port, from which Balearic beats boomed out of a state-of-the-art sound system. 'They're just some friends of mine, in film.'

'Perhaps,' Tara replied. 'We're quite enjoying just chilling here over drinks, but we may wander on up in a bit.'

'Gotcha,' Larry said, high-fiving them both before jogging backwards away from the table then turning and running back on to the boat. He gave out more high-fives as he climbed aboard.

An hour later, when the dregs of their cocktails were beginning to congeal, the pair strolled over to the yacht. Like Reza's, it was gleaming white inside, though slightly smaller, but there were film posters on the walls and, outside, the seating was made up of a smattering of director's chairs. Everyone was gathered on the large deck at the front. The girls spotted Larry immediately. He was standing to the side, looking out on to the water, and Abena realized with a jolt that he was surrounded by some of the cast of *Lost*. Tara helped herself to a drink and went in search of a bathroom. Abena started to walk towards Larry but was intercepted by a tall man with a shock of grey hair, a kind, weathered face and sparkling light brown eyes.

'Hello. And what brings you to this party? Friend of Larry and Rufus?'

'Actually I don't know anybody,' Abena admitted. 'I was just having a drink on the port with my friend Tara who is … well … she's in here somewhere, and Larry approached us and invited us to the party! It's a great bash though, glad we came,' she said, looking around.

'Ah, so you met Larry – brilliant director. I've worked with him on a couple of projects.' A knowing grin illuminated his face.

'Oh I see, then you must be an actor? Producer?'

'I produce films.'

'Really?' Abena's eyes widened with interest as she gazed up at him. 'What sort of stuff have you done?'

'Oh, you know, a few films you may have heard of: *Winter Sunrise*, *My Father*, *Constance and the Colonel*, and then of course *Red*, which was nominated for best film at the Oscars, and *Surface*, which won best director and best producer. *A Day in Siberia* won best female lead …'

'Oh, you must be Carey Wallace! *Winter Sunrise* is one of my all-time favourite films! I think it may actually be the only film adaptation I've ever seen that has exceeded the strength of the original book.'

'Yes I am. And, wow, thank you. Actually, of all I've done, *Winter Sunrise* is my favourite too.'

'How was it to work with such an experimental director?' Abena asked. 'I loved his use of language – high register for street kids and low for the poncy society lot – it was fantastic, just so clever.'

Carey smiled. 'Good question. But actually it was awful. Sure he thinks he's so liberal-minded, but he didn't want to work with any actor who he felt wasn't bright, because of course his scripts are incredibly "intellectually taxing". Yawn, yawn, yawn! He upset a lot of great actors who he vetoed even though they would have been mega box-office draws. He's an even worse snob than the people he writes about. Social snobbery is funny because it's so absurd, but intellectual snobbery – that's a whole different thing. I've seen many a man broken by intellectual snobbery, utterly humiliated.'

He laughed. 'Here, would you like one of these?' he asked as a waiter passed by with a tray of glistening Kir Royals.

'Love one, thank you!'

'So, tell me about you, what's your name? What's your thing?'

Abena was enthralled with Carey's tales of producing high-grossing hit films. It seemed a whole different world to what went on around the mostly struggling, low-budget, British films for TV or DVD that Mallinder ended up trying to distribute internationally.

An hour later they were still engrossed in conversation when Larry approached with a man who Abena vaguely recognized from television but couldn't put a name to.

'Hey, you can't monopolize her all night,' Larry teased Carey. 'This young thing is dying to meet her.' A scene from last Monday's episode of *Lost* swam enticingly through Abena's mind. It featured this rugged, lean actor running shirtless across a tropical island, muscles glistening with sweat. But she mustn't let her mind wander; she was just getting to arranging a meeting with Carey in London.

As if out of nowhere, Tara appeared and made a beeline for Larry, midget complex clearly on hold. Anyone would have thought Larry was a long-lost relative judging by the way she launched herself at him before shimmying strategically into the tight gap between him and the actor. This was exactly the distraction Abena needed to turn her attention back to Carey and she smiled and left Tara to do her worst with the star.

'Well, so …' Carey said, picking up where they'd left off. 'I always stay at the Charlotte Street Hotel when I'm in London, so we can catch up for lunch in the area soon. I fly home to LA tomorrow, and we'll wrap up principal photography on the current project next month, so I may be in London a little after that. I'll definitely call you.'

'That would be fantastic,' Abena beamed.

Just as the two were about to part company, they were interrupted by the screams of three women as they tried to throw a bearded, bespectacled old man overboard.

'Hey, Bendy!' Carey shouted at the laughing captive, who had now regained his balance and composure. 'Come and meet Abena, she lives in London too; you guys should talk.'

'Bendy' came over immediately and introduced himself as Benedict, or Ben. Abena was shocked to realize he was probably in his late twenties – not an old man at all. She felt an irrational annoyance at young guys who did the whole beard and glasses thing, especially when they hid what looked like attractive features, probably thinking it made them look intellectual. Ben was tall and slim with dark skin and a slightly lopsided grin. His thick-rimmed spectacles almost concealed his eyes. Unable to place his looks, Abena wondered where his family was from. Other than the long beard, his hair was short and the darkest brown. He wore a sixties-style billowing white shirt over a pair of Levi's cut off at the knee.

'This is Abena. *Winter Sunrise* is her favourite film,' Carey announced proudly.

'I'll bet it is,' Ben said drily, already bored by the thought of yet another empty-headed groupie trying to pull a rich Hollywood mover and shaker.

'It was actually a book first, but oddly enough that didn't seem to capture the imagination of the unthinking masses the way the film did.' He looked at her scathingly. 'How about *Sorrow*, did you like that?' he asked.

'Yes. But as a member of the "unthinking masses", of course I prefer *Winter Sunrise* – the leading man had better abs.' Abena couldn't be bothered to defend her choice seriously to someone who had clearly already decided she was a bimbo.

'Ben also worked on *Winter Sunrise*,' Carey said.

'Oh?' Abena asked. 'In what capacity?'

'I was a runner.'

'A runner?' And after all that showing off, she thought.

Seeing that Carey had been waylaid by an actor and was now engrossed in a new discussion, she thought she'd better continue their conversation. 'How come you're out here with Carey?'

'Carey knows my parents – they used to work for him – so I've helped out on quite a few of his films. He flew me out here as a birthday present. There's no way I'd be able to afford a holiday like this otherwise – and it's not as if I could just flirt my way into a party like this.'

Abena was furious. This guy didn't know the first thing about her, so who was he to judge? And besides, he'd only wangled his job – as a paltry runner – through contacts of Mummy and Daddy.

When one of Ben's previous captors re-emerged and grabbed his arm, Abena was only too pleased to wander off into the crowd.

# Chapter 7

There was a colossal difference between Abena and Tara's flight in, and their flight back. Without Reza, the girls had to make their own way to Nice airport, from where, to their bitter disappointment, they would be flying cattle-class to Heathrow. Tara gazed wistfully at first-class check-in and was horrified to spot a little girl of no more than three years old carrying a tiny customized Hermès Birkin Bag.

'Oh my God, Abena, look at that kid. Tina's been on the waiting list for one of those for a year.' Her mother liked to be referred to by her first name as it made her feel young.

'Probably a good thing they won't sell it to her if she's in as much debt as you say she's in?'

But Tara was too busy seething over the bag to hear. She didn't want to feel this way about a three-year-old, but she couldn't help envying her. Imperious little cow in her high-heeled jelly shoes and mini-Birkin.

'Piss off,' she muttered inaudibly as the bewildered child toddled past.

The girls reluctantly joined the economy-class queue behind three large teenagers sporting a uniform of velour tracksuits with matching pouches of flesh hanging over their waistbands. As Tara turned to point this out to Abena, the biggest teen swivelled round, put a hand on her formidable hip and gave Tara a petrifying stare. Taken aback, more by the pinkness of the adolescent's sunburnt face than by the venom of her gaze, Tara bit back a giggle. This girl was clearly susceptible to a condition Tara liked to call 'fattitude', and she had no intention of suffering the consequences of a sudden outbreak.

Never had the differences between the haves and the have-nots been more clear to Abena – well, apart from when she holidayed in her sprawling family home in Ghana, designed and built by her wealthy grandparents long before Abena was born and raised in England. They had wanted to be sure that no matter what, the many children and grandchildren they hoped to have would always have somewhere full of love and joy that they could retreat to.

'It's going to be a long flight,' Abena said, grinning at Tara.

'Anyhow, we haven't had a proper chance to catch up about last night. Did anything happen with that actor, I didn't catch his name?'

'What? Oh him, yeah, no, I wasn't really interested in the end so I didn't pursue it. Anyway, he was so up his own arse he was practically tickling his tonsils,' she huffed. 'Great party though, who was that old guy you were chatting to all night?'

'Only the most talented man in film,' Abena announced smugly.

Finally the girls arrived back at their ground-floor flat in Ladbroke Grove.

'And we're home,' Abena said, taking in their colourful surroundings. The decor consisted of shoes and exotic dresses strewn everywhere, clashing gloriously with the hundreds of pictures tacked haphazardly on almost every spare surface, a shameful number of which were of themselves. Abena tried to suppress the dull dread building up at the thought of returning to work the next day by browsing the ASOS website for an affordable fashion hit before checking her emails. She perked up when she saw a note from Sarah about going to interview some star – she must invite her over for a drink so they could swap gossip.

Meanwhile Tara was in the kitchen, chatting on the phone. 'Yes Papa, Natalya Ozolin. Why, do you know the name? I don't think you'd know them – she only came over here a few years ago … Anyway, how are the little dogs? Are they missing me?'

Tara ended the call and groaned, flouncing into the sitting room and throwing herself on to the sofa. 'Ugh! Work tomorrow …'

'Where are you this week anyway?'

'Still on reception at that hideous novelty paper-clip manufacturer run by Harry the Hobgoblin. How can such a tiny, odious little thing have his own company?'

'Is he really that gross?'

'Abbi, he's shorter than you, he's perennially pompous and hideously smug. Monday to Thursday he's just about tolerable to look at I suppose, because he wears a suit, but dress-down Friday kills me every time.'

'Oh God, the Sad Friday Outfit – tell me about it. Just when you think someone's looking amazing, they swap their hand-tailored Savile Row suit for a pair of granddad jeans pulled up really high and then belted so it gives them a wedgie.'

Abena closed her eyes as she conjured up the unpleasant image in her mind, adding mischievously, 'You know what I think? I think men should be born into one female-approved, standard outfit and have to apply for a licence and take a test before they're allowed to dress themselves.'

'Oh my word, yes!' Tara shrieked with glee. 'Yes, something simple and classic, no coloured lining or any of that vulgarity.'

'Oh my God, listen to us!' Abena laughed.

\*\*\*\*

Reza and Henry were ensconced in the spacious basement office at Reza's Mayfair home. Giant screens covered every wall, on to which share prices were constantly projected, so that even while eating a power breakfast Reza was always on top of any market fluctuations. He removed his tailored suit jacket, classically cut and in elegant navy, but lined in a sumptuous purple silk. He finished the business section of his newspaper and quickly skimmed the gossip pages. Its contents made him spit with rage.

'How could the Sorellensens have missed my party to go to Billionaire in Sardinia! Pah! I have much, much more money than Flavio Briatore,' he spat. 'Why shouldn't *I* have my own nightclub?'

'Oooh,' Henry said, his eyes flashing, 'you'd be a brilliant club proprietor. But you'd need to do something bigger and better than anything out there at the moment.'

'Go on.' Reza looked pensive.

'Well, I don't know exactly, maybe a new idea like, like a club on ice, or on water.'

Reza banged his hand down hard on the desk and a vein at the side of his neck began to throb.

'I have an idea!' he roared. 'A floating nightclub. I'm going to buy

92

another boat – a motor yacht four times the size of *Deep Pleasure*, with a huge helipad for guests to fly in from all over – and create the world's only floating nightclub.' He rose and began pacing the room. 'Yes, and people will pay to come – no fifty-euro entrance fee here, men will pay in the tens of thousands, but women will come for free. All guests will have to be invited to pay and party. It will be … a members' club of sorts. Henry, take notes.'

Henry was already scribbling away in his Filofax, nodding his head furiously.

'We will cultivate an aura of exclusivity so potent that men will do anything to become members, and pay anything. And every beautiful woman the world over will kill to set her painted toe down on this historic vessel. It will be wonderful—'

Reza was interrupted mid-flow by the ringing of one of his phones. Henry looked to see who it was.

'It's your brother.'

Reza paled. 'Answer, for me Henry, tell him I am not here.' He loosened his tie and waited.

'Er, OK,' Henry said. He never, ever passed on messages to Reza's brother. He was the only person in the world who Reza seemed truly in awe of, maybe even a bit afraid of, despite, or perhaps because, he was the polar opposite of Reza and adored by all who knew him. He was quite simply the kindest, most loving and trusting of men. He didn't have Reza's financial acumen but he was comfortable enough, and much of what he did make he gave away to charitable causes, including a foundation run by his beloved wife that funded educational projects across South East Asia.

'Good morning, Reza's office,' Henry sang.

Reza watched Henry's plucked eyebrows express shock, pity, and finally resignation as he listened to his brother shout, cry and rant down the phone for five minutes. Finally the tirade stopped and Henry cleared his throat to speak.

'I can see why you'd suspect your brother, of course, given the circumstances, but I know that Reza certainly did not sleep with your wife that night.'

There was a pause, then Henry continued, 'No, no, no, I know that for a fact because Reza was at the hospital with me.'

Another pause.

'Yes, it was a severe asthma attack and when that happens it's a matter of the utmost urgency. There was no time to wait for an ambulance and we were already near the hospital so Reza instructed the driver to take me there. Now, although my boss is a very special man, I can say for sure that even he couldn't get to Dubai from London in the space of twenty minutes.'

After the final pause, Henry began to laugh. 'Yes, yes, it's quite alright. I know the feeling. When we love someone that much we all sometimes become a wee bit oversensitive don't we. Oh of course not, no of course I won't tell him you suspected him of anything. That'll be our little secret. Aha ... Alright, bye bye now, I'm so glad it's all been cleared up.'

Henry hung up the phone and looked at Reza. 'I just hope he doesn't ring the hospital to check.'

Reza rang a bell by the side of his desk and a uniformed maid appeared at the door.

'Bring me the Montrachet 1978.'

'Sir.' She bowed and left the room, and returned carrying a dusty, ancient bottle of white wine. She held it reverently in her arms as though it were a newborn child. Reza took the £15,000 bottle and handed it to Henry.

'This is my most valuable bottle of wine. It's for you.' Henry wiped away a tear.

'Enough of that. I'm off to my meeting. Organize some girls and a dinner for tonight.' With that Reza turned and left the room.

# Chapter 8

Natalya had returned home to find a red slip from the Royal Mail in her letterbox. Someone had sent her a parcel and she couldn't wait to pick it up. It can't be from Gregory, she reflected; she had just come from his place and he hadn't mentioned anything. If he'd sent her something, he wouldn't have been able to resist gloating about it. He didn't buy her enough presents, but when he did, he wouldn't let her forget about it for months afterwards. 'Wait a minute, Natalya. Look at that ring in the window over there. Blimey, how much is it? It's a bit like the one I got you, only the stone is smaller.' How pathetic. No, this package was not a gift from Gregory. Her mother couldn't afford to send her anything. And she had no friends. By process of elimination Natalya reached the conclusion that best suited her. The gift was from Claude.

There was a time when she'd juggled multiple wealthy men. That had been lucrative, but she'd had to stop after the dangerous stunt she'd pulled last Christmas when she'd been seeing Oleg and Gregory simultaneously. Oleg could have bought Gregory a hundred times over, so when she'd met him at a party she hadn't hesitated in going back to his house. They began seeing each other and each time they met she came dressed up in costume according to his instructions. Gregory must have sensed something was up as he started beating her soon after she met Oleg, once smashing her head so fiercely against a wall that it left a dent. Oleg had seen the bruises and was outraged that she was sleeping with someone else.

One day, she arrived at Oleg's door hunched and small-looking in a man's greatcoat. That evening she was playing the part of a down and dirty street-walker, and everything from her ripped stockings to the cheap PVC bustier was designed to arouse him. 'Leave me your tramp stamp!' he demanded. 'Leave your mark on me. I want your hoe-bag lipstick on my schlong and your filthy scratches on my back. I want the world to know I was savaged by a street-walking slag.'

So she used her long red costume nails to leave deep scratch marks all over him.

Although her bruises had healed, Oleg's rage had plainly not subsided. No sooner had he come, he began to cruelly taunt her that he'd lied about his feelings for her, was sick of her and it was time for a replacement. Devastated at yet another rejection, she thought she could make some money by blackmailing him and threatened to lie to the police that he was beating her up.

To Natalya's surprise Oleg was more secure in the legality of his fortune than she imagined and went to the police himself. Finding no evidence of physical abuse on her body, but discovering the deep scratches all over Oleg's torso, the police made two formal charges against *her*: one for perverting the course of justice and the other for a serious physical and sexual assault on a senior citizen. In the end Oleg slipped the officers a wad of cash and told them to drop the charges. But she'd learnt her lesson; having more than one man on the go was dangerous.

Since then she'd decided to concentrate on finding one man who could single-handedly fulfil her needs. She would marry him and they could have a little baby, and she would love her baby and he would love her and they would keep each other company. She would buy a big, charming place for her mother and she'd have her over to stay all the time as well. Married and with a child she could receive her mother without embarrassment. She would no longer need to lie about where the money came from. Getting married made more sense than pulling stunts like that.

So, would Claude be her knight in shining armour, if such a thing exists? Natalya turned her mind excitedly to the contents of the parcel. Could it be jewellery? No, that was too extravagant so soon after they'd met. Perhaps it was something thoughtful, like a luxury Smythson version of the scruffy notebook she'd left with him. But then again, he looked like a diamond man to her. Maybe it was jewellery after all.

Now at the front of the post office queue, Natalya felt her heartbeat quickening and her palms becoming moist. She ripped open the packaging as soon as it was in her hands. 'Arrrrrgh!' she screamed, and hurled the contents of the package across the room, startling the elderly ladies behind her. They stared, alarmed by the angelic blonde flinging a tatty blue notebook across the floor with such anger.

Moments later Natalya's phone rang. She wrenched it open and snapped 'Natalya'.

Claude's laughter was soft and indulgent. It was as though he was a fly on the wall at the post office and was enjoying the turmoil he'd created.

'Did you get your notebook?' he asked.

'Yes,' Natalya sulked, walking over to retrieve it.

'Then why do you sound so angry? You know, when I realized you had dropped it and I had your address, I was going to send you a wonderful gift, but I worry about these things in the post. I have it waiting at my house in St Tropez if you'll do me the great honour of visiting me there one weekend. Or come visit me in Geneva, Gstaad or Shanghai?'

'You can't buy me,' Natalya retorted, thinking that if she were Pinocchio her nose would be a mile long by now. Happily, though, her nose was as flawless as the rest of her. She looked the picture of innocence.

'I don't want to buy you. I just want to get to know you. So far you know that my name is Claude, that I own a plane and homes in St Tropez, Geneva, Shanghai and Gstaad, that I like blondes and that I am considerate enough to return lost property to its rightful owner. If it weren't for your notebook I would know nothing about you, other than that you fully take my breath away. How is that fair? Give a little, ah?'

Natalya had to concede a laugh.

'I take that as a sign that you'll have mercy on me? I will book your flight today. When can you come – first weekend in June?'

'I think I am free then.'

'Good, then it is sorted. And my full name is Claude Perren, if you want to look me up before you come and check that I am not a serial killer.'

He added, 'Goodnight my heart', before hanging up the phone.

Placated, Natalya rushed home. She couldn't wait to look him up on Google: things were starting to get interesting.

Beep beep. A text message. Claude? No, Henry, and he wanted her to come to one of Reza's dinners at Cipriani. Gregory was busy with the wife, thank heavens, so, yes, she would go. Natalya didn't expect to meet anybody there and she had no particular desire to see Reza, but she didn't wish to spend the evening alone.

****

Abena's decision to attend the meal was equally strategic: she was hungry and she liked Italian food. Tara had a mysterious dinner date, but would cut it short and join Reza's do if he turned out to be a bore. She was rarely tight-lipped about her men so Abena decided he must be a weirdo – one of the kinky eccentrics she liked to indulge in every once in a while but was too ashamed to come clean about.

At Cipriani, a crowd was gathering for Reza's bash. As usual, the female-to-male ratio was about ten-to-one. For randy businessmen this was the attraction; for would-be oligarch's girlfriends it was an annoyance; and for everybody else it didn't matter either way. The spectacle was fantastic, the atmosphere electric, and the mix of people varied and fascinating.

After greeting Reza, Abena took a seat beside another woman who had come on her own, who turned out to be an impressive gynaecologist from Latvia called Beatrise. There was also Lisa, a successful fund manager from West London. Abena noticed that Reza hardly paid any attention to them even though they looked sensational. Opposite Abena were three sultry brunettes who lived in Knightsbridge but appeared to have neither an occupation nor an interest in anything around them, other than Reza. Everybody was expensively and seductively dressed. Lots of fierce, black Gucci and tight, nude Versace. And killer heels were de rigueur. Without engaging anyone in conversation, it would have been difficult for an onlooker to tell the call girl from the City high-flyer. Which was precisely why Abena was embarrassed when she felt a tap on her shoulder and turned to see Sebastian Spectre from St Tropez standing beside her.

'Sadly, it seems the leopard *does* change her spots. Atahari isn't it?' Sebastian smiled down at Abena.

'Sebastian. We meet again. Well I'm glad my bikini made an impression on you, even if my name didn't. It's Abena.' They kissed on both cheeks. 'Are you with your brother?' Tara needed to invent an emergency with her dinner date and jump into a cab to Cipriani this second.

'No, just a friend. Alex might join us later.'

'Great, I think Tara's coming later also – you know, zebra print?' she replied, taking in his outfit. He looked amazing in worn brown cotton drawstring trousers and three T-shirts layered over each other. He really had perfected the I'm-so-laid-back-but-actually-awfully-well-connected-and-wildly-privileged look. The simplicity of his casual–cool ensemble only enhanced his smouldering looks. It was as though he was saying 'I don't need to wear a jacket and brush my hair because I'm Sebastian Spectre'. But his choice of footwear gave him away. No one, Abena thought drily, could truly be blasé about fashion if they were wearing Prada men's sandals, especially when those sandals – as she knew through Tara, who was almost as obsessed with men's fashion as with women's – were not yet on sale to the general public.

102

Sebastian let his eyes flicker over the other diners at Abena's long table. 'Come and join me, darling.'

He was so presumptuous. She hated how her heart sang when he called her darling. 'That would be a bit rude now wouldn't it? I'm gonna have some grub with this lot but we could catch up for a drink later?'

'I'll be at my regular table, come find me whenever you like.' He glanced briefly at Reza, who wasn't looking, before sauntering off.

'Oooh la la! And he was …?' Natalya asked, hurrying into the restaurant on Henry's arm.

Abena looked up in surprise. Natalya was usually too bored to make conversation but seemed in peculiarly high spirits today.

'Sebastian Spectre!' Abena and Henry giggled in unison.

'You can sit here.' Abena pointed to two spaces near her. 'Where have you two been?'

'I had to sort some last-minute invites to this dinner and picked Natalya up on the way. I hope Lisa made it?'

'Yes, we've been chatting, but why does Reza even bother inviting her, or me for that matter, when he doesn't pay us any attention?'

'Oh he adores you, honey,' Henry reassured her, 'but he also understands the rules. To make a good party you need a variety of people – all attractive of course – and now and again his business partners prefer a more cerebral lady who can, you know, speak.'

The girls both laughed. 'Of course Reza prefers the ones who can't speak. Smile and giggle, remember! But he's a real sweetie.'

Natalya and Abena exchanged doubtful looks.

'You see, you need to understand how people like Reza work. People who can build empires worth billions—'

'Do tell us Henry.' Natalya leaned in. There was a look of determined concentration on her face, like that of a child trying to get her head round her maths homework.

'Well,' began Henry, relishing his rapt audience, 'there are three qualities that are almost universal among self-made tycoons. The first is their singular ability to focus – on an entirely different scale to a normal person. They're able to be completely single-minded when necessary. And Reza's in a kill-or-be-killed world.'

'So what are the second and third qualities?' Natalya asked.

'Mr Tycoon doesn't have to be well educated or clever, not in the recognized sense, but he needs to have a strategy, and also to be opportunistic enough to benefit from unforeseen circumstances. I mean, Reza's doubled his bank balance in the credit crunch.' Henry took an extra-long sip of wine while Abena and Natalya waited expectantly.

'The third quality is that they are delusional – which, oddly enough, actually helps them. Their inflated sense of their own power and importance becomes self-perpetuating and helps them gain even more power and importance. Let's face it, when we're told something enough times we start to believe it, and when Reza tells me he rocks my world, I can't help but shake.'

Abena devoured a beef carpaccio, seafood salad, a plate of tagliolini with shredded ham and a slice of tangy lemon meringue pie without any trouble at all. As Sarah was always grumbling, anyone else with her appetite would be clinically obese by now. In the mood for some dangerous flirtation with Sebastian, she said her goodbyes and made as if to leave. Then she sneaked off to the adjacent room, hoping that Reza wouldn't see she'd jumped ship. She felt suddenly very aware that it had been a long time since her

104

last proper boyfriend, Kunle, and allowed herself a brief surge of nostalgia for the last time she'd felt really, truly happy.

Kunle was a young Nigerian lawyer. They'd met at Oxford when he returned to the university to cheer on his old college at a boat race. When she first set eyes on him the rowers had long since paddled by but he was still by the water, staring deep into it. It was a striking and romantic picture. She'd wandered past, and perhaps he'd caught her image in the water beside his own. He turned. They chatted and began dating. The next thing she knew she was in the intense heat, humidity and hectic social flurry of a Lagos Christmas. They ate succulent, spicy food at the Sky Bar, enjoying its panoramic views across the city. They strolled hand in hand along the beach. They scoured markets and exhibitions for exciting pieces of contemporary art. They danced and partied at Kunle's friends' houses, swam and relaxed at his home, and ate the sweetest, ripest mangos she'd ever tasted, lazing in his grounds while cooks prepared an endless series of welcome feasts. He read plays to her and wrote her poetry. She fell deeply in love. They stayed together for a year, but when his law firm seconded him to New York and he'd demanded she ditch her degree, marry him and follow him out there, she'd realized that Kunle loved Kunle even more than she did.

Whoah. Abena snapped out of her daydream and steadied herself by placing a hand on the wall before approaching the boys. She must have had more to drink than she'd realized; she was finding it difficult to focus. Sebastian and two friends were laughing raucously and Abena was struck once again by the self-assuredness that punctuated his every movement. The easy way he sat in his chair; the relaxed abandon with which he laughed; the chiselled perfection of his profile. A twist of longing pulled at the base of her stomach.

'Oh Sebastian ...' She sang, rather than called, his name. All three looked up instantly, first in surprise and then with mild amusement as they noticed her swaying. They rose from their chairs to greet her as she slid into the free seat beside Sebastian.

'Sebastian, you've got to hide me. I've got to hide,' she giggled, leaning her head on his shoulder. 'Reza thinks I've gone home but I haven't, I'm here, you've got to hide me!' This time she steadied herself on Sebastian's knee rather than the wall.

Sebastian threw his head back and roared with laughter. 'I'll hide you, baby, don't worry, stay with me.' Turning to his two friends, he explained, 'She's a friend of Stefano Banio – you know, Banio Insurance.'

'Oh yeah, Stefano – what's he up to these days?' Stefano was clearly a source of great interest to the boys.

'Alex and I bumped into him in St Tropez. He's in good shape, joining the firm.'

He turned and beckoned to a waiter. 'Could I get another bottle of the Allegrini La Grola, and an extra glass?' And turning to Abena, who had by now removed her head from his shoulder, although her hand was still lodged resolutely on his knee, he asked, 'You'll have a glass of wine darling?'

'Oh no, I really shouldn't,' Abena protested. 'I'm absolutely wasted, I ha—'

'Come on Grandma, one glass won't kill you,' cut in Sebastian. 'Here, try mine.'

Abena raised Sebastian's glass to her lips, savouring the aroma. 'For such a "casual" guy, you certainly know a lot about luxurious wines,' Abena whispered into his ear, her mouth just brushing his earlobe.

By the time the bottle was empty, Abena's hand had moved from Sebastian's knee to his taught upper thigh. She almost couldn't believe her own conduct, but by this stage of the evening there was no hope of reconciling action with reason. The restaurant emptied around them and waiters hovered pointedly by the table, loudly clearing and tidying the surrounding area.

'I think they're trying to tell us something,' Sebastian remarked, throwing a black American Express card on top of the bill. He didn't bother to check the amount. The two friends immediately proffered their Coutts cards, and Abena made a feeble and token reach towards her purse, knowing that she wouldn't actually be allowed anywhere near the bill. This suited her fine; she was all *for* equality between the sexes, just not at dinner time.

'Come on, I'll drop you home.' Sebastian held out a hand to Abena and ushered her into a waiting taxi. As the cab trundled off in the direction of Chelsea rather than Ladbroke Grove, it occurred to Abena that Sebastian hadn't asked where she lived. She was about to point this out when he smoothed a strand of hair falling across her face.

'God you're stunning,' he said, staring at her mouth. 'I've been wanting to kiss you all evening.' Abena looked up at him from under her eyelashes. Her heart was thumping as he gently pulled her closer.

Sebastian's über-modern flat was gigantic, open plan and minimalist. The glossy grey kitchen stretched seamlessly into an oval living room the size of a small bowling alley. The floor was composed of vast slabs of light-grey stone strewn with differently

107

textured cream rugs. A pale brown leather sofa, which must have been made to measure, formed a perfect semi-circle against half of the curved white wall. At the other end of the room stood a long Perspex table so thin that at first Abena thought the rows of magazines arranged artfully on its surface were floating on air. The only respite from the clinical-looking, high-design elements were a couple of vibrant flower arrangements that added the obvious, yet striking, finishing touch. From all this Abena inferred he must have an interior designer and very efficient cleaner. She longed to take a peek at his bedroom and look for more of a personal touch and was just imagining what she might find there when her eye was caught by a pair of sophisticated red-soled high heels. They had evidently been lined up neatly to one side by the cleaner. Sebastian followed her glare and offered nothing by way of explanation.

'Come over here, darling,' he called, walking to an adjoining room she hadn't noticed. 'Let's watch a film.'

She stepped into what turned out to be a home cinema. The screen spanned the entire wall but there were only five soft, oversized chairs, upholstered in red velvet like those in a commercial cinema. He turned off the lights and pressed PLAY. Abena had no idea what the film was – it could have been *Sesame Street* for all she cared. She was conscious only of the proximity of her body to Sebastian's as he moved to stand behind her. She needed him closer. He slid a lazy hand inside her dress and cupped her left breast from behind, letting out a soft moan as he unzipped her short black silk dress and let it drop to the floor. Abena turned and kissed him furiously, pressing herself hard against his erection. She knew she shouldn't give in on the first date if she wanted him to fall for her, but her decidedly lacklustre attempt to wiggle free from Sebastian's strong embrace only succeeded in getting him even more excited.

'Stop it,' she giggled, 'I mustn't. Not on the first date – I wasn't brought up like that.'

'Technically speaking, it wasn't really a date was it?' murmured Sebastian. As he slid an expert finger inside her white lace panties, Abena realized just how hard it would be to resist him for much longer.

\*\*\*\*

'Where did you get to last night, you sly thing?' Tara asked. 'The background noise was so loud on that message you left, I couldn't really hear you. I thought you said you were with Alex Spectre, but you couldn't have been, could you? I mean, I guess you weren't – not out with him all night?' Tara's face was whiter than usual. Her eyes darted about the room but wouldn't meet Abena's gaze.

'Oh God, no, not with Alex. But Sebastian was at Cipriani with some friends of his and you're not going to believe this—'

'You slept with Sebastian! That's amazing,' Tara screamed, a rosy flush restored to her cheeks.

'Wait, wait, hold on! Firstly, I did not *sleep* with him. We were just flirting outrageously. I mean, so outrageously it was embarrassing. Anyway, we ended up back at his and – my God, Tara, his place is incredible—'

'Does he live with Alex?'

'No, no, let me finish. He lives on his own and Alex has an apartment in the same block. Anyway, so we get back to his, and I am totally wasted. But he suddenly makes a move on me. And, well, we kind of ended up very scantily clad and then I … I don't know, it just didn't feel quite right. So I told him that I didn't want to take it any further because I wasn't ready and things were moving too quickly, and … I'm really shy with boys.'

Abena caught Tara's eye and sniggered loudly.

'Anyway,' Abena continued, wiping a tear from her eye, 'I think it was a good move because this morning when I woke up he was already awake, staring at me.'

'Aaaaargh!'Tara pounced on Abena and threw her arms around her. 'And now there's no excuse for me not to meet Alex. It's clearly *meant* to be.'

# Chapter 9

The following morning Abena was late to work as usual. So late, in fact, that she didn't even have time to worry about whether Sebastian would call. She rushed into her cramped offices, flustered as always, and went straight to her desk to make sure there were no missed calls from Olympia. Despite being the boss and owner of the thirty-strong company, Olympia liked to micro-manage everything – particularly Abena. Although Abena was diligent about making up lost time by staying late into the evening, Olympia – who rarely made it into the office until midday – had taken to finding silly excuses to ring in at 9.05 a.m. True to form, Abena had three missed calls from Olympia, as well as one from her assistant, Wendy. Unable to face Olympia right now, she called Wendy back, surprised she wasn't in the office. As Wendy answered the phone, Abena heard a dog howling loudly in the background and steeled herself for a terrible announcement.

'Oh it's you,' sobbed Wendy. 'I called in earlier to say I'm on my way to the vet. It's … it's awful …'

'Wendy, what's wrong? You sound dreadful. Is … is it Bruno?' Wendy would fall apart if Bruno had to be put down.

'He's not eaten in twelve hours and he's been throwing up all night, I don't know what the problem is but I'm terrified. I'm ever so sorry, I'll be in just as soon as I can.'

'Not at all. Just make sure he's alright and I'll see you when I see you.' Abena was relieved it didn't sound too serious but she hoped Wendy would be back in soon; her inbox had enough red flags to start a communist revolution.

By mid-morning Abena was battling with PowerPoint, putting together a detailed presentation on the latest mediocre producers Mallinder had taken on. She had just identified the one or two who might one day actually end up being worth something, but the fun stopped there. This was essentially an exercise in manipulating figures and creating graphs on Excel and it was incredibly dull. Not for her the glitz of Cannes or the parties at Sundance. She'd be lucky to go to the premier of an Asda advert. Parties and wining and dining the producers was Olympia's domain, and although Abena had a ton of ideas for how Mallinder could promote these producers and create more press coverage about them internationally, she'd long ago stopped bothering to share them with Olympia, who dismissed Abena as a jumped-up young thing – and then nicked her ideas anyway.

At 11.30 a.m. Olympia flounced into the office in a light grey, floor-length trench coat, a red beret perched on the side of her head. Underneath the coat she had on a tight grey ruffled dress and chunky red knee-high boots. As Olympia strode towards her, Abena stared intently at her screen and tried not to giggle. An upright and majestic-looking woman, Olympia liked to dress quirkily, but she was no spring chicken. Nobody at Mallinder knew for sure how old Olympia was, it was a secret she guarded closely, but it was thought she was a well-preserved fifty. She considered herself a big hit amongst the producers she represented and was blissfully unaware that her clients only came to the office because they fancied either Abena, the tarty blonde on reception, or one of the trendy-looking wannabe film-director boys who, like Abena, had taken jobs at Mallinder to realize their dreams and had ended up ordering in boxes of A4.

Abena groaned inwardly, remembering that she hadn't returned Olympia's calls and was probably in for a bollocking. Instead, Olympia announced smugly, 'We've just added a new freelancer to our database. I've had a little tête-à-tête with him and he said we'd been recommended by Carey Wallace! *The* Carey Wallace.' Olympia smirked. 'If word's out to the likes of him, it won't be long before we have Oscar winners in our catalogue! Right! I'm off to a screening at Bafta and then a late lunch with the Simpson boys.' She gave Abena a naughty smile, which clearly said 'I'll use my wit and sex-appeal to charm the powerful Simpson brothers into investing in our dismal back-catalogue of films'.

'That's fantastic,' Abena stammered. She didn't point out that the only reason Carey had heard of Mallinder was because of her, nor that, at sixty, the Simpson brothers were far from 'boys'.

'Oh,' Olympia added, 'and I'll need that presentation I asked for by first thing tomorrow morning.' With that she turned and stalked into her plush corner office, knowing full well that the original deadline had been next Friday, and now Abena would have to stay in the office all evening to get it done.

The afternoon was greatly improved, however, by a text message from Sebastian. She held her breath as she clicked on the little envelope icon.

*Watching the sun set over Paris from my suite at George V. Shall we watch it together next time? S.*

# Chapter 10

Sarah was desperately low. Her interview with Willy Eckhardt a few weeks earlier had been, by all accounts, an extraordinary success, giving the paper a full mailbox of reader feedback for the first time in months, much of it from young people describing their own struggles with bulimia. The *Gazette* had acquired a younger, punchier image as a result of this touching celebrity exclusive, but still there had been no mention of a permanent position and a salary. There was only one week left to go until the end of her internship and then she would be out of a job.

The last time she'd been in touch with Willy it was to email him a long list of things to do with his wife and kids in London and Oxford. She'd included a little-known production company that put on enchanting musicals, tailoring them to suit individual families by renaming iconic characters such as Peter Pan and Mickey Mouse after the children in the audience. She'd also spoken to Abena about high-end builders and designers and had got a recommendation from Olympia, whose Hampstead home was a riot of colour and showcased her vast collection of modernist furniture, all shaped like a teapot. Sarah really hoped he liked her suggestions, even if he hadn't got back to her.

She rose from the soft single bed she'd slept in since she was ten and pulled open the curtains to inspect the weather. Raining. Anyone would think it was February, not the first day of June. Having showered quickly and thrown on a mismatching bra and pants, she reached for the nearest pair of trousers, happening upon the black ones she'd worn yesterday. She raised them to her nose and sniffed. They'd do for one more day. She added an old black V-neck jumper from Hennes and a pair of plain black lace-up plimsoles. Calling goodbye to her parents, she trudged down the stairs and flicked through the pile of post on her way out. To her surprise, there was an official-looking envelope addressed to her. Probably the Student Loans Company wanting payback.

Sarah opened the letter and scanned it quickly. Then she read it again, more carefully this time. She read it once more just to be sure. Then she closed her eyes, grinned until her cheeks began to hurt, and jumped up and down as fast as she as could. The fourth time she read the letter, she whispered the words aloud:

*Dear Ms Hunter,*

*Further to your meeting with Mr Eckhardt, he is delighted to be able to make you a formal offer of employment. Should you accept the position of personal assistant to Mr Eckhardt, your key responsibilities will be as follows:*

*1) You will be responsible for the organization and upkeep of Mr Eckhardt's schedule.*

*2) You will oversee correspondence between Mr Eckhardt and his fans/clients/suppliers/colleagues.*

3) You will attend business and social functions with, or as a representative of, Mr Eckhardt, should your presence be appropriate.

4) You may on occasion be required to undertake personal tasks for Mr Eckhardt, such as the supervision of his children or the arrangement of familial and social engagements.

5) You will give your neighbour a great big hug at the end of each day. A Willy world is a happy world. :-)

You will receive twenty-five days paid holiday.
The salary Mr Eckhardt has proposed for you will start at £35,000 per annum with a review after six months, and the position is available immediately.
Should you wish to discuss any of the terms of this letter, please do not hesitate to contact me.
I look forward to hearing from you as to your availability.
Yours sincerely,
Ms Gloria Dwyer,
Publicist to Willy Eckhardt

Sarah floated to the *Gazette* office on a great sea of happiness, not even noticing the wind or the rain.

\*\*\*\*

'Natalya, do you have a problem with nudity?' The woman cocked her head to one side and her eyes travelled slowly up and down Natalya's slender body. Then she fixed her stare on Natalya's breasts, taking in how they appeared both small and yet, in comparison to the slightness of the waist and the daintiness of the ribcage, voluptuous.

'No.'

'Fine. Could you take off your dress for me, leave your undies on, and I'd like you to walk slowly to the other side of the room. Stop for five seconds, turn your head and then walk back to us. That's right isn't it Emilio?'

'Exactly, if you can do that for us please …' a bored-looking Emilio glimpsed the name at the top of the model card in front of him and added 'Natalya'.

Natalya glanced behind her at the queue of models waiting for their turn and sighed. The queue had grown longer and the row of girls now stretched through the door and out into the hallway. Most of them were the same height as her with blue eyes and hair falling just short of shoulder length, which was the particular look they wanted at this casting.

Natalya scrutinized her competition. Some looked bored or tired. Others were nervous, particularly the new faces, who hadn't yet had time to build a portfolio of pictures and must rely solely on the impression they were about to make in their two-minute window. These new faces were visibly intimidated by the regular models' experience and confidence. Natalya knew so well how they felt, plucked from the school gates or their local shopping mall and thrown into the world of fashion modelling. Despite dreaming of this day from the age of ten, they would have been stunned by quite how difficult the job is to get the hang of.

The hardest thing is learning how to walk. Natalya had watched countless adolescents miss out on the chance of a lifetime because of the particular rhythm with which they placed one lanky leg in front of another, caught out by shoes that have transcended fashion to become sculpture. And yet despite all the angst and struggle of initiation, new faces have their own weapon against the more established. They have bodies that are not yet battling the onslaught of womanhood. They have not yet succumbed to the ruinous invasion of hips, breasts and thighs.

Natalya stared enviously at two identikit blondes chatting gaily with each other. She couldn't understand girls like this. They thrived on the travel, the constant flow of people and the glamour, and whether they were walking for a poxy graduate or the biggest designer in the world, they retained an affinity and camaraderie with each other that never ceased to surprise her – didn't they realize they were competitors? Even the make-up artists had their favourites. This was a cut-throat world and Natalya trusted nobody.

She undressed slowly, undoing each popper at the side of her tight green dress individually, although they could have been easily peeled apart in much less time.

Emilio drummed his fingers on the table and exchanged a look with the woman beside him.

'If you could hurry please, we've quite a lot more to get through today,' the woman said.

Finally, Natalya was down to her sheer thong and bra and she started to walk, as instructed, to the other side of the room. Halfway there, she heard the woman laughing. Natalya spun round to find her poring over a series of photographs on Emilio's digital camera. From the sound of her giggled whispers, the photos apparently showed Emilio's young goddaughter, wearing fancy dress and with a finger wedged up Emilio's nostril.

The woman looked up. 'Keep going,' she snapped.

Seconds later and before Natalya even had a chance to stop and turn, Emilio put up a hand. 'OK, that's enough, thanks for coming. Who's next?'

There were two piles of model cards on the table: a large one and a small one. He placed Natalya's card on the large pile, raising an eyebrow at the woman, who nodded. Natalya just had time to retrieve her dress before the next girl strutted to the centre of the room to pose for her Polaroid, looking unsmilingly into the camera lens and hunching her shoulders so that her back was concave and her thin body appeared skeletal.

'Mmmn, great bone structure,' Emilio murmured to the new girl as Natalya stalked out, looking as nonchalant as she could in sheer bra and thong.

Natalya got dressed in the corridor and reached into her bag for her scrappy blue notebook, which, after its postal adventures, was by now almost falling apart. The address for her next casting was Dean Street. At least that was still in W1. She'd been to five castings already today and had one more to go. Walking to castings was a good way to keep fit, but she often had to rush to get to them on time so it was easy to end up spending a fortune on taxis. She clutched her portfolio – her 'book', as the agencies called it – and flipped through the pages: Natalya on a beach frolicking by the shore; Natalya in a series of evening dresses and haughty hats; Natalya and a sultry boy in matching tweed outfits; Natalya entwined round a perfume bottle. She stopped at the perfume campaign. Now that had been great money – not that she'd seen much of it. She remembered with bitterness that the agency had kept most of her wage to pay the rent on the model flat in Paris, where she'd done the shows for a season. The grotty apartment crammed with malnourished Eastern Europeans, Brazilians and a Sudanese girl had felt more like a camp for asylum seekers than a chic Parisian base, and she was sure the agency had held back far more than it was worth.

Suddenly she felt weary. She resolved to skip the last casting and run herself a relaxing bath at home. Oh and she could look Claude up on the net again, in case there was something she missed.

The first entry that appeared when Natalya typed in 'Claude Perren' was a Wikipedia biography she already knew by heart. It read:

> Swiss self-made billionaire and business tycoon ... Raised in Geneva ... By the 1990s, Perren entered the Forbes top 100. Forbes estimated his personal and family's fortune at $7.3 billion on its 2009 list of the world's richest people. The bulk of his fortune was made in construction and property, and Perren has interests stretching from Shanghai to Paris... A dedicated family man, Perren was devastated by the death of his wife Helen in May 1999. ... In 2000, on the occasion of the graduation of his son from Harvard University, Mr Perren made the naming gift for what became the Claude F. Perren Building, home of the university's...

Jackpot! Natalya shut off the computer and glided to her en-suite bathroom to pour some essential oils into the bath. The female booker's tinny laugh rang in her ears, mocking her. I won't need to pander to the likes of you for much longer, she thought, as she slid into the water and closed her eyes. Natalya was unaware that a dark, new chapter in her life was about to begin.

****

'Willy Eckhardt offices,' said a deep bass voice.

'Oh, good morning sir, could I speak to Ms Gloria Dwyer please?'

'Speaking,' the voice boomed.

'Oh, er, oh I see, sorry, er Ms Dwyer. I … I'm calling about the job. It's Sarah.'

'Ah, Sarah. Good. Well, what do you say?'

'I'll take it. Thank you so much. I'm delighted. I'll take the job.'

****

The first letter arrived the next day. An elated Natalya, assuming it was from Claude, felt a sudden chill shoot through her body when she saw how her name had been scrawled on the envelope in a handwriting that was both childish and menacing. The writer had pressed the blue ball-point pen with such force upon the envelope that the imprint of her name could be clearly read on the paper it encased. The letter itself was brief. It had been typed on a computer, and the two lines of small black font seemed absurd on the A4 sheet of plain white paper.

> Natalya,
> If you want to stay safe, get out. Go home. I know about Stan.

Shaking, Natalya collapsed back on to the red leather sofa, one of the only flashes of colour in the luxurious but bland cream-themed apartment that Gregory had rented for her. She knew that many people were jealous of her, some even despised her. But nobody – absolutely nobody – knew about her father. She always lied about him if people asked. She would tell them her real father had been dear Janis, who had died so suddenly and so needlessly, from a curable illness for which he hadn't been able to afford treatment. She had never written about Stan, never said anything; she hardly knew a thing about him herself. Other than that she loathed him.

She closed her eyes and thought back to the moment her mother had told her what had really happened on the night of her conception. Natalya had been eight years old. Until then, she had thought her father was a charming man called Stan who had gone to live in England where he could work hard and earn lots of money – enough to buy Natalya a big pony. That he wanted Janis to keep mummy company, but that he loved his daughter and would come back to find her. But at just eight years old, Natalya, hardened by poverty and the weight of supporting her mother emotionally since Janis's death a year earlier, had begun to question this story. 'Mummy, is my real daddy really going to come back? I don't believe that he really loves me,' she had asked one day while she helped weave a basket she would sell in the market at the weekend. She had stared at the big basket in her small hands, which, if she was lucky, would fetch enough to buy a few days' worth of vegetables. She could not bring herself to look at her mother because she had known, just known, that she was about to learn something terrible.

'Your father got me to do something I did not want to do. That

I should not have done,' Daina began.

She took Natalya's hands in hers and her voice was choked with tears, although Natalya didn't look up to see them. She didn't understand, but she sensed that something was deeply wrong. She felt a sadness and something more. Something that was to feature greatly in her life and which she was later to identify as disgust. She had felt dirty. And now, thirteen years later, Natalya was frustrated that she couldn't actually remember the rest of what had been said in that conversation, a conversation which had shattered a delusion that had comforted and sustained her for years. Her traumatized eight-year-old mind had immediately blotted out the details, the horror, the odd tone of her mother's voice that had frightened her, leaving only a sense of intense revulsion.

For a short time after that conversation she had hated her mother, though she hadn't known quite why. She'd felt revolted every time her mother touched her, or called her name. Was it because of what had been done to her? Or because she had shattered a dream? Or something entirely different? She hadn't really known, but life wasn't the same after that. Then, four years later, her attitude towards her mother changed again.

Natalya was twelve years old. It was sunny outside and she was doing as she always did on a Saturday morning, helping her mother sell the woven baskets at the market. She was wearing a battered old dress of her mother's, cinched in with an old leather belt, and didn't care in the least that it looked silly. She just wanted to sell as many baskets as possible.

She had just set up her stall as nicely as she could when she noticed a tall, thin man of about forty staring intensely in her direction. Pleased, she adjusted the baskets; he didn't look like the sort who usually bought them, but he had been standing there a while so she supposed he must be interested. Slightly nervous under the ferocity of the man's continuing stare, she fiddled with the baskets again, piling them on top of each other until one fell off the rickety old table. Natalya bent down to pick up the basket, and inspected it crossly. Glancing up at the man, anxious that he would still want to buy something, she saw that his gaze had now moved from her face to her chest. She looked down and was embarrassed to see that the oversize dress was hanging well away from her body and her small budding breasts were completely exposed. Clutching the thin material to her, she quickly rose and repositioned the basket.

But she noticed something in the way that man had looked at her chest. He had been *enraptured*. It had been a look stranded somewhere between intense pleasure and intense pain. Suddenly Natalya understood what lust was. She sensed it was a powerful force; certainly more powerful than her poor, lovely mother, who had been only three years older than herself when she had first given birth.

But Natalya also sensed that such lust gave a woman power. At that moment in the market when she saw the man's eyes mist over, somewhere beneath her disgust and fear she had enjoyed it. *She* had caused such a reaction. Instinctively, she smiled at the man, who flushed slightly and moved on. He never did buy a basket.

It seemed that after that incident boys and men watched her everywhere she went. They watched the sway of her skinny hips as she rushed to and fro. They watched her long, long legs, which were always on show for she was taller than most and could only afford second-hand clothes. These men were irrevocably drawn to her nipples when she wore dresses made out of thin fabric. They were mesmerized by her soft skin, which was lightly tanned and flawlessly smooth. And most of all they looked at her face: at her red lips, which had developed a fullness to match her growing breasts, and at her eyes, which were big and innocent and the brightest blue. It was a face as vulnerable and as beautiful as an angel's, and though she was young, she knew her height made her appear older than she was.

## Chapter 11

'See you later, hon, we're off.'

Abena waved a final goodbye to Tara as she raced down the front steps to Sebastian's black Range Rover. She could see Tara through the kitchen window, pouring herself a glass of wine. Taking in the plush car and Abena's sexy version of country dress – skinny denim, tight cashmere, and slouchy flat boots – Tara raised an eyebrow and winked. Sebastian was about to drive off, when Tara emerged, barefoot, on the road. She'd pulled a pale blue chiffon skirt over her chest to become a sheer dress, and a Prada turban was perched on her head. She leaned into the car through Abena's open window.

'Just before you go, Sebastian, I was going to suggest that you and Alex come round to ours for supper one evening? We can have an intimate little St Tropez reunion …'

Sebastian thought for a moment then shrugged. 'Not a bad idea.'

'Don't sound *too* excited.' An indignant Tara forced a laugh.

'I'm just not sure what Alex's movements are for the next few weeks. I think he said something about Ibiza and Paris.' And then, turning to smirk at Abena, he added, 'And besides, I want to be …

alone with this one. Can you blame me?'

'For Christ's sake let's go before we make Tara sick,' Abena laughed, elated. The car pulled away in the direction of Sebastian's family's estate in West Sussex. 'And put some clothes on, Tara,' she shouted back at her friend.

Sebastian squeezed Abena's leg and leaned forward to put on some music. Abena shivered at his touch, and then screwed up her face as Coldplay's Chris Martin assaulted her ears. 'Aaaaah-woooooo-oooo' he wailed through the speakers, like a cow in labour. 'Noooobody saaaaid it was easy … no one ever saaaaid it would be soooooooo-OH hard …'.

'Obviously I love Coldplay – who doesn't – but I'm in the mood for something … more upbeat?' Abena pleaded. After all, if she felt like listening to an ex-public schoolboy having a good old whinge then she could talk to Sarah's boyfriend. 'I see you have Buena Vista Social Club, how about that?'

'Whatever the lady wishes.' Sebastian watched appreciatively as Abena threw her arms up above her head and wiggled in time to the invigorating Cuban beats. His eyes squinted when he smiled and his uneven teeth gleamed white. He became more dazzling each time she saw him.

'So, er, what do you do?' she asked. Crazily, her leg still tingled from his touch.

'Shocking question.' Sebastian leaned over and kissed her.

'Drive, Sebastian, please! I'd love to be alive for my first ever visit to your country house.' From his reluctance to answer, Abena guessed he did nothing.

'But you, darling, must be a model?' Sebastian looked again at Abena and nearly veered off the road.

'What, are you joking? Come on, I'm only five foot three!' Abena laughed. 'I just graduated actually, from Oxford,' she said with a hint of pride.

'I couldn't be arsed with university, Sebastian countered. 'I'd much rather get stuck into business straight after school than waste time in some college bar. Anyway everyone gets a degree these days, there's no cachet any more. I left school five years ago and did internships for a couple of investment banks, and now I'm taking time off to see if I want to do the family thing, or something of my own.'

Abena realized it was Daddy's advertising empire bankrolling five years of 'casual' dinners at Cipriani every night. The summer internships would only have been ten weeks long. Five years was a long time off to choose a path.

Changing the subject, she remarked that they must be roughly the same age then.

'Exactly. I guess I seem older?'

'Actually, yes, you do.'

'I guess not going to uni matures you. You know, you're out there working before your contemporaries.'

After a couple of hours, Sebastian announced they were nearing his home.

'You'll love it here darling, it's my hang-out. I'm so glad you're not just one of those model party girls. I'm fed up with that shit. I like a woman with a brain, so we can hang out and talk about things – you know, life … philosophy … life philosophy.'

The tall black gates to the estate opened and Sebastian's car sped down the gravel drive, through acres of neatly landscaped garden, to the house. Abena got out and surveyed her surroundings. Alongside the gigantic mock-Georgian main house were some cottages, presumably for the staff, as well as grass tennis courts, a squash court and what looked like an entire golf course. She looked back at Sebastian, who had taken off his sweater and unintentionally pulled his T-shirt off with it. She tried not to stare at the neat ripples of muscle that lined his stomach and torso; he was perfectly worked-out without being bulky and clearly made regular use of the sporting facilities.

'I'm not surprised this is your hang-out!'

'Come on,' Sebastian took her hand, 'I'll show you round.'

Inside, the house was like a five-star hotel: immaculately clean and tidy, with furnishings made from the highest-quality materials and not a hint of shabbiness. There was trophy art on the walls, including a Picasso, the frame of which must have been lovingly shined-up on a regular basis. Even the large pillows on Sebastian's super-king-sized bed were blindingly white and perfectly plumped up atop the smooth white duvet. She looked around for books or any sign of culture, but all she could see by way of personal touches were countless photos of Sebastian partying with good-looking people, most of them well-known models or the kids of famous musicians. Then she saw a row of postcards of stunning women, most of whom she'd watched in films. Picking one up she turned it over: 'Sebastian, sweetheart, amazing working with you. You're welcome to come stay in LA anytime. Pamela A x'.

'Oh, you found those.' Sebastian waved a dismissive hand. 'I had a crush on her as a kid so I got my father to hire her for one of our ad campaigns. She's become a friend now. Good girl actually.'

Before Abena's jaw could drop, Sebastian strode across the room. 'But *you* are irresistible,' he said, lifting her into his arms and kissing her, then collapsing on to the bed with her still firmly in his grasp.

'Aren't you supposed to be giving me a tour of your grounds?' she teased, shaken once again at how aroused his touch made her, and desperate to retain some composure.

'I think, sweetheart, after all that driving the least I deserve is a snog-break.'

Abena felt herself melting as Sebastian slipped his hand under her sweater and gently squeezed her breasts. He dropped his head and kissed the nape of her neck, then he pulled off her sweater and let it fall to the floor. He unhooked her silky black and purple bra and buried his face in her chest, moaning softly before taking her left nipple in his mouth and sucking it, pinching the right one as he did so. Growing more frantic, he tugged at her tight jeans and growled 'Take these off.' Before she had even finished pulling them down he had ripped at her lace thong and now she was completely nude. Still fully clothed, he pulled her on top of him and ran his hands greedily all over her skin, grabbing at the flesh of her high, round bottom, enjoying every curve of her soft but toned body. 'Do you have a johnny?' Abena whispered, in between his frenzied kisses.

Sebastian undressed faster than Abena had thought humanly possible. As he stood at the foot of the bed enjoying her with his eyes, she marvelled at him too. His impressive cock stood hard and upright under his flat, tennis-honed belly. Abena knelt on the edge of the bed and pressed herself up against him, stroking and kissing him greedily. He pushed her back down, parted her legs and positioned his face so he could tease her clitoris with his tongue and squeeze her erect nipples at the same time. As she began to shake with the first throes of orgasm he climbed on top of her and thrust himself inside her. When he could contain himself no longer, he rolled her over so that she was on top of him, arching her back in ecstasy. 'I ... I ... I'm coming', he breathed, closing his eyes and grabbing at her tiny waist, bouncing her feverishly on himself.

Then his face contorted as though he was in pain and the strong hands around Abena's waist squeezed her so hard that she really *was* in pain. He raised his head and let out an almighty howl. Then he howled again for five full seconds and his pelvis shook and jerked a few more times before he dropped his head backwards and relaxed, staring at Abena with a glazed expression.

She lay on top of him, and they remained, wordlessly, for minutes while he slowly stroked her back. She smiled dreamily down at him and kissed him lingeringly on the mouth, feeling him grow hard once more.

Sebastian resumed the tour of his estate three and a half hours later, and Abena sheepishly avoided eye contact with the maid hovering outside the bedroom. They moved on to the living and dining areas, which, Abena was disappointed to see, were decorated in cream and beige colours with lots of dark varnished wood.

'I think Dad would like to be a bit more adventurous with the decor, but Mum's reined him in unfortunately. She read somewhere that simplicity is more tasteful.' He gave Abena a look that suggested he thought his mother was a nightmare.

Abena was flabbergasted at just how many different places the Spectre family had in which to eat. They could lunch up on a high gallery that spanned the width of the splendid double-height library, looking over unread books covered in a thick layer of dust

– 'We aren't what you'd call readers,' Sebastian had grinned. They could dine at a round mahogany table in the middle of a circular space connected to the central, gleaming, restaurant-sized kitchen. They could breakfast outside on any of the ivy-canopied terraces. They could face south in summer or north if they fancied some shade. They could eat intimately *à deux* beside the temperature-controlled outside pool or they could dine in the main hall with two hundred guests.

Next stop was the wine cellar, followed by the home cinema, which could seat at least fifty. The house seemed designed for entertaining and Abena wondered idly what sort of films the Spectres liked to watch there. There were sixteen huge, theatrically decorated bedrooms, each with its own his-and-hers bathrooms. Sebastian showed her just three, beginning with the 'Out of Africa' bedroom, which came with a full-size genuine lion-skin rug, and a stuffed buffalo in the corner. In the 'Renaissance' room, two maids were arranging flowers and plumping pillows on a four-poster bed covered in gold-leaf and draped in damask silk canopies. Most indulgent of the lot was the master bedroom, which had its own chute leading directly to the Olympic-sized indoor pool two floors below; this enabled Sebastian's father to simply slide from his bed straight down into the pool every morning, with no excuse for not doing his daily thirty power laps.

Just as Abena and Sebastian were about to take a stroll through the grounds, the front door slammed shut and Alex appeared in the hallway.

'I thought we were alone tonight,' Abena whispered.

'I thought he'd be at his place in Chelsea this evening. But don't worry, he's usually got company so he'll keep out of our way.'

As Sebastian said this, a woman appeared behind Alex and kissed his neck. She was not a natural beauty, Abena observed, but she knew how to buy it. Her hair was highlighted multiple shades of blonde, which lifted her complexion, and the height of her blow-dry formed a becoming frame for her face. Her simple, cleverly boned black dress gave the impression of a streamlined silhouette and her high heels added four elegant inches to her height. The dress was cut low at the front to show off the woman's ample chest, but pearl earrings and minimal make-up lent a demure tone to what might otherwise have been a sluttish ensemble.

'Is she the girlfriend?'

Sebastian laughed. 'Shouldn't think so.'

'How's it going, big man?' He embraced his brother and the two banged each other on the back with gusto.

It emerged that Alex was putting Isobella up for the night as she'd missed her connection at the airport.

'It's awful. I just flew in from Zurich and was literally five minutes after closing time for my Miami flight. That's all, but it was too late. So I had to call Alex, as we're all the way over in the Cotswolds. He was so sweet to come and get me,' Isobella simpered. Abena tried hard to remember when she'd last seen someone in a cocktail dress and pearls on a flight and found no memories forthcoming.

'How are *you* anyway, Sebastian? It's been ages.' Isobella bit her lip and smiled too intimately.

'Very well Issy. Alex, you remember Abbi from France?'

'Abbi, hi, how are you?' Alex air-kissed her on both cheeks, showing no sign of recognition whatsoever.

134

'Are you in town for a bit? Because Abbi's friend … er … er … the blonde, do you remember?'

Alex looked blank.

'Well, anyway, she's invited us over to theirs … For dinner at some point.' Sebastian looked meaningfully at his brother, his face impish.

'Yes, I'm sticking around for June but I've quite a lot on. Why don't you chaps arrange something and if I'm free then I'll come along. He reached out and rested a hand on Isobella's bottom. Come. I'll show you to your room.'

Sebastian picked up the internal phone in the hallway and dialled the kitchen.

'I've a starving African in my arms and she'd like to be fed. Any news?'

Abena laughed. That must be Romilly, the newly acquired Michelin-starred chef he'd been telling her about.

Romilly had run a superb restaurant in a nearby country-house hotel for the past fifteen years but some months ago had begun fantasizing about letting his staff take the strain so that he could lead a quieter life away from the constant stream of demanding customers. Sebastian's father, Simeon Spectre, had always been a fan of the restaurant, and when he offered Romilly the position of personal chef to the Spectre family, Romilly jumped at the chance. The arrangement was going swimmingly. Romilly and his wife had moved into a large, comfortable cottage on the estate, he was paid handsomely and given free run of the kitchen, and was able to take his time and experiment with exquisite and unusual dishes. It was a particular relief not to still be churning out his signature lobster mousse every day – he could produce a batch of *mousseline de homard au champagne et caviar* literally with his eyes closed.

As for the Spectres, they found that Romilly's home-cooking surpassed even the gastronomic thrills of Chez Romilly and were constantly surprised with wonderful new dishes. A weekend at their country house had become the most sought-after invitation in the Home Counties.

\*\*\*\*

Harry, the diminuitive owner of the novelty paper-clip company where Tara had just finished temping, reached for a bottle of fizz and climbed on to the booster seat behind the wheel of his Jag. He punched Tara's Ladbroke Grove address into the satellite navigation system and set off.

When he arrived, he could see Tara through the window, glass of wine in one hand, black nail polish in the other, and one long, slender leg stretched out on the kitchen counter. He got a stiffy instantly.

'Come in, it's open,' Tara called through the window. He found a place to park then let himself into her flat.

'Harry, trust you to arrive on time! I haven't done my toes yet,' she frowned.

'Let me,' said Harry. 'But make yourself comfortable first.'

Tara grabbed the half-empty bottle of wine and led the way to the sitting room, followed by Harry, clutching the champagne and two flutes. She sat down on the sofa, removed her turban and shook out her hair. She looked mockingly at him.

'So now what?'

He knelt at her feet and kissed them both. 'Now it's my turn to get on my hands and knees for *you.'*

Tara stared at the top of Harry's bald head and loathed the sight of it. Then she gasped as he lifted her left foot and brought it to his lips. He let his tongue flicker out to gently probe the soft skin between her unpainted toes, before taking one fully into his mouth. He licked and sucked it with his eyes closed, as though his life depended on it. As though nothing known to man could taste better than that toe. Tara leaned back on the sofa and closed her eyes too. She said nothing until all her toes were slippery and wet and she had finished climaxing. When she finally opened her eyes she looked down and saw that he had started to paint her toenails for her. He ran the small brush in careful, straight lines along every nail until each one was black and glossy. Tara rested her head against the back of the sofa and sighed. This would be the absolute last time.

# Chapter 12

Natalya removed the small mirror from between her legs. Satisfied that her bikini line looked in perfect shape from every angle, she reached for her Crème de la Mer and rubbed the moisturizer all over her body. The extortionate price she had paid for it would yield good returns. Every man up until this point had felt like a warm-up, but this was no rehearsal. Claude was the main event and Natalya was not prepared to screw this one up. She unwrapped a parcel of newly purchased red underwear and stepped into it, relishing the luxurious feel of silk against her skin. It was a present from Gregory. It hadn't been difficult to persuade him to buy it for her, for him. Only it wasn't for him; it was for Claude. But Claude would not of course be allowed to enjoy it fully on this occasion. It was too soon. Perhaps he would glimpse just a hint of red bra as she let the straps of her dress fall down her shoulders on a balmy night. He might see a flash of scarlet silk knicker as she crossed and uncrossed her legs, causing her dress to slide up her thigh. He would have to work hard before he saw her in nothing but the silk underwear. He would have to earn it.

Glancing at her watch, Natalya saw that she had an hour and a half to go before her car was due. Just the right amount of time to finish making herself up. Her crocodile-skin weekend bag was ready and waiting in the hallway. She had planned its contents meticulously and packed it days in advance. She entered the bathroom and washed off her face mask.

An hour and a half later she was ready to go. In a form-fitting blue dress and towering heels, her face largely hidden behind oversized black sunglasses, she cut a striking figure. Her hair had been cut short into a peroxide-blonde elfin crop for a test shoot she'd been booked for. It was the first time she had done anything so drastic with her hair, but Mario was a top photographer, and even though test shots were unpaid, a shot by Mario in one's book was highly sought after, and she was pleased with the result. Every girl was doing the LA-style long honey hair thing these days, and to look like every girl was the last thing Natalya wanted. The car arrived on time and the driver leapt out of his seat to carry her bag and hold open the door.

'Heathrow inn'it?' he enquired, his eyes glued to her image in the rear-view mirror.'

'Yes. Terminal One please.'

'Okey dokey. Where you going to then, my love? Is it work or play? You look like you're famous or somefink.'

Natalya did not wish to make conversation with the driver.

'France.'

In full view of the man, who was still mesmerized by her reflection, she reached into her handbag, switched on her iPod and put her earphones in place. It didn't work.

'What you up to in France then? There's a lot a people heading up that way this time a year. I took Madonna up to Heathrow once. She were going a St Tropez wiv that ex-hubby a hers.'

Natalya gazed silently out of the window, trying to keep her mind off the horrifying letter she'd received. She realized with annoyance that the driver was still talking, telling more anecdotes about celebrities, most of whom had pots of money and no talent. They didn't know what hard work was. She despised them, and right now she was ill inclined towards this tedious man too.

Eventually she snatched out a headphone and snapped 'What?'

'Oh sorry, you was listening to yer music was ya? I was just sayin' that it's a real honour ta get ta drive lovely ladies such as yourself around. Hope ya don't mind me sayin' so. You're a right cracker you are.'

Natalya's eyes rolled behind her shades; someone change the record *please*!

Aloud she said, 'Thenk you. I will sleep now until we reach Heathrow.'

Natalya's flight was delayed by half an hour, so she whiled away the time in the business-class lounge, mildly annoyed that the airline only offered first class for long-haul flights. Forgoing the free food on display, she helped herself to some Perrier and flicked through a copy of *Vogue*. She usually found business and first class fertile hunting grounds, but this time she was uninterested in collecting business cards.

Once, she'd spent the night with a businessman she met on a flight out to Milan. They'd had a champagne-fuelled night of passion in a Milanese hotel. The next morning she'd woken up, flushed and happy at the thought she might be in love for the very first time, to find an empty space beside her in bed where his body should have been. She'd called him in a panic, only to be met by a foreign ring tone. Finally he answered, 'Baby, I'm in Mexico.'

The jerk had pronounced it Me-hi-co and there was no hint of regret or embarrassment in his tone. She had hung up the phone and been about to cry, tears of frustration more than sadness, when she'd glanced at the table by the bed and spotted an envelope with her name written on it. In the envelope was a wad of cash. She never saw the man again, but she had herself a great few days in Milan, and returned home with a suitcase full of gorgeous clothes. Every cloud has a silver lining.

This time, though, nothing would distract her from Claude. Natalya boarded the aircraft without removing her dark glasses and found her seat near the front of the plane. She dozed lightly until the food and drinks trolley arrived, at which point she declined the food and requested a glass of champagne instead. She asked the stewardess if she could borrow a pen, but before she could fetch one a previously unnoticed gentleman three rows back thrust his Mont Blanc in Natalya's direction. Thanking him, Natalya ripped out a couple of pages from her notebook and started a letter to her mother. It had been so long since she had written regularly in Latvian that she preferred to write in English. Her brothers, who had become proficient in English at school, could translate for their mother.

Darling Mother,
How are you? How are the boys? Did Bendiks like the books I sent him? What about Juris? How did his exam go, my little dumpling? I miss you all terribly but things are going great here and I'll hopefully be able to come and see you soon. I'm actually on my way to France now – I've landed a fantastic assignment there. I'm modelling

*for a wedding dress designer in St Tropez. I've heard*
*it's supposed to be beautiful there. I came across this*
*picture of me taken backstage at a show and thought you*
*might like it.*
*Do let me know if there is anything you need me to send*
*you urgently.*
*All my love,*
*Natalya*

She ripped out the photograph of herself from the *Vogue* that she'd sneaked out of the business-class lounge. The photo had been taken during graduate fashion week. Not as prestigious as the main shows, and the graduates didn't have much of a budget to pay models with, but they were the stars of the future and she'd been pleased to be snapped there. She slipped the photograph and the letter into an envelope and put it in her bag to post from France. Then she handed the pen back to its owner.

Claude was waiting to greet her in person when she arrived in Nice. Natalya had expected he would send a car, which would have enabled her to touch up her make-up before seeing him. So she wasn't in the slightest bit cheered to spot him sweating in the arrivals lounge, clutching a huge bouquet of orchids.

Natalya's irritation appeared to go undetected by Claude as he gathered her up in his arms and lifted her into the air.

'Mmmn …' He sniffed her hair, her neck, for what seemed like ages. All the while his eyes were closed and he murmured again and again, 'My sweet child … my darling heart.'

Natalya was repulsed by this grievous invasion of her personal space. The deviation from her plan had unsettled her and she was incensed. She took a deep breath and slowly counted to ten in Latvian, something that her mother had taught her to do whenever she felt fear or anger.

Regaining both her composure and control of the situation, she took a step back and said, 'Monsieur Perren. I was not sure you would recognize me with my hair like this. Do you like it?'

'I know your face very well. I have seen you hundreds of times. I looked at all of your pictures on the web. Even when dreaming, I see your face.'

Natalya giggled, looked down at the floor then back up at him in what she hoped was a shy glance. As she did so she noticed a thickset man in a smart suit standing a couple of metres behind and slightly to the left of Claude.

'Do you go everywhere with protection?' she asked, as Claude reached down to carry her case, declining the bodyguard's offer of help.

'Outside the confines of my own property, then, yes. Everywhere.'

The silent bodyguard led the way to the helicopter waiting to fly them to St Tropez. A peculiar little man with a long, pointed beard and a shock of haphazard curls was waiting with a briefcase beside the aircraft.

'My doctor; he flies with me everywhere,' said Claude, ignoring him. 'So, now, I hope you won't mind, but I have taken the liberty of organizing a party for this evening, to welcome you to my home.'

'But that is so sweet!' Natalya gasped. 'I am overjoyed.' And she was. A 'party' meant crowd, and a crowd would take the pressure off her interaction with Claude. If she could, she would avoid being alone with him in a romantic setting for a while. Only then could she prolong the courtship and retain the power.

'Good. It will be dinner and dancing at my place. I hope you have something spectacular to wear? Or you would like us to go and buy something now?'

'No, no, absolutely not. I think I can put a little something together. I don't want you to buy me a thing; you have treated me far too much already.'

In the past, Natalya would never have turned down the offer of a shopping trip, but this time she figured she would forgo a dress right away, in favour of a diamond ring on her wedding finger in the future.

Natalya racked her brains for something to talk about with Claude during the twenty-minute chopper flight and, failing dismally, decided to stay quiet and demure unless he initiated a conversation. He didn't. But he smiled at her and told her, in French, to relax and enjoy the views. Compared to Reza's private jet the aircraft was small, but it did have vast floor-to-ceiling windows that offered far-reaching views from every angle. She felt dangerously close to the elements. It was as though their helicopter was a delicate bubble in this great expanse of blue sky, soaring above a mythical forest of green. Natalya wondered at the bounty of the trees and the endless azure ocean and felt a twinge of sadness, seeing such beauty spread out beneath them. Why did humans always have to spoil the fairy tale?

'*Tu aimes ça, ma petite chérie?*' Claude looked up from his Black-Berry, himself unaffected.

'*Mais oui. C'est magnifique!*'

They landed at Claude's sprawling white villa, which was

classic and beautiful, but nothing Natalya hadn't seen before. As if sensing she was unmoved by the size of his St Tropez headquarters, Claude guided her straight through to his garden at the back. Strangely, the door seemed to be unlocked.

'Oh!' exclaimed Natalya. The garden appeared to go on forever and the view over the hills and valleys of southern France extended as far as the eye could see. The landscape looked as striking as it had done from the air.

'This … is why I bought the place. For the view. And the security. I have the most secure home in France. Every inch of this place is under constant surveillance. There are no house keys, just retina-recognition technology. Nobody but me, my staff and the people I let in can enter.'

By late afternoon the crocodile-skin bag was unpacked and Natalya had time for a brief swim before starting to get ready for the party. She freshened up and changed into a black string bikini. She deliberated for a few minutes over whether or not to add heels, then decided that as Claude liked to call her his 'sweet child' he must prefer the young look. She kicked off the wedges and slinked barefoot through the villa and out to the pool area.

'Wow!' Claude rose from his deckchair and clasped her hands in his. Then, taking a step back, he looked her up and down. His rheumy eyes were filled with such devotion that Natalya feared he might fall, sobbing, at her feet.

Natalya winced imperceptibly at his Speedos. They were tight, red and far too small for him, and to her utter horror a thicket of long, wiry grey pubic hair curled from beneath them and stalked down the insides of his upper thighs. His belly paunched over the top of the elasticated waistband, making the Speedos seem even smaller. When he was clothed Natalya could concentrate on his face, which might once have been handsome, but in Speedos there was no escaping the truth. As her resolve wavered she closed her eyes and visualized the squat she'd grown up in. Then she opened her eyes and took in the vast swimming pool, shimmering in the afternoon sun, and the Ruinart champagne cooling in an engraved silver ice bucket beside it. She could learn to love him.

The first party guests were due to arrive at 9 p.m. Staff had spent the day preparing a feast of fresh seafood, gourmet salads and beluga caviar. Fifty-eight tables clad in brilliant white linen and set with gleaming silver were scattered around the pool. An immaculately turned-out string quartet were busy tuning their instruments, positioned beside the main entrance in readiness to greet the first guests. Upstairs, Natalya was watching from the window of her marble bathroom, which was almost as big as her entire flat in London. Butterflies danced in the pit of her stomach. Claude had invited tycoons, celebrated actors and actresses, European royalty, powerful politicians, and even one head of state, and although he maintained that this evening was in her honour, she knew from her research that he regularly entertained at his homes around the world.

Claude wanted Natalya in position early to welcome the very first arrivals at his side.

'You are a princess.' Claude's voice was hoarse and his eyes misted over when she emerged, dressed in a floor-length emerald gown. Natalya was pleased she'd decided to shun her sexy mini-dress, and even more pleased to see that Claude, now in black tie and no longer sweating, looked a lot more presentable than he had earlier by the pool.

'Come, I have something for you. Remember I told you on the phone that I have a gift for you. Well here it is.'

Natalya flushed. 'You meant it! I thought you were teasing me. Thenk you.'

She unwrapped the small box Claude handed her. Inside was a pair of sparkling diamond-drop earrings. It was the single most exquisite gift she had ever been given. Short of words, she kissed Claude's cheek as tears streamed silently down her own.

'My pleasure. Oh it is my pleasure,' Claude soothed. He hugged her tight to him and kissed her tears. He slid his hand up and down her exposed back and over her tight schoolboy's bottom, where he let it rest. Then he took her face in his two hands and planted a cold, wet kiss squarely on her scarlet lips.

'Ah, Mr and Mrs Ambassador De La Fontaine, welcome to my home. So good to see you both. Please meet Natalya Ozolin, perhaps you know of her from the fashionable pages of the papers?'

Claude thrust Natalya forward to be admired and then left her with the ambassador's wife while he led the ambassador aside for a quiet word.

'Yes, I have certainly seen your work before,' said the ambassador's polite wife.

'Thenk you. Claude has been greatly looking forward to welcoming you, and, er, your husband, to his home.' Natalya attempted to make small talk and was relieved when Claude quickly returned and handed the woman back her husband in readiness to receive the next guest.

Natalya couldn't remember the last time she had felt so important. Couple by couple the distinguished guests arrived and

Claude introduced her to each one as 'the accomplished Natalya, a top model and brilliant linguist'. She had not, by any means, reached the top of her profession as a model, neither did she consider herself a linguist. But she had been speaking broken French with Claude, a language she had picked up from spending time in Monaco and the South of France. She could converse in Italian because of ex-boyfriends who had not known English. She had taught herself German almost purely though Mozart's opera's. She had not found Russian difficult to learn, and her English, as well as her Latvian of course, was fluent. On reflection, maybe Claude was right about her linguistic ability. For the first time, Natalya felt special, more than just a hired body. By Claude's side she was really someone.

An elegant couple in their late fifties wandered past, champagne glasses in hand, and she watched as the man, who had been carrying his wife's silk shawl, now wrapped it around her thin shoulders as the night closed in and the sea air began to cool. Natalya was struck by the tenderness of the gesture. She continued watching as the woman looked up and smiled at her husband; a true, loving smile of thanks. Her eyes creased and twinkled, shining as brightly as the diamonds at her neck.

'Oh, Madame Perren,' the woman turned away from her husband to face Natalya, just as Claude appeared behind her, 'what a breathtaking gown! You have wonderful style.' She delighted in Natalya's appearance with a motherly warmth. 'We're summering on the Italian Riviera this year – you and Claude *must* come and stay with us on the boat.'

'We would love to, Your Grace,' cut in Claude, pressing a proprietorial hand on Natalya's shoulder and closing it in a vice-like grip.

\*\*\*\*

Sarah took a deep breath and looked herself over in the mirror. For her first day at Willy Eckhardt Productions she had opted for a smart and conservative knee-length cream dress she'd bought specially from Zara and plain brown shoes with a small heel. She was a little worried about how the others in the office might receive her, knowing that Willy had offered her the job over dinner. She needed to look elegant and presentable, but not as though she'd flirted her way into the role. As she made her way to the tube station she tried to control her nerves by breathing deeply. It wouldn't do to throw up on her first day at her new job.

And then there was Willy. What a joy it would be to work so closely with Willy. Even though she hadn't spoken to him since their dinner at the Wolseley a month ago, she felt sure she was going to like being his assistant. She just hoped she could do a good job.

Sarah arrived at 10.25. She took a minute in the street to smooth down her dress and hair, then marched into the office and introduced herself to the receptionist.

'Good morning. I'm Sarah Hunter, Willy Eckhardt's new assistant.'

'Oh, hi Sarah, nice to meet you. I'm Linda. If you'd like to take a seat I'll buzz Gloria. She'll be looking after you this morning until Willy gets in. He tends not to arrive till much later.'

'OK, great.' Sarah sat and surveyed the reception area. The balance sheet of this production company must be very healthy indeed. The furniture was new and expensive. The offices themselves, in the heart of Mayfair, must surely be costing a bomb.

'Lovely premises, aren't they,' she said to Linda. 'How long have you been up and running? I understand this started up long before Willy himself arrived in the UK. It must be doing well already. I mean, wow!'

'No, not long at all actually. The company was set up ten months ago, specifically to produce *Britain's Next Musical Megastar*. Before that Willy was still tied up with all the songwriting stuff. Excuse me a moment— Goooood morning, Willy Eckhardt Productions, Linda speaking, how may I help?'

'Ah hah. The talented Ms Hunter.'

Gloria's voice thundered through the reception area, causing Sarah to jump from her seat, spilling the cup of coffee that Linda had handed her on arrival. Sarah groaned as she watched a dark mark form on her cream dress. What a way to start the day. Red-faced, she extended a hand to meet Gloria's outstretched one. Just as she had on the phone, Gloria really *did* sound like a man – and indeed looked like one too. Gloria pressed her sturdy fingers around Sarah's and shook her hand so vigorously that her entire body shuddered with each rise and fall of the arm.

'Don't you worry about that,' Gloria boomed, moving her stocky hand to pat the wet patch at Sarah's crotch. 'It'll dry in no time.'

She handed Sarah a print-out.

'Here's your itinerary for the next couple of days. Are you familiar with editing pictures? Good. I have a selection of photographs that will go out to the press but I need you to go though them all and make Willy's teeth whiter in each one. Then there's a phone conference with Simon Cowell you'll need to arrange, which takes us to one o'clock, when you'll have lunch with Willy.'

Sarah nodded eagerly.

'Tomorrow you'll go to Willy's recording studio and meet with executives from his record label, and then you may be required at a dinner with Rupert Murdoch in the evening, to promote the show. Does that all sound fine to you?'

'Oh goodness, it's more than fine. It sounds amazing!' Thinking back to her first days at the sleepy *Wimbledon Gazette*, she almost laughed out loud. She felt as though she'd been transported to a different universe.

'I'm glad. It's hard work too though. It might all sound fun and glamorous, but our job is to make sure that it stays that way for Willy. Just always remember that *he* is the performer, not you, and you'll be fine. But you look as though you've a good sound head on those shoulders.'

Sarah was so filled with gratitude that she didn't even mind Gloria's manhandling. The statuesque publicist was now guiding her to an office, resting a hand on the small of her back to steer her through the door. She took in Gloria's outfit. Slouchy trousers and a white shirt with a navy blue suit jacket. Her shoes were flat Italian loafers like the ones Sarah's dad wore. She was robust but not fat and her hair was already a distinguished grey, which complemented her air of no-nonsense efficiency.

'You'll also need to get yourself a smart new wardrobe. We've a number of big events coming up, and Willy tends to attract a lot of press attention, so he likes his whole team to look sharp. I've booked a stylist for you this afternoon.'

Oh God, thought Sarah, envisioning a wardrobe of tight Jane Norman pencil skirts. But when she met up with Tulip at the MAC cosmetics counter in Selfridges, it was clear Willy's stylist had other ideas.

'Darling, *hi*, I'm Tulip,' announced a striking, stick-thin fashion-ista with jet-black hair, alabaster skin, kohl-rimmed eyes and blood-red lips. She looked like Snow White on heroin. 'OK, now, stay right there, no, no, no, noooo, don't *move*, just let me *look* at you!'

Sarah stood awkwardly on the spot while Tulip looked her up and down.

'Do I meet with your approval?' she asked nervously.

'Darling, you're fabulous!' exclaimed Tulip before signalling to a staff member for assistance.

'Oh yes, hi, I'll need some *very* heavy-duty contouring bronzer, I need to create cheekbones in a fat face—'

'"Fat face!"' Sarah spluttered.

'Oh no, darling, you're fabulous, don't you know, people with round faces look so much *younger* – just age *wonderfully*.' Turning back to the shop assistant, Tulip added dark eye make-up to the list. Worried that without make-up Willy's colleagues wouldn't take her seriously, Sarah made no objections.

With make-up sorted they headed to the women's designer-wear floor and talked briefly about the 'look' Sarah was going for. She stuttered, not entirely sure herself, that she was after a few different looks.

'I'll tell you what *I* think,' drawled Tulip as Sarah steeled herself for humiliation. 'I'm thinking a little bit edgy but still sophisticated and most of all capable, after all you *are* a secretary and you *do* have an office job to do.'

'Well, I'm a personal assistant for now but I—'

'Oh whatever, darling, the main thing is you're fabulous! Now come and try this on for me sweetheart, it's Westwood – simply di-*vine*.'

Sporting a pair of cut-off hot pants over lurex leggings, chunky high heels, a baggy gold top and a bowler hat – the sum total of which was £3500 – Sarah laughed at her reflection then stepped out of the changing room.

Tulip frowned. 'OK, so at least now we know the edgy look doesn't quite *work* for you darling – that's absolutely fine. And we won't do legs – legs don't quite *work* for you either. Who was it who put larger girls on the catwalk last season? Was it Mark Fast? Let's go for fitted longer dresses, let's do cleavage; that *works* better on … on girls like you.'

'I'm a size ten to twelve thanks, I don't have to buy two seats on a plane *just* yet!' Sarah spluttered.

'Oh no darling you're *wonderful*, gorgeous, of course you are – you have a fabulous hourglass figure and lovely natural tan. Let's make the most of that!'

Sarah was tentative at first. Used to buying clothes on the high street, and relying on ethnic trinkets found on her travels to lend outfits originality, she didn't know where to start when faced with several floors of different designers, about whom she knew nothing other than that their prices were stratospheric.

She picked out a white-and-blue Moschino knee-length dress that looked exactly like one she'd bought a couple of years ago at Gap for £30. This one was £700 so she tried it on just to prove a point. As soon as the zip was up, though, Sarah had to admit defeat. The dress worked like a corset, streamlining her entire silhouette and emphasizing her firm waist, which appeared smaller than it actually was. When she added a push-up bra, her breasts seemed triple their usual size. She stood on tiptoes to imagine herself in high heels. The dress fell marginally below the knee and was just the right side of slutty. Tulip suggested she get it in black too because it was such a versatile colour.

'Excuse me, excuse me, can somebody help me?'Tulip shrieked across the shop floor, gesticulating wildly so that everybody turned to stare.

'Can you help me? I need this in black too but they've run out of the really *large* sizes. Can anyone do something or will I have to order it in especially? My client's a *bigger* girl.'

There was a flurry of activity on the shop floor and to Sarah's relief, just as Tulip was about to make an announcement over the tannoy, a young shop assistant triumphantly located a size twelve.

Tulip and Sarah added stretch jeans, some spiky, dominatrix-style heels, and silk shirts in every colour of the rainbow to their collection of eight dresses. They decided to forgo jewellery as they didn't have a big enough budget for that and Tulip declared that if it wasn't diamonds then it wasn't worth wearing. Besides, the clothes were so striking and colourful that it would look less garish to keep accessories minimal.

'You mustn't look like you've tried too hard,' shuddered Tulip. Sarah found this hilarious coming from a woman sporting a denim playsuit and heels, a jet-black pudding-bowl haircut, scarlet lips and a tattoo on her left arm that read 'Mama didn't love me'.

'Right, come on darling, let's pay up now and go sort your hair out and get you some beauty treatments.'

The shop assistant didn't bat an eyelid. 'That'll be £11,130 please.' Sarah gripped the counter to steady herself as Tulip handed over Willy's company credit card.

Despite wanting to murder Tulip, Sarah returned home with a spring in her step. A new haircut framed her face and swung elegantly around her shoulders. She wasn't sure whether it was simply because she was looking out for it, but she sensed she was turning more heads than usual on the tube. She could hardly wait to show Si her new look.

# Chapter 13

'Hi Elton, this is my girlfriend Abbi.'

Sebastian shouted above the noise as the paparazzi clicked away in the background. Sir Elton and Abena kissed hello before he moved on to greet the Beckhams, in town for a few days. A photographer moved in to collect Abena's details.

'Hi, what's your name please?'

And then to Sebastian, 'Sebastian Spectre, this way please.'

Sebastian ignored him.

'It's Abena Ankrah, should I spell that for you?'

'Ooh yes please! I'll need help with that one!' the photographer replied.

'Let me write it for you. Who are you with?'

'*Hello!* magazine.'

Delighted, Abena made a mental note to pick up a copy next week. It would be wonderful to have a record of her and Sebastian dressed up together without having to ask him for a photograph and risk looking over-keen. On the other hand, hadn't Sebastian just referred to her as his girlfriend? It struck Abena as much too soon, especially given his playboy reputation, but she was elated nonetheless. She was determined to forget past broken-hearts and not be too guarded with him. She would do everything to make this work. Right now they were at Elton John's White Tie and Tiara Ball and she hadn't had such a fun evening out since she and Tara had gone wild in St Tropez. Waitresses were circulating with trays of champagne, weaving through the six hundred guests milling around on the perfectly manicured lush green lawns.

The theme of this year's ball, held in the Old Windsor home of Sir Elton and his partner David, was inspired by sixteenth-century Mogul India. Sitar players and the tinkle of temple bells on dancers' ankles made enticing background music for the spectacular scene, lit by flickering candles and the last glow of the evening sun. Men in dress coats, white bow ties and colourful waistcoats strutted like peacocks among the women, dramatic in floor-length gowns and sparkling tiaras. It seemed that every other person was famous, and those who weren't were discreetly managing, finding, and paying the famous, be it to appear in their films or advertise their mega-brands. It was people-watching heaven.

Dinner was served in a magnificent white marquee designed like a miniature Taj Mahal and decorated with tropical vines and huge lanterns. Abena picked up a menu and thought she'd gone to heaven. Courgette blossoms filled with feta, toasted walnuts, lamb and morel korma with truffle oil and basmati rice, followed by platters of exotic fruits and pistachio ice cream.

She was seated between Sebastian and his father, Simeon. 'Hands off, Dad,' Sebastian said. It was clearly meant to be a joke but there was no laughter in his eyes.

Simeon grinned at Abena, who couldn't help but notice that hotness was a Spectre family trait. She grinned back. Simeon's latest girlfriend, who'd been invited despite his wife's presence on the table, was to his right. Alex and his date – a hair-tossing brunette called Sammie – completed the picture.

Drink loosened the revellers' tongues and conversation soon flowed freely. Abena and Simeon found themselves in a light-hearted debate about *droit de seigneur* in the medieval period. After conceding that maybe Abena had a point, and that allowing rich men the right to sleep with any maiden on their lands on the night of her wedding was *not* a civilized way to run a country, he ran his eyes appraisingly over her body and reached over to slap his son on the back.

Turning to Abena, he asked, 'So what did you bother with studying for?'

'Sorry? Er, to give me options, I guess.'

'A girl like you has enough options already, no? I'm sure you could take your pick of the men here.' He winked suggestively. 'Oh, wait a minute, don't tell me you mean *career* options?'

He turned to the rest of the table. 'Help!' he cried. 'This one's about to take off her bra and burn it.'

'Now this I'd like to see,' drawled Sebastian.

'Off with your bra!' shouted Alex across the table.

Simeon picked up his knife and fork and started banging on the tabletop, chanting, 'Off! Off! Off! Off! Off!'

The two brothers joined in.

When Abena giggled, showing no sign of offence, Simeon turned to his youngest son. 'You've got yourself a goer here, son. Better look after her.'

Sebastian leaned over and whispered in her ear, 'I knew my folks would love you.'

Abena wasn't so sure about his mother. Lucy's steely glare

had pierced the side of her face throughout the meal, and when Simeon rushed off to the bathroom, his wife jumped at the chance to seize his seat and interrogate Abena.

'What a delightful dress you have on. Elie Saab, no?' Lucy enquired.

Abena glanced down at her dress, a designer gem she'd found languishing at the bottom of a pile in a Notting Hill thrift shop. 'Yes, it's Elie Saab, and yours is fabulous too.' So far so good, but she was still cautious. Her face had been burning with the heat of Lucy's stare.

'Thank you, I thought it looked pretty with these.' Lucy fingered the string of pearls nestling in her crêpey bosom. 'They were passed down from my grandmother. I think she wore them with her debutante ball dress. We're a very old family; Sebastian has a long tradition to uphold.' She tittered.

Abena smiled back sweetly. She knew that Lucy's grandfather had been a relatively successful tradesman, but by no means the aristocrat Lucy would have liked him to be. She also knew that Lucy had been a struggling waitress when she and her husband had first become acquainted, long after Simeon had built his advertising empire from nothing.

'Where do you come from ... A-bee-na is it? Do forgive me; I struggle with African names.'

'Yes, it's Abena. I was born in London, and my family is originally from Ghana.'

'Oh.' Lucy's eyes widened. 'It must be very different for you here in the English countryside. How long have you been in Britain? You sound almost more English than I do.' Lucy gave another shrill titter.

'I was born in London,' Abena repeated, 'but my family are based in Kent. I went to school in Sussex and then on to Oxford, where I would often venture out with friends into the Oxfordshire countryside.' Abena didn't mention that those breaks had usually consisted of alcohol-fuelled rampages through the woods, organized by the cross-dressing party boys of the weird and wonderful Piers Gaveston Society – an Oxford institution. 'So I suppose I am fairly used to the English countryside.'

Happily, Abena didn't have to carry on the conversation, for all of a sudden the chattering that had filled the marquee stopped, and the charity auction was announced. With lots including a luxury trip to India accompanied by Richard Gere, and a Bentley Continental GTC, the marquee soon raised an incredible £4 million. But it was the final item that really got everyone excited: the chance to have a medley of award-winning singers record a personalized CD in the winner's honour. The bidding was furious. When the bid reached £500,000 Abena thought that must be the limit, so she was shocked to see a mumsy red-head on the adjacent table throw off her jacket and shout across the room to the previous bidder, 'That all you got? I'll raise you £100,000!' The crowd whooped, cheering on the charitable largesse. The auctioneer was in his element.

'You gonna top that then or what?' he shouted to the other bidder, a fat man in his forties. 'You gonna let a woman trample all over you?'

The crowd roared with laughter.

'£650,000,' retorted the fat man.

'Ooooh, someone's got a small penis!' mocked the auctioneer. 'Come on lady, please. Someone needs to put this show-off in his place!'

'That someone is me,' she screamed. She took to her feet in excitement and shook down her curls from their uptight bun. 'One million pounds!'

All eyes swivelled round to see if her competition could top that. He waved the auctioneer away in good humour and shook his head to signify defeat. Victory was the red-head's and the crowd put their hands together and clapped her on.

Sir Elton even took to the stage and serenaded her.

By now, even po-faced Lucy had relaxed. She beckoned Sebastian to follow her on to the dance floor and began a strange variant of the tango, cackling as she led her son across the floor. Simeon had sloped off with his girlfriend and Alex appeared to have been kidnapped by two sweet gay guys who clearly fancied him rotten. Annoyed with Sebastian for deserting her, Abena gathered up her clutch and went for a wander through the grounds.

Having done a fifteen-minute circuit, Abena was just about to sit back down at her still deserted table when she caught sight of someone who looked vaguely familiar. She realized with a jolt that it was Benedict Lima, the bearded man on the boat in St Tropez, now with a very seductive-looking woman on his arm.

'Ben!' she called, grateful for somebody to talk to even if they hadn't exactly hit it off when they'd met. She hurried across the marquee's shiny floor in her precariously high heels, conscious that she was tottering in the way that always really annoyed her in other girls. 'We meet again!'

'Abena!' Ben started in surprise, catching her about the waist as she tripped and fell slightly.

'These shoes are a bloody nightmare!' Abena cursed.

'Well, at least you look good.' Ben smiled, disparagingly.

Abena checked out his date – a doe-eyed, wavy-haired Indian girl with that enviable combination of a slender body and naturally large, shapely breasts. How on earth did he pull her, and what was he doing here in the first place?

As if reading her mind, Ben announced, 'My friend Hasna is an actress – we met when I was working on a film she was in and she invited me along.'

'Oh right. I'm here with my boyfriend, Sebastian Spectre,' Abena said proudly, turning to point him out. They both looked in the direction of her table, where Sebastian and Alex were playing some sort of drinking game with two very excitable raven-haired actresses. Sebastian had taken off his waistcoat and one shoe and was shooting Alex amused looks.

Sensing her embarrassment, Ben drew Abena and Hasna off to the dance floor. Filling glasses for all three of them, he started to dance with both girls, until Abena had cheered up slightly.

Abena watched Ben dancing. He had rhythm and danced in an easy, unselfconscious manner, but as he noticed her watching him he camped it up, wiggling obscenely to make her laugh.

'We love to dance in Brazil,' he smiled.

'Oh, is that where you're from?'

'My family is, yes, but I've been living in LA until pretty recently. I—'

'Angel, where have you been?' Sebastian charged over and grabbed Abena around the waist, kissing her and singing love songs into her ear, loudly, off key and completely at odds with the music that was playing. He tried to slip a hand down her top but Abena hit his hand away playfully, ecstatic to have him back. She was oblivious to the look on Ben's face as he watched them, and to the flirtatious glances Sebastian was giving Hasna over her shoulder. All Abena was aware of was Sebastian's magnetic presence, and how dull she felt when, seconds later, he was off again.

'Well, it worked for a while at least,' Ben muttered.

'What worked?' Abena asked, surprised.

'You made your boyfriend jealous ... Nice to know I'm good for something, huh?'

'That's ridiculous! I don't *need* to make my boyfriend jealous. And what business is it of yours anyway?'

'None. But I know girls like you, tripping about in your heels, expecting everyone to fall for you – twisting men round your fingers.'

'What do you mean, girls like me?'

'Well, you know ... gorgeous, but ... you know, just flirt their way through life, not a care in the world.'

Abena shivered as the evening began to cool, annoyed but also slightly flattered.

Watching her, Ben removed his dress coat and went to drape it around her shoulders when, suddenly, the marquee fell silent. Abena looked up to see an ocean of awestruck women with their mouths hanging open and turned to find out what was causing such a stir. She caught her breath as she watched Sebastian stride coolly through the parted crowds, wearing nothing but his Calvin Klein underpants and a single Turnbull & Asser sock. Beating Ben to it, he enveloped her in a bear hug and kissed her ravenously.

'I'll keep you warm, darling,' he whispered, wrapping his toned arms around her, a brazen, nearly naked figure in a marquee of men and women dressed in their most formal attire.

She should have been mortified, but in his arms she felt deliriously happy.

\*\*\*\*

Gregory's bitches were out of control. His wife had grown even fatter and lumpier in her pregnancy, and today he'd received a postcard from the strangely addictive young slut he'd been juggling for the past five years. The picture on the front had shown the port of St Tropez, and the message on the back had been short and clear.

> Gregory,
> Things between you and me are no longer working. I can't be your mistress any more. I have met somebody else, so please do not try to contact me again. Your wife should find an honest man who likes women, not schoolgirls. You should seek help.
> Natalya

'Natalyaaaaaaa. Natalyaaaaaaa.' Gregory howled her name through his sobs. Who else would indulge him like she did? He'd booked himself into a hotel, telling his wife he was off on a work trip. He didn't give a shit that she deserved his support; whoever said women glow with pregnancy was a lying toad. He just needed to be alone. Curling his weedy body up into a ball, he rocked back and forth on the bed. He had been to the little tramp's apartment but she didn't seem to be back from France. Well, he could wait. He was going to find her. And when he found her he was going to ruin her. He was going to make her scream louder than she'd ever screamed for him in bed. No designer would dream of paying her to model again, and no man would want to fuck her after he was through with her face.

# Chapter 14

Tara climbed into the driver's seat of Harry's Jaguar XKR, snorted the last of her charlie off the top of the dashboard and sped off down the M40 towards Gloucestershire and her ancestral home. She thought back to how she and Harry had fallen into this clandestine kinkfest in the first place.

It had started with an email. 'We've got a problem here, Tara, can you come into my office.'

Uh oh, she'd thought. She knew she'd been rude on reception. She'd had a terrible day, was fed up with being a receptionist and so, when someone with a nasal, whining voice had called up and said 'I wonder if you can help me?', Tara had drawled 'Sweetheart, there's no helping *you*.' It had turned out to be Harry's biggest client.

The client must have complained, and now awful Harry wanted to see her. Crap. She crept to Harry's office door and he beckoned her in.

'The bad news is, Tara, you're fired. The good news is we're now no longer breaking company policy if I do this …'

He pressed a button on the remote control he was holding and the projector screen in the middle of the room rose to reveal a desk piled high with a selection of sushi, strawberries and cream, and chilled champagne, some of it already poured into two glasses.

He dialled his PA's extension. 'There's a problem to be dealt with here, Karen. I'm not to be disturbed for the next hour.'

He walked over to the door and locked it. Then, turning to face Tara, he quietly and calmly said, 'Remove your dress.'

When she stood there open-mouthed, he raised his voice an octave. 'Do it.'

Something compelled her to comply. Perhaps it was the sheer crazy unexpectedness of his request. She had no time to take in the situation, let alone consider it rationally, so in unthinking, auto-pilot mode she did as she was told.

'And the rest,' he whispered. Then Harry lifted her up on to the desk, dipped his forefinger in a glass of champagne and slid it into her mouth. He moaned softly as her lips closed around his finger. Afterwards he reached for a piece of sushi and fed it to her. One by one he fed her every piece of sushi on the plate until she'd consumed the lot.

Despite the bulge in his trousers Harry had still not touched her anywhere other than on her mouth. As he moved on to the strawberries, Tara suddenly came to her senses. What in God's name was she doing sitting naked on her boss's desk? But it was too late to turn back. No matter, she would just have to assert herself instead. With the back of her hand she smacked the platter of cream across the room, where it splattered all over the wooden floor. She stared defiantly at Harry, who ran his eyes all over her body, boring into her in a way that made her shiver and thrill.

'A Care in the Community type spent all day scrubbing that floor,' he said, his moist lips forming a twisted smile. 'Get on your hands and knees and lick it off.'

And so there she was, butt naked and spread-eagled at his feet, licking cream from the floor and desperate for him to reach out a sweaty palm and touch her. But he never did.

'Get up,' he smirked. 'Put your dress on and go. I'll be at your house at 8 p.m. tomorrow to take you for dinner.'

Still speechless, she had done as he'd told her and for the next twenty-four hours had been unable to think of anything but him. He was a smug, repulsive dwarf in his Sad Friday Outfit, and yet he'd managed to manipulate her like that, to get her tingling and wet between her legs, excited to be sitting there naked in front of him, gagging for him to touch her.

After their dinner, the orgasm he'd given her had been her most intense ever. But afterwards she had wanted to barf. She knew she could never love him, never date him, never even enjoy his company. Alex was the sort of man she needed to be with.

It was time to end this dalliance with Harry – she needed more from a man than just a freaky orgasm. It was no big deal. She would return his car. When he called her she'd be busy then forget to call him back. This would anger him at first and he'd pursue her more, spurred on by her lack of interest. Soon afterwards the calls would slow down. He'd get bored, give up, meet somebody else. Someone on his level. She had no particular desire to hurt him; the fling would simply fizzle out by itself, with no need for a dramatic or emotional break-up. In the meantime, his car was proving useful.

She glanced at her watch and groaned. Poor Connie hated it when she was late for Sunday lunch. Her faithful old nanny and now housekeeper had worked for the Wittstanleys for as long as

Tara could remember and was virtually family. She and the gardener were the only permanent staff the Wittstanleys retained. Both of them septuagenarians, they stayed out of loyalty and were paid virtually nothing, though they did enjoy free lodgings. Tara stepped on the accelerator. Ignoring angry hoots behind her as she swerved, struggling to control the powerful Jaguar, she turned the radio on loud to wake herself up. She had called Tina earlier to warn her that she would be late but her mother's mobile had been off. When she phoned home instead, her father had snapped that Tina hadn't yet returned from dinner at her sister's last night, claiming to be too drunk to drive – which seemed odd to Tara because Tina had, at Papa's request, cut off most of her family after her marriage and hadn't seen her sister for years.

Tara reached Willowborough Hall in record time. Driving through the gates, she was struck, as she always was, by the drama of her imposing home. The vast, stucco-fronted, pale grey Regency mansion was built in neo-classical style, spread over three storeys, with two symmetrical wings leading off the main section. Tall mullioned widows glittered in the sun, and through the lower bay-windows she could see the mahogany-panelled Great Hall, designed for entertaining on a palatial scale. Stone statues of grave-looking ancestors and other notables gazed imperiously down as she climbed the curved marble steps to the huge front doorway.

Those Regency walls had seen so much over the centuries. An intricate painting in the Great Hall, one of few remaining original artefacts, portrayed Willowborough Hall and the surrounding village as it had been all those years ago when her family had been gloriously influential. She loved to study it whenever she returned home at weekends. But these days the house was no longer in its prime. The ivy and wisteria were out of control, the furniture had been patched many times over, and the fountain, whose magnificent spray had once reached almost to the window of her third-storey bedroom, now stood dilapidated and dry.

Lady Tina rushed out of the house, letting the heavy front door slam behind her.

'Hello, darling!' She took Tara in her arms and hugged her, standing on tiptoes to kiss her cheek. 'Gosh, you have grown thin, are you sure you've been eating properly? And gosh, Tara, where on earth did you get that car?'

'Oh, it's just a friend's. Is lunch served? I'm starved.' Tara raced past her mother and into the house.

'Papa, Papa, I'm home.'

She ran down the hallway, shivering. The cost of adequately heating the house was something her father had never been prepared to entertain, but it now seemed even colder than she remembered.

'Tara-Bara. Welcome darling.' Lord Bridges emerged from the library where he had been reading the *Telegraph*, followed closely by Ferdy and Lamb, the two little white-and-brown-flecked Jack Russells. 'You look well, got a bit of colour to your cheeks. Have you been spending more time outdoors?'

'Yes Papa,' lied Tara, glad she'd added some extra blusher. 'Is it just us today or are we having anybody over?' She bent to scoop up Lamb, who was yapping at her feet, and he licked her sunken cheeks worriedly.

Hugo's jaw stiffened. 'Your mother has invited somebody from the Committee over. A young chap, goes by the name of Orlando or—'

171

'Orlando heads up the National Trust Committee,' Tina cut in. 'He's been an invaluable help with the sale.'

'What sale? You didn't tell me you were selling anything?' Tara said accusingly, dropping poor Lamb in her surprise.

'We've had to sell four hundred acres of the estate to the National Trust, darling, there was simply no other option,' Tina pleaded.

'What! I can't believe you didn't even see fit to consult me! Well, how much did you get for it anyway, can you at least pay off my student loan now?'

Hugo was becoming irritated. 'We received £2 million for the land, Tara, just part of what is owed to the bank. We've paid off a little of our debt and the rest has already been spent on restoring this dump. Now be quiet.'

Not for the first time, Tara felt a deep sadness that came with the knowledge that she would probably be the last Wittstanley to grow up at Willowborough. Even if the family could find a way to avoid eventually having to sell the entire estate, there was no way she or any of her cousins would be able to take on the burden of its maintenance.

Connie crept in, sensing tension. Then she cleared her throat and announced, 'Lunch is served.'

'Well, what of Orlando? He's late.' This time Hugo snapped at his wife.

Tina was spared from having to fabricate an excuse when the doorbell rang. She rushed to open the door and Tara shuddered as her mother's most flirtatious giggle echoed around the hallway.

'What do you know of this Orlando guy, Papa?' Tara whispered. For an innocent Sunday lunch there were more sequins on her

mother's outfit than in an entire series of *Strictly Come Dancing*.
'Do I have to be nice to him?'

'Staff' was her father's curt reply. 'I've never met him, but your
mother said he is simply staff at the National Trust.'

'Well,' Tara retorted, sensing her father's indignation, 'if Tina
says he's "staff", then I shall bloody well treat him as such.'

'Do behave yourself, dear,' Hugo admonished, but not before
shooting his daughter an approving smile.

Hugo took his seat at the head of the large table and Tara sat at
his side. As Tina entered the room Hugo rose slightly to acknowledge her then seated himself once more, barely even nodding
at Orlando. When all where seated, Hugo said grace. The meal
kicked off awkwardly but drink soon raised Lord Bridges' spirits
and Orlando and Tina seemed unable to stop themselves giggling
like schoolchildren over Committee jokes. The only person present
who remained unamused was Tara.

\*\*\*\*

Natalya felt as though she was walking on air as she boarded her
flight back to London. 'A glass of champagne please,' she said to
the air stewardess. She had good reason to celebrate. The weekend
had flown by and she was secure in the knowledge that Claude
was besotted with her. It was sooner than she had anticipated, but
the decision to end things with Gregory had been the right one.
The rent for her apartment was paid in advance for the next three
months and Claude was finalizing the purchase of a London home
for himself, which she could no doubt move into afterwards. She
wondered how Gregory would take the news. He had never loved

her. She knew that. For him it was a sexual thing. When she'd wanted him to leave his wife he would not even consider it. She was glad of that now, but at the time it had hurt. When you are sixteen and alone in a new city you cling to the first person who happens to find you. After five years alone, however, you adapt to your situation and you exploit it in any way you can. There is no choice but to do so.

Natalya's plane arrived on time and she hailed a taxi back to Knightsbridge. She picked up her letters from her mailbox, nodded at the concierge and took the lift to the fifth floor. Scrabbling in her bag for her key, she paused. Was she imagining things, or could she hear someone in her apartment?

She opened the door.

A hand grabbed her through the darkness and she screeched, dropping her bag and the letters in terror. Gregory put one hand over her mouth. The other was still clamped around her neck, his body pressed against hers. She could smell his sweat and stale breath. Had he been waiting there all weekend?

'Who is he?' Gregory yelled. 'Who is he?' He dragged Natalya to the kitchen and reached for the bread knife, letting go of her mouth.

Holding the knife to her throat, he whispered, 'If you scream again, I'm going to use this.'

Natalya whimpered, then started to cry. Would he do this? Would he really hurt her? He had been violent before, but a knife?

Gregory put the knife slowly back down on the counter. Natalya exhaled audibly, but still did not dare to scream.

'H-h-how did you get in here?'

'Thought you were clever, didn't you, you bitch, changing the locks so I wouldn't be able to get at you. Well it's a good thing your friendly concierge knows who I am.'

'Gregory, please, let me go, you're hurting me, I … Can't we sit down and talk about this properly?'

'How could you do this to me? Not now, after everything I've done for you?' He released Natalya from his grip and fell against the counter sobbing uncontrollably.

Natalya edged slowly away. She was very shaken, but also disgusted by the sight of his puny frame, quivering in the corner of her kitchen as he wailed like a little girl.

'Who is he, Natalya? You have to tell me.'

'You would never leaf your wife for me. You can't. I need to move on, Gregory, I'm not the girl I was when you met me.'

'I'll kill him. Tell me who he is, where did you meet him?'

Natalya thought quickly. 'He is in property, we met in St Tropez. His wife died, Gregory. He is lonely, and he wants a new family.'

Gregory frowned at this and Natalya went on, hastily, 'You and I would drive each other crazy; we do, and you know it. There is no future for the two of us, Gregory. Please, just let me try to be happy with somebody of my own.'

Gregory stood and lunged, as though he was about to hit her.

'Don't!' she shouted. 'If you hurt me now, there are witnesses. The concierge knows you are here. You can leaf now. Go back to your pregnant wife and she will never know what you hef done to her.'

That seemed to hit a nerve with Gregory. He stopped in his tracks and looked away.

'Well, give me back all the jewellery then. And you'd better get the hell out of this flat. Just see how long your new man will support you after he gets bored of fucking you. You'll be back.'

'I don't hef your jewellery.'

'What do you mean YOU DON'T FUCKING HAVE MY JEWELLERY?'

'I don't hef it, Gregory! I don't hef it. I gave it to my mother in Latvia.'

Gregory walked slowly towards her and grabbed her once more by the neck.

'You listen to me, you whore. I pity you. You're gonna be trampled on and used and abused. You'd better steal a hell of a lot more from this sucker than you've stolen from me all these years because you have nothing. Nothing! You're gonna get old. And ugly. You'll be alone, and what will you do for money then? You're already losing your looks – you're nothing like the beauty I met five years ago. You and this cunt deserve each other.'

He threw Natalya across the room, turned on his heel and walked out of the apartment.

As soon as his footsteps faded from earshot, Natalya rose and slammed the door shut, leaning her back against it. She closed her eyes and imagined what he might have done if she hadn't thought quickly and brought his wife into it. The man had left her with many bruises in the past, but he was weak, and terrified of his wife – and her minor fortune – leaving him for good.

She bent to retrieve her letters and for the second time in half an hour was stricken with panic. There, underneath her telephone bill, was a plain white envelope bearing her name in that peculiar handwriting. Shaking, she ripped open the envelope with her brown, manicured fingertips.

Its contents were as vile as the first one.

Hurling the letter against the wall, Natalya burst into tears. As she tried to gulp down the sobs that threatened to overwhelm her, she realized this was the first time she had completely let go since she had arrived, alone, in London six years earlier. Crumpled on the floor, her slight frame shook as she wept. Who would do this?

Panicked now, she ran back to the door and double-locked and bolted it. Her heart was thumping; she had never been so petrified. She took a breath and tried to focus. Who could be sending these letters? Not Claude or Gregory, surely. One of the first things Natalya had learnt about men was not to give away more than the bare minimum of information. Not only did it keep them intrigued and keen, it kept her protected. They could not know her past to use it against her and she could disappear from their lives in the blink of an eye. One moment she would be the centre of their universe, and the next, she would be gone.

No. She knew that the letter could only be from *him*. The person she had really been thinking of when she'd said yes to the model scouts. The man she had come to England to find. Her father. Now, somehow, he had found her, and he wanted her out of his life. He wanted no record of her; of his dreadful history. Natalya shivered. He wanted her dead.

*Part Two*

# Chapter 15

'This is insane!' Abena shrieked as she climbed out of Henry's convertible and followed him and Tara into Reza's villa.

'I can't believe we're back in St Tropez again!' Tara agreed. 'Henry, you could have given us some notice – I haven't even had time for a wax!'

Henry laughed. 'Sorry, girls, but Reza only decided to sail her here a few days ago. We were in Sardinia all last week for the first launch parties, and of course we've had to keep everything hush hush as we haven't finished arranging all the licences.

'A floating nightclub – amazing! I can NOT wait for the party later!' Abena enthused.

'Hell YEAH, baby! And we've decided to call the club *Sin*. Reza liked *The Sea-Stalking Stallion*, but boats are female really, aren't they?'

'So come on, what's the deal – how much is membership? Who are the founding members? I know Sebastian is dying to join!'

'I'll definitely see what strings I can pull for *him*, sweetheart. I'll smuggle him onboard inside my wetsuit if I have to. Reza wants word to spread amongst those who can afford it, but he's told me not to sell any memberships for the first few months, to get people hungry. When they do go on sale, membership will be five-hundred grand a pop and obviously based on referral. Members can stay on the boat whenever they wish and the party never stops. There's dance music at night, lounge music by day, live performances, non-stop first-rate haute cuisine, booze or whatever else one might wish for …' Henry broke off. 'Sorry, I sound like a brochure don't I? But I tell you, this place is going to blow your Jimmy Choos off. We've already turned away interest from a state president because Reza didn't think he was influential enough! What these boys will get for their membership is the chance to socialize with the brightest and the best in a secure, exclusive environment, away from the paparazzi, away from the tax man and away from their wives.' Henry smirked. 'But there are only three founding members at the moment. There's Reza himself, of course, then there's a financier and co-investor in the club called Bertrand Brampton Amis, and the third member is … yours truly.' He puffed out his chest proudly.

A maid appeared out of nowhere with a tray and three glasses of champagne and they each thanked her and reached for one. 'To *Sin*,' they roared, holding their glasses high above their heads.

A few minutes later a horn tooted in the driveway.

'Oh. My. God.' Henry raced to the window and pressed his nose against the glass in time to see Sebastian Spectre pull up in a vintage sports car, looking like a forties movie star with swept back hair and dark glasses. Sebastian jumped out of the car, stormed in through the open front door and grabbed Abena's hand without bothering to say hello.

'Come on, let's go,' Sebastian said.

'B-but we've got to get ready for the party tonight. It starts in an hour!' Abena protested.

'We're going for a swim first,' Sebastian grinned, pulling Abena out and back towards his car. 'We'll meet you guys on the boat,' he called over his shoulder at a swooning Henry and bitterly jealous Tara. There was no sign of Alex.

'Darling, can you sort me out a little something for tonight?' Tara wandered over to the window to join Henry.

'Leave it with me,' he replied. 'You sure can get through that stuff can't you?'

'Not really!' Tara retorted. 'I mean, I never really buy – just do the odd line at parties if I'm offered it. Well, *sometimes* I buy, but I take it with all my friends. It's a perfectly civilized and social thing to do. And anyway everyone and his dog does coke these days, it's not like I'm out robbing old ladies.' She laughed shrilly. 'What?'

'Nothing,' Henry said.

'Well then why are you looking at me like that?'

'Come on, get ready my love, it's nearly time to go. I'm going to check on the Frenchies then come back for you.'

Tara felt great as she arrived at the harbour in the early evening, dressed in a Grecian-style draped ivory silk dress and flat jewelled sandals. She was to take a speedboat out to the club – Sin was far too big, not to mention exclusive, to be moored in the port. A gentle wind tousled the sea and as her boat surged forward, lurching on the uneven water, flecks of spray hit Tara's face and her dress billowed in the breeze. She felt exhilarated and free.

There must have been two hundred people on the boat already when Tara arrived at *Sin*. Not that it felt like a boat. The wide jet-black deck was furnished with long, black, luxuriously soft outdoor sofas that curved around the gleaming black sides of the ship, beneath its solid-gold gunwales. Tara pushed her way into the covered central area, wondering how on earth she'd find Abena in the crowd. Inside, the walls were also jet black, and the crystals and mirrors embedded in the padded silk gave it a clubby feel. An oval bar, also apparently of solid gold, dominated the immense space. Behind it an army of busy bar staff were preparing fantastically outlandish cocktails. Tara watched, riveted, as pure cocoa was melted into a glass of champagne and sprinkled with what looked like pepper. Circling the bar a flashing revolving dance floor moved in time to the music. It was spinning slowly but Tara had a feeling things would get faster as the night progressed. There were excited whispers that Jay-Z and Beyoncé were to perform later. The whole boat buzzed with suspense, as though everybody was waiting for something.

Behind the bar Tara could see a casino. The only people who had been allowed to wear bikinis instead of party dress were the girls handing out complimentary chips to Reza's guests. She wandered over to the blackjack table and a pretty girl gave her a gold case. Tara laughed at her own naivety when she realized that the bikini was in fact painted on, and the girl was naked. She was about to start a game when there was an announcement over the speakers.

'Will all guests please proceed to the front deck.'

Tara stashed the case in her bag and followed the throng out on to the deck.

At once all the lights went out and there was an awed hush. The sea seemed to part as a sleek black speedboat charged towards the big yacht. Behind it, an upright figure, his head haloed in light, appeared to walk on water. It was Reza, illuminated by a strong spotlight fixed to the boat, balancing on a single golden water-ski and clutching a golden tow-rope in the boat's wake. He twisted and turned skilfully, easily manipulating the ski. His hair blew in the wind and his body, tense with thrill and exertion in a skin-tight wetsuit, was so low to the sea that he was almost horizontal as he zigzagged over its surface.

A DJ activated the outdoor speakers with the press of a button and a deep voice thundered out: 'Introducing … REZA! Billionaire! Philanthropist! Visionary! And founder of … *SIN*!'

The guests stomped and clapped in appreciation, whooping and cheering. Tara was laughing so hard, her cocoa-and-pepper-cocktail came out through her nose. Oh where was Abena!

'Fuck. There she is!' Tara covered her mouth with her hand as, right behind Reza, and completely ruining the effect of his grand entrance, Sebastian and Abena, dressed in casual beachwear, motored up to the floating club astride a jet ski. Abena sat cringing behind Sebastian as over two hundred surprised faces peered out at them. They overtook Reza, now in his speedboat, and climbed aboard the yacht. They'd obviously just been swimming. Sebastian shook his head and slicked back his wet, dark hair with his hands. He looked deadly in swimming trunks and a blue cotton shirt that clung damply to his perfect torso. Abena looked dreadful. Her hair dripped down in wet tails either side of her face, framing her mascara, which now ran in dark lines down her cheeks. Her nose was running, she had salt in her eyes and her sundress stuck unflatteringly to her bottom.

'Erm, sorry,' she muttered to nobody in particular as Sebastian sauntered off in search of a drink.

Tara grabbed her friend's hand and pulled her aside, staring her up and down gravely. 'Men can just pitch up on a yacht fresh from the sea, slick their hair back and look wonderful. Women … we need things. We need hairdryers, and make-up and pretty dresses …'

'OK OK OK. I didn't exactly plan this. Let's go find the loo and sort me out.'

Abena freshened up in a belted purple jumpsuit and pretty flats, then they emerged and made their way to the casino. Sebastian was nowhere to be seen so they settled down at a blackjack table. In a fabulous run of beginner's luck Tara kept finding herself with unbeatable hands. Abena started to think that the bikini girl dealing the cards had taken some sort of shine to Tara. After half an hour Abena had already lost all her chips.

'I'm off to find Sebastian,' she said.

'Stop mooning after him,' Tara replied, not looking up from the game. 'No wonder you haven't made anything here, you're obsessed. Look how well I'm doing – if only this was real money!'

'Oh it is, you can cash it in over there,' the dealer cut in.

As Abena skipped off, Tara looked down at her £4000 worth of chips, drooling over the amount of coke that would fetch her. She strolled over to the cashier.

Abena scoured the deck but couldn't find Sebastian. Returning to the casino, she found Tara doing the moonwalk on the revolving dance floor, singing a Michael Jackson tune to herself even though the DJ was playing a house remix of Madonna. Reza had also hit the dance floor and to Abena's horror was closing in on Tara, pulling the bikini girl behind him. Suddenly realizing she was naked, Abena was shocked to see the girl grind her painted gold bottom against Tara. Distracted, Tara turned round to see Reza's lips inches from her own.

'Let me show you something.' Reza took Tara's hand and dragged her behind the bar. Pushing a barman out of the way he pressed a button under the counter and a small hole appeared in the floor. 'Come, I want to give you something very special, I can tell you like a bit of this.'

'OK, just quickly,' Tara faltered. She climbing down the rickety steps into the abyss, envisaging a whole cellar full of drugs. Reza followed her hastily before any of the guests could notice. He pressed another button and the trapdoor closed above him. Dim lights flickered on, illuminating a small room lined with mirrors. A selection of handcuffs were chained to one wall, with various oils and ointments lined up beneath them.

Tara let out a crazed scream, for once totally lost for words.

'Aaaaah, you like a bit of role play, don't you?' Reza closed in on her. 'Pretending to be scared like that; pretending this isn't what you wanted from the very first time you laid eyes on me.'

'Let me out right now!' Tara demanded.

'You women are so cute when you pretend,' Reza said.

Tara made a dash for the button Reza had pressed but found it needed a code to work. She heard Reza laughing softly and spun round to face him. He was already naked. She looked around desperately for any kind of escape route but all she could see was Reza, reflected in every mirror from every angle. She screamed again.

Reza reached for an ominous-looking tube, squeezed its oily contents on to his left palm and rubbed his hands together. He held Tara's eye throughout. Tara gagged.

'How long have you been wanting me like this, baby?' He bit his lip. Then he pushed her up against a mirror and squashed her face with his greasy hands. Tara bucked and struggled, jerking her head violently from side to side. But Reza was too strong for her and covered her mouth with his.

'Stop!'Tara shrieked, in floods of tears.

Reza released her arms.'But I thought this is what you wanted? You and Abena have been fighting over me from the start, both so jealous of all my girls—'

There was no time for a stunned Tara to reply because at that moment the trapdoor flew open and Sebastian Spectre landed at her feet, naked, bruised and horrendously drunk.

'Darren!' Reza shouted up to his minder as he scrambled into his trousers.'I told you to deal with him outdoors.'

Tara seized her chance. She scrambled up the steps and into the light. Never had the sight of two hundred plastered party-goers been more welcome.

# Chapter 16

'At last!' Natalya whooped with joy as she slid the key into the lock and stepped into Claude's brand-new Mayfair house, an enormous, double-fronted mansion on the same tree-lined street as Reza's home. She had often lingered outside Reza's house, on her way in to one of his parties, imagining what it would be like to own one of these properties. Claude hadn't allowed her to attend the St Tropez opening of Reza's club, but she didn't need Reza any more. She was already his equal.

After a carefully orchestrated display of enthusiasm for sourcing furniture and trawling interior-decorating websites, Natalya had been put in charge of getting the house ready while Claude attended various meetings in Paris and Shanghai. She now had a fortnight to add the finishing touches. The prospect of two weeks alone in this palatial mansion was marvellous. But it did not feel strange, or exciting. Rather, Natalya felt as though she had returned home after a long and uncomfortable journey. She sensed that this was where she belonged, that this was the life for which she had been born but which, by some perverse joke, had been withheld from her until now.

Natalya had surprised herself – a rare occurrence – by finding that she really had enjoyed the decorating process. She surveyed the house and felt an unusual emotion swelling within her. She was proud. This house was her first big project, and it mattered to her that Claude liked what she had done. She'd thought of everything, even having the driveway repaved to include under-floor heating so that in winter any snow would melt, easing entrants' passage – and particularly her own what with her collection of hazardously high heels.

The master bedroom was on the first floor but she took the lift up anyway, just because she could. The lift door opened straight on to the vast room and she threw herself on to the enormous white bed. It was firm on her side and soft on Claude's – she found soft beds intolerable after the wooden floorboards of her childhood. Stretching out her long legs and arms as far as they could go, she laughed disbelievingly at how much space there was. She'd barely have to touch Claude.

She skipped over to her crocodile-skin weekend bag – her other bags had been unpacked by the staff but she had left specific instructions that this one should not be touched – and pulled out an old wooden jewellery box. It was carved with her name and the word 'Mīlestība', which meant 'Love' in Latvian. She pulled out the pieces that Gregory had bought her with his wife's money over the years. A beautiful watch inlaid with rubies, two small pairs of diamond studs and a pearl necklace. She fingered them carefully and added them to the exquisite jewels that Claude had given her. Gregory might expect her to have nothing when she's old and ugly, but Natalya had the beginnings of a very healthy pension plan in the form of all these jewels. She doubted she'd need to use it, not if she got married. But she had learnt the hard way that one must always be prepared for when life deals you a bad hand. When that happens, you either resort to Plan B, or you don't survive.

****

'Papa, I honestly don't know how it's happened again in such a short space of time. These big banks are supposed to be really secure. Perhaps it's internet hackers? I *have* started online banking now. Maybe that's put me at risk.'

'Online banking is no less secure than other forms. I thought you said they'd frozen your account. Look, I'll transfer some money but you'll need to return it as soon as you've sorted this thing out. Shall I speak to the bank this time?' Hugo Bridges grumbled down the phone to his daughter.

'Oh no, no. No need for you to speak to them. I … I just spoke to the bank and they assured me that an investigation is under way, and that they'll refund the money as soon as they know what's happened.'

'Right. How much did you say you'll need?'

'Oh, a grand should see me through.'

'I can send you £500 max, Tara. You'll have to get a proper job. And do you have any plans to return home at any point? We haven't seen you at Willowborough for a few Sundays and your mother is worried about you. Are you eating properly?'

'Yes, yes, I'm fine. I'll be down soon, I've just, well I told you, I had to go to that thing last Sunday and I … I'll come over next weekend. So when do you think I'll have the money?'

'I'll get it to your account by tomorrow.'

'Oh thank you, Papa, that's perfect. Well, I'll see you at the weekend. Do take care and love to Tina.'

'Goodbye Tara.'

Tara put down the receiver and rang her dealer. The money would be with him tomorrow.

The next morning Tara woke up late, and decided not to go into work that day. Dark circles had formed under her eyes recently, even when she didn't feel tired. She lay there unable to get back to sleep, not helped by the noise coming from Abena's bedroom. Abena had taken a week off work as Sebastian had promised to take her away to make up for embarrassing her at Reza's club, where he'd managed to get beaten up by Reza's minder and nearly tossed overboard. As far as Tara was aware, Sebastian hadn't kept to his word. Instead of whisking Abena away somewhere and leaving Tara in peace, the couple hadn't left Abena's bedroom in days.

Three hours later, Tara still hadn't got up. She knew she had to eat something and start the day but she felt so lethargic. Spotting a wrap of cocaine down the side of her bed, where she'd hidden it away from Abena's prying eyes, she reached for it and snorted a little. Just a treat. A special breakfast so that she could face the dismal day. Before long the entire wrap was empty.

At 8 p.m. Tara heard Abena knock on her door and buried her head under the pillow. She wasn't in the mood for gossip now.

'Hey,' Abena said and sat down on Tara's bed without waiting to be called in. 'You OK? Sebastian and I are going out for dinner soon. You've been in your room all day.'

'Yes, yes, I'm fine. Just had some stuff to do in here. You know, sorting out my CV. I might apply for that fashion PR thing I was telling you about.'

'That's fantastic,' Abena said, a touch too brightly. 'Really awesome. You should definitely do that, temping is so unreliable and I really need that money you owe me. I can't pay your rent next month.'

'Sure, whatever, but let's not talk about money now, it's … I'll sort you out, don't worry.'

'Yeah, no, whenever, I was just reminding you that's all. Have you eaten? There's pasta in the kitchen if you like.'

Tara got out of bed and made for the door. 'Thanks, I'll have some now. Have a romantic dinner.'

'Um, aren't you going to get dressed first?' asked a horrified Abena. Tara was wearing only a pair of low-waisted white knickers. 'I'd appreciate it if you didn't wander around naked while Sebastian's here.'

Tara shrugged and reached for a short, sheer kaftan lying on the floor. Abena gritted her teeth but said nothing.

'Hey Tara, how's it going?' Sebastian materialized in the doorway.

'Very well indeed, thank you, sweetheart,' Tara replied, wiping a smudge of Abena's dark brown foundation off his nose.

'Come on, Sebastian, let's go.' Abena rose and stalked out. She didn't like the way he looked at Tara – and why couldn't she put some clothes on for God's sake?

# Chapter 17

Abena had just sat down with a cup of coffee and *The Sunday Times* 'Style' magazine when her phone rang. Irrationally cross, she glanced at the screen and saw that the number was withheld. Probably a salesperson.

'Hello?' she snapped.

'Hello, is that Abena?' a deep American-accented voice enquired.

'Er, yes, speaking.' Abena racked her brains to try and identify the voice. Perhaps it was a potential employer. She detested her job and had been casting around for escape routes. But on a Sunday?

'It's Carey Wallace, we met three or four months ago in St Tropez, at Larry's party. Remember me?'

'Oh, Carey, hi, how are you? Amazing to hear from you – of course I remember you, the super-duper producer!'

Carey laughed. 'You're too kind.'

'So where are you – which country are you calling from?'

'I'm … in London!'

'Yippee! Me too! What are your plans? How long are you sticking around for? We should catch up.'

'Well, that's exactly why I'm calling. If you're free tonight then you should come join me and a couple friends for dinner.'

'That sounds great. Where are we going?'

'How about Roka? On Charlotte Street. Do you like Asian food?'

'Mmmn, sushi is my favourite.'

'Good. Then we're off to a fabulous start. Come to the Charlotte Street Hotel at eight and we'll stroll down together.'

'Looking forward to it.'

Abena lay back and grinned. She couldn't wait to see Carey again – their evening in St Tropez had been the most fun night of all. She wondered whether Benedict would be there too – he'd been so sweet to her at the ball, despite Sebastian's appalling behaviour.

Abena spent most of the afternoon planning her outfit and daydreaming about the future. She mustn't jump the gun, but if this guy was interested in her then it could lead to anything. She imagined herself starring in Carey's next blockbuster, a gun-toting and leather-clad hottie with Will Smith as her on-screen lover. She'd never been under any illusions about the acting world – she'd seen too many girls stump up colossal sums for good drama schools only to end up waitressing while waiting for the breakthrough part in an unglamorous East End production. The odds were unfavourable, the output simply not worth the effort. Besides, she was far more interested in the writing and producing side of things; that was more her style, more intellectually and creatively challenging. But hey, if Carey wanted to catapult her right to the top after a few suppers then who was she to say no?

By 8 p.m. Abena was dressed and ready in a ruched white jersey dress, over which she'd thrown on a lightweight mac with a massively oversized collar, inspired by 'Style' magazine's 'More is More' fashion spread. Despite her traffic-stopping outfit, every taxi she waved at sailed past. She became hot with frustration and anxiety. She hated to be late, yet she always was. Finally, at around a quarter past eight an empty black cab pulled up.

'Charlotte Street please.' She climbed in and, turning on the light inside, reapplied her powder and studied her make-up in her compact.

'You look great,' chuckled the taxi driver, appraising her in the rear-view mirror.

'Sorry, terribly vain of me. When I took my driving test my instructor told me I was the first person he'd ever failed not for *neglecting* the mirrors, but for looking at them far too much,' Abena joked.

She arrived at the Charlotte Street Hotel bar half an hour late and spotted Carey immediately. Nervous that someone like him would be unused to being kept waiting, she called his name. 'Carey?'

He turned round and her anxiety evaporated. Carey had a broad grin on his face. 'Hi Abena.' He bent down and she went to kiss his cheek but he enveloped her in an enormous bear hug.

'I hate being late, I'm so sorry to have kept you waiting.'

'Uh-huh, when I said 8 p.m. I didn't mean African 8 – I've lived in Ghana for a while and know that over there 8 means anything from 9 p.m. to 8 a.m. the next day.' He was milking his advantage but Abena didn't mind.

'Ha ha! What were you doing in Ghana – filming *Red*?'

'Indeed. So what have you been doing since France?'

'Well, in between trying to escape the wrath of my boss, who blames me for everything from the messiness of the stationery cupboard to the global recession, I've been having rather a fun time. I was back in St Tropez just a few weeks ago – I'm not surprised so many films have been shot there, it really is a bizarre place.'

'So what film would you shoot there?' Carey asked idly.

'Well, um, actually, you'll probably think it's silly, but I've always had this idea to make a glossy, modern version of Thackeray's *Vanity Fair*. Obviously it was written centuries ago, but everything's still kind of the same. There's still a war for the boys to go off to. We still play, we still pretend, we still want more … And we still love with all our hearts.' Abena paused, embarrassed, and looked at Carey, but he was listening intently. Emboldened, she went on. 'And I would hire that director you used for *Winter Sunrise* – I remember you said he's difficult to work with but he has such an extraordinary way of taking an apparently unambiguous concept and turning it into a delicious enigma. You leave the cinema confused, when you came in so grotesquely sure of yourself and your opinions and … Anyway …' She trailed off. What was she doing, describing her dream to one of the most influential men in cinema? But to her surprise, Carey smiled.

'That sounds very interesting. Yes, he is good. You've really thought this through. What sort of style would you go for – are we thinking trendy art-house or big-budget commercial?'

'I love everything, but I've never understood the school of thought that says something is only good if nobody gets it. If you've got something worth saying then why not say it in a way that everybody can understand? And film is a business. Like every business it needs to be sustainable – so big and commercial for sure!' Abena laughed. 'And a nice hunk like Djimon Hounsou in the lead role.'

At nine-thirty they strolled over to Roka, where Carey's friends had already assembled. Abena had to bite her lip to stop herself from squealing when she saw who they were eating with. What Carey called 'dinner with a couple friends' was in fact a banquet with a whole host of famous faces, many of them American. Carey sat Abena beside him, and again she had to suppress a disbelieving laugh. To her right was Bryan Jones – *the* Bryan Jones! – whose star-turn as the hapless twin brother in the sitcom *Smithy & Smith* had accompanied her through many a hung-over Sunday. Across the table, a young actress who Abena recognized as the arm-candy of a more accomplished actor – and who seemed to have the opinion that nudity in films was only OK if it was completely gratuitous – introduced herself as Marcie Wharton. Completing her end of the table were actress-turned-political-activist Gizzi Bryson, who had starred in lots of films and adopted lots of babies, and Tom and Kimberly Thompson, a husband and wife who wrote wildly contrasting books. Luckily Abena had read both the husband's biography of Thomas Cromwell and the wife's exuberant bonkbuster satirizing the super-rich. They were thrilled to meet somebody who read books purely for enjoyment. 'They're usually totally illiterate in the film business, and the few who aren't only see books as the basis for a film adaptation,' confided Tom.

Carey nodded at her. 'I knew *you'd* be fine with these guys. Some people are intimidated by fame.'

'Oh we're all just people,' Abena countered blithely. She sure as hell wasn't prepared to let any of them know how star-struck she was.

Secretly, she was also thrilled to prove to herself that she could have such a glamorous evening without Sebastian. She'd noticed lately that, every time he mentioned or took her to anywhere fabulous, he would ask her patronizingly, 'Do you know it?' or 'Have you been here before?' As though he'd somehow plucked her from a mundane world where high-octane luxury meant a speedy M&S delivery and was now introducing a touch of much-needed Sebastian excitement into her life.

With the exception of Abena, everyone present had met before and knew each other's work. Unsurprisingly, conversation soon turned to Abena's occupation.

'So what is it that you do, Abena? You're not an actress or I'd know you. Do you do music?' Bryan asked.

'I think she's in fashion,' announced the author husband.

'No,' Marcie said slyly, looking Abena up and down. 'Your outfit's far too perfect for that – people in fashion don't let it show how hard they've tried.'

'I hope you're a producer? The industry needs more young women coming into the profession. I'll certainly be encouraging my adopted girls,' said the more experienced Gizzi.

Abena stalled for time. As an unknown friend of Carey's she could be anyone. Not just someone who filled in Excel spreadsheets for an ungrateful harridan. Just as she was about to fabricate an elaborate lie, about working undercover at Mallinder as part of her research for a private detecting mission she'd been commissioned to undertake by Kroll, Carey jumped to her rescue.

'Abena's actually just graduated from Oxford.'

The Americans really sat up at the mention of such an old English institution.

'Really?' exclaimed Marcie, still competitively eyeing her outfit. 'That must be a challenge. Do you like it there?'

'I've left now, but yes, it was a lot of fun. It's a stunning place.'

'Oh my Gaad, soo so nice,' Kimberly the society satirist added with unnecessary enthusiasm. 'Taam,' she nudged her husband, 'dontcha remember, we did a talk there with all those great kids, up in Aaxford? They wanted to know all about *Lifestyles of the Rich and Famous* and *Daddy I Want a Pony*. They just couldn't believe I'd written them both in such a short space of taaam—'

'Just took you three months each, didn't they baby?' Tom cut in.

'And the film version was my absolute favourite part ever,' added Marcie.

'Yes, your tits did a fantastic job. Had a commanding screen presence.' Bryan ducked as Marcie threw an edamame bean at him.

'*Behave*!' said Kimberly, theatrically holding up a heavily jew-elled hand. 'Abena you *must* read my next naarvel. I think you'll like it – it's all about underachieving kids in the ghettos ...'

'Intriguing ...' Abena smiled.

'Abena, you absolutely must come and stay with us in the Hol-lywood Hills if you're ever in that part of the world,' offered Gizzi. Her eyes were so bright and her toothy smile so dazzling that Abena wondered whether she was angling to adopt her too. Gizzi was clearly enthralled by her, and though Abena clicked fairly fast that she was just another means by which Gizzi could try and ingratiate herself with Carey, it was thrilling all the same.

'Ya know, I'd like to go back to Aaxford? I'd like to go and do another reading,' cut in Kimberly. She turned to her husband. 'I just find when I read in front of students it's sooooo *rewarding*.'

Now that the writers had coaxed the conversation back to the topic of themselves, Abena relaxed and started talking to Carey, continuing the chat they'd begun at the hotel bar.

'It doesn't sound as if you've even started to find your thing at Mallinder Films,' Carey said. 'You're finding it difficult to know what to do because you're torn. But don't take the easy route just because you can. Don't try to, I don't know, act, just for the sake of it, or get into show business because it sounds sexy. You need to stretch yourself. Produce something, produce a film, or start your own company. It's fine for you to do something serious – you're glitzy enough on your own account, you don't need to go looking for it.' Abena was unnerved by the intensity of his stare, and the feeling it stirred within her.

'Wow, you're pretty forthright with those opinions on someone you've only just met.'

'Sorry, I say what I think. Some people don't like that.'

'No, no, it's great. I … I suppose I just wasn't expecting such an accurate psychological analysis quite so soon.'

'I like you, Abena. I think you're a great girl, and you're driven, ambitious, but you've got a good heart. I wanted a lot too. I like that and I'll help you in any way that I can.'

'Well, I'm flattered. I respect your opinion immensely. I'd love to learn from you.'

'I'm happy to teach – your curiosity inspires me.'

And so began a mutual fascination between the two: mentor and protégé, artist and muse.

# Chapter 18

Abena walked into the living room of her flat to find Tara curled up on the sofa, naked apart from a small towel wrapped around her chest, which barely reached the tops of her thighs. She appeared to have just stepped out of the shower and was rubbing moisturizer into her legs while she watched television. Sebastian was sitting on the opposite sofa, watching her.

'I thought you said you were going home this weekend,' Abena said with barely disguised annoyance.

'Can't be bothered,' Tara replied without looking up from the TV screen.

'Why are you getting changed here, Tara? Is there anything wrong with your room? Or the bathroom?'

Tara looked up. 'I felt like watching television, if that's OK with you? This is my flat too.'

'Right, and since when have you ever watched daytime TV? Why don't you go out and do something? You've been moping around the flat all week.'

Sebastian cleared his throat and dragged his eyes away from Tara's legs. 'Come and stay with us in Sussex, Tara, there's plenty of space.'

Abena turned on her heel, marched to her room and threw herself on her bed. She tried to hold back the angry tears she could feel welling in the corners of her eyes.

'You OK? I was just trying to include Tara.' Sebastian had followed Abena back to her bedroom.

Abena couldn't believe what she was hearing. Tara was being a selfish cow, and when did Sebastian become Mother Teresa? But there was no way she was going to play the jealous girlfriend. She got up from the bed and yawned.

'Sure, that's sweet of you. Shall we make a move soon? I don't think it's a good idea that Tara comes with us. She normally goes home for Sunday lunch and she hasn't been in weeks, her family are worried about her.'

'Fine, I'm ready, I was just waiting for you to get your stuff together.'

Abena packed the last of her things and Sebastian took her overnight bag out to his Range Rover. Abena made to follow, pausing to pick up the cash she thought she'd left on her bedside table. She was sure she'd left six £20 notes there, in the vain hope that she could get through an entire week on £120, but it was gone. Perhaps she'd spent it and forgotten, or maybe Sebastian had taken it, mistakenly confusing it with his own. She'd better go.

'Darling, you didn't see any money lying around my room did you? I seem to have misplaced £120?'

'No I didn't, but you don't need any money now, babe, find it later – it's probably in one of your handbags.'

'Yeah, I'm sure you're right,' Abena said, getting into the car as Sebastian revved the engine impatiently. She wasn't so certain though.

They broke the drive to West Sussex with a long lunch at a country pub. Sebastian ordered a beer for himself, a glass of red wine for Abena, and two steaks, cooked rare. Talking excitedly through a mouthful of beef, Sebastian began to tell Abena about a new business idea that had occurred to him during a recent trip to Paris. 'What I'm going to do,' he began, 'is set up an environmentally friendly clothing range.'

'Tell me more.' Abena raised a sceptical eyebrow. She couldn't see how this fitted with his expertise or talents.

'It's a fucking joke what we're doing to the planet,' he continued. Abena nodded and glanced out of the window to where Sebastian's shiny Range Rover was parked.

'But our generation can do something to offset that. In Paris I was talking to my mate Charles-Albert and he came up with the idea. We were thinking we could use only recycled stuff, you know, recycled paper in our offices, and all the clothes would be tie-dyed. Of course nobody wears tie-dyed stuff but we'd hire all the hottest models to advertise our brand. It'll be awesome – it'll go totally global and revolutionize the retail industry.'

Sebastian's eyes were twinkling in anticipation like a toddler on Christmas Eve.

'That sounds like an ambitious start-up. You'd need loads of seed capital for that, even for the advertising alone. Would Simeon finance it?'

'My Dad wants me to do something with my life, so, yeah, he'll chip in a few mill, but it'll be my thing. I'll make it successful myself and pay him back. I can build just as huge an empire as he has.'

'Hmmn, sure. But what about the modelling agency you wanted to set up last week, or the restaurant?'

Sebastian stared at her like she was an imbecile. 'Obviously, I still wanna do that too. It's all about delegation. That's how you take over the world, darling.'

He took a triumphant swig of his beer and leaned across the table to kiss her. His total unwillingness to engage with reality was so irritating but as usual she completely melted at his touch. Looking into his eyes, she kissed him back and convinced herself it didn't really matter what she thought because it would never happen anyway. She knew that in twenty years from now Sebastian would still be hell-raising all over the world on his father's fortune and dreaming of building an empire. In a way, his idealism was quite sweet.

'By the way, what are you doing Monday evening?' Sebastian asked as they prepared to head off.

'I've got plans, I'm going out with Carey Wa—'

'Cancel your plans. I've been invited to the Tringate Charity Fundraiser and it's pretty hard to get a plus one for that kind of thing, but I did. You'll love it, darling. Honestly, you've never seen anything like it.'

'As I was saying, I've got my own plans. I'm going to a private film-screening with Carey Wallace and some other friends.'

'Who's Carey? Not that old guy you were telling me about? Du-ull. Well this thing is gonna be more of a laugh than some crap film, but no worries, we can hook up afterwards – if you want to see me at all that is.'

'You're more than welcome to come out with Carey and me.'

Sebastian ignored her.

\*\*\*\*

On Monday afternoon Natalya decided to attend the Mirror Mirror casting. Always aware of her Plan B, she'd felt she should at least keep going to the prestigious castings – you can forget the hair shows or wedding catalogues – until she had a ring on her finger. She'd still have just enough time to return home and get ready for the Tringate Charity Fundraiser. Claude was the chief benefactor, and she was to attend in his absence.

She strode confidently to the casting table and placed down her card. Even on the table's cluttered surface her magnificent image stood out. She knew there were many more breathtakingly beautiful models to come after her, and they were all in competition with each other. She knew that the chosen model would earn upwards of £60,000 to be the face of Blue Whisper perfume, and all the others wouldn't receive a penny. But this time Natalya didn't care. She needn't pander to power-happy bookers any more. She had been freed. She exuded the nonchalance a Mirror Mirror model needed to project.

'Great face,' the tired-looking woman behind the desk commented. Her own face was distinctly not great and Natalya wondered what had made her take such a job in the first place. Was it deliberate masochism?

'What's your availability at the beginning of January?' she asked mechanically.

'I really couldn't say right now. I'll let you know nearer the time if it becomes relevant. Thenk you.'

The woman's eyes widened. Models at such high-profile castings never spoke to her like that. Unsure quite how to respond, she pursed her lips and scribbled a note on the back of Natalya's card. If her intention was to unsettle Natalya, it didn't work. By the time the woman had taken the lid off the pen, the audacious beauty with the elfin haircut had already left the building.

Hurrying back to Mayfair, Natalya worried she may have been unnecessarily rude at the casting, but it couldn't be helped. She needed to have enough time to dress for tonight's event, and as she was a sponsor, or representing one at least, all eyes would be on her. She might even bump into some old conquests. She'd show them how far she'd come.

She rushed to her closet, a converted bedroom, and pulled on a skin-tight floor-length backless silver gown. At the front, the dress was slashed to below the navel. Once she'd taped it in place, it moved with her body like a second skin. She slid on vertiginous silver heels, which took her to well over six foot, and reached for the outrageously expensive diamond-drop earrings that Claude had presented her with. She slicked her hair to one side in a quirky, fashion-forward style. There was no point going to the salon when her hair was so short. She admired herself in the mirror. She looked like a mermaid that had been taught to walk.

Natalya was pleased she was going alone. She thought of her third visit to St Tropez and shuddered at the memory. She had decided the time was right to offer Claude her body. So that evening she came down to the poolside in a pink baby-doll nightie, claiming she felt unwell.

'Please,' she said in a soft voice, 'put your sweet child to bed.'

Claude looked at her, a strange expression on his face, and she recognized it immediately – the no-man's land between pleasure and pain that she had seen in the market all those years ago, and then every day after that. Claude gathered her into his arms and sucked her nose. She suppressed an appalled yelp and looked deep into his eyes.

'Let me take you up,' he whispered.

Then he lifted her off the ground and carried her to the lift and into the first-floor master bedroom, where he laid her on the bed. Although she was far from heavy, he took a moment to stop wheezing from the exertion. When he had recovered, he removed her nightie and his own shirt and linen trousers and lay beside her. They did not make love that first night or the night after – it took Claude a few attempts to achieve an erection, but he was content to simply enjoy the sensation of her naked flesh against his whenever he wasn't able to get it up, and on the third night they did it. On two occasions he requested she insert a newly manicured finger into his anus. That was particularly unpleasant.

Shaking her head to banish the image, she picked up her mobile phone and took a photo of herself. The picture was a triumph, and the earrings glistened, illuminating the entire image. She sent it to Claude's BlackBerry, accompanied by the message: *I am wearing your earrings and thinking of you. N. xoxoxox.*

The Tringate Charity Fundraiser was held in a grand converted Georgian stately home outside London. Inside, it was dark and atmospheric, filled with antiques and ancient oil paintings in heavy gilded frames. The evening was to begin with a five-course meal, after which there would be fireworks and dancing in the open-air ballroom. In the concert hall, the Royal Ballet were warming up before their performance of a specially choreographed dance. The biggest draw for most of the guests, however, was the promise of the first live performance in years by legendary band The

Samsons, who had re-formed specially for the occasion. This was where Sebastian Spectre expected to spend the vast majority of the evening. First, though, he had to eat, and he was delighted to be seated next to a stunner in a positively indecent silver dress and a cute boyish peroxide-blonde hairdo. In the absence of his girlfriend, she'd do very nicely indeed.

'Hi. Sebastian Spectre,' he said, extending a hand towards the girl.

She looked at his hand, then gingerly touched his fingers with her own.'Natalya', she said shortly, and turned back to her truffles.

Why was this mere boy seated on the top table and seated beside her, the sponsor? She recognized him from somewhere and he was unnervingly attractive; she'd tried not to think about how many years it had been since she'd spent a night with a hard-bodied youth.

'And what is your involvement with the Tringate event?'

'I've sponsored it.'That should teach this haughty model.

'You? You've sponsored this?'

'Well, my father has, last year and the year before. What's your involvement?'

'I'm this year's main sponsor.'That should put this handsome rich kid in his place.

'You?' Sebastian asked.

'My partner is Claude Perren.'

'Ah, Mr Perren. How do you keep up with him?' Sebastian mocked.

Natalya pierced him with an unsmiling stare.'What?'

'Just he's doing big things in Paris at the moment, isn't he? Is he ever going to slow down?' Sebastian asked, playing innocent.

'Yes, he is. And no, he's not.' Natalya answered both questions curtly, torn between wanting to gloat about her famous connection and wanting to pretend that she was kind of single. She'd be foolish to jeopardize her future with Claude but the thrill of enslaving a man was addictive, particularly if he was good-looking and rich.

A waiter came round with a choice of red or white wine. 'I would like vodka,' Natalya said imperiously.

'Certainly Madam,' came the waiter's polite reply and he returned immediately with a bottle of Grey Goose.

'I'll have some of that too,' Sebastian told the waiter. He was about to ask for some tonic when Natalya picked up her glass and downed the contents in two gulps before calling for some more. Steeling himself, Sebastian swallowed his in three sips and tried not to splutter. Natalya tried not to betray her amusement.

'So where is Daddy tonight?'

'He's at our place on St Barts. Where is Mr Construction?'

'Buying the rest of France,' Natalya smirked. 'Do you have a girlfriend?'

There was a long pause. Sebastian downed another vodka and filled both of their champagne glasses from the bottle of Cristal on the table.

'I'm kind of seeing someone,' he said.

'Lucky girl,' Natalya whispered.

'It's nothing serious,' Sebastian said.

Sebastian's readiness to be ensnared was beginning to ruin Natalya's fun. But then she caught sight of his thigh, taut and toned against the velvet chair. She took a long sip of Cristal and looked again at the gold name-card in front of Sebastian's plate.

Where did she recognize Spectre from?

Sebastian stole a closer look at the marvellous cut of Natalya's dress. He was devastated to realize that it didn't reveal anything when she moved or leaned forward. What a tease. He felt his BlackBerry vibrate in the pocket of his trousers and remembered he'd told Abena they'd hook up later. Guiltily he set the machine to divert all calls to voicemail. The truffle plates were cleared away and tender fillets of rainbow trout appeared on the table. Natalya wasn't in the mood for fish so she placed hers on Sebastian's plate. By the time the duck arrived, served on a bed of meltingly soft foie gras, the pair were laughing so much they neglected to eat anything. When the waiters came to clear pudding, Natalya was licking lemon and chilli soufflé from Sebastian's quivering fingers. And by the time the petits fours were set down, Sebastian and Natalya were nowhere to be found.

'Get it out!' Natalya ordered.

'What? Now?'

'Get it OUT!' Her fingers trembled as her hand found its way to the bulge in his trousers. Sebastian was alarmed and aroused in equal measure. His cock strained against his jeans but the stony expression on Natalya's face was terrifying.

Eyes flashing, Natalya ripped open the top of his jeans and knelt down. And then suddenly her mouth was on him.

'Sweet Jesus!' He gasped as her tongue flickered across his cock. 'And I thought you weren't hungry earlier ...'

'Shut up!' Natalya came up briefly for air. 'I don't want to talk.'

She grabbed Sebastian's hand and pulled it between her legs. She moaned loudly at his touch, and then, suddenly, she was straddling him, rocking gently at first, then building up to a frenzy. And even though he was talking all the while, groaning, murmuring and stammering his encouragement, all Natalya could hear was the sound of angels and cherubs playing the violin while they floated, pink and chubby, in the clouds above. Yes, she thought, this is what heaven feels like.

Sebastian had taken Natalya to his country estate, having correctly guessed she'd be more impressed by his Sussex mansion than his London flat. Besides, he'd been fantasizing throughout dinner about sliding her naked down his father's chute and having scorching sex in the pool.

So they made love, more slowly, in the pool, and again, frantically, on a sofa by the south terrace. Finally Natalya was sated. She knew she wouldn't come again, so while Sebastian was going down on her she calculated the value of the house and its owners. About £9.5 million for the house, she decided, and £350 million for the Spectre family's net worth – nothing on Claude. And besides, this one was clearly not the settling-down type. She realized his head was still between her legs.

'OK, thenk you,' she said, bringing her knees together sharply and sitting upright on the sofa. 'I want to go now.'

'Oh. OK, well, I'll drive you to London, I'm going that way too. I reckon we've had a pretty good innings already.'

Natalya rolled her eyes. Why did the English always have to bring cricket into it?

Sebastian couldn't resist showing off his Chelsea pad and Natalya couldn't resist another orgasm, so they stopped for one last quickie on the way. Finally he dropped Natalya back home in Mayfair.

# Chapter 19

For the fourth time in as many minutes, Abena checked her telephone for a sign that Sebastian had tried to contact her. She'd left a message saying she was going to stay overnight in Bristol and that she would see him tomorrow. She had thought the screening was in London, but it had turned out to be part of a three-day festival near Bristol. So she'd booked into the boutique hotel that Carey was staying at. As it happened, Benedict Lima was staying there too.

'So anyway, what did you think of the film?' Benedict asked Abena.'Yet another new adaptation of *Romeo and Juliet*, and still it had me wiping away a tear.' He grinned sheepishly.

'Really?' Abena's eyes slanted suspiciously.'I didn't exactly have you down as the romantic after all those withering remarks about my boyfriend at the ball.'

'Please. That wasn't love, that was a grand gesture from a spoilt attention-seeker. All the world's a stage …'He trailed off when he saw how hurt Abena looked.

'Sorry,' Benedict shook his head, 'but that's not what I'm talking about. Imagine meeting somebody who is everything to you. Really everything, so that when they aren't there then nothing is left in this life; you die because you can't go on. I've sure as hell never loved like that.'

'I hope you never will.'

'You don't want me to experience passionate love?' Now it was Benedict's turn to look hurt.

'I want everyone to know life-affirming love. A love that makes you happier just knowing it exists. An honest love that doesn't masquerade as passion when really it's poison.'

'But what about when it doesn't exist? What if your lover dies, like in the film?'

Abena paused for a moment. 'I think maybe the love can live on – just evolve, and change. The energy can be shared, transferred, grown, whatever. Why should it stay the same? I just don't think love should cripple, make us less equipped to deal with the world around us. I think it should strengthen us and make everything we encounter more exciting.'

Benedict was looking at Abena intently, a rapt expression on his face.

'What?' she said, quite sharply. 'Can't a girl who wears nice shoes have a real opinion?'

'If you'll stop treating me like a pretentious über-intellectual because I wear glasses, I'll try to get over your stilettos. Deal?'

'But I didn't …' Abena paused and laughed. 'Deal.'

'Have you heard anything from Mr Universe then?' He watched Carey wonder off to the other side of the hotel bar to talk shop with some industry acquaintances over from New York.

'No, it's strange. Perhaps his BlackBerry is out of juice. He's crap at charging it. It's no big deal.'

'Idiot!' Benedict muttered with seemingly uncharacteristic

aggression.

'Hey, it's no big deal!' Abena laughed. 'After all, I'm the one changing the plan – or at least I would be if he'd answer the damn phone!'

'Actually it is a big deal. No one cares about manners any more but it's just plain rude. No one deserves to be treated like that by their boyfriend, even an independent girl like you who can look after herself.'

'How very eighteenth-century of you,' Abena said drily. 'Sorry, that was rude. Thanks for sticking up for me. And for looking after me at the ball. It was very sweet.'

'I detest that word,' Benedict cut in.

'What, "sweet"? Why?'

'Oh you know why! "Sweet" is what girls call their little brothers. Or their dogs!'

'Nonsense, brothers are exasperating and dogs are smelly. Fine, don't sulk. You're clever. And a romantic. And sweet. How's that?'

'Hmmnn … Getting better …' He offered her his arm and led her, slowly, in her precariously high heels, to the bar to buy a drink.

'What would you like to drink?'

'A glass of red would be great – you must let *me* get it this time,' Abena pleaded. She remembered on the boat he'd said he was a runner, one of the few people in the world who earned even less than she did.

'Don't be silly, let's get a bottle,' he replied, pushing her £20 note away and handing his card to the barman.

As Benedict ushered her over to the corner and on to the comfiest seat, Abena was aware that she should really be trying to network with the high-powered crowd mingling in the bar. But she realized with a shock that really the only person she wanted to talk to was Ben, even if he could be infuriatingly stubborn regarding the central message of *Romeo and Juliet*.

Looking at her watch sometime later and seeing it was past midnight, Abena realized they'd been arguing and chatting for over two hours.

'Look at the time! No wonder my stomach's growling, we've forgotten to eat anything.'

They trawled the streets of Bristol in search of somewhere serving anything other than dodgy kebabs. By 1 a.m. it was pouring with rain. Benedict looked at Abena, drenched and shivering. Her hair was in two dripping pigtails, and what was left of her make-up was smudged about her eyes. He was struck by how adorable she looked. He forced a laugh.'How about room service?'

Benedict's room was delightful, with hand-painted white floors, a cosy log fire, a king-sized four-poster bed and a vintage Chesterfield sofa in the corner. In an adjoining room were two distressed leather sofas into which they both collapsed.

By now quite drunk, the pair woozily discussed the other films they'd watched, until the arrival of two big, juicy burgers cut short their analyses.

'My God it's exciting to be allowed a burger once in a while!' Abena whooped as she removed the silver cover on top of her plate. With Sebastian she always felt like a bit of a heffalump eating anything this awkward and greasy.

Once they'd eaten they moved into the bedroom to listen to some music and, sinking on to the Chesterfield, Abena swiftly realized how tired she was. Looking at Benedict, who had now slumped on his bed and removed his glasses to rub his eyes, she guessed he felt the same.

'Wow! You should take off your glasses more – I had no idea you had those striking eyes … It makes me wonder what you're hiding under that beard!'

'You don't like my beard?'

'I'd just like to see your face, that's all.' Abena yawned. 'I suppose I should really be going now.'

'Stay a second, just one more song, my favourite?'

'OK,' Abena jumped up to join Benedict on the tall four-poster bed piled high with satin throws and plumped-up pillows. As the mournful voice of Bob Dylan caressed her ears she drifted off to sleep on Benedict's shoulder. Gently he removed her shoes and covered her with the duvet. For a few minutes he watched the rhythmic rise and fall of her body. Then he stood, slowly so as not to wake her, and switched off the lights. He let himself into Abena's empty room a few doors down and climbed into bed, alone.

\*\*\*\*

Natalya,
If you have come to revisit the past, it will come back to haunt you a thousand times over. The past is DEAD and BURIED. Be careful.
Stan

Natalya's tormentor had caught up with her and there was nothing she could do about it. It was the day after the Tringate Charity Fundraiser and she felt impotent and vulnerable. She knew that

219

the police wouldn't bother with her case, not after her false claim against Oleg. And besides, despite the insinuations, nothing in the letters was actually abusive. How were they to know how dangerous her father really was? She had no proof of anything, just her mother's word that a man had come from England in search of a good time and in the process had ruined her life. He had destroyed her self-esteem and her confidence, and demolished her dreams.

Natalya didn't dare contact her mother about these letters. It would only upset her, and make her beg her firstborn to return to Latvia. No, frightened as she was, the only way forward was to ignore the letters and not allow this ogre to control her life. Not when she was so close to her dream of untold riches, of financial freedom, for the first time ever. She was not about to throw all that away and return to hawking baskets in Riga's Old Quarter. She would not be cowed by the evil that was her father. She would face him. And she would kill him.

If he did not kill her first.

Suddenly Natalya heard a voice and realized with a jolt that somebody was in the house. Her heart seemed to jump right out of her chest and as the figure advanced towards her she let out a long strangulated scream and backed away until she was stooped, trembling in his shadow.

Then she saw his face.

'Claude!'

She sighed with relief as she jumped up, crushing the letter into a ball, and flung herself against him, nestling her head in his neck as though he were her beloved soldier husband returning from a war zone.

Claude smiled to himself as he kissed the top of her head. The strange, delicate thing loved him so.

****

Just five grand doors down the road from Monsieur Perren's newly acquired residence, Reza reached for the loo roll. He was out of paper and made a mental note to fire the head housekeeper first thing in the morning. Sighing at the inconvenience he reached into the back pocket of his chinos and pulled out his wallet, from which he extracted three crisp, new £50 notes. Standing up, he reached behind and gave his rear a couple of vigorous wipes before scrunching the money into a ball and flushing it down the toilet. He pulled up his chinos, washed his hands quickly, ran a comb through his thinning hair and hurried out of his mansion. His Bentley was waiting to drive him to Southwark for an interview with the *Financial Times*.

# Chapter 20

Abena decided to spend extra time on her getting-ready ritual that evening. She hadn't seen Sebastian for a while and was surprised at how painfully she missed him. She knew it had been her decision to stay overnight in Bristol, but still, the number of times he called had dwindled from a few times a day at the height of his pursuit to absolutely nothing for a week. But at least he'd texted earlier and explained that he'd been busy with 'business', whatever that amounted to, and that he'd make it up to her over dinner. Well, she'd blow him away tonight. Every so often a man needs to be reminded of how lucky he is. She hadn't been sweating it out walking to work every day for fun. She did it to look as good as she could, and she hated to have to blow her own trumpet, but: toot toot!

Examining herself in the mirror Abena was finally satisfied with her softly applied make-up, the 'natural' look being, as usual, the most lengthy and laborious one to perfect. Her eyelashes seemed endless, framing her dark eyes, and the gold shimmer on her cheeks lifted her complexion and lent it an air of sunny vitality. The dark circles under her eyes, the result of late nights spent rowing with Tara about her habit, were untraceable underneath a deftly applied layer of Touche Eclat. Her lips were full and inviting and her long dark hair fell in tousled waves about her face. She threw her keys, phone, lip gloss and a spare pair of undies into her clutch bag and treated herself to a taxi.

Sebastian had excelled himself in his choice of restaurant, food being one of the only passions the couple truly had in common. He watched with amused appreciation as Abena devoured in record time a first course of *lingua di manzo, salsa verde* – ox tongue being a speciality of the exclusive Italian restaurant. He adored girls with good appetites. Women who didn't cultivate and indulge their sense of taste were usually disappointing where other sensory pleasures were concerned. And by that he didn't mean women should stuff themselves senseless on pies, burgers and sausages, rather that he was attracted to those with distinguished palates and adventurous tastes.

Sebastian seemed unable to take his eyes off Abena, so she banished her last lingering doubts and, confident that he still fancied her like crazy, relaxed and allowed herself to enjoy her food. They drank a fruity red that was as old and full bodied as they were young and slender. Pudding was sweet and sticky.

With the meal over, Abena's mind wandered to what lay ahead. Sebastian was obviously thinking the same thing as he placed his wine glass down purposefully, moved the candle to one side and leaned forward to bring his face right up close to Abena's. Nina Simone was playing softly in the background and Sebastian added his own baritone slurs to her throaty purring. 'I put a spell on you …', he sang, 'Cos you're mine …' Abena joined in: 'You better stop the things you do … It ain't right … OOOOOH IT AIN'T RIGHT'. She belted out the last line like a true diva, and fell about laughing.

Sebastian jumped up and grabbed his girlfriend's hand. 'Come on, let's get out of here.'

Full of wine and mischief, Abena began to perform an impromptu Nina Simone karaoke-cum-striptease in the car.

'Birds flying high ... You know how I feel ...', she sang, her voice rich and low as she slipped her foot out of her stiletto and stretched her bare leg high in the air, letting her blue silk skirt slide up her thigh as she bent her knee and brought her toe to rest on the dashboard. Sebastian swerved the car and the driver of a beat-up Ford behind hooted and made a 'wanker' gesture.

'Sun in the sky ... You know how I feel ...', Abena continued, and her white cape came off. 'Breeeeeeze driftin' on by ... You know how I feel ...' Now she peeled off her white silk vest. 'It's a new day ... It's a new dawn ... It's a new liiiife ... Foooor, meeee ...' She sang louder as she shimmied out of her skirt, to reveal her black lace underwear.

'And I'm feeeeeeeling good ...'

Sebastian was so fired up he could barely open his front door. Running inside the apartment with only her cape wrapped around her Abena headed straight to the bedroom and threw herself backwards on to the bed, arms thrown wantonly above her head.

'Come and get me,' she cooed, laughing at Sebastian, who had tripped over his jeans in an effort to remove them and run towards her at the same time. Then Abena turned her head to the side and the sight she encountered caused her heart to stop.

'What are these?' She rose from the bed, slowly, uncertain. In her hand was a pair of sheer Agent Provocateur panties.

'Either you're a secret cross-dresser or you've got some explaining to do.'

Sebastian's face fell. It was all Abena needed to know. In a single casting down of the eyes, he had surrendered. Still, he tried to fight back.

'What the … I can't believe Alex would do that to me. He obviously brought some girl back here and she must have left them in my bed.'

'Why the hell would Alex come here when he's got his own place to bring girls back to?'

'Uh, yeah. Yeah, but he's been having some work done to his place so he's been staying here.'

'He had work done to his place weeks ago.'

'Well, I … I don't know, they must have been here for weeks.'

'Oh right, I see, so you've been sleeping with a pair of stripper pants in your bed for three weeks and just happened not to have noticed. For that matter your housekeeper hasn't changed your sheets for three weeks either. You can do better than that, Sebastian.'

At once his face hardened. 'Baby, this is who I am. It's how I roll.'

Abena was stung to the core. Had nothing in the last five months meant anything to him? Deep down, though, she'd known.

'How does it feel … To be on your own … Like a rolling stone …', she murmured sadly under her breath.

'Do you want me to drive you back?' Sebastian asked.

She looked at him, a wan smile on her face. It was a smile for all the fun they had shared, but tempered with hurt and sadness.

'I'll get a cab. See you sometime … I guess.'

She turned and walked, wretched and alone, into the icy, dark night.

****

'Tara?'

Abena banged harder on Tara's bedroom door.

'Tara?'

No answer. She pushed the door and walked in. Tara was in bed with the light off, so Abena didn't notice the translucent pallor of her friend's skin, nor the almost imperceptible shivers of her bony body.

'What is it?' Tara asked crossly.

'Sebastian's been cheating on me – we broke up.' Abena gulped down her tears.

'Why d'you break up?'

'B-b-because he cheated on me.'

'Oh.' And then, 'Hon, do you have some cash I can borrow?'

Abena let out a loud sob. Tara had so many of her own troubles. Sniffing noisily, Abena shuffled off to bed alone.

****

Abena wolf-whistled as Sarah arrived for Sunday brunch in one of Notting Hill's trendy cafés. 'You're really looking amazing these days, Sarah.'

'Thanks! I feel great. Things are going so well with Willy – you won't believe the people I'm meeting and the stuff I'm doing. I've organized a celebrity karaoke for Willy's natural disaster rescue charity, which is going to be covered by all the glossies, and it's been dinners, dos and parties non-stop in the evenings, and manic meetings and emails in the office all day, so it's exhausting but I love it there.'

She paused for breath and gabbled on.

'I just wish Si would appreciate me a bit more. He's the only person who hasn't said they like my new haircut and he's the one who should love it the most! I invite him out to Willy's events and he just stubbornly refuses, saying he's sick of me out with all these lecherous TV execs breathing down my cleavage every night when they wouldn't be able to if he'd only come to stuff with me and … Oh my God, Abbi, are you OK?'

A fat tear slid down Abena's cheek. 'Yep, yes, I'm sorry,' Abena sniffed. 'It's just, Sebastian and I broke up – he's been cheating on me.'

'Oh, sweetheart!' Sarah embraced Abena, comforting her in that motherly way that made all the boys do whatever she wanted. 'Poor thing, tell me everything. What happened?'

Abena began telling the story and by the time she got to the ridiculous bows at the sides of the frilly Agent Provocateur knickers, she was in a much better mood.

'Obviously, compared to you and Si, it's nothing, I mean, I was only with Sebastian for five months or so, and it was hardly serious – just a bit of fun, you know…'

'Hon, five months is more than enough time to fall for someone. And especially someone like Sebastian Spectre, well he's … Anyway, you're so much better off without him Abbi; infidelity is inexcusable.'

Abena looked uncertain, so Sarah carried on, 'You know I've never told anybody this before, but my parents were almost torn apart by my mother's affair.'

'You're kidding! Your family seems like the perfect little unit.'

'I know, and my mother's a complete prude like me! But my dad had a few too many rums one Christmas and told me the story.'

'So what happened?'

'Well, it was the internet that caught them out. Mum's not very computer-literate and didn't realize Dad could read her emails if she didn't sign out. He stumbled across an email to Mum from their friend Nigel that said "My cock is hard thinking about you". So of course my dad was absolutely furious. He hit the reply button and wrote to Nigel saying "If you have any more bulletins about the state of your cock then kindly direct them to your own wife". Then he went rummaging through the rest of her emails and came across the message that made him demand a divorce.'

'What was the message?' Abena was trying seriously hard not to laugh.

'It was my Mum's reply to Nigel that did it. He'd sent her something really smutty about how he wanted to do her all weekend in a seedy hotel, and she'd replied, "Yes, wouldn't it be lovely, with crisp, white linen sheets and the sunlight streaming in." My dad thought that if that was the foxiest thing she could come up with then Nigel was welcome to her – said it was symptomatic of all the problems they'd been having in bed for years.'

'I'm astounded! Well, at least they worked it out in the end.'

'Yes, but imagine if they hadn't! You were right to break away from Sebastian, these things often get worse.'

Abena waved at a waitress and ordered two Bloody Marys.

'Could you ever have an affair with a married man?' Sarah asked.

'No,' Abena answered immediately. 'Nothing to do with the morality of it all; after all, his marriage is not my responsibility. It's more that I just hate the thought of the sort of married man who still has affairs. He puts on this front as a libidinous alpha male,

229

but behind the mask he's a spineless beta. That type of man just isn't attractive to me.'

'Me neither,' Sarah agreed.

Both girls slurped at their cocktails and thought about men.

'Let's do something tonight,' Abena said, feeling more upbeat. 'Go out – I just need to do something.'

'Do you fancy Annabel's?'

'Is this really Sarah Hunter I'm talking to?'

Sarah laughed. 'Bertrand Brampton Amis, who manages all Willy's financial affairs, is hosting a dinner there. He's super-rich and super-posh and extra girls are always welcome at that kind of thing.'

'I'm on it – anything to stop me thinking about my miserable love life. I'm going to drag Tara out too.'

Sarah's face fell, she'd always thought Tara's bitchiness was the wrong side of fun.

'I just need to get her out of the flat – and I need to watch her.'

They celebrated their decision with a toast to 'bizarre life experiences', swiftly followed by toasts to independence, to making the best of life, to love, and, as an afterthought, to world peace.

By the time Abena was ready to stumble home she felt an urge to call Benedict. She didn't quite know why. She supposed she wanted somebody else to talk to about things. When he didn't pick up, she left a teasing message:

'Hi there Ben, it's Abena, romantic shoe fetishist, remember? He he. Well, just wondered if you and your mesmerizing eyes wanted to come to a party at Annabel's tonight, 9 p.m. Don't forget to comb your beard – dress code is smart! Ha ha.'

She put down the phone. Whoops! Was she *flirting* with Ben?

How silly. She didn't even fancy him – and imagine how boring it would be dating a broke student type after the excitement and glamour of being Sebastian's girlfriend! Anyway, she didn't need anyone. She could be alone. Yes! Alooone … Humming tipsily, Abena headed home to change.

**\*\*\*\***

There is something about being in a loud and glamorous group that makes people who are usually graceful behave like brats. As Sarah strutted into Annabel's, followed closely by Abena and Tara, male eyes followed the sway of their hips admiringly. Female heads turned too, but with a mostly competitive glint in their eyes.

'Everyone's staring at us,' whispered Sarah, simultaneously self-conscious and exhibitionist in her very merry state. She was aware of how high her breasts were, pushed up in the most dramatic of her newer dresses, and newly tanned from an embarrassingly excessive sun-bed session after yoga. She herself could not help but stare down at them every so often, strangely aroused by the power they wielded over those around her.

As Tara announced, 'If I weren't us then I'd stare at us', Sarah guffawed with disproportionate vigour and arched her back to accentuate her curves.

Spotting Bertrand, who, in the absence of Willy, was holding court at the head of a large table, Sarah sashayed towards him, pausing mid-movement to nod and smile at a 'silver fox' raising a champagne glass at her from a neighbouring table.

'Bertrand, hello, so lovely to see you. Meet my friends, Abena and Tara. Girls, Bertrand Brampton Amis is *the* most accomplished man you could ever meet. He is one of the top bankers in the City and his family have owned the private bank that oversees all Willy's financial affairs since … since the beginning of time!'

Bertrand looked embarrassed and gestured for Sarah to sit down. 'You look incredible, Sarah. Glad you could make it. And this elusive boyfriend of yours?'

'He thinks Berkeley Square is the epitome of Western corruption.' Sarah grinned. 'But life's too short not to have fun. And anyway, I'm trying to cheer my friend Abena up – her boyfriend's just given her the sack.'

Bertrand glanced down the table at Abena. 'What a silly boy. So it looks like we're all partnerless tonight. My wife's out of town.'

'What are we drinking, Bertrand?' Sarah said quickly.

'You can have whatever you want. Just promise not to do any fussing or organizing tonight. Willy's not around and you can relax.'

Sarah decided she liked Annabel's. She liked the old-school glamour, the men in shirts and jackets and the women mostly in smart black dresses, not a ripped denim trouser in sight. Old favourites and nostalgic dance anthems made for festive music, but it was not so loud it ruled out conversation. She remembered what she'd heard about the place being reassuringly expensive. At the time she wasn't sure she liked the sound of that. But she liked it tonight. Yes, Sarah decided, it was all very civilized indeed. What a shame she'd never be able to bring Si here. He always wore jeans and, outside of work, he refused to wear a jacket.

Bertrand, on the other hand, wore jackets fabulously. His skin was tanned the same honey colour as Sarah's, although his was real as he'd just returned from a break at his wife's family's estate in Tuscany. Sarah had never been into older men, but she had to admit Bertrand was remarkably handsome – in an austere, poker-up-bottom sort of way, anyway. And it was flattering how he rose from his seat to stand, erect and straight-backed, every time she left or rejoined the table.

'Come on, let's dance.'

Sarah found his clipped, old-Etonian tones sexily authoritative; masterful, even.

Bertrand took Sarah's hand and led her to the small dance floor at the back. Moving his feet deftly in time to the music, he spun round and snaked backwards on to the floor, jiving all the way. Tara and Abena watched open-mouthed as this seemingly reserved middle-aged man in a suit transformed himself with one move into a hybrid of James Bond and Carlos Acosta. He moved with the agility of a trained ballet dancer but the arrogance with which he did so was pure sex. With each movement he dared his audience to laugh at the absurdity of his talent, so blatant and unexpected that it seemed not quite right, and yet it was amazing.

Abena finished yet another glass of exquisite Châve au Cheval Blanc and held her breath as she waited to see how Sarah would retaliate. Sarah had many talents, but dancing was not one of them. Moments later, her worst fears were confirmed when Sarah began to sway.

Emboldened by drink and carried away by her own voluptuous-ness, Sarah started wiggling her hips in a large circle and clutching at her breasts and her head in turn. It was unclear to what beat she was moving.

'Oh no, she's going for the "dip-down" again.' Abena exchanged a look with Tara and they both watched in fascinated horror as

233

Sarah parted her legs and shimmied down to the floor, banging the ground hard before struggling to wiggle back up again.

Abena turned away and thought of how she'd last been at Annabel's with Kunle. But now images of Sebastian were swirling through her head and then morphing into parts of Kunle. His long, broad back. Now it was Kunle's powerful hand, the darkest brown on one side and lighter on the palm, fingers splayed, and his lifeline etched deep and sure, heralding a grand future. Suddenly Abena's failed romances ganged up on her and made her miserable. She was desperate for a diversion. She jumped out of her seat and ran to join Sarah and Bertrand on the dance floor.

Abena grabbed Sarah and the two of them shimmied down to the floor together, working it like a pair of Las Vegas showgirls, forsaking every last shred of dignity in exchange for one inebriated moment of forgetting. As they slid down to the floor for the final time, Abena noticed that Bertrand was unable to take his eyes off them, nodding his head in time with each gyration of their hips. The look on his face was sheer lust. Abena beckoned him closer and wherever she whirled and fell across the dance floor, Bertrand followed behind. He moved lithely like a snake and in her sozzled mind Abena felt she entranced him as though she were his snake-charmer.

So wrapped up was Abena in the music and in Bertrand, she didn't notice a familiar figure push through the crowds towards the dance floor. Or perhaps she didn't recognize him, after all he was wearing contact lenses and had shaved off his beard. Benedict Lima had also donned a blazer to comply with the strict dress code, even though it wasn't his thing. He was taken aback when he was approached suddenly by a seductive older female who reeked of expensive perfume but had a look in her eye that was thrillingly cheap.

'My first husband was for love,' she purred. 'My second for money. My third was for status, and *you*, handsome … I want you for sex.'

'Objectify me any time, beautiful!' Benedict laughed, 'but I'm afraid I'm here for someone else.'

It didn't take long to find Abena, grinding on the dance floor with a dirty old man. Cursing himself for bothering to show up, he turned and raced out of Annabel's.

Tara, meanwhile, was deeply bored. She was making painfully dull small talk with Abdullah from Saudi Arabia, who was seated to her left, and she was just about to ask him if he had any cocaine on him when, out of the corner of her eye, she spotted Alex Spectre making his way through the club with a slim, Savile Row suited man in tow.

'Alex!' Tara shouted, starting up, ignoring the outrage of Abdullah, who'd been about to proffer his business card. 'It's me, Tara.'

'Hi,' Alex stopped by their table and ran his eyes quickly over the rest of the party. There was clearly no one there of interest and he made as if to leave but Tara grabbed his arm. He looked at his friend and then turned back towards Tara.

'Was there something else?'

'Stay and have a drink with us!' she begged.

Alex's friend shrugged. 'I'm Jasper,' he said.

The two sat down cautiously, both perched on the ends of their seats, weight still on the balls of their toes, ready to shoot off the starting block at the earliest possible moment. Alex craned his neck to see who was on the dance floor.

'Oh, Bertrand Brampton Amis. I'll just go say hi.' And with that, Alex and Jasper were off.

'Probably sucking up to get ahead in the City,' Tara grumbled to herself. Her end of the table was now deserted so she concentrated on watching with some satisfaction as Alex was politely dispatched by Bertrand, who had Abena's bottom to attend to and certainly didn't want to think about work now.

Gradually the music faded, the revellers thinned out, and the night began to draw to a close. Tara, who'd been bored silly all evening, was about to go and interrupt Alex and the deep discussion he'd been having with Jasper when he sauntered up to the group to ingratiate himself with Bertrand once more. After inviting Bertrand to watch a Chelsea game in his father's box the following week, he turned towards Tara and fixed his green eyes on her. He hadn't looked at her so intently since the first time they met, and it was as if a thousand-watt light bulb had been switched on inside her, making her cool eyes sparkle with exhilaration. His gaze dropped to take in her seventies vintage black cocktail dress. It had once been figure-hugging but was now too big for Tara's ever-shrinking frame.

'Stunning,' Alex concluded. Tara flushed, he'd called her stunning!

'Vintage I suppose?' he added.

Flustered, and furious she'd been outdone by her own dress, Tara snapped sarcastically, 'No, I got it new last week.'

No sooner had she spoken than she regretted it. 'No, not really. It *is* vintage.' She flushed deeper red.

'Oh you comedian, you.' Alex seemed to enjoy her discomfort. He let her stew for a while longer, then added to her confusion by resting a hand firmly on the small of her back and asking how she planned to get home.

Seeing that with Alex's hand on her bottom, Tara was utterly incapable of answering, Abena slurred that they'd hail a cab back to their flat.

'Nonsense,' Alex announced. 'I'm dropping Tara home.' He smiled at Bertrand. 'I suppose you'll see that Abena gets home safely?'

Bertrand returned a conspiratorial smile. 'Of course I will, Alex. And you can tell your father that I'll definitely be joining you at the game.'

Abena looked up at this married, forty-something billionaire financier. Through a haze of alcohol, an inner voice whispered 'Out of the frying pan, into the fire', but she pushed it away. Why shouldn't she have some fun? Before she could change her mind, Bertrand grabbed her hand, and quicker than you can utter the words 'My wife doesn't understand me', they were in his car and speeding towards his Belgravia mansion.

Once inside the Belgravia townhouse, Bertrand showed Abena into the drawing room and offered to fix her a drink. 'Sure,' she replied, half-taking in the varnished mahogany floor, the high white ceilings and the huge bookshelf crammed with well-thumbed classics that spanned the width of an entire wall. 'Incredible plaish!'

She perched precariously on an ornate velvet-upholstered chaise longue, which looked like a family heirloom. Bertrand's formidable-looking wife stared coolly out of an antique silver photo frame on the mantelpiece. A harbinger of doom. Abena shivered and stumbled towards the picture, then she turned it face down so she could no longer see Mrs Brampton Amis's accusing eyes. It was not too late to leave. She tottered in the vague direction of the door but was intercepted by Bertrand, returning with a magnum of Krug. He set the drinks down and folded her in his arms. They collapsed on a sofa and lay together, holding each other tight. Not moving, not talking, just breathing. Deep and slow, until their breaths were in tandem. They breathed as one. Before long they were naked, and then they moved together as one.

# Chapter 21

Tara tried to sleep. She'd been awake all night although she hadn't left her room, and now it was morning and Abena would be in soon to hassle her about why she was still in bed. God she was so nosy and miserable these days. She probably wanted Tara out of the flat so she could move someone else in in her place. Maybe Abena would prefer some guy who doted on her and would cook and clean and be an ideal flatmate. Tara sulked. Nobody seemed to care about her. Her father and mother had become weird and preoccupied and she hadn't had any action since Harry.

At least there was heavenly Alex. She thought back to that night after Annabel's. He'd driven her home, and before speeding off he'd kissed her goodnight. She'd tried to invite him in, but he obviously didn't want to take things too fast. His lips had fleetingly moved from her right cheek to her left, tenderly brushing her mouth in between. There was no mistaking the way he'd stared at her afterwards: he was clearly just taking things slowly. She would simply have to be patient.

But now her phone was ringing – her father again. What did he want? Probably to shout at her to return the money she'd taken. She ignored the call.

After an hour had elapsed, Tara felt she should at least get up and wash her face. Oh fuck, the door was opening; Abena must be home. She scrabbled under her bed for the rest of her cocaine and snorted it all in six full lines before Abena reached the bedroom door, hurriedly hiding the evidence. She simply needed a little push to get up and face the day. Oh God, why was Abena leaning sorrowfully against the door? Poor, hard done by Abbi. Why was she such a bloody martyr?

'Hey, hon,' Abena whispered, 'do you want me to turn your light on?'

'Er yep, yes, thanks,' Tara muttered. She shot up in a sudden burst of energy.

'What's up, sweetheart, we haven't had a proper chat for ages. Let's go party somewhere tonight shall we? Let's get Sarah and Bertrand out. Yeah that'd be fun. I'm really on form and feel like going out and doing something, and work's going cool, you know, and getting good feedback from the applications I sent out – and it's, yeah, it's all good. And Tina called to say that her friend Orlando has already brought me a really nice Christmas present – maybe I can flog it for some serious dosh and—'

'Hey, hey, hey! Slow down! I'd love to do something tonight but just, let's relax. Hon, when was the last time you ate something?'

'What? Oh yeah, I'll go eat something now,' Tara snapped.

'No, don't worry, I'll get it. You just look really, really thin, hon, and not in a nice way – you look rough, and your eyes are swollen and red. This isn't like you, Tara, you've … you've got a problem.'

Tara's eyes darted around the room looking everywhere except at her friend.

'What are you doing?' Tara watched, annoyed, as Abena stepped into her bedroom and opened the window before picking up several discarded T-shirts and panties off the floor.

'I'll wash these for you. I don't think you've done any laundry for over a month.'

Tara stormed out of the room and into the bathroom, locking the door behind her.

In Tara's absence, Abena took a good look around her friend's room, her heart beating twice its normal rate as she steeled herself for a particularly unpleasant discovery. Before she could look underneath the bed, Tara's mobile rang again and the word 'Papa' flashed up on the screen. Abena picked it up.

'Hello, good afternoon, how are you? It's Abena.'

'Oh, hello, Abena, I'm well thank you. How are you? I hope you girls aren't causing too much havoc in town?'

'Well …'

'I've been trying to contact Tara but I suppose she's left her phone with you – is she out?'

'No, no, she's in, she's just gone to have a shower.'

'Oh I see, I see … Well I, er, I called to tell her that I'm coming to London.'

'Fantastic,' Abena squealed. There was nothing Tara needed more right now than some guidance from her parents. If they saw her they would surely do something.

'Are you just visiting for the evening?' Abena continued.

'I'm afraid I'll be expecting to stay rather longer than that.'

'Oh, right. Wonderful.' That sounded ominous but Abena didn't feel it was her place to enquire any further. Perhaps she was imagining things, but she thought that Hugo's speech had sounded distinctly blurred.

'Well, if you could let Tara know that I'll pick her up for dinner at about eight?'

'Yes of course, I will do. See you soon.'

'Take care, Abena.'

Abena was nervous as she hung up the phone, she simply couldn't tell whether a prolonged visit from Tara's father would be for the best or if it would give rise to even more complications.

When Tara emerged from the shower and heard about her father's visit she seemed mildly surprised.

'He's not bringing Tina with him?' she enquired, wiping her runny nose with the back of her hand.

'Apparently not,' Abena replied. 'But just be ready at eight. Shall I help you get ready? You know, do some make-up for you?'

Tara froze Abena to the spot with her icy stare. 'I'm not an invalid. I can get myself dressed.'

'Fine.'


The impromptu visit from her father was the kick Tara needed to pull herself together a little. She arranged for Joe, her dealer, to drop off some more coke, then began to get ready for her father's arrival. Her hair was dull and limp so she pulled it back into a neat ponytail instead of leaving it to frame her face as she preferred. She put on a pair of tracksuit bottoms that she used to go jogging in and then a pair of jeans over the top. Likewise, she layered her sweaters, opting for two thin ones and a thicker baggy one on top. The disguise made her appear a stone or so heavier, and the November cold would ensure she didn't overheat. She slathered her face in a slightly darker foundation than she normally used and applied concealer around her eyes and nose to cover the bags and the puffy redness. Then she added liberal amounts of bronzing powder and blusher in an attempt to create a healthy glow. Surveying herself in the mirror she decided that she couldn't be described as 'hot' but that it would have to do. At least she didn't look as rough as she felt. Next she went to work on her room and stashed whatever she could under the bed before gathering any clothes that had escaped Abena's audit and throwing them into the bottom of her wardrobe. Finally, she gave the floor a quick hoover even though she was exhausted.

Lord Bridges arrived just before eight and Tara could smell that he hadn't bothered to wait for her before starting to drink.

'Hello, Papa.' She kissed his cheek and beckoned him into the flat.

'Tara-Bara,' he beamed. 'You look nice. Good God, it's suspiciously tidy in here.'

'We're always tidy, Papa, we're domestic goddesses,' Tara sniffed. 'Would you like a drink?'

'Actually we'd better go; the table is booked for eight.'

The two walked arm in arm down the road to the small French restaurant where their table was ready for them.

'So where are you staying? Where's Tina?' Tara enquired while she played idly with a bread roll, tearing it into little pieces on her plate.

'Do eat properly, dear,' Hugo grunted.

He beckoned the waiter and ordered a bottle of red wine.

Once their glasses were filled and they had ordered, Hugo took a deep breath and announced to his daughter, 'There is something I need to tell you.'

Tara put down her glass. 'Oh?'

'Your mother and I have decided to separate.'

Tara's immediate reaction was a sigh of relief. For a brief moment she'd feared that she'd been busted and that she would be packed off to Gloucestershire, locked away and not allowed any drugs.

'Oh, oh really? My God, that's …'

'It was your mother's idea of course. She claims I drink far too much, which is, frankly, ridiculous. And of course that silly National Trust fellow, Orlando, hasn't helped matters.'

'Hmmn, no I didn't like him at all.'

'So, for the foreseeable future I shall be staying with Uncle Rupert in Fulham.

Tara's face fell. The last bloody thing she needed was for her father to be in London, wanting to spend more time with her and with her pretty young girlfriends.

'I'm so sorry.' Hugo couldn't bear to see his daughter look so forlorn.

'I'll talk to Tina,' Tara said. 'You can't just turn your back on years of marriage. What will I do?'

Tears began to roll down Tara's cheeks and her perpetually runny nose was streaming violently. 'Please excuse me,' she sobbed, rising and running to the bathroom.

While Tara took her time in the loo, Hugo had some fun watching the awkward couple two tables away. Must be a first date. Hugo thought their clothes very odd indeed. The man's bony elbows poked out of his shirt. Why was he wearing a short-sleeved shirt instead of a proper one? In November? Surely one just rolls up one's sleeves if one is hot. She, however, was dressed prettily in a flowery dress and had sat through the meal with an undisguised look of disbelief, as though her date was not at all what she'd bargained for. That's the internet for you, Hugo thought.

Hugo watched the bill arrive and the couple both sit there staring at it for a rather long time, neither of them moving. He wondered why the chap didn't just get out his card and settle the thing. Finally the tight-fist reached into his breast pocket, pulled out a pair of supermarket reading glasses and squinted at the bill for another few minutes.

'Right,' he said, 'so, OK, so you had the lemon tart and the large glass of vino, but—'

He looked up in surprise as his date threw down enough cash to cover the whole meal and stomped off to get her coat.

'Oh, er, oh I see, I thought we could go Dutch, or er, just pay for what we had – after all I did have the extra pork and herb sausage …' he shouted after her. 'But if you want to do it like this, then fine, I'll get it next time.'

Put out that this rather amusing drama had ended, he switched his attention to a table in the corner. A pinched-looking husband looked on in silence while his wife ordered for them both with a voice loud enough to be heard clearly across the room. 'I'd like the steak and wine pie but without the steak, I'd like it just on the side. And then I'd like some greens, except not spinach, no leaves of any kind and no peas or broad beans. No, no, you can give me beans, but I'd like the beans to be skinny and not broad. I'd like a sesame seed roll on the side and a side salad, but without leaves and no seeds in that. I'd like a French dressing but no vinegar, it's far too acidic. And give me the Eggs Benedict for my husband but without the bread and I don't want the eggs to be poached – I want them boiled so that they're not runny, and no vinegar for him either, the acid doesn't help with his bowel problems ...' And then, 'Oh and a glass of champagne for me, but hold the bubbles – plays havoc with my digestion.'

After twenty minutes Tara re-emerged, appearing to be more composed. Watching his daughter's expressionless face as she returned to their table, Hugo breathed an inward sigh of relief. Given the circumstances, she had taken it exceptionally well. She'd made no comment about his drinking and hadn't become as hysterical as he'd feared.

'You know, Tara, once we've all had time to get used to the idea, we may be able to arrange it all quite conveniently. There is no need for either of us to move out permanently, not necessarily. I don't see why your mother and I shouldn't be able to take a wing each and live on quite happily. We've had separate bedrooms for over a year you know.'

'Have you? Christ!'

'Of course, if that doesn't work,' Hugo continued, 'then I want custody of the dogs.'

Tara pouted, then laughed.

'Shall we go on somewhere for an after-dinner drink? It's a real treat to catch up with you, dear, even in such regretful circumstances.'

Tara knew that her father was more interested in the drink than in her, but she also felt that any kind of intoxication was better than none, so she nodded her head in agreement.

'Yes, there's an alright bar across the road, Papa. Come on, I'll show you.'

'What about Abena? Do you want to invite her along too, or any of your other friends, I'd love to treat you.'

'Thanks Papa but nobody's around at the moment.' Tara was saddened to realize this was the truth.

As she left the restaurant, Tara bumped straight into a very slim girl with short platinum-blonde hair. Tara noticed enviously that was carrying the latest Balenciaga handbag. 'Sorry,' she muttered, although the girl could have looked to see where she was marching.

'Hi Tara,' said the willowy blonde.

'Oh, it's you – Natalya.'

'Yes, I hef not seen you since St Tropez, how are you?'

Before Tara could reply, Hugo had stretched out an eager hand. 'Hello, Hugo Bridges. How do you do?'

'Natalya shook his hand and looked quizzically from him to Tara.

'My father—'

'I'm her father.'

Tara and Hugo spoke as one, each eager, for different reasons, that Natalya should not think them a romantic couple.

'What are you doing now, Natalya? Would you like to come and join us for a drink across the road?' Hugo was unable to tear his eyes away from this ravishing Latvian or release her hand.

Tara was mortified by his stupefaction. She knew her father had an eye for the ladies but she'd never seen him react this strongly to anyone. Maybe the separation was sending her father potty? As the reality of her parents' split began to dawn on her, she felt the beginnings of a panic attack coming. Her life was disintegrating before her eyes and she was powerless to stop it.

Natalya felt uncharacteristically moved by the invitation. To see such a distinguished-looking father enjoying an evening with his precious daughter made her wistful, comforted and angry all at once. She couldn't remember the last time she'd shared a drink with someone purely for the sake of good company rather than because they could be of use to her in some way. She was pleased to have been asked.

'Yes, thenk you, I will join you. My partner is away and I do not relish the idea of a night alone in our huge place in Mayfair.'

Tara, forced to snap out of her inner turmoil, couldn't remember anything of either a 'partner' or a huge place in Mayfair from their brief conversations in France. She'd obviously got lucky in the meantime.

The lounge-bar Tara had picked was dimly lit and bass music rumbled from the speakers. Hugo bought a glass of port for himself and vodka tonics for the girls and settled himself beside Natalya on one of the low leather sofas. He was staring at her moronically and Tara felt a flash of shame.

'Where were you educated, Natalya?' Hugo asked. 'Tell me about you? Your life? Your childhood?' The questions tumbled randomly out of his gibbering mouth.

Natalya flashed a steely smile. 'I went to the school of poverty, misery and hard graft, but beleaf me, I can tell you more about philosophy and economics than your most learned Oxford professor.'

She looked Lord Bridges in the eye and he gave a strangulated wail.

'Well …' Natalya lifted her glass in a toast before taking a sip.

Hugo downed his sweet port and went to get another.

Tara leaned across and asked Natalya whether she had any coke on her.

'No, sorry,' Natalya replied. 'Thet stuff is not for me. I can't beleaf you and your father get wasted together, it's so cool you've got such a close relationship.'

'He knows nothing about me,' Tara spat. 'He drinks so much that he doesn't even stop to think about what I'm doing, or how I'm feeling. He doesn't know about my life – probably still thinks I play with Barbie dolls.'

'He loves you, Tara. You should appreciate thet at least. I ... I would keel to have a loving father.'

'Oh. I didn't know you weren't on good terms with yours. I'm so sorry.'

Tara called across to Hugo at the bar. 'Papa can you get us some more vodkas?'

Hugo turned and fluttered his eyelashes drunkenly at Natalya. Then he stopped and peered at her, as though he was studying a bizarre museum exhibit.

'Aaaargh, I'm so sorry about Papa,' Tara groaned, burying her head in her hands. 'You just have to ignore him when he gets like this.'

Natalya laughed. 'Thet's OK, he's sweet really, harmless. We both know what horrors are out there.'

Both girls thought immediately of Reza.

'So, tell me about your partner,' Tara said, downing the last of her vodka then staring at the bottom of the empty glass.

'He's ... rich.' Natalya shrugged her shoulders.

'Good start.' Tara grinned and clinked her empty glass against Natalya's.

'He's one of the richest men in the world, actually. And he gives me whatever I want. He dotes on me and he ... he tries to control me. But thet's men for you, I guess.'

'Sometimes I think you hate men.' Tara was slurring now. 'Me too, I hate men too, they're stupid. Look at my father for Christ's sake.' Tara gave a hoarse laugh and threw herself back on the sofa. 'Shall we get some coke?' she asked.

Natalya shook her head and reached for her phone, which was vibrating in her bag.

'Hello bébé,' she shouted above the music. Then, apologizing into the phone and signalling to Tara that she'd be back, she ran out of the bar so that she could better hear Claude.

'Where are you?' Claude sounded angry.

'I'm just having a quick drink with a girlfriend on the way home.'

'A girlfriend. Who? No men?'

'No, no men, of course not, just an old friend, Tara.'

'I don't like you going to bars without me all the time.'

'No, no, Claude, I don't, this is just a one-off.'

'I think it's time I got you a full-time minder.'

'Wh-what …? But nobody even knows who I am,' she pleaded. 'Thet is not at all necessary, darling.'

'*Everybody* knows who *I* am, and they know that you're with me. You're mine. I've got to go to my meeting, it's 9 a.m. here. Go home now and send a message when you're back.'

'Yes. Yes alright. I love you.'

Natalya hung up and returned inside. She could see that a swaying Hugo had been watching her through the big glass windows for the duration of her phone call and he now caught her by the waist as she approached the sofa.

'Where did you get to young lady? Don't tell me you're a naughty one – just like Tara-Bara.' He guffawed loudly as Tara wrinkled her nose in distaste and took four large sips of her vodka.

Hugo had by now switched to vodka as well, so he'd bought a bottle. Minutes later, the bottle was empty and the girls watched, horrified, as first Hugo's knees buckled and then the rest of his body collapsed in a thud to the floor.

Tara had seen her father drunk on many occasions but had never seen him collapse before. She had no idea how to respond. She was sure he'd come to, but she couldn't very well send him off to Uncle Rupert in this state.

Natalya, however, was unfazed and she quickly mobilized into action. 'Come and stay with me,' she said. 'I've plenty of rooms.'

Tara wanted to get home to her own flat because she thought she had a little coke left but Natalya seemed so focused and together that she found herself passively following orders. Natalya hailed a cab and got someone to help them hoist Hugo into the back seat, reassuring the reluctant cabbie that he wouldn't throw up all over the newly cleaned interior. She handed Tara one of the bottles of water she'd demanded from the bar before leaving. 'Drink this,' she said. Then she opened another bottle and forced it into Hugo's drooling mouth.

Natalya felt a surge of compassion for Tara. In St Tropez she'd envied her, but, looking at her skinny frame and blotchy skin, and at her daddy, she saw that here was somebody whose problems might even rival her own. She herself had learnt to cope, and now she could help Tara, she wanted to help her, and the knowledge filled her with joy. Perhaps she and Tara could even become friends.

Hugo had not, as the cabbie had feared, been sick on the journey home; instead, even more humiliatingly, he'd wet himself.

Unable to face the grisly sight of her father's sodden, naked body, Tara left Natalya to undress him and put him to bed – on his front so he wouldn't choke if he threw up in the night. By the time Natalya had finished dealing with Hugo, Tara had already fallen asleep upstairs on the master bed. Natalya climbed in beside her, remembering to first send Claude a message saying that all was well, that she missed him, and that she was in bed thinking of him. Natalya looked down at Tara, restless in her sleep, and kissed her temple.

# *Chapter 22*

Abena didn't know what she was still doing with Bertrand. That amazing night after Annabel's should have been a one-off. But Bertrand had had other ideas, and what had begun as a sexy dance was now a torrid affair.

So here she was again, back in Bertrand's gorgeous Belgravia house, sneaking in a couple of passionate days while his wife was away on another business trip. Despite what she'd said to Sarah, Abena knew it was wrong and she felt horribly guilty. But she lacked the strength to end the affair herself. The prospect of months and months of nothing but Mallinder, without Sebastian's wild hedonism to offset it, was too depressing to contemplate. And she wasn't even welcome at Reza's glamorous events any more – after her disastrous entrance with Sebastian at *Sin*, she'd become *persona non grata* with him.

Shutting herself into one of Bertrand's many bathrooms, Abena picked up her phone. She needed to talk it through with someone. She went to call Tara, the only friend she could rely on not to judge her even a tiny bit, but stopped herself – after all, the girl was in no fit state to offer a valid opinion. And she could hardly talk it through with Sarah after their chat about infidelity the other day.

She thought of Benedict. She longed to speak to him, and had a funny feeling he might not judge her either, but then he hadn't returned her last call, and neither had he shown up at Annabel's, so she guessed he hadn't enjoyed her company that much.

What the hell. She was enjoying herself with Bertrand so why beat herself up with guilt? She grabbed her make-up bag from where she had slung it, on the teak lid of the toilet seat, and put the finishing touches to her face. A night on the tiles was just what she needed.

'Oh hellooo,' purred Bertrand in as seedy an accent as he could manage. Abena giggled.

'You certainly scrub up well. Can it really be just half an hour ago that you were sweaty, naked and dishevelled on my bedroom floor? Come, let's go, angel.'

They clambered into Bertrand's Bentley and he directed the driver to a Mayfair casino.

'Precious, I'm afraid my wife returns home tomorrow afternoon, so I will need you to be out of the house tomorrow morning.' Bertrand sounded apologetic.

'No worries, I was only imagining I'd stay for a couple of days anyway,' Abena breezed. At the back of her mind, she hoped that his wife's return would put a natural end to this delicious affair.

'So. Casino hey?' Abena teased. 'What makes a man who looks after other people's money want to throw all his own away?'

'Oh, I'm not a gambling man, but it's a very social casino and the real money is made over the entrecôte steak, long before the gaming begins.'

'I don't know why you want to make any more – you've already far more than you know what to do with.'

Bertrand was silent for a while and Abena feared she'd angered him in some way. After all, now that bankers were being vilified in the press for bringing about the recession, he might be racked with remorse for earning so much from his stake in the bank.

'Sorry,' she backtracked, 'It's none of my business.'

'Oh no, it's fine, good question.' Bertrand leaned back and threw a lazy arm around her shoulder. A broad, deeply contented smile split his face. 'I was just trying to work out the answer. I think it's the thrill of the chase, and the acquisition. It's the same for everything in life really. Once I've made it, I move on and try to make more elsewhere. I don't need it, don't always spend it or use it, or treat it with the respect I should. But I enjoy the process of making it mine.'

'Oh,' Abena said. The rest of the journey passed in silence.

\*\*\*\*

Natalya had been thinking a lot about Tara, and decided to pay her a visit. She had seen an unexpected side of her the other night, quite different from the spoilt, carefree English rich kid she'd taken her to be. She had always despised girls like that, who seemed to look down on her for trying to better her life; who seemed to consider themselves too well bred to care about money, even though they would lose every shred of self-dignity if it were taken from them. But Tara had shown her that even those girls could be miserable. Maybe happiness really wasn't connected to wealth and status. Maybe that old chestnut was true: all you need is love. No, not for someone like her, anyway.

Stopping off at Harrods' food hall and then Hermès, where

she bought a little scarf for Tara with money from the allowance Claude had set up for her, Natalya took a cab to Tara's Ladbroke Grove flat. Claude was keen to assign her a personal driver but Natalya wanted to put that off for as long as possible as it would be yet another way for Claude to spy on her from abroad.

'Hey, come in.' Tara let Natalya into the flat. 'Sorry it's such a mess,' she sighed, and sank down on to the sofa, pulling a thick duvet on top of her. 'Sorry I look a wreck; I think I'm coming down with something.'

'I can get you a cleaner?' Natalya offered, stepping gingerly into the room. 'This is for you.'

Pinched and drawn as she was, Tara's eyes lit up when she saw the Hermès packaging. 'Wow, thank you darling.' She opened the parcel and smiled before dropping the package and its contents on to the floor and sighing once more. 'So, how are you?' she asked Natalya. Natalya could tell that she didn't really care what the answer was and so didn't bother to respond. Instead she plunged straight in.

'You can still kind of manage your habit, Tara, but you should seek help, otherwise you might end up like your father.'

Tara couldn't even muster the energy to get angry. 'My father doesn't take drugs.' She wiped her snotty nose on her sleeve.

'No, but he is an alcoholic,' Natalya replied. There was no point in pussy-footing around at this stage. She reached into her bag and arranged the various treats she'd bought in the food hall: some sushi, a selection of salads, and some Krispy Kreme doughnuts for a sugar boost. 'Eat something.' It was more of an order than a question, so Tara reached for a doughnut and took a couple of nibbles.

'Now, I know a very good place for you to go to, and your father too if he wants. It's called Appletons Rehabilitation Centre. It's expensive, but is supposed to be excellent. Many models go there. They hef a 99 per cent recovery rate and only 2 per cent relapse.'

'I've been to rehab before,' Tara sulked.

'Seriously, when?' Natalya asked.

'At school, when I was caught smoking weed, but I didn't really need it then. I guess I need it now.'

'I guess you do.'

'I'm not gonna spend Christmas in a fucking loony bin – it's not the glamorous jolly that all the celebrities make it look like.'

'I know this.' Natalya was sympathetic.

'I have to go home for Christmas. And then maybe I'll think about it.'

'Progress, at least. Eat some more.'

Natalya moved closer to sit beside Tara and slid her own body under the duvet. Then she reached out a hand and stroked Tara's greasy hair.

They lay together, wordlessly, for a long while. Natalya let her eyes close as she savoured Tara's listless company. She tried to think of other things, but she couldn't force *him* out of her mind. The father that didn't want her around – didn't want her alive? Would he really go that far to protect whatever life he had culti- vated in England since that fateful night twenty-one years ago? Natalya supposed he had a family now, a wife perhaps, and new children – legitimate ones. He had warned her not to come near 'us', whoever 'us' entailed. She sensed it was simply a matter of time before they would come head to head. The feeling repulsed and frightened her. Yet somewhere deep down she was strangely excited. Whatever he was, he was her daddy. And if he killed her, he would have to acknowledge her first. Natalya tasted bile rising into her throat and forced her thoughts back to the present. She hugged Tara tightly. 'It's OK, honey,' she whispered.

****

Abena and Bertrand were staying at a country-house hotel for the weekend. The beds were enormous and feather-soft, each room had a roaring fire, and there was a three-Michelin-star restaurant and a world-class spa on hand to feed body and mind. The hotel was famous for its service and boasted more than thirty staff members to every one guest. Staff who would find themselves mostly idle tonight as Bertrand had booked all twelve of the rooms to ensure that he and Abena wouldn't be disturbed. They were lying facing each other on parallel massage beds, being pummelled and stroked by expert masseurs in spotless white uniforms. Scented candles encircled the beds and the surround-sound speakers played the sound of a sea rippling under a soft breeze and lapping the shore again and again and again.

Abena had almost dozed off when she realized Bertrand was talking to her.

'I'm going away to France for work next week. Merging one of Willy Eckhardt's projects with a foreign investment of mine, so your pal Sarah will be coming along too. She's brilliant, very capable and efficient in the office and a good professional attitude.'

'Well, whatever you do, don't tell her about us.'

'Are you mad, angel?'

The waves continued to lap and then Bertrand began talking

again. 'I've been thinking. Let me take care of your rent, precious. I hate the thought of Olympia being mean to you. Let me take care of you.'

Abena closed her eyes and pretended to sleep.

That night, after the staff had left, she offered to give Bertrand her own, special massage. Not for the faint-hearted.

'Baby! Yes please!' He gazed at her, eyes shining.

Chuckling to herself, she tied Bertrand to the bed so that he couldn't escape.

'Ow!' Bertrand yelped as she slammed a fist into his shoulder blade. Another blow followed. And then she pummelled, jabbed and beat the man until he was whimpering and sobbing into his pillow.

'Baby, this isn't quite the type of massage I had in mind.'

Abena brought her elbows down sharply on his lower back for the last time, and leant to speak in his ear.

'B, please don't ever ask to "keep" me again.'

'Oh, baby, is that what this is about? I'm sorry, I didn't mean to disrespect you. It's just you seem so upset about your career, and your friend Tara. And the money really is negligible to me. I thought it would be a nice gesture – one less thing in your life to worry about.'

'Worry about my pleasure, darling, not my rent.'

After an hour had passed, Abena untied him, kissing the sore marks on his skin where he'd been bound. Bertrand rubbed his wrists and looked at her slyly.

'Well, you've taught me my lesson, so I better teach you yours …'

Abena ran whooping through their suite, bracing herself for the mother of all punishments.

\*\*\*\*

Tara's emaciated back bobbed up und down in quick, convulsive movements as she retched into her blood-splattered pillow. It was three days since she'd last had a hit but her nose still bled intermittently. Despite pains in her chest and her arm, she couldn't stop wanting more.

The highs were fleeting, but so intense, so euphoric. The lows were not fleeting; they lingered. The lows made Tara feel as though she might as well end it. That it didn't matter if she died of a heart attack one of these days because she didn't care. She didn't care that her friends were beginning to hate her. She didn't care about her parents' relationship. About that goaty man that her mother was so taken with now. She didn't care that her father was always drunk. None of it mattered except her next line.

And then there was the fear. Fear of how she would cope if she couldn't get hold of more cocaine. And fear of what would happen to her if she got hold of more than she could pay for. Joe wasn't so nice to her any more. He didn't have time for poor little rich girls whose pocket money had dried up. She'd met other men who could give her what she wanted, but only if she gave them something in return. A blow for some blow. Fuck. Why was she seriously contemplating it? She wasn't an 'addict' for Christ's sake. She was an intelligent, well-bred girl. She wouldn't suck a cock for a gram of coke. Would she?

# Chapter 23

'Wow,' said Sarah, as she ran her hand along the shimmering cocktail bar on board *Sin*. 'I never thought, not in my wildest dreams, that I'd find myself on a super-yacht in the South of France. Thank heavens Willy took a chance with an inexperienced PA. Which reminds me, we need to organize a Chairman's Reception for you for next year when you'll be chairing Willy's board. I was thinking the Dorchester—'

'Sarah, you're not working now – stop fussing.'

'Of course I'm working, Bertrand, why else would I be here? I feel like this isn't me, like I'm having a weird out-of-body experience. And where on earth have all these women come from? These are like … mythical people, you know, those breathtaking beauties of fable and fairy tale, who you never actually know or see in real life …' Bertrand silently congratulated himself and Reza on hitting the spot with their floating club. Sarah went on, 'I'm glad my boyfriend and I broke up – he definitely would not approve. In fact I'm not sure I do.' She looked around, open-mouthed at the solid-gold opulence of the bar at which she stood. 'And please keep this Reza character well away from me, I've heard some real horror stories about him.'

Bertrand glanced in the direction of a smallish man in tight snakeskin trousers doing the limbo under a girl's outstretched leg. He bit his lip.

'To be honest I don't think you're his type. Ahem, far too classy,' he added, after Sarah looked offended. 'When did you break up with your boyfriend?'

'I'd seen it coming for a while. He said if I got on a plane out here today then that was the end of us. He thinks my job is taking over our relationship and that my values are melting.'

'Melting?' Bertrand looked amused.

'"Melting" was his word. Values that were once solid are apparently turning to slush. They've become a sticky pool of depravity – he's awfully melodramatic for an accountant. And anyway it's not true.'

'Sticky pool of depravity … Good God, that sounds blissful!' Sarah shot him a warning look and he changed tack. 'Sarah, you skilfully manage a team of thirty people directly and hundreds indirectly; you've helped thrust Willy Eckhardt back into the collective consciousness of an entire nation; you've masterminded events that have raised hundreds of thousands for charitable causes; and you've more than likely saved Willy's marriage with all the anniversaries, birthdays and children's treats you've organized. What has your boyfriend done as a trainee accountant?'

'Thanks, Bertrand.' She treated him to a genuinely warm smile. 'Well I couldn't have done any of it without your mentoring. Anyway, enough about him. Let's get another drink. I am determined to catch up on all the years of fun I've missed out on with that silly boy – and it's not every day I get to drink Russian cocktails out of imitation white skulls.'

'Hear! Hear!'

The theme of Reza and Bertrand's Christmas party was white. On the deck of *Sin*, two huge Christmas trees sculpted in white gold by that year's Turner Prize winner gleamed in the moonlight. Diamond rings hung off the delicate upturned branches – a little souvenir for each of the female guests. Taxidermy was having a fashion revival so stuffed tarantulas clambered up each tree and crazed-looking stags and does were positioned around the deck. Security had been discreetly ramped up tonight, and hidden in waterproof casing underneath the boat's golden gunwales was a newly installed anti-paparazzi device that could detect any unauthorized camera activity for miles around and obliterate the images.

And what fantastical images they would have been. The dress code was head-to-toe white: apart from the staff in black, Reza was to be the only exception in a tight denim shirt and snake-skin trousers. Although most of the women were in floaty ethereal silks, and the men in tailored linen shirts and white jeans – perfect for showing off gleaming winter tans – there were a few outfits that really stood out. Sarah passed a man smoking a cigar, his slicked-back silvery grey hair complementing his white silk pyjamas and monogrammed slippers. And who was this haughty-looking woman? In a belted white satin suit jacket with matching harem pants, clear PVC courts and white floppy ears atop a head of lustrous black hair, her look was 'Bugs Bunny does the couture shows'. Next to catch Sarah's eye was a family dressed entirely in white feathers. A fresh-faced teenager in a feathered mini-dress was furtively eyeing the men while her parents, both dressed in long feathered coats, were talking animatedly to Reza.

'No, it's probably best you don't engage Rhiannon in that superb limbo dance. It looks hilarious but the poor dear's still recovering from a lacrosse injury at school—' laughed the mother, scarily shrill.

'Incidentally, Reza,' cut in the father, seeing Reza's eyes snake down his daughter's coltish legs, 'did you know, I flew in straight from a record-setting shooting weekend in Hampshire. I'm now so adept with a gun I could shoot the cork off a bottle of Dom from an astonishing distance.'

Sarah laughed and moved on, doing a double-take as a girl glided past wearing nothing but pearls, vast strings of them draped around her to form a bandeau dress that shimmered and tinkled as she moved. The girl looked at Bertrand out of the corner of her eye, holding his gaze for a few seconds before prowling on. Sarah glanced despairingly down at her own white dress, which Tulip had picked out for her. It clung to her curves a bit too lovingly.

Bertrand looked as debonair as ever in deck shoes, linen trousers and a simple white shirt. He'd rolled up the sleeves to reveal a slim watch – with a fat price tag, Sarah noticed – and although he'd undone too many shirt buttons, he'd avoided a Rezaesque greasiness by ensuring there was plenty of room to breathe in it. He began to bounce in time to the blaring house music. Reza had flown in a hot new DJ fresh from a private gig in Ibiza, and the star mixer was already working the boat up to a frenzy.

'You look really great today, Sarah. White is definitely your colour.'

Sometimes Sarah forgot Bertrand was twice her age; when you gave him some alcohol he seemed to revert to his teens. She could see him stealing glances at her cleavage whenever he thought she wasn't looking. She really ought to pull the dress up a bit. She didn't.

Neither did she resist when Bertrand grabbed her hand to lead her to his clients.

'Ouch!' Sarah shrieked, as her foot was pierced by a spiky metal heel. 'This boat is way too crowded. Are you sure you're adhering to health and safety regs?' she grumbled, but her comment went unheard above the music. The tracks were getting faster and as a low, deep voice boomed 'The world is mine', the fervour of the crowd intensified. Sarah would definitely have preferred something more soulful.

Eventually Bertrand found the clients he was searching for, clustered inside on a white leather banquette. The stage and casino had been collapsed for the night and the revolving dance floor stilled, leaving one gigantic space in which to dance, chat and play. One of the clients was the man with the monogrammed slippers, though Sarah didn't quite catch his name above the din. He shook her hand and, still puffing on his cigar, offered her another drink. Although the second of the clients, who introduced himself as Theo, was much younger and better looking, somehow it was the first that Sarah couldn't stop scrutinizing. There was something in his manner that suggested he wielded immense power, and it was strangely thrilling to be around him. She finished her drink in one gulp to steady her nerves.

Scores of women were circling their table, zeroing in on Bertrand like tigers stalking their prey, while at the table opposite, three amazing-looking women were dancing gracefully on the banquette seating, moving with agile abandon. Sarah was watching them in awe when she felt a hand on her back encouraging her too to get up and dance. Downing yet another vodka tonic to give her courage, she climbed on to the cushioned bench and started to sway nervously, embarrassed. It felt like Team Bertrand was trying to top the other table and Sarah felt shamefully aware she was probably letting the side down. But, whatever! She was free and she was here. Since she didn't have to give a damn what Si thought for the first time in years, she would try to relax.

As the alcohol worked its wicked magic on Sarah and she was starting to really move, building up to another 'dip-down', the music came to a sudden stop. An immense drum roll thundered to an impressive climax and a team of nimble waiters appeared, bearing five bottles that were spitting huge flames and sizzling like indoor fireworks. Thinking that a magic show was about to begin, Sarah drunkenly started to applaud. The flaming bottles were borne across to the table opposite Team Bertrand, illuminating the slinky dancers and their three male companions, one of whom stood on his seat and lit a cigar from the flames. As the drums continued to roll, he smugly blew out a perfect smoke ring, held one of the bottles aloft, and shook its contents over a blonde in a white bikini. Sarah was amazed and revolted to realize it was a magnum of Reza's exclusive *Sin* champagne he was spraying – about £5000 worth! The *Sin* champagne was the only drink that wasn't free that evening – and so the only one everyone wanted to be seen ordering. Sarah could see at least four unfinished magnums on the table beside the five new bottles. There was no way they could drink all that.

She felt sickened at such a shameless display of decadence, but Bertrand caught her eye and just shrugged, as if to say 'that's the way the cookie crumbles'.

Ten minutes later, the drums began to roll again. To Sarah's horror, this time the waiters were heading in her direction. Thankfully, they focused on Theo, who theatrically surveyed the number of magnums that had been brought to their group. Not five like the other table, but six. He lit his cigarette in the flames, leaned forward and blew the smoke defiantly in the direction of the opposite table. With a smile he turned to check that the monogram-slippered mogul approved. Team Bertrand had triumphed. Their status as top dog was secure.

Sarah shot another disgusted look at Bertrand.

'I don't judge, Sarah. Maybe they gave ten million to charity last night. Did you? Relax, enjoy yourself.'

Sarah looked at Theo, now sandwiched between two brunettes and groping both of them simultaneously. 'Maybe they did, but then again, maybe they didn't. Anyway, I just think it's vulgar and it's unnecessary.'

She slurred on, 'The world's finances are in a terrible state, people are looshing their *homes* and, and, and, their *livelihoods*, and yet theesh people are just spending and spending like there's no tomorrow. Wassit to them if they lose a few million to the drop in property values – they've still got another fifty mill hidden away offshore so that's alright then!'

Bertrand had never seen her this worked up. Now there was a spark in her eyes and a rosy flush to her cheeks that was making him exceptionally randy.

'Good God you're gorgeous!' He shook his head in wonderment, making Sarah even more incensed. He wrapped his arms around her and hugged her as she collapsed against his chest. Willy had left the party hours ago; Scheherazade, the winner of

267

*Musical Megastar*, had disappeared too, and Sarah knew nobody else here but Bertrand. As angry as she was, she felt protected with his arms around her.

'Darling,' Bertrand said, 'I'm not defending all this per se, but what do you think will happen to the economy if these people stop spending? Don't you think even more businesses will go bust, and even more people will be unemployed? Don't you think governments will collect even less in taxes? What will happen to public services then?'

Sarah looked up, but before she could reply Bertrand suddenly cut in again, 'Say, have you met Rory?'

Rory shook Sarah's hand and she smiled back, forced to calm down now that they had company. Tall and slim with dishevelled dirty blond hair, he was, Sarah guessed, probably in his mid to late thirties. Rory smiled shyly. He looked like he'd be more at home in the corner of a jazz café than at this raucous party, and she couldn't agree more – the music really was much too loud. As if echoing her thoughts, Bertrand leaned over and shouted that they ought to have a drink somewhere quieter.

Bertrand led them away from the main din and towards the yacht's exit but instead of disembarking he glanced around and then pressed a button concealed behind a small mirrored tile. A side door slid open to reveal a spacious and pristine white cabin.

'Wow! I thought you said there were no cabins.' Sarah had never seen anything like it – an open-plan living room and kitchen so dazzlingly white she had to blink several times. It was like walking into a luxury igloo.

'That's what we tell the members but of course Reza and I have our areas. There's an office and various other little rooms hidden

268

about the place – some of which I've never even seen.'

They sat down together on a long sofa covered in ice-white mink.

'Has it really been that long since we saw each other? We used to get up to all sorts of mischief,' Rory chuckled at Bertrand.

'Must be ten years now. God I'm getting old.' Bertrand smiled at Sarah with an assuredness that showed no signs of abating with age.

'Let me fix you both a drink,' Sarah slurred, assuming a hostess role that felt surprisingly natural. If Rory had any questions regarding the absence of Bertrand's formidable wife, he kept them to himself. Instead, he seemed unable to tear his eyes away from Sarah, who was now leaning against the door in her tight dress, hair falling over her face and one arm thrown upwards. She'd grabbed hold of the doorway to try and steady herself – she felt dangerously tipsy – but it had the effect of a fit young bitch's mating call to two naughty dogs who were seriously on heat.

Bertrand strolled over to Sarah, eyeing her. In full view of Rory he ran his hand over her bottom as he kissed her gently and slipped a probing hand inside her dress.

Sarah gasped, 'Oh my God!'

She tried to feel indignant, but somehow she didn't. She wanted him.

She gave an involuntary moan and pulled Bertrand's head close so that she could kiss him violently. Suddenly Sarah's dress was up around her waist and she stood pushed up against the door in high heels, a lace thong and a slip of a white dress as Bertrand grabbed her firm butt with both hands and pressed his body tight against hers while he kissed her. His feral urgency was at odds with his gentlemanly appearance and it excited her wildly, as did the knowledge that they were in full view of Rory. Sarah writhed and moaned as she reached for Bertrand's hair and pulled his head towards her breasts as he grabbed at the straps of her dress and pulled them down. Opening her eyes, she peered over Bertrand's head and glanced at Rory, still seated languorously on the sofa. He had undone his flies, and he looked calmly on while he pleasured himself, massaging his cock up and down with one hand in fast, rhythmic movements. His dusky blond head was thrown back slightly, his breathing loud and deep.

Sarah smiled coyly at Rory, slipping her arms fully out of the dress and allowing Bertrand to quickly unhook her strapless bra, freeing her pendulous breasts.

'Christ!' Rory wailed from his vantage point, his face contorted with longing. He could take it no longer; he had to touch her. Jumping from his seat he kicked off his slacks and boxer shorts, and, as an afterthought, his cashmere socks, and hot-footed it across the room. Sarah was utterly shocked at her own unhesitating compliance and how could this feel so damn natural? She knew it was slutty, and yet it didn't feel wrong. She had never felt so sexy, so adored and so turned on in her life.

Joining Bertrand in his animal ravaging of Sarah's curves, Rory stripped her dress from her body and tossed it to the ground before sliding behind her so that she was gripped tightly between the two friends. He dropped his head to kiss her shoulder and slid his hand down in between her thighs, slipping a gently probing finger between her legs. He gave a guttural groan. Sarah's own cries were getting louder now and Bertrand decided it was time to move into the bedroom. He lifted Sarah, still in lace thong and high heels, and carried her next door with Rory in hot pursuit.

Bertrand threw Sarah on to the bed and ordered her to strip. By the time she had kicked off her heels and wiggled swiftly out of her skimpy thong, all three were naked. Bertrand raced across the room to dim the lights and paused by the switch with a raging hard-on as he watched Rory and Sarah exploring each other's bodies on the Egyptian cotton sheets. Sliding on to the bed beside them, he stroked Sarah's breasts before gently edging Rory aside to position his head between her legs and lick her to orgasm, while Rory took each of her nipples into his mouth in turn and flicked and bit them gently.

Just as Sarah thought that she might melt if she had any more pleasure, she felt Bertrand enter her and then the waves of excitement mounted once more until she could think of nothing but the exquisite feeling between her legs. She wanted to be wholly consumed by both of them, but she sensed from the way Bertrand asserted complete control that if Rory took her it might cross some irrational line. Closing her eyes she reached down to feel Rory's erection and brought him to orgasm just before Bertrand brought *her* to orgasm for the second time that night.

Afterwards, damp, exhausted and euphoric, the three lay entwined on the bed, Sarah facing Bertrand, one leg draped over his, and spooned by Rory, until they slowly drifted to sleep. Sarah never told Bertrand that later in the night she'd been woken by the slow rocking of Rory's pelvis from behind and that she'd let him slip himself inside her and had rocked him gently to a climax while Bertrand, who had rolled over to the other side of the super-king-sized bed, slept soundly. Likewise, Bertrand never told Sarah that he'd been far too hot and damp to sleep properly and that

271

he had watched wordlessly while Sarah was taken by one of his oldest and dearest school-friends, just as he had done twenty-four years ago when they'd shared Georgina after Rory's sixteenth birthday party.

*****

Olympia had just had a blow-dry and now tossed her poker-straight newly red bob in slow motion, like someone in a shampoo advert.

'Mallinder hasn't been profitable this quarter as you all know,' she announced during the last company meeting of the year, 'so I've decided to cancel tonight's staff Christmas party in order to save money. Instead I'll be cutting it down to a dinner just for me and all the producers. None of you'll be needed at the dinner I shouldn't think, so there's an extra evening's holiday for you right there.'

'But we normally get the hours of the Christmas party off in lieu anyway,' whispered a disappointed Wendy, holding back a tear. The Mallinder Christmas party was the only time she was ever taken to a restaurant where the sauces didn't come in sachets.

'What was that, Wendy?' Olympia snapped. 'Speak up! Oh, and Abena, seeing as you know the most about the producers, I'd like you at the venue beforehand to oversee the seating plan and help organize. You can make yourself scarce once the boys arrive, I'm sure you've got other things to do this evening anyway what with your ritzy social life.' She shot Abena an envious or disapproving stare.

'Actually, Olympia, I've nothing on tonight as I had the

Christmas party diarized. But of course I'll be there, since it's my job.'

'I'll need you from 5 p.m. onwards – actually you'd better stick around throughout the evening in case there's a problem. The producers will start coming at six-thirty so at that point you can go across the road – there's a seafood place where you can sit and get yourself a bite to eat, and don't worry of course you can expense that.'

Abena perked up. Sheekey's was a wonderful fish restaurant, even smarter than the place Olympia had booked for the party. 'Sure, I'll wait at Sheekey's and you can just call if you need me.'

'Sheekey's?' Olympia's lips twitched. 'No, I meant that fish and chip place nearby. What's it called … Dandy Dan's Fish 'n Ribs? Something like that anyway. Right, now we've overrun. Get back to work everyone.'

Dejected, Abena wondered idly how Bertrand was getting along in France. It was almost five o'clock and she'd had no time to change before rushing to the restaurant to help. Not that it mattered seeing as she was now disinvited along with the rest of the staff. Or not as it turned out. She looked at the name cards on the table and saw that the acquisitions manager and the sales manager had both been included. Why on earth had two such insipid and uninspiring men been allowed to join the party?

Moments later, Olympia flew into the restaurant, sighing loudly. 'So much to do and so little time.' She smiled at Abena. 'Great, you're here already. So how should we do the names?'

'Well, I'd been thinking that the producers should be seated next to those they might have creative synergies with, that way they

273

could end up working together on co-productions, which means bigger budgets and potentially bigger money for Mallinder?'

Olympia thought about it for a nanosecond then shook her head. 'No. I think I should occupy the central position.'

She picked up her name card and placed it in the middle of the table, 'And then we can have the most important producers beside me, becoming gradually less important the further away from me they're seated.' She looked at her watch. 'Right I'm off. Back at six so I'll leave you to get on with things here. Oh, and have a read through this speech; the acquisitions and sales managers wrote it together, pretty good right?'

Abena felt like puking as she read the first few lines of the speech. No, Olympia was not 'as inspirational as President Obama, as serene as Buddha himself'. She was amazed that they'd actually extracted their noses from up Olympia's majestic bottom in order to write the thing. She couldn't bear to read any more so she put the speech down and turned her attention back to the names. All the usual suspects were there – but hang on a minute, was that Benedict Lima? She thought back to Olympia smirking that she'd added a freelancer to the database who had heard of the company through Carey Wallace. But he wasn't a producer. He was just a runner. Puzzled, she placed him towards the end of the table.

Eventually, having liaised with the staff and chefs, checked on the music and finished the names, there was little else for Abena to do. Olympia had returned, sporting an ill-advised thigh-skimming shirt-dress and a trilby hat. She looked Abena up and down. Abena was purposefully scruffy today in beat-up denim and high-tops. 'Quick, get out before the producers see you,' Olympia shrieked. So Abena went and sat in the dreary chippie opposite, sulking as she watched the dinner kick off through the clear glass.

She saw the mostly male producers file in to the restaurant, though there was no sign of Benedict. She noted with satisfaction that many failed to show and those who did looked bereft at being cheated of their chance to get the delightfully accommodating receptionist and other young staff under the mistletoe. It was clear that, by ignoring anything so profit-friendly as compatibility and synergy, competitors and bitter enemies had ended up side by side, and nobody got to network effectively. And the seating hierarchy was so obvious that Abena could see people frowning as they took their place in social Siberia, egos irreversibly dented. It was safe to say that Olympia wouldn't be seeing the two at either end of the long table again.

From her lookout, sitting at a booth between a junkie and a hobo who smelt faintly of urine, Abena tried not to laugh at Olympia's misfortune. She was just about to sink her teeth into her pungent kebab – the best of a bad bunch – when she felt a hand on her arm.

'Abena, is that you?'

She gawped at the tall, dark, clean-shaven man with intense eyes and thick black lashes.

'Ben! I didn't recognize you.'

'Likewise – do you normally spend the festive season eating kebabs by yourself in a Leicester Square chippie?'

'You won't believe it but I'm supposed to be at the Mallinder party. I got told to piss off at the last minute by my boss Olympia and to wait here in case she needs me.'

'That's disgraceful! Well I'm not going in without you. Looks like it's kebabs all round.'

They were interrupted by a brunette running into the chippie calling 'Benedict, Benedict, where are you?' She was petite and stunning, with a smattering of freckles across her upturned nose.

'Hey, we're over here. Abena, this is Lee.'

Abena put out her hand and smiled but the woman stepped away, repelled by the greasy remnants of kebab on her fingers. 'What's going on Benedict? Where's the party?'

'Across the road, but we're not going in unless Abena's allowed in.'

Lee turned and stomped off down the street.

Abena winced. 'You'd better go after her. Sorry, I think I've scuppered your date. What are you doing here anyway?'

'Carey mentioned Mallinder to me – I wanted to contact every distributor in the country just to have all bases covered while I'm here. And don't worry, she'll calm down. But, actually, I'm glad to see you ... You see, I got your message, and I just wondered—'

'You got my message? So why didn't you call? I thought manners was your thing!' Abena didn't quite know why she felt so indignant – it was only Ben after all.

'Well, actually, I did come to Annabel's but you seemed to have your hands full, so ...'

Abena felt hot with shame. 'Oh, oh God, Ben that's awful. You came all that way and I, I—'

'Shhh,' Ben said, 'it really doesn't matter. But if you must know, the reason I came all that way was because I wanted to tell you something.' He looked Abena fiercely in the eye, daring her to stop him. 'Even when you were clearly plastered, with that scumbag all over you on the dance floor, I still couldn't stop looking at you. You're the most incredible girl I've ever met. I think, Abena, I think I might be falling for you.'

Abena looked into his eyes, troubled pools of molten chocolate, and leaned forwards to brush his lips with hers. The kiss sent
shock waves through her body.

'Uh-oh,' she thought.

Benedict's date flounced back into the gritty chippie and he and
Abena jumped apart before she spotted them.

'Really, Benedict, let's go now. We're late as it is and after that
Olympia woman's gushing letter about you being the guest of
honour I think it's very rude of us not to show,' she said.

'Guest of honour? I thought you said you were a runner on film
sets?' Nothing was making any sense to Abena.

'That's what he always tells ditsy, greedy girls who he doesn't
like,' spat his date. 'And I know all about you, trying to get into
Carey Wallace's pants! In fact, Benedict runs a film-financing company he set up five years ago straight after film school in LA. He
started out on film sets but now he earns pots of money raising
eye-watering sums to executive-produce films he cares about. But
because he's low key, and discreet and modest,' she rested her
hand on his shoulder, 'you vacuous star-fucker types who suck up
to all the Hollywood bigwigs have never even heard of him. Well,
one day he's going to be bigger than anyone.'

'Is this true Ben?' Abena asked him sadly.

'About the job. Yes. That's what I do, but—'

'Sure Ben, d'you know what, don't bother waiting for me. I'm
just fine here. Why don't you and your charming girlfriend go and
join all those clever, worthy, non-vacuous people across the road,
who of course care nothing for status and aren't greedy in the
slightest. You all deserve each other. And when you're gone, don't
ever come back.'

'Abena don't be—'

'Ignore her, Benedict! Come on, we're leaving.' Lee grabbed his arm and pulled him out of Dandy Dan's Fish 'n Ribs mid-sentence.

Only when she was alone did Abena let out a sob. With a deep breath she tried to pull herself together and, just for something to do with herself, she reached down for her soggy kebab. It was gone. She looked to her right and noticed that coincidentally the smelly homeless man had also done a runner. Looking to her left she saw that the junkie was staring at her in disgust, shaking his head as if to say 'Sort your life out, love'.

Abena went home to sleep off the evening's events, and woke up just as miserable. At work she found that Olympia had disappeared off to her holiday home in Gstaad, leaving a to-do list that kept Abena working frantically until the morning of Christmas Eve. Just as she was finishing an inventory of furniture in Olympia's office – grumpily comparing Olympia's soft leather chair to her own back-ache-inducing piece of tat –Olympia called the office from a mountain-top restaurant. 'Abena, hi,' she shouted over the tinkle of toasting wine glasses. 'Before you leave, can you just do something for me quickly. I'm thinking about installing an en-suite dressing room in my office so I can head straight from there to my dinner dates with the industry boys. So much more efficient, no? Get me some quotes.'

Miraculously, Abena managed to get everything done, but she had almost reached breaking point by the time she left and headed, deflated, for the train station to travel to her family home.

\*\*\*\*

Natalya had been desperate to return home to spend Christmas with her mother but Claude had insisted she come to Geneva with him. She loathed it. The usual party-circuit locations were always exciting in parts, even with Claude. But unlike in St Tropez, or Paris, or London, where people treated her as part of the Perren power machine, Switzerland was hideously boring, like one great big old-people's home. Civilized people migrated to the mountains or a far-flung beach over the Christmas period, but this was Claude's time to switch off. So they would probably spend much of their time in just each other's company, in the hideous prison of a home Claude had had built on the outskirts of Geneva. When she was not with him, she would be expected to engage with his ghastly relatives, with whom she had absolutely nothing in common.

So it was with reluctance that she had boarded Claude's plane a few days earlier and arrived in a land where every street was clean and tidy and nothing was out of place. And it was with even more reluctance that she forced his chef's stodgy, carb-laden food into her super-slim body. How can a man who had all the ingredients in the world at his disposal exist on a diet of cheese, potatoes, bread and chocolate?

'You must eat everything you have been served,' Claude wheezed, scraping up the remains of the lamb goulash on his plate with a hunk of granary bread. 'And afterwards you will go to the bedroom, put on your blue gown and wait for me on the bed.'

Natalya wanted to drown him in a vat of melted Emmental. Instead, she stabbed at a fried potato with her fork and surveyed the building. He had literally built himself a fortress here. A fifteen-metre wall made of solid rock surrounded the entire property, penetrated only via a secret sliding stone door, which, as with all of Claude's properties, had been programmed with retina-recognition technology. Natalya's eyes had now been approved and entered into the system but she had no idea how Claude had obtained a 3-D scan of her eyeball.

Once through the wall and into the compound she could move freely through the 'garden' – if you could call a grassy courtyard covered overhead with bulletproof glass a garden. At the end of the garden you reached the main building, a horribly dark cavernous space with tiny windows to ensure that, even from the air, it was impossible to see inside.

The interior was furnished as Natalya had come to expect – with the best of everything, but in peculiarly functional style. Claude had torn down anything personal after his wife died, since when he'd had neither the time nor inclination to refurbish.

Strangest of all was the small chamber beside the panic room. Natalya had stumbled upon it one evening and let out a blood-curdling scream. 'What is it my darling heart?' Claude had come running. Natalya pointed at the shrouded figure on the floor, shocked into silence.

'Oh yes, did I not tell you I have preserved my wife? So that she might be with me always. I did not like the idea of the doctors cutting her open, violating her.'

Natalya shivered. She never had found out how it was Claude's wife died and there was little information to be gleaned from the net.

Just as dessert was being served, Claude's very serious son and daughter-in-law silently entered the dining room with their own son, his grandson. Only they were allowed to be late. Claude beckoned his son to his side and sent the other two to sit on either side of Natalya. His son sneered at her across the table so she turned away, assessing the wife, wondering how such a plain, straight-looking woman had snared a Perren for herself. She felt the child's sticky fingers tap on her knee. Irritated, she was about to slap his hand away when she saw that Claude was watching, curious to see how she was with youngsters. She put on her wedding cata-logue smile and stroked the boy's curls.

'Yes? What is it my dear?' She lowered her face so that he could speak into her ear.

Pulling at her diamond earring, he whispered, 'I hate you.' Then, laughing, he jumped off his seat and ran round the table to clam-ber on to his father's lap.

\*\*\*\*

As the train trundled away from the station Abena stared out of the wide window and watched the lightest flakes of snow land softly on the track, melting as they made contact. She'd been long-ing for this Christmas fortnight at home with her family in Kent, and there was the family skiing holiday in Switzerland to look forward to as well. Bertrand was trying to engineer a clandestine visit too. She still had misgivings about their affair, but it did at least help take her mind off work and assuage her loneliness post Sebastian. Not to mention the constant drain of having to watch over Tara. Thank God Tina had come to pick her up yesterday – some time relaxing at home could be just the therapeutic break her friend needed.

The snowflakes were becoming bigger and harder now and as the train picked up speed they pelted Abena's window in relentless, rhythmic thrusts. She loved the passion and unpredict-ability of the weather, loved that any minute now the clouds could clear and give way to revitalizing sunshine. She let the rhythm of the beats against her window soothe her into an almost trance-like state. And so it was a few seconds after the man had walked by that her mind registered his passage. Jolted out of her reverie, Abena leapt up, forgetting her bag in her haste, and dashed down the aisle into the next carriage.

She just caught sight of his back before the carriage door closed behind him. Was she destined to keep missing him? Well she wouldn't give up this time. She pursued him to the far end of the train, where she finally caught up with him, breathing hard. 'Ben!' she shouted. 'Ben!'

The man swivelled round and looked at her blankly. He was not Benedict.

'I'm so sorry, I thought you were somebody else,' a shamefaced Abena explained. Her cheeks burned with embarrassment and she didn't dare look at anybody else in the carriage as she hurried back to her seat and slumped down into it. Probably a good thing it hadn't been him. She was furious with him anyway and had no idea what she would have said. The rest of the journey dragged on, but she put on a cheerful smile to match that of her father, waiting happily for her at the station.

Abena's three older brothers and their wives, girlfriends and children had already arrived at the family home. The pretty, detached farmhouse house was filled to busting with informal family photographs, irreverent modern European art and ancient African artefacts. Big, comfy, worn sofas were everywhere apart from in the main living room, where a smart Roche Bobois suite shared the space with tall, tribal, throne-like chairs – both wedding presents from her respective grandparents. Her oldest brother's chubby twin toddlers, Kwame and Jojo, were dancing in reindeer romper-suits by the front door and Abena found her spirits instantly lifted.

'Hello Jo,' Abena giggled, as she scooped the first gurgling child up in her arms while the other ran off with her handbag. She took Jojo and went to seek her mother out.

'You look nice, Mum,' she commented, having found her preparing yet more food in the big kitchen, the hub of the home. She was cooking sweet plantain and a tomato-rich rice dish, no doubt to add to the mountain of goodies already laid out about the house and piling up on the kitchen counter. Her mother, normally kitted out in smart suits for her job as a top lawyer in the City, had put on a colourful hand-dyed and woven dress decorated with intricate embroidery and beading.

'Thanks, darling.' She kissed both her daughter and little Jo on the cheek, commenting on how handsome the toddlers were growing. 'They really are developing Ankrah cheekbones aren't they? Any nice boys around you, darling? I was just chatting to General Ampofo the other day and his youngest son, you know, the unmarried one, he's just qualified as a barrister…'

Abena backtracked quickly out of the kitchen, grabbing a marinated roast potato to share with Jojo.

Her mother called after her, 'Abena can you give the living room a quick tidy before your aunt and uncle arrive with the children. They're staying for three nights.'

'No probs.' She wandered off to help with the last of the preparations. Big family Christmases were fun and it was customary for everybody to chip in and help out.

Christmas Day was as manic as usual. Twenty-five relatives, five of them babies, had flown in from all over and were now seated around two long tables, enjoying the feast that Abena's mother had been cooking up for days. Comforted as always by the warmth of her extended family and the general feeling of goodwill that was evident everywhere, from the happy gurgles of the youngest babies to the contented toasts of her parents and their siblings, Abena hoped that Tara was enjoying such a heart-warming break and felt sad when she had to admit that this was unlikely.

After the meal and prayers it was time for the playful 'opening ceremony', and with so many people there were literally hundreds of presents under the tree. The children and babies were the most spoiled, receiving toys, clothes and books. Inquisitive young Kwame's favourite new toy, however, was not wrapped up. He had ransacked Abena's handbag earlier in the day and was now enjoying chatting to a nice man called Bren-ne-dic. 'Gagaga ... Ahh ...' he cooed down the phone.

'Ab-en-a,' the funny man was saying to him.

'Wooooooooo!' Kwame screamed back, this was more fun than bath-time with his duck family.

'Please can I speak to your Aunty Abena?'

'Abena eat Christmas pie ...'

'But can—'

Oh, where had the funny man gone? Kwame had just pressed a shiny red button. 'Bye bye Bender,' he shouted down the empty line.

****

284

In Gloucestershire, the atmosphere was uneasy. Hugo and Tina had decided that for the sake of a happy Christmas they would forget their marital problems and attempt to be jolly. Tina had also begun to suspect that Hugo was not the only one developing a substance-abuse problem, and was keeping a close eye on Tara. For the sake of decency, Tina had not invited Orlando to join them, but his absence made her irritable, as did Hugo's drunkenness and Tara's sullenness. Joining the Wittstanleys for Christmas Day were Tara's Uncle Rupert, his wife Anya, and their three girls, in matching purple dresses and hats. The only other guests were Hugo's other brother, Edward, and his wife Annabel. It was an uncharacteristically sombre affair, with conversation consisting mainly of the two uncles and their wives making awkward plans to meet up in Klosters for the New Year.

'Stan, old boy, you in Klosters too?' Edward raised an inquisitive eyebrow at his brother. Even after more than five decades the Wittstanleys still found it hilarious to refer to each other using their shortened surname. The talk of Klosters, however, put paid to any hilarity as Tina pursed her glossy lips and Hugo's red face deepened in colour. They, of course, could not afford such a break this winter. Tina didn't mention that she had already made alternative plans to go to Courchevel with Orlando and that she hoped to bring Tara with her.

'Shall we open presents?' trilled Anya, worried the tension would ruin the day for her little ones.

'Yes, yes, yes!' chanted the girls, who were delighted with almost all of their dolls and puzzles and even loved the Bob the Builder and Fireman Sam books Tara had picked up from a discount

285

bookshop last minute. They were the first kids' books she came across and she'd been too exhausted to search for anything more girlie. Tina was less impressed.

'Fireman Sam! Bob the Builder!' she spluttered. 'What *is* this preoccupation with *workmen* in children's literature? No wonder society is going downhill. What's wrong with Harry the Hedge-Fund Manager? Or Frederick the Financier? Far more appropriate reading material for an impressionable four-year-old.'

Tara, slumped on a sofa half-watching TV, could barely muster the energy to roll her eyes.

# Chapter 24

Tara's relief at having escaped a torturous skiing holiday with her mother and Orlando was short-lived. In order to get Tina to agree to this, Tara had had to promise to see a doctor about her 'problems'. Tina had never actually mentioned the word drugs, referring instead to her daughter's weight issue, eating habits and skin condition. Likewise, Tara had studiously avoided creating a scene and delving deeper into the heart of things, and so they had both been complicit in cultivating an absurd atmosphere of denial within the big house. The visit to the doctor, therefore, was a huge jolt to both mother and daughter.

At Dr Nicholas Lawrence's practice, Tara was informed that she had a serious dependency on the class A narcotic cocaine. She learnt that her addiction was psychological rather than physical, but that this type of dependency was just as dangerous. She was informed that she was putting her heart under serious pressure, that she was severely malnourished, and that due to reduced blood flow from ingesting so much cocaine, she suffered from severe and potentially life-threatening bowel gangrene. Speaking very slowly to ensure that both women understood the seriousness of the situation, the doctor leaned forward and asked the sinfully attractive, busty mother in front of him if it might be easier for him to speak alone with Tara. Tina had by now become almost as pale as her addict daughter. She shook her head slowly. They both needed to hear this.

Dr Lawrence ended his appraisal with the ominous words: 'Your fragile body is ailing and not half as robust as it should be at your young age. The next hit could kill you.' At which point Tina fainted.

By the time Tina came round, Tara had been prescribed medication for her bowel gangrene and been recommended a number of NHS institutions to clean herself up. Dr Lawrence also gave Tina a directory of publicly funded rehabilitation programmes, and slipped his number inside, just in case she needed a little support after hours.


Back in London, Tara was now morosely recounting the tale to a transfixed Abena and Natalya. Caught up in the drama of her own story, Tara began to sob. At first the tears were gentle, then the floodgates opened. She parted her red lips as far as she could and let out an almighty wail.

'Oh,' she howled, 'You don't know what those NHS programmes are like. He said I'm depressed. They'll section me in a mental hospital with a bunch of weirdos and perverts and kids from children's homes. I'll probably get raped and stabbed to death by crack addicts from Br-Br-Brixton ... Oh my God, what am I going to do?'

Natalya waited for Tara to pause for air and cleared her throat. 'Bébé, I told you already, I know a place. A good place, with nice people. And it's clean, and beautiful, and comfortable, and they will support you, and help you recover at a pace thet is right for you, and without judging you.'

'Ooooohhhhhh.' Tara resumed howling. 'How the hell can I afford something like that? Do you think my parents give me a fucking penny?'

Natalya nodded, her lovely face creased with genuine concern. 'I know, I know,' she soothed. 'Let me take care of it.' Tara stopped crying for a moment and looked up quizzically at her new friend.

'All my life,' Natalya continued, 'I've worried about money. But when you worry about it, it takes over your life. Now, for me, for the first time, money is not a problem and I want to help you now because I am able to. I want you to forget about money and just concentrate all your energy upon getting well.'

Abena wiped a tear from her eye and smiled at Natalya.

'That is the single most kind-hearted thing I have ever heard. You are literally saving my best friend's life.'

Tara too, was still sobbing, but this time the tears were of gratitude rather than anguish. 'Oh my g— I can't. I can't accept that – how will I ever repay you? Oh I will pay you back I swear, I swear, I'll go and I'll get better and I—'

'Don't worry about thet now. Just get better and if you feel you must pay me back then you can pay me back when you are recovered.'

She smiled and reached for Tara's cold, heavily veined hand, caressing it in hers the way her own mother had done to her when she was a child. Abena and Tara felt suddenly ashamed of their aloofness towards Natalya in St Tropez.

Abena glanced down at her vibrating phone and saw that Tina was calling again. Shocked into action and now feeling horribly guilty as well as petrified for her daughter's life, Tina had temporarily joined her alcoholic husband in London in order to keep a closer eye on Tara.

'Yes, we're making really good progress,' Abena reassured Tina. 'She has agreed to check into Appletons pretty much immediately.'

'She seems to want to fight this now, that's a relief. But, oh Christ, I can only imagine how much it costs to be treated there. I suppose we can sell the piano, or even the house – not that that will do much good the number of times it's been re-mort—'

Abena could hear the panic in Tina's voice rising to a crescendo and cut her off before she could babble on any more about her dire financial situation. She wondered whether Tina had taken herself off the waiting list for that Birkin bag yet.

'It's been taken care of. A friend has very kindly offered to pay for Tara's treatment.'

There was a long silence before Tina falteringly enquired who he was. It humiliated her, somehow, to have strange men paying for things that she, the mother, should be buying.

'It's not a he, it's a girl. Natalya, a friend of ours.'

'Natalya? I don't think I know her. How kind. Where on earth will she find that kind of money?'

Tina was heartened to hear that the unknown sponsor was not some sleazy man with all sorts of dishonourable intentions towards her little girl.

'She's a very successful model.' Abena decided not to mention Claude Perren.

'Well, can I speak to her? I must thank her, and come to some sort of arrangement as to when and how we can repay her.'

'She's here now. She says Tara is already booked in – she can head up there later today.'

'Oh yes, yes, wonderful. You've been such a brilliant friend to her. I know what a handful she can be – takes after her father. I simply don't know how I'd have coped without everyone rallying around and helping. Yes, why don't I come over to the flat now and we'll all drive down together. That way I can meet Natalya too. Yes that's a great plan.'

She sounded quite upbeat, and as an afterthought added, 'Of course that means that I won't need to spend another night in London and can get straight back to Orl— I mean to Willowborough.'

At that moment Abena felt even sorrier for Tara than when she had caught her retching and clutching her stomach on the bathroom floor. At a time like this, how could a fling be Tina's primary concern? She clearly loved her daughter, but her self-obsession was rivalled only by Tara's and even then Abena felt that Tina had the edge.

'If you'd like some time alone with Tara I can arrange for Natalya and I to leave the flat after you arrive?'

'Please, no!' Tina cried. 'Who'll calm her down if she makes a scene? I'm simply too fragile at the moment and she'll ... she'll want her friends around.'

Tina arrived at the flat later that afternoon and rushed towards Tara's bedroom. As always her make-up was immaculate and she was still tanned from skiing. Her freshly cut dark hair was glossy and had plainly just been blow-dried. When she lowered her shades, though, the enlarged grey bags underneath her reddened eyes spoke of many sleepless nights. Tara was curled up in the foetal position on her bed and didn't even look up. For a brief moment, Abena found herself annoyed. Tara must take responsibility for her own addiction – it hadn't been forced upon her. Yet she somehow managed to look so frail and ill and utterly innocent.

'Come on darling.' Tina kissed her daughter gingerly and helped her up off the bed. 'Your father's outside in the car. We're all coming to see you off.'

Turning to Abena, she asked, 'Is she all packed?'

'Yep, we've packed her bag – it's in the hallway.'

Abena pointed out Tara's large leather bag, which she had packed with enough clothes, toiletries and books for a couple of months if necessary. Although Natalya and Abena knew that clothing shouldn't be a priority, they hadn't been able to resist including Tara's favourite Matthew Williamson party dress and a classic sexy LBD just in case the in-patients got to go on a few jaunts to London. They'd also packed all of Tara's make-up and were dying for her to use it. The moment she started bothering with things like that again it would be a sign she was on the road to recovery.

Glimpsing the mahogany coloured Tod's bag that had gone missing from her own dressing room eight months ago, Tina pursed her lips but kept silent. Outside, Hugo had nodded off in the passenger seat of his wife's second-hand Audi and was snoring loudly. Natalya emerged from the bathroom, which she'd been giving a good clean, and smiled shyly at Tina. Tina was utterly charmed by such flagrant beauty and all thoughts of the usurped leather bag were forgotten.

'You must be Natalya!' she squealed, running to embrace her.

Abena deposited the contentious bag in the boot of the Audi and climbed in the back with Tara. A short while later, Tina and

Natalya emerged from the apartment arm in arm and giggling like old friends. Hearing his wife's cackle, Hugo woke with a start, promptly banging his head against the steering wheel. He opened his eyes narrowly and was delighted to see that his wife had morphed into a slender young blonde, then realized he was looking at Natalya, and that his wife was following closely behind her. He stared at Natalya in a way that unsettled her – it was as if he couldn't quite decide whether he loved or hated her.

Settling into the driver's seat, Tina peered round and squawked 'Everybody in?'

'Yes', everyone chorused, and as Tina set off with a girlish giggle they could have been on a school trip to the theatre, not a rehabilitation clinic. Tara, the star of the show, was massively nervous but also overwhelmed with hope and relief. At the clinic she could finally escape the threats from angry dealers, who she'd finally paid off, though far later than she should have. And more wonderful than that was the chance of ending the pain. The pain of giving up would surely not be easy, but the pain of continuing would be excruciating.

Tina was euphoric that here was a potential solution to her daughter's suffering that was not only comprehensive and reassuringly expensive, but was far enough away from home to create minimum upheaval in the horrific period she was going through herself. She would have some much needed 'me time', particularly if she could persuade Hugo to check into that grotty NHS alcoholics' clinic they had looked at. Orlando was right, she was forever looking after her demanding family and nobody ever thought about her, about her needs and wants.

All Hugo could think about was when he would be able to

sneak a few swigs of the vodka in his hip flask. Perhaps they'd stop at a service station en route where he could rush off to the loo. He was aware that Natalya was sitting behind him and he glanced round at her. She squeezed his shoulder and his hand moved instinctively to hold hers.

Abena and Natalya looked at each other knowingly. Having both worked tirelessly to persuade Tara to seek help, they had developed a mutual respect for one another and now felt a weary satisfaction that something constructive was finally happening.

'Are you OK, Natalya?' Abena whispered

'Yes, I'm fine … It's just …'

'What is it? You can tell me.'

'It's nothing, I'm fine.' Natalya smiled but her eyes were downcast. It had been lovely to feel like part of a family. Even one as dysfunctional as Tara's.

As the sun went down, the car drew up at Appletons Rehabilitation Centre, a beautiful Victorian house set in acres of landscaped grounds surrounded by the rolling farmland of Kent's North Downs. It seemed the setting might really offer the peace and tranquillity necessary for successful recovery that the brochure had promised. Dr Lynne Tomlinson came briskly out of the clinic and into the driveway to welcome Tara personally. She was dressed casually in blue jeans and an orange sweater and Tara was relieved to see that she wasn't carrying any odd doctor's paraphernalia to prod and jab at her with.

The entire party was offered soft drinks in the cosy reception area, which was warmed by a log fire and felt snug under its heavy, low wooden beams. Afterwards they were taken on a tour of the clinic, which had the capacity to house forty-three patients on an in-patient basis, with several halfway houses in the nearby village for day- and out-patient care. Tara was to be an in-patient and they were taken to see her rooms. She had her own private living room for entertaining, which, like her bedroom, was plainly decorated in creams and magnolias with a few simple paintings of pastel-coloured flowers and fruits on the walls. It wasn't exactly hip but the overall impression conjured was of welcome cleanliness, calm and serenity.

'Each programme is individually tailored according to the patient's needs,' Dr Tomlinson explained as she showed them round. 'The process towards recovery normally takes eight to twelve weeks, but we provide a further extended care period if that's needed. Once Tara returns home, we'll allocate a recovery partner from the clinic who'll continue to communicate with her for a year after that. We do things properly here,' she summarized with pride.

The doctor led the guests through to the spa pools in the modern annex at the rear of the building, and elaborated on the centre's facilities. 'Treatment in the Narcotics Unit involves a varied programme of counselling and recreation, including sessions with an art therapist and a music therapist, as well as the choice of tennis, swimming or riding. This will begin tomorrow,' she said, turning to Tara and putting a hand on her shoulder, 'so you'll need to make sure you eat well tonight to keep your strength up.'

Tara wasn't really listening and felt a fleeting surge of pain at the thought that she wouldn't have a chance to see heavenly Alex for at least eight weeks.

Moving on to the tennis courts and then the stables, Dr Tomlinson continued, 'As you can see it's not all serious here. Patients get to enjoy outings to places of interest, and we actively encourage them to socialize with and strengthen each other through regular group interaction *and* a three-course dinner every evening, cooked by a wonderful chef who used to work for the *royal family*.' She glanced at Tara as though she hoped that might impress her. Passing through the dining hall, Tara thought idly that it looked like the inside of Cipriani in New York – the grand uptown one, not the cooler downtown restaurant. Hugo reflected morosely that if someone would pay for him to go here then it would be a bloody good incentive to tear himself away from the bottle.

At length it was time for the group to leave Tara in the capable hands of Dr Tomlinson. Hugo broke down in uncharacteristically loud sobs as he put his arms round his daughter. 'I'm sorry,' he stuttered, his deep voice breaking in a futile attempt to pull himself together, which only made him cry harder. Tara herself felt numb. She couldn't cry, only stand listlessly, while her father, who had always been so strong, leaned the entire weight of his shaking body on her thin shoulders. His breath smelt of alcohol and it seemed absurd to Tara that she and not he was the one being made to seek help. 'I'm sorry,' he repeated. Tara could see in his eyes he had given up. The youthful hope that had filled Tara's throbbing chest in the car journey to Kent was something that Hugo didn't understand.

Only then did Tara's eyes begin to water, and after that everybody followed suit. Dr Tomlinson took a few steps back to give the party some privacy. As the Audi eventually rolled off she put an arm around Tara's shoulder and led her slowly back into the clinic.

# Chapter 25

Arriving back at Claude's Mayfair house, Natalya jumped as she heard her phone ring. Her heart stopped beating momentarily and she braced herself for the worst. Seeing that it was just her booker calling she let out an audible sigh of relief.

'Hello, Gaby.' She wondered what her booker wanted from her; she hadn't called for a while.

'Hi, Natalya. How are you today?'

'Fine.' Natalya wished she'd get to the point. Some bookers might pretend to be your friend, but Natalya knew that the motive was and would always be money. So why the small talk?

'Well, I've got some very exciting news for you, Natalya.'

Natalya inspected her manicure in the moody light of her bedroom.

'What is it?'

'You got the job!' There was an expectant pause.

'What job?'

'The Mirror Mirror campaign, Natalya. You know, the big, prestigious Blue Whisper job that all the top girls were considered for? And you got it, over everybody else! They need you for two days. You'll earn £70,000 for two days' work.' Gaby enunciated her words slowly, as though she were speaking to somebody with learning difficulties.

'Oh yes, I remember.' Natalya thought back to the unattractive, po-faced woman at the casting who she had shocked with her nonchalance. She hadn't had a big job in years. How ironic that one should come along now when she was hardly in need of the cash. But she'd do it anyway. It was always a nice thing for a man to be able to say that his girlfriend, or, hopefully soon, fiancée is a model. Of course she'd be expected to give up work once married but she would take this job.

'When is the shoot?'

Gaby was becoming angry at Natalya's impassiveness. 'They told you at the casting, it's in a week's time. On the 15th and 16th of January. There'll be a couple of other girls there too but you're the main one.'

'Very well, thenk you, Gaby.'

Natalya snapped her phone shut and rang Claude in Dubai to check she was allowed to accept the job.

\*\*\*\*

At 7.50 p.m. on Tara's first night at Appletons, a young nurse knocked on the door and then let herself in with her key. She ignored Tara's sullen look and bustled into the room.

'Hi Tara, I'm Nurse Allison but I prefer to be called by my first name, so call me Nurse Sally. Oh, that's a nice outfit.'

Abena had packed only Tara's most flattering clothes, which forced Tara to look a little better than she intended. She longed just to pull on her cotton tracksuit bottoms and her holey college sweater from Oxford, but instead she wore a pair of once tight and now baggy dark blue Chloé jeans and a tight-fitting bright blue mohair jumper, which brought out the striking blue of her eyes.

'Have you washed your hair like the doctor ordered?' asked Nurse Sally bossily.

Tara felt like retorting that no, her hair was just naturally wet, but she refrained and was surprised when Nurse Sally reached for the hairdryer and brush provided by the clinic and proceeded to blow-dry her hair into a voluminous silky golden curtain. Tara would never have styled it like that herself, preferring something flatter and edgier, but she had neither the energy nor the inclination to argue. And after all, she did look prettier than she had in months. She followed Nurse Sally to the dining hall and thought about the other patients she was about to meet. Probably all spoilt brats and self-indulgent mentalists – she'd have been better off in an NHS hospital with people who had real problems to overcome like she did. She was suddenly immobilized with fear and an intense craving for some coke.

Putting her hand flat against the wall to steady herself, Tara stopped still and breathed heavily in and out. She was hyperventilating. Had she been at home she would have taken something, anything that she could get her hands on, then and there. But there was nobody she could turn to for drugs in this prison. Nurse Sally waited a few metres away, casually examining the clear nail polish on her own neat, short nails, first one hand, then the other. Tara was still gulping down air, panic clutching at her chest. 'There, there,' Nurse Sally smiled, but she made no attempt to move closer. Eventually Tara calmed down and turned as if to return to her room.

'Where do you think you're going?' Nurse Sally asked.

Sighing, Tara swung back round again and followed Nurse Sally into the dining hall, where she was ushered to a seat near a nondescript brunette in her late thirties, a slight blond man in his forties, a pretty teenager, and an obese man in his twenties. Tara couldn't help noticing that all were dressed in upmarket, well-cut clothes.

'What are you in for?' the teenager asked, wide-eyed.

'Cocaine. You?'

'I've been clean from heroin for three weeks now.' The pride in her voice was obvious.

Tara nodded, wondering what the boring-looking people on either side were being treated for. She turned to glance at the man to her left, who muttered 'Alcoholic'. The teenager reached across and squeezed his hand and the nondescript brunette gave an encouraging nod. 'I'm an alcoholic too,' she said. A sweating, overweight middle-aged man across the table chose that moment to join the conversation.

'Thex and love. I juss can't ssshtop having thex …' he wheezed. 'I want it all the time … I want to do it when I'm s-s-sssad, I want to do it when I'm happy. I want to do it when I'm alone and when I'm in public … I want to do it with boys and girls and men and women and …'

When the rest of the party greeted this disturbing outburst with empathetic nods and smiles, Tara turned away, disgusted.

And then she noticed him. In her heightened emotional state his presence in the dining hall was like an epiphany. If Alex Spectre had taken her breath away, this man was her reason to breathe again; her reason to live. He sat at the table opposite, apparently conversing amicably with those around him, and yet he seemed somehow distant from them. While they gesticulated and talked frantically, he remained still. He watched them intently and with kind interest, and yet he seemed to be holding something back from the conversation. He was tall and slim and there was a distinguished quality about him and his restraint, but Tara saw at once that it was not arrogance. His dark, wavy hair was longer than was fashionable, falling to just above his shoulders, but it showed off his face perfectly, like a beautiful, unusual frame around an Old Master. His face was long and thin, gaunt even, but his complexion was healthy and naturally tanned and his light-brown eyes were encircled by thick, dark lashes. Tara wondered what his history was. A tortured artist perhaps? Then she took in his outfit: a sumptuous chunky black cashmere cardigan with red corduroy trousers and dapper red loafers. Well, thought Tara, perking up, the only thing better than the romance of a tortured artist, was a super-stylish and evidently well-heeled man with the *looks* of one.

He met Tara's gaze and gave her a welcoming smile. He hadn't seen her around the clinic before, so he raised his glass of sparkling water in a toast. Tara noticed the beautiful old watch on his slender wrist. Probably a relic from a distinguished ancestor with excellent taste. She lifted her own glass of water and smiled, feeling distant stirrings of something she'd not felt in a long time. Hope.

That first night at rehab, Tara lay in bed and closed her eyes, but sleep never came. She ached all over and cried softly into her pillow. Every so often an agonizing pain would sear through her entire body and she would shout for a nurse to come and hold her, but that didn't help. Eventually she stopped even calling for a nurse. She simply clamped her mouth shut and buried her head under her duvet.

On the second night Tara placed her pillow over her face and pressed down, hard. She felt like her lungs would burst but each time she gasped for air her hands loosened. Finally she threw the pillow on the floor and let tears roll down her face. Later she managed to sleep for around two hours. She slept for between one and two hours every night of the first week yet during the daytime she would sleep for hours at a time and wake up disoriented and severely depressed. She just knew she would be unable to make it.

\*\*\*\*

It had been a surreal week for Natalya and her booker Gaby. Once the press release had gone out that the glamorous Latvian with the quirky hairstyle had secured the Mirror Mirror campaign, Natalya's profile within and without the fashion industry shot up instantly. Gaby fielded countless calls from fashion houses dying to book the hot new model, the overnight sensation. She didn't bother to point out that Natalya had been struggling from go-see to go-see for years and had in fact already been seen and rejected by a number of the people enquiring about her now. The fashion world was full of sheep. The only problem now was Natalya's annoying reticence. The imbecile was turning down ridiculous sums of money and had said yes to only one in ten offers. Gaby felt like shaking her at times.

She needn't have worried. Playing hard to get never fails. The more offers Natalya turned down, the more in demand she became, and the more she ensured she would not become too quickly overexposed. Natalya knew how to extend her own shelf-life.

The shoot was to take place in a large, eccentric house beside a sandy beach in Devon. Natalya was amazed to be given her own dressing room and a personal runner who delighted in bringing her anything she wanted to eat or drink. In the outdoor shots, instead of freezing, scantily clad, in between photographic sessions, she was sent to warm up in her own mobile waiting room kitted out with nibbles, champagne and cashmere wraps. She recognized the other models, Irma and Anastasia, from the fashion pages, but although they were also well known and therefore well treated, she was undoubtedly the star. She invited them into her own fancy quarters so that they could while away time chatting about their homeland, Russia, which Natalya had visited a few times and whose language she had taught herself.

'Well ladies, *na zdorovie!*' Natalya poured out three glasses of champagne. She was pleased that it was perfectly chilled.

'Mmmn … Just what the doctor ordered,' purred Irma, rolling each syllable in her deep, seductive, Russian-accented voice. She took a long sip and closed her eyes, savouring the bubbles in her throat before emitting an indulgent moan. Anastasia and Natalya looked at each other and burst into a fit of giggles. Irma was known in the industry for being a notorious man-eater, rumoured to have broken the hearts of several Hollywood actors and a minor royal.

'These poor boys have no chance in the face of that!' drawled Anastasia.

'Exactly,' agreed Natalya. 'No wonder Lord Talveston developed a heart condition after dating you – and the poor guy was only in his thirties. You nearly gave me a cardiac arrest right there.'

Irma pretended to slap Natalya, then finished the rest of her glass in one long sip.

'Ah, it's so good to finally meet you both,' Natalya said. 'I've heard a lot of great things about you.' She looked from Irma's ice-white hair and translucently pale skin to Anastasia's olive complexion and short black bob with its heavy asymmetric fringe. Both were even taller and thinner than Natalya, with razor-sharp cheekbones and narrow, Slavic eyes. She adored the extraordinary, almost alien-like beauty of the other girls and revelled in the picture that the three of them together must create. She found herself thinking once more, as she'd noticed with Tara, that it was surprisingly good fun to spend time with like-minded girlfriends.

'Natalya, sweetie, you're on again. Are you ready or you do you need some more time?' called Mia, the creative director. Stark-raving mad, and an absolute genius, Mia had worked in the industry for many years and was renowned for her collection of bizarre belts, which were extraordinary even in the world of high fashion. Today she had her live pet python wrapped around her waist, pulling in an otherwise billowing silk dress.

'You look incredible, Natalya honey!' appraised Anouska, the shoot's achingly cool stylist. She shook out her own scruffy black hair and re-pinned it in a towering beehive while she admired her styling of Natalya.

Natalya stepped out of her trailer and on to the beach in a strapless golden taffeta dress rucked up around her calves to reveal a pair of green Hunter wellies in an intentional clash of styles. Everybody stared, dumbstruck. She stood on tiptoes and jokingly sashayed down a mock catwalk, nose high in the ear, haughty hand on hip.

The rugged photographer and his young assistant began to sing, deep and slow, 'Sheeee's a model and she's looooking good ...'

Natalya collapsed, laughing, and then the photographer pressed PLAY on his retro portable stereo. In their secluded location they didn't have to worry about the noise.

'Dance for me, baby!' he cried.

So Natalya jumped, skipped and leapt around outside, long legs everywhere, arms flailing, unselfconscious and gloriously happy.

The laughter didn't stop once the cameras started rolling. Respected and admired for the first time within her profession, Natalya relaxed. She had nothing to prove. Instead, she forgot herself, forgot about Claude, genuinely forgot about her faceless, fearsome father, and she became the mysterious beauty of the campaign. She took on a whole different persona and for a few hours she was transported to the better world she'd always dreamed of.

'OK, Natalya,' directed the photographer, 'your man is back home after three months away. You're newlyweds and you're totally in love. You see him at the other end of the beach. Show me how much you want him.' He kept clicking away as Natalya bounded, smiling, across the shore. 'Oh yeah. Baby, you're gorgeous!' he shouted. 'Oh you're beautiful, that's it, give me another turn.'

Natalya threw herself into character. As she worked her way through the dozens of scenarios the photographer called out, she was struck with little flashes of inspiration. 'Why don't I stand this way,' she suggested, 'so that the cut of the dress appears even more asymmetric?' And then later, 'If I look down this way then you can catch the shimmer of gold on my eyelid, which is the exact same gold of the dress.'

As the winter sun faded from the sky, the shoot started to get more intense. 'Now that it's getting dark,' said the photographer, 'I want to really sum up the essence of Blue Whisper. Give me your natural, sensual side. Oh yeah. Oh yeah, Natalya, you're so fine! That's it, now look at me, keep moving!'

Natalya threw herself on the ground, rolling in the sand as she gazed straight up at the camera, an expression of pure bliss on her face. Nobody spoke.

'That's it,' said the photographer. 'That's the money shot. That's gonna set a million women's hearts alight.'

They didn't wrap up until 10 p.m., after which everybody enjoyed a light fresh fish and salad dinner, huddled together at their cosy beach-house hotel.

The next day the gaiety started all over again at 9 a.m. and after two hours of hair and make-up the photographer began, once again, to capture the splendour of the models and their surroundings. It was a shorter day of mainly group shots this time. The three girls pretended they were old friends – who just happened to be exceptionally good-looking – strolling along the golden sandy beach. They laughed and gossiped and fooled around, playing tricks on each other, doing cartwheels and giving each other piggybacks. The scenarios were contrived but the rapport between the girls and the wider team was genuine. As the final stunning shots were achieved, Natalya felt a wave of bittersweet happiness.

At the end of the day, a driver chauffeured the three models back to their respective homes in London. It was with heartache that Natalya parted from Irma and Anastasia. For two days they had shared in the same fantasy scenarios, and for those two days they'd believed in them. Now she was back in the real world. The girls swapped phone numbers and vowed to meet up for drinks, although each quietly suspected their drinks date would never materialize. It didn't matter though. They had shared a wonderful experience, which Natalya could add to her portfolio of memories. She hoped that one day the joyful memories in her life would out-number the sad ones.

Bathos. That was the first word Natalya learnt in London just for herself. From the sublime to the ridiculous. The last two days had been sublime, but, as she opened the door to find Claude already home and fiddling with a new security gizmo in a pair of yellow silk pyjamas, she knew that the euphoria was to be short-lived.

'Hello, my child. Take a seat.' Claude didn't crush her against his bulk and smother her with kisses as usual.

'Hello, bébé, welcome home. I was just going to the bathroom.'

'No. Sit down first.'

Natalya perched wearily on the edge of a chair.

'You wait, Natalya,' Claude ordered, snatching up his ringing phone and speaking, eerily quietly, into it.

'I own that entire region, and I don't like selling it now at a third of the price I paid only two years ago. But understand this. I can bring down governments just by uttering a sentence.'

He snapped the phone shut and turned to Natalya. 'I see you have been out and about. You have a lot of fun without me, ah?'

He couldn't still be upset about that night with Tara? She rose from the chair and leaned in to kiss him, if only to shut him up.

'No, baby. Not now.' Claude grabbed the hand she had stretched out to embrace him with and held it with such force that she thought he might cut off the blood supply to her fingers.

'How do you explain this, baby?' From his breast pocket he

pulled out a magazine cutting. It showed Natalya and Sebastian Spectre deep in conversation at the Tringate Charity Fundraiser. The picture had been cut out meticulously with a pair of scissors into a perfect rectangle.

'You … you told me to go as your representative.' She struggled to get the words out.

'But I asked you to bring security to watch you. Did you do it? No. And I did not ask you to go half naked.' He let the picture flutter to the floor.

'You will stay in this house for a week.'

'What? I don't understand.'

'I said, you are not allowed to leave this place for a week. It is your punishment. Do not disobey me again.' He roared the last sentence so loudly that a cluster of staff gathered at the door to see what the commotion was.

'I'm sorry,' Natalya breathed.

He turned and left the room without a backward glance.

'Claude, I'm so sorry,' Natalya wailed after him.

Natalya waited on the magnificent bed for an hour, but still he did not come. She was wearing the girlie pink panties Claude liked her in. She had to make it up to him. She just had to. How could she ruin everything at this stage, when she was in the home stretch? If she could make amends then she was still in with a chance of marrying the man. Yes, she was making modelling money now but that was negligible beside Claude's mountain-moving fortune.

Finally she heard the beep of the lift, signifying its arrival on the first floor, followed by heavy, lethargic steps coming towards the bedroom. Her throat was dry and her head throbbed with anxiety.

Claude stood for a moment in the arched doorway.

'I'm so sorry, Claude. I should not hef gone against your wishes. I will never do so again.'

Claude entered the room and sat heavily on the bed. Then he gathered Natalya in his arms and squeezed her body tightly. He closed his eyes and lowered his face to her neck. He inhaled deeply, breathing in her scent, his nostrils flaring as he did so. Then he kissed her neck and her cheek, her eyes and her nose and her mouth, all the while murmuring 'My dear, dear Natalya', over and over again. 'You are so dear to me. I am only making you do this so that you will understand what you have done.'

Natalya cried tears of relief. He loved her so. That's why he was possessive and controlling; because he loved her to the point of barbarity. And his work was so stressful – particularly now when he had just lost a chunk of money. Wasn't that what he'd said? But he'd make it all back on the Argentine deal. Claude was a genius and his talent was finance. All geniuses are crazy – capricious, fanatical – abnormal by their very definition.

'Promise you will never disobey me again?'

'I promise.'

And you will give up this … modelling?'

'I promise. Anything.'

They fell into horizontal positions on the bed, still entwined, and lay like that until Claude dozed off. At which point Natalya opened her eyes, removed his shoes and tucked him into bed before sliding herself back into his arms and falling into a troubled slumber.

\*\*\*\*

Down the road, Reza had just returned from a rare walk around the block. Shunning all of his cars, he had taken advantage of the crisp winter air to get some exercise and clear his head so that he could rethink some trading strategies. He decided to pick up a copy of the *FT* en route and have a read of his interview. On his way out of the late-night newsagent he passed a dirty-looking man selling *The Big Issue* and stopped to buy a copy. He tossed the man a £50 note.

'Keep the change,' he said.

'God bless you, sir. You're a good man.' The homeless vendor's mouth hung open as he watched Reza retreat into the distance.

****

'My name is Philip Avery Hampton and I'm here on a dual diagnosis: post-traumatic stress and severe depression. While here, I've learnt that depression is not something I'm naturally prone to, rather it's a direct result of a childhood trauma. I am anti-drugs of any kind, so, rather than treat my condition with prescription drugs, I've decided to try counselling for the first time in my life. I've been at Appletons for eight weeks now and am really starting to feel the beneficial effects of therapy.' He paused, waiting for the supportive clapping to die down.

'I've never been under any doubt that the death of my Greek mother when I was five has had a profound impact on the way I feel, even to this day, and that it has exacerbated the melancholy side to my character. I've never needed a therapist to tell me that. But what I did need, I suppose, was someone to talk about it with.'

'Thank you for your honesty, Philip,' the therapist soothed. 'We can all learn from each other through shared experiences, stories and recovery, that is the key purpose of group therapy. Tara, do you feel ready to share something of yourself with us today? We would love to draw you closer and strengthen you as your presence strengthens us.'

'I feel stronger already,' Tara replied, looking at Philip rather than the therapist. 'Philip's story has touched me, he drew me out of myself.'

'Great.' The therapist looked pleasantly surprised. 'Philip, would you like to tell us more? Or is anybody else inspired to share something of themselves with the group?' She looked at the other four patients who were still digesting Philip's history and shook their heads.

'If … if it helps Tara, then I'd like to say more.' Philip stood again, flushing.

'I was brought up in London, Oxfordshire and Athens by my English father, who remarried a remarkable English woman shortly after my mother's death. She looked after me. She brought me up as her own. She loves me as her own. She went on to have three more children with my father. They have … the same ruddy complexion and fly-away auburn hair as both my father and step-mother.' He smiled. 'It's beautiful.'

'Do you feel … different, Philip?' probed the therapist.

Philip considered the question for a long time. 'I feel very different. Not the same as those in my family, and not the same as those around me.'

Nobody spoke.

'Oh boohoo, get out the violins,' Philip laughed. 'I feel very silly now.'

'Don't be embarrassed, Philip. Your story is special to us.' The therapist's eyes kept flitting from his to Tara's.

'My father is often described as righteous and kind.' Philip pushed a wayward strand of long hair out of his face and looked through the window at the rolling green hills. 'He set an example to me of what a real man should be. He respects the past but he doesn't dwell on it. He's ensured that my family's farmland remains productive even today and he's bred world-class race horses. He has grown our family businesses to even greater heights and written five volumes of bestselling memoirs at the same time. He's a … a doer, not a talker. Our family is pretty well known, I guess you could say that. Well, not me, as I'm not into all that'– he looked bashful –'but you'll often see my half-siblings photographed in a variety of weird and wonderful outfits as they flit from launch party to society ball to fancy-dress gathering.' He half laughed, half winced.

Something clicked in Tara's brain: the Avery Hamptons. She remembered an article she'd read about them somewhere. It had been very rude about Philip – clearly he hadn't cooperated with the piece, probably finding the publication too silly for words. In fact, yes, it had reported that Philip had once said the party scene was 'as empty as the cupboards of my fashionably emaciated half-sister's kitchen.' It was due to his low profile, then, that Tara hadn't recognized him. She'd actually met his 'fashionably emaciated half-sister' on quite a few occasions.

# Chapter 26

The view across the Swiss slopes from the height of the ski lift was breathtaking. Abena was only a beginner but she hadn't thought twice before agreeing to join Bertrand, a seasoned skier, off piste. It was the only way to ensure none of her family would spot her.

This tranquil twenty minutes in the chairlift, enjoying the sunshine as they inched towards the mountain top, was the first time the illicit duo had managed to engineer some time together.

'Where's your wife?' Abena asked.

'Told her I'm here with clients. She's on St Barts with the kids.'

'Oh God, I keep forgetting about your kids,' Abena groaned.

'Sweetie, do just that, forget about them – they're my problem. Now, do you think anyone's ever had sex on a chairlift?'

'Hmmn … well, what with four layers of clothing to get through, libido-zapping thermal underwear, fibreglass feet and being suspended a gazillion metres above ground level, I would think you'd need some serious skill. It would be quite a lovely way to die though.'

Bertrand threw an arm around her shoulders and pulled her close, nearly knocking off her sleek Chanel goggles – pinched from Tara's wardrobe before she left. Abena may not have been skiing before, but she'd begged, borrowed or stolen all the gear and had perfected her ski-chic look long before she learnt to walk in the clunky ski boots. Repositioning her eyewear and smoothing down her fitted black ski suit, she leaned back in the chair, closed her eyes, and breathed in the lush air.

'I love it here. I'm absolutely dreading going back home,' she said. And then, 'B, when you first saw me, did you think I was just a vacuous, mercenary cow?'

'Oh, darling, we've been through this. Are you still talking about this Benedict fellow? I told you, first impressions are often completely deceiving and we're all mistakenly taken in by them. After all, everyone always thinks I'm a perfectly nice, uptight, well-behaved, old-fashioned English gentleman.'

'True.' Abena grinned. 'When really you're a devilishly hand-some, international man of mystery.'

'Quite.' Bertrand smirked.

They removed their protective helmets to kiss. It was an awe-some sensation at such a high altitude and Abena felt giddy. Then Bertrand pushed the bar up on the ski lift, grabbed her arm and pulled her whooping and shouting through the trees.

As Abena finally slid to a controlled stop at the bottom of the mountain she caught sight of her mother in the jam-packed restaurant nearby, balancing a giant serving of raclette on a paper plate as she tried to wade through the crowd in her unwieldy ski boots. She was clad in the highest-spec ski-wear despite having stayed well away from the slopes all day. Abena stifled a giggle. Her mother was the real reason the family rarely went skiing. She had a weakness for hearty West African specialities, especially pounded yam, and goat meat pepper soup, and over the years her waist had, slowly but undeniably, spread. Eventually the day came when she realized that if she tried to balance her entire bulk on two thin strips of fibreglass and then propel herself down a crowded mountain, there was little chance of her arriving at the bottom in one piece without having crushed a small child along the way.

Bertrand slid to a halt beside Abena and spotted her mother easily.

'Abena! Fancy seeing you here,' he grinned.

'Piss off, Bertrand,' she muttered in a panic. 'We're supposed to be meeting at your chalet!' But Bertrand was in a playful mood and wouldn't let up.

'Oh there you are, Abena, I was worried about you,' called her mother, stepping gingerly out of the restaurant and clutching at her husband as she tried not to slip. 'You've found a friend?' She looked suspiciously at Bertrand.

'Erm, Bertrand works with Sarah Hunter. We just ran into each other actually.'

'Well, come and have a drink with us, Bertrand.' Abena's father had been feeling outnumbered and was pleased to have some male company. Abena swallowed, eyes wide with fear. They moved on towards the bar and ordered a round of Glühwein.

'Do you have any children, Bertrand?' asked Abena's mother when they'd run out of conversation about how good the snow was.

'Yes, two girls.'

'How lovely, how old are they, do you have a photo?'

'Actually, yes. Yes I do. But I'm not sure it's, er, appropriate.' He saw Abena's parents exchange a concerned look and realized he

315

sounded like someone barred from public playgrounds.

'No, of course I'll show you if you'd like to see. They're five and seven.' He just had time to flash up two adorable kids on the screen of his phone when it began to ring. 'In fact that's probably them now.'

He put the phone to his ear, 'Hi poppet, can I call you back later? Oh does she? OK, put her on quickly.'

Abena could just make out a child singing 'Twinkle, Twinkle, Little Star' at the top of her shrill voice. She felt sick and ran to the washroom as fast as her cumbersome boots would let her. She would end this affair as soon as she got back to England.

On her return to the bar, Bertrand offered to get the bill before leaving, but was refused. He shook Abena's father's hand, kissed her mother on both cheeks, and then turned to Abena herself.

'Wonderful to bump into you. I do hope you enjoy the rest of your holiday.'

With that he was on his way.

'Well, he seemed perfectly nice,' Abena's mother announced. 'A little uptight maybe, but a true old-fashioned English gentleman.'

That evening after dinner, Abena met up with Bertrand at his chalet. An unconventional combination of pinewood and thatch on the outside, with gadgetry and glass inside, it was like stepping from a charmingly traditional Swiss cottage into a cosmopolitan Berlin penthouse. A real log fire blazed and enchanting arias filled the room, thanks to a discreetly placed Bang & Olufsen speaker system.

Abena and Bertrand lay facing each other on a fluffy rug by the fire. This time there were no layers of clothing to separate them. He traced the outline of her lips with his finger and then ran the

316

finger down the side of her body, bringing his hand to rest on her bottom. Abena stared at him, taking in his physique, neither soft and flabby nor hard and firm. The way he looked at her was a more powerful aphrodisiac than any vibrant youth's muscled stomach. She really felt truly, exquisitely beautiful and desired.

After some time had elapsed, Bertrand rolled Abena over to take in her back view. God she was marvellous. And she made him feel so very youthful. In fact, with such a pert young bottom in his hands, he could be back at Eton.

# Chapter 27

Tara snorted as yet another therapist explained the benefits of his particular session.

'As you know,' Dr Jacowski began, 'immersion in art encourages the true expression of our inner fears and hopes. I believe that even through the medium of A3 paper and felt-tip pen, each of my patients can come to know themselves and each other.'

Tara tried to catch Philip's eye so they could laugh together at the ridiculousness of the whole thing. After weeks of waiting they had finally been assigned as therapy partners for this session. But he was leaning forward in his chair, earnestly looking up at Dr Jacowski, so she decided to try and give the process a chance. She thought fondly of Abena; if she'd been here the two of them would be on the floor weeping with laughter by now. She couldn't help but yawn out loud. She hadn't slept soundly for three weeks and was suffering from chronic fatigue.

'Tired?' Philip asked, as soon as the therapist left the room in search of crayons. 'It must be tough coming off coke so suddenly like that. How are your withdrawal symptoms?'

Tara was touched by his sympathetic tone and considered milking her condition a little in the hope of maybe getting a hug, but there was something about the way his gaze penetrated her that made her unable to be anything but straight with him.

She reflected for a moment. 'It's been hard. Really, really hard. But, now … I feel I'm coping with it a bit better than I thought I would.'

'Really?'

'It's … it's strange,' Tara continued, 'I mean, the first two weeks were horrific, just awful, and I didn't sleep for a week, and I was … shaky … and nauseous – I mean physically sick quite a lot. Sorry, I know that's really unattractive! But now I suppose it's just combating the depression …' She didn't add that things got easier when she could dream about him as a diversion from the pain. And that now that she'd met him, life at the clinic gave her more hope of eventual happiness than anything waiting for her back in London.

'I know the feeling,' Philip replied.

'But you … I know I barely know you, but you seem so together and fulfilled and kind and … I'm sorry, I'm babbling, but you just don't come across as a depressive person.'

'Thank you! That's sweet, Tara. I suppose I try not to, and in fact when I've company, things aren't often so bad, it's more when I'm alone. And then I tend to become very introspective. And I bottle it up – my therapist says I don't talk about things when apparently I should. I need to socialize a bit more – loosen up!' He smiled at Tara and raised an eyebrow as if to say 'Well, here it is – this is who I am, I know I'm peculiar but I've bared my soul to you and you can take it or leave it.'

Tara tried not to stare at him but his face still took her breath away. Close up, rather than appearing more human than his almost unnaturally elegant profile, he seemed even more otherworldly to her.

'I love to talk.' Tara blushed at how stupid her words sounded. 'Talk to me whenever you need to.'

If Philip felt that she was silly, he didn't show it. His haunting eyes misted over and he squeezed Tara's hand.

'Thanks,' he whispered, his voice hoarse.

The therapist returned armed with a bunch of multi-coloured crayons. After explaining what to do, he poured three cups of green tea and settled down to his drawing. Tara couldn't help feeling like she was back at prep school, but she reluctantly reached for one of the coloured sheets of paper and a felt-tip pen and settled herself next to Philip, who was sprawled on the floor and scribbling intently. She observed him with undisguised interest for a good five minutes before starting on her own drawing, quietly cursing her father for having passed down to her his addictive personality rather than his remarkable artistic flair.

After half an hour, the trio stopped drawing and exchanged doodles. Dr Jacowski had managed to rustle up a quite outstanding picture of the clinic and the greenery that surrounded it. Tara had drawn an antique table in the dining room at Willowborough, and Philip had gone for a very abstract set of different coloured lines and overlapping circles. The three discussed the pictures for twenty minutes, without coming to any illuminating conclusions. Just when Tara was congratulating herself on her correct assumption that this was all bullshit, Dr Jacowski announced that that had just been a warm-up. Now that they'd had a chance to become acquainted with one another, they were to draw portraits – either a self-portrait or a portrait of each other. They had to sit at separate ends of the room, and without looking in a mirror, at photographs, or at each other, they must draw from memory.

Tara concentrated so hard she quite forgot to be sceptical. After the hour was up Dr Jacowski, who hadn't drawn anything himself this time around, asked Tara to talk them through her sketch first. She held up her self-portrait for all to see and grimaced as she heard both men gasp. Her portrait bore a strong resemblance to herself but it had been manipulated to become a massively distorted representation. Emerging from a scrawny neck that could have belonged to a chicken were not one, but two heads. One of the heads was a simply drawn but perfectly attractive sullen blonde with Tara's long, imposing nose and red mouth; the other was a grotesque, enlarged, pock-marked head with squinty, reddened eyes and greasy, lank hair sticking to its forehead. When nobody said anything, Tara took one more look at her portrait and burst into tears.

Dr Jacowski contemplated the sketch for several minutes, leaning right back in his chair and tilting his head at different angles. Eventually he said, 'Let us first see what Philip has come up with and then we'll discuss both drawings together.'

Tara was astounded when Philip produced his own drawing. Unable to meet her eyes, he gazed down at the floor in front of him while she gawped at the picture. Staring out from the large white sheet of paper was an extraordinarily lovely woman. She had the same blue eyes as Tara and the same red lips – plumped up to Angelina Jolie proportions. Her complexion had been smoothed out so that the pimples she was still plagued with, and which she covered painstakingly with concealer each day, were not apparent. But most striking about the picture was the expression that Philip had drawn on Tara's face. She was fun-loving and smiling, with a sparkle in her eyes that he had quite literally drawn in with a dash of gold pen. Tara's tears continued to flow through the laughter bubbling in her throat.

The session drew to a close and both patients made to leave for the next appointment on their strict timetables. Philip was only a couple of steps out of the door when he turned around.

'Tara?'

'Yes?' she replied, swivelling round instantly to face him.

'Would you like to come over and listen to some music before supper? I've really enjoyed talking to you.'

Tara nodded. 'Yes. Yes, I'd like that.' She bit her lip.

Philip's face reddened. 'Great, it's Room 31, Staircase 3. Shall we say … 7-ish?'

'That sounds perfect.'

For the rest of the afternoon Tara barely thought about cocaine, her mind full of Philip, and what she would say to him, and, most importantly, what she should wear. She fingered the two dazzling dresses she had with her but decided that they would be too much for going to somebody's room to hang out. Philip seemed shy so she didn't think it would turn into anything more than an intimate chat, and anyway, she herself wasn't up to anything more than that. But it was a very good start.

She picked up a pair of jeans she no longer liked – Abena must have confused them with her Notify pair. They were already extremely holey and thin so she ripped them further across each thigh. Stepping into what was now a pair of tiny denim hot pants, worn over a pair of grey woollen tights, she surveyed her reflection and noticed happily that all the enforced exercise and riding had given a bit of definition to her long, thin legs. She added a slouchy, duck-egg blue, long-sleeved T-shirt and a pair of chunky-heeled boots. Not bad, she thought, pleased with her enterprise. She did wish she had something a bit sexier though. Then she pulled off the T-shirt and removed her bra. Pulling the T-shirt back on, she checked that the outline of her breasts was visible and that her nipples could be made out through the material of the top, but that the effect was subtle and could pass for accidental. Perfect. She applied eyeliner and glossy pink lip gloss for the first time in months, then she reached for the chocolate brownies she'd baked herself. It was amazing how domestic one became when there were no drugs or alcohol available.

Checking her reflection one last time, she waltzed out into the corridor and towards Staircase 3. Out of the corner of her eye she could see Nurse Peterson watching her from the office at the end of the corridor.

Tara knocked firmly on the door of Room 31 and was gratified to see that Philip had also made an effort. He had changed since she'd last seen him and was now wearing a timeless classic: jeans, a light blue shirt and a very slim-fitting blazer.

'I like your blazer,'Tara blurted out immediately.

'Oh. Thanks, I er, had it cut extra slim, otherwise they tend to look too old-school and stuffy and … anyway, what the hell, you look amazing!'

'Thanks, it's just, well … I didn't really bring any of my nice stuff with me.'Tara blushed.'I made these earlier – do you want some?' She handed him the brownies.

'Oh, you're lovely!' Philip laughed and embraced her in a huge bear hug.'You'd make someone a fantastic wife,' he teased.

Tara's pulse was racing.'Well, you need somebody to look after you. Clearly.'

'Clearly?' Philip pulled away to look Tara in the eye but left his arms around her waist.

'Well, you said you've nobody to talk to about the things that matter to you … about your mother … your PhD, what you want to do with your life. I could talk about that kind of thing for ever. Come on – you already know about my dysfunctional family and dire job situation – it's your turn now!'

Philip released Tara from his embrace and led her into his living room, where he poured her a cup of tea. Schubert was playing softly in the background and the room was dim, lit only by candles he must have smuggled in.

'Sorry. I'm not trying to seduce you,' Philip grinned, 'I just think it's a bit more atmospheric like this. The bright light was far too harsh.'

'Yes, I know, my rooms are the same – sooo clinical.'

She looked around the room, noticing that, like her, Philip hadn't bothered to decorate it for such a short stay. There were a couple of photographs, though, which had been tossed irreverently to one corner of the floor. Tara picked them up and looked at them. In one she recognized his father and stepmother and three half-siblings. The other was a plain, mousy woman in her mid-thirties.

'Is that your natural mother?' Tara asked.

'No,' Philip threw his head back with an amused chuckle, 'that's my girlfriend, Diane.'

Tara dropped the photo, stricken. 'You haven't mentioned her before!'

'It never came up.' Philip shrugged.

'Is she quite a bit older than you?'

'Not really, well, a couple of years older, she's twenty-nine.'

'How long have you been seeing her?'

'Oh Christ, years now. We've grown up together – she might as well be my sister.' He rolled his eyes fondly. 'She's studying for her PhD too, but we met when we were first-year undergrads.'

The track came to an end so Philip switched over to some jazz and turned it up loud, sensing that the atmosphere needed to be lifted. Turning to Tara, he grabbed her hand.

'Come on let's dance.'

'What?'

Tara wrinkled her nose and looked at him as though he were mad, but he wouldn't give up. He reached for her other hand and pulled her up off the sofa, twirling her round and watching her spin across the room. With her emotions all over the place from countless penetrating therapy sessions, not to mention Philip's sudden revelation, Tara felt light-headed, almost as though she were drunk. She was overcome by an excruciating need for a fat, juicy, invigorating line of coke. As if in a daze, she wiggled half-heartedly to and fro in time to the music, utterly shocked by the horrifying discovery of Diane.

\*\*\*\*

Meanwhile, Tara's father was struggling with his own addiction. He picked up the empty litre bottle of vodka in front of him and threw it against the pristine white wall of the guest bedroom at his brother Rupert's house in Fulham. He'd been about to do it today. He'd finally summoned the strength to make his way to an Alcoholics Anonymous meeting as Tina had suggested. He'd agreed to go and see a doctor and get help from a local NHS clinic. He had thought that Tina would be happy about this; happy that he was finally doing something about it. But when he'd picked up the phone and called Willowborough there had been no answer. He'd stopped communicating effectively with Tina years ago, but he felt suddenly so alone and never more in need of her. So he tried her mobile. It rang, and rang, and rang, and he was about to hang up when a cold, male voice answered.

'Orlando speaking,' the voice barked.

'Oh. I see, well, is my wife there?' Hugo asked.

'She's bathing. Can I pass on a message, Lord Bridges?'

Hugo was sure he detected more than a hint of sarcasm in his voice. 'Tell her, tell her I … Oh never mind.' And he hung up.

He never did make it to that AA meeting. Instead he had shut himself in his room, and he had drunk a bottle of vodka. Now it was finished and he was incensed. Incensed at the way his life had turned out. He leaned out of the window and surveyed the tree-lined street. His brother had a happy marriage, a loving wife, children, money. He and Tina had only been able to have one child, and he had been a terrible father – concentrating all of his energy on drink and keeping Willowborough in the family. He'd probably neglected Tina too. It was no wonder she'd turned to Orlando.

He could fight his demons and get better. But for what? He was too old to get a decent job and provide his family with the comforts he should have given them decades ago. And anyway he had no family now, not really. Tina had as good as left him, and Tara-Bara was in real trouble. He'd messed her up so much. She'd probably be better off without him. He picked up his pen, took out a sheet of thick white paper and started to write a suicide note.

Reaching under the bed for his prescription painkillers, he tipped a large handful on to his palm and threw them into his open mouth, attempting to wash them down with some water. He promptly gagged and regurgitated the lot. He stood, anguished, and staggered to the kitchen, where he found the pestle and mortar and took it back to his room. Crushing the remaining contents of the jar, he poured the powdered painkiller into his glass of water and drank it down.

After half an hour Lord Bridges was sweating profusely and struggling to breathe. After one hour, with a final sudden jerk, he collapsed backwards on to the bed. Arms and legs spread, eyelids closed, mouth contorted in pain. His last thought was of Tara-Bara, eyes sparkling with mischief, dancing round Willowborough with Ferdy the Jack Russell in her arms.

# Chapter 28

Abena was glum as she hopped off the tube at Notting Hill. The flat seemed so empty without Tara in it, and she resolved once more that she must move out. She missed her friend desperately and felt so guilty over her affair with Bertrand that even he couldn't cheer her up. Work was miserable too; today she'd edited a 20,000-word document for Olympia only to be told she'd been given the wrong version and would have to do it again tomorrow. She left the station lost in thought – and ran smack into Sebastian, who was sauntering past on his way to a date at The Electric.

'Oh, hi.' Abena's hand flew automatically to her head and she smoothed down the tendrils of hair, all sweaty and dishevelled from the hot, sticky tube journey back from work. Sebastian, who never travelled anywhere by public transport, was perfectly put together in trainers, his beloved well-worn jeans, a white shirt with a tank top over it, and a jaunty leather bomber jacket that Abena hadn't seen before. He was tanned a deep caramel colour. God, he was sexy.

'Hi,' he replied, far calmer than she was, although Abena thought she could detect a hint of embarrassment. 'Great to see you! How's it going?'

'Yeah, yeah, good. Just yeah, work's the same – looking around elsewhere actually. Had a great break, went skiing. You?'

'Nice one,' he replied. 'Yeah, I'm not long back myself actually. We got that place in Punta del Este in the end, so we were all there for New Year's.'

Abena felt a stab of pain as she remembered how he'd invited her to see the year in in Uruguay with his family and him. Of course they'd broken up well before she'd had a chance to do that.

'How's Tara? he asked. 'Alex has been asking after her.'

'Oh really? She's not been doing too good actually, she's in rehab.'

'Shit, things get that bad? Where's she at?

'Appletons.'

'Oh yeah? They should be able to sort her out – easy.'

Abena was embarrassed to feel tears pricking at the back of her eyes. She said, too brightly, 'Yeah I spoke to her last night and things are looking OK for her. She'll be pleased to hear about Alex!' And then, still sounding far sunnier than she felt, 'Well, good to see you. I've got to dash as I've got a dinner to go to in a bit and I need to get home and change.'

'Yeah, yeah … you take care then. And let me know if you're having trouble finding something – jobwise. I can hook you up with one of Dad's mates if you like.'

'Yeah thanks, I think I'll be OK though. I've had quite a few offers – just trying to work out which one I should go for.'

Two lies in a row.

'Well, cool! See you around.'

Abena stood on tiptoes to kiss him on both cheeks and turned and hurried off before Sebastian could notice how shaken up she was.

Philip's course of treatment had finished some time ago and he'd been out of rehab for a month now. With Philip gone, Tara was fed up with rehab. She still sometimes craved drugs but felt that the worst was over and that she'd regained control. All the physical withdrawal symptoms that she had suffered from at first, including her aching back and sleepless nights, had disappeared. She was keen to go home to Willowborough. Of course she was sad not to return to her old life in Ladbroke Grove, but Abena had moved out, and besides she needed to be far away from her dealers and druggie friends in London. Yes, she thought, living at home in the country for a bit would be relaxing. She wouldn't need to work, and though she wasn't sure what state her parents' marriage was in right now, surely, as the returned prodigal daughter, she'd be fussed over and spoilt regardless. Her mother had said something about a slight mishap with her father ending up in hospital, but apparently it was nothing that Tara needed to worry about. Probably another case of gout. What a hypochondriac!

Checking her post, she beamed to see another small cream envelope with her name on it scrawled in Philip's idiosyncratic handwriting. It was always such a thrill to receive his elegant missives. She would read each letter again and again, and then spend an entire evening formulating her reply. His letters weren't flirtatious and Tara knew he was the faithful type and wouldn't dream of cheating on his girlfriend, but the way he wrote made it clear that he saw a deep connection between Tara and himself. He'd never spoken about his late mother with Diane in the way that he had spoken about her with Tara. Nor had he held Diane's hand and wiped away her tears and soothed her shakes when she was suffering, the way he had with her. Diane, from the little he'd told her, was very sensible. She'd never get herself into silly scrapes like Tara, she was more like Philip's father. She held herself together at all times, practical and unemotional. But Tara had sensed that he'd enjoyed helping her. It had drawn him out of his own sorrows and given him a sense of pride and strength and purpose, whereas Diane seemed to make him feel weak and dispensable.

In the privacy of her living room she devoured each word he'd written. He always told her she was beautiful, in every way possible. Tara suspected he had read too much into her grotesque self-portrait. But still it was nice to hear, and she was starting to believe it again. Even when she'd lost faith in herself, her friends had all stood by her and she felt so much renewed love, in particular for Abena and Natalya, without whom she'd probably be sleeping with some gross old man in return for coke. She took out her laptop and started working on her CV. When she got out, she was going to stop being such a brat, and get a job, and pay back everything she owed, and get all of her wonderful friends mind-blowing presents to apologize for months of ingratitude.

The next days passed torturously slowly, but they passed nonetheless, and at long last it was time for Tina to come and fetch Tara from the clinic. With so much time on her hands, Tara had spent her last days making petal-covered thank-you cards for her favourite therapists, who were all sad to see their most glamorous patient leave. Indeed, she was glamorous once more. Forced to attend supper every evening and surprised by the excellent quality of the food, she'd put a stone back on and was delighted to see her little breasts regain their perkiness, after months of having a chest like a ten-year-old boy's. She had seen a dermatologist at the clinic and her skin was back to normal; her bowel gangrene had subsided too. She knew she had caused some irreparable damage to her body, and she was well aware that any relapse would have severe consequences, but right now Tara felt like she could take on the world.

Tina jumped out of the Audi, followed by Hugo.

'Papa!'Tara exclaimed over the shoulder of her mother, who had buried her head in her daughter's chest and was hanging on for dear life.'I didn't think you'd be coming too. I half expected you to have moved out! What a treat. I've missed you both so much. Did you bring Lamb? And Ferdy?'

'Oh, darling,'Tina stood on tiptoes to kiss Tara's nose,'we've had such a terrible time without you. So much has happened. But your father and I have decided to give our marriage another chance.'

Tara stood, speechless, staring from one parent to another.

'Come on Tara-Bara, let's get you home and we'll explain everything.'

She didn't have a clue what had happened while she was away, but it must have been good if her parents were back together. Now all that she needed was for Philip's frumpy old bore of a girlfriend to disappear and everything would be perfect.

Once they arrived home, Tina poured everyone a glass of sparkling elderflower cordial. Having already sneaked a peek in the drinks cellar, Tara knew that all the alcohol had been cleared out of the house. Taking her cordial, she reacquainted herself with Willowborough's treasures: the intricate painting in the Great

Hall, her father's fun portraits of Lamb and Ferdy, the comforting warmth and smells of the Aga-heated kitchen. Inspecting her father's bedroom, she was pleased to see evidence that Tina had moved back in. She might be rehabilitated now, but she needed to know her father was too. She searched high and low for a secret stash of booze, knowing every possible hiding place as she'd used them all herself, and found not a drop of alcohol. Good. She was about to leave the room when she noticed a letter poking out of a sketchbook on the windowsill, clearly bearing her father's handwriting. She picked it up and read it.

Her father was on his way upstairs when he heard Tara's crystal glass hit the floor and shatter loudly into fragments.

'Tara-Bara is everything alright? What was that smashing sound?'

'Papa,' she sobbed, on her hands and knees with grief. 'You tried to kill yourself?'

Hugo went to hug her but she shrugged him off. Tina was not so easily shaken off. She held her daughter tight and refused to be pushed away. For the first time in her life Tina demanded the right to act like a mother. She held her daughter in the way she'd so desperately needed to be held all these years but was too proud, or too embarrassed, to ever ask for.

It soon emerged that events at home had been far more remarkable than those at the clinic. Tara learnt, with increasing incredulity, of how her father had ended up in A & E, saved just in time by his little niece, who'd skipped into his room to show him her picture and found him passed out and soaked in sweat. He had been put on a life-support machine and had very nearly died.

'Why didn't anyone let me know?' screamed Tara, furious.

'You had your own problems, darling. I was only thinking of you. And anyway, I knew he would live. And do you know how I knew that? Because at that moment, when I saw him there, on the life-support machine, I realised that I couldn't live without him. That I needed him, I needed him to live.'

Tina and Hugo exchanged looks of such unadulterated longing that if Tara hadn't still been struggling to take in the dreadful details she would have felt quite queasy.

'By the grace of God, your father pulled through, but it still wasn't over then. He started to hallucinate and experienced a fit of mini-seizures, which the doctors said were the symptoms of alcohol withdrawal. With the amount your father had been drinking, it was going to be dangerous for him to just stop immediately, so they kept him hospitalized for a few more weeks, gradually reducing his intake.'

'I only got out a week before you did,' Hugo cut in. 'And I'm sorry for not being there, for not helping you.'

'Papa, I'm sorry for not helping *you*!' Tara clasped her head as though it would burst open at any minute with the horror of what she was hearing.

'So,' Tina concluded, 'the struggle is not over for either of you yet, but we're all going to work together to help each other out. Firstly, none of us will drink alcohol in the house, or in front of your father. And I'm going to be attending AA meetings with him; you're welcome to come too while you're here, darling. And, most importantly, we're going to keep in touch!' A rueful smile played about her lips.

'It had got to the point where the three of us were leading completely separate lives, and it was only because of this, this neglect on all of our parts, that none of us realized the extent of everybody else's problems. So as of today I'm reinstating the Sunday Lunch rule.'

The Wittstanleys went to bed early that evening. Each of them had a lot to think about. Tara opened her diary and started a new month and a new chapter, which she called 'Hope'.

****

Sebastian Spectre sauntered over to his brother's apartment a few doors down from his own. Despite living so close, he hadn't seen Alex for a while. Probably too busy lady-killing, he thought. He'd just pop over and say hi, see if he wanted to go and grab a quick beer. He thought fleetingly of his encounter with Abena. She'd been looking super-hot. Even though he was seeing Jemima now, he'd been disappointed that Abena hadn't invited him in for a drink. They'd been practically outside her flat, and he missed her soft luxuriant skin and sinewy body.

He knocked on his brother's door.

'Come in – I left it open for you,' Alex called in a breathy voice. Clearly his brother was expecting company. He pushed open the door and whistled as he walked inside. The dining room table was set for a three-course meal for two, the lights were dimmed and a delicious scent emanated from the kitchen. Both brothers were foodies but they rarely got around to actually cooking. Alex was making a big effort for some lucky girl.

Taking a peek into the kitchen, Sebastian saw a leg of succulent-looking lamb roasting in the oven. In the fridge were two bottles of the rare vintage champagne that had gone missing from their father's wine cellar.

Laughing to himself, Sebastian made his way to Alex's room, expecting to find his brother arranging his hair in preparation for whichever beauty was on her way.

Hearing footsteps, Alex called out naughtily, 'Baby, I'm waiting! Come on in ...'

Sebastian suppressed a snigger and opened his brother's door, to be confronted with Alex sprawled unclothed across his bed, both hands behind his head, legs spread wide and a comely smile adorning his face.

'What the fuck?' both men spluttered in unison.

Alex grabbed a towel and wrapped it around his waist while Sebastian, now over the shock, bent double with uncontrollable laughter.

'Sorry, mate,' he laughed through his tears of mirth, 'were you expecting someone else?'

Jesus! If this was the way Alex got his 'highly sought after yet harrowingly elusive' reputation with the girls, then he was no longer remotely jealous. You'd never catch *him* doing anything so humiliating.

Suddenly Sebastian heard a sound that made the hairs on his neck stand on end.

'Cooeee! Baby, are you in there? I'm coming ...'

'W-wait!' Alex tried to protest, but it was too late.

Henry, Reza's gay assistant, was already in the bedroom. 'Yummy!' He licked his lips when he saw the back of a second man. 'You didn't tell me we'd be having company, Alex, you naughty thing!'

Sebastian spun round to face him. Henry! And, bloody hell, that was a bottle of Montrachet 1978 in his hand!

Then, as the scale of this seismic revelation hit him, Sebastian collapsed on to the floor by the bed. Alex hung his head, brow furrowed in anguish.

'Now,' Henry said, as calmly as if he were making a cup of tea before settling down to watch *EastEnders*, 'don't you tell me you've never imagined your brother might be gay?' He placed a hand gently on Alex's shoulder. 'Hellooo! Wake up and smell the skinny latte!' he shouted so loudly that everybody jumped.

'How long has this been going on?' Sebastian asked his brother.

'What? Gay? Or you mean Henry and I?'

'Well, I ... I ... both I suppose.'

'I've always known, Seb. But it's always just been so much easier to pretend. The girls were ... so easy. It was just like, I'd smile at them, and they'd fall at my feet! And I'd take them for the odd dinner, play with their breasts, or whatever. But mostly I'd just get us all pissed or high and we'd ... sleep. And then I got this ... reputation. And I was a god, and everyone wanted me and to know me and to hang with me – guys and girls – and yet nobody really knew me.'

Sebastian said nothing.

'I'm sorry.' Alex shrugged. 'Sorry for living a lie. For not telling you. But, but I'd never, you know, done it with boys either. Well, a little fumble at school—' He saw the distaste on his brother's face. 'Sorry! But you know, I'd never done anything ... serious, until I met Henry. And he made me face up to who I am, and be OK with it. I was going to tell you and Dad and Mum and everyone, I was just trying to work out how.'

After a few minutes, Sebastian got up and walked out of the apartment. Alex lay face down on his bed and sobbed into his pillow while Henry rubbed his back.

# Chapter 29

Natalya was running, savouring her new-found freedom. Finally another week of solitary confinement in Claude's house had come to an end. Her meals had been rationed this time too and once she'd even passed out because she was so hungry. When she came to, she couldn't immediately remember why they'd argued in the first place. Then it came back to her. It was a look, a glance she had given the director of a children's charity at a dinner he had held in honour of Claude, their main donor. She wasn't to look at men like that, to let her eyes meet theirs unnecessarily.

When they returned home from the charity dinner, Natalya had had to sit through a two-hour lecture from Claude on appropriate behaviour. 'It always happens like this!' Claude had hissed at her. 'You girls always start off sweet, grateful for the wonderful life I provide for you. But then you get used to it, take me for a fool, start to cast your loose eyes around at parties.'

Natalya knew she must never underestimate Claude's need to be in control. To never let anyone get one over on him. When Claude had started out in business, he had wanted to make $10 million. Then it became $100 million. Then $1 billion. There was always somebody richer for Claude to try and outshine – and there was always a hungry young chancer waiting to pounce if he messed up. He could never take his finger off the pulse. He must remain in control at all times.

Natalya ran through the historic streets of Mayfair and down to Piccadilly, past the Wolseley and the Ritz and then into the tranquil oasis of Green Park. Claude wanted her back in half an hour, but it felt wonderful to breathe some fresh air at last. She kept looking over her shoulder, jumping at every shadow. She could never quite feel free, even when she was alone. Amid the crowds of shoppers and tourists, she didn't notice the small Korean man training his long lens on her from inside his nondescript car. He took another photo before placing the camera in the glove compartment beside his loaded gun.

\*\*\*\*

Tara couldn't believe how quickly the weeks had flown by. It seemed ages ago now since she'd been at rehab, and so far she hadn't relapsed. Her father's condition had affected her more than she let on; it wasn't so much the alcohol, it was the overdose. As miserable and misunderstood as Tara had thought she was, the thought of losing her life was appalling. She didn't want to die, so the fact that her father had deemed life so hopeless that he was prepared, no, *willing*, to give it up had had an immensely sobering effect on her.

Lately, Tina had been the most loving and selfless wife and mother Tara had ever known her to be and, for her part, Tara was avoiding histrionics or confrontation of any kind. It was blissfully relaxing to be in the country and she so enjoyed riding through the lush Cotswold hills and spending time in the library reading books and magazines, even rediscovering some of her old texts from her English course at Oxford. But there was still something missing. She longed for Philip. His letters had dried up now and she assumed that, for him, their friendship had gone the way of all friendships made in such intense, artificial situations. The two of them had felt so intimately connected through their shared problems, but now that their issues had been resolved and they'd each returned to their normal lives, perhaps he couldn't even remember any more how close they'd been. But Tara remembered. She missed Philip every minute of every waking hour – and most of her sleeping hours too.

She tried desperately to forget him by getting stuck into her work. Abena had suggested Tara try to launch herself as a freelance fashion stylist, which would give her the freedom she needed as well as the chance to indulge her creative side. She had already started sending out emails to friends at magazines to let them know of her plans, and she was organizing a bunch of test shoots with model and photographer friends so she could create a portfolio to show prospective clients. She hoped Natalya would test for free. Now that she'd been booked for the Mirror Mirror campaign, Natalya was becoming quite a name. She wouldn't contact her just yet though. Not many people knew that Tara was already out of rehab and she wasn't quite ready for the inevitable flood of calls, which might tempt her to start partying again. When the time was right she would rejoin her old life.

\*\*\*\*

Simon Tamarand had reacted to the painful break-up with Sarah, the only woman he'd ever been in love with, in the only way he knew how: he threw himself into his routine. Like clockwork he was up at 6.45 every day, fitting in an hour at the gym before work. He found it invigorated him, and it gave him less time to torture himself with thoughts of Sarah. In addition to his tennis at the weekend he had started playing Sunday League football, and every Friday night without fail he went out drinking with the lads who worked in credit-control at his office.

The upside of this post-break-up routine was that his body was incredible. His torso was rock hard and his arms and back rippled. There was not a spare ounce of flesh on him, and this didn't go unnoticed on a lads' night out. Having been with Sarah for most of his adult life, he was both amazed and pleased at how easy he found it to pull.

This particular Friday evening was cold and gloomy, but Simon was excited, or as excited as he could get these days without Sarah in his life. The big boss had intimated only a few hours earlier that Simon was up for promotion very soon, but he just had to have a word with Simon's immediate superior, Dan, about the exact remuneration package. Consequently Simon was determined to try and impress Dan – a legendary drinker – when they went out that evening.

Simon hated the competitive point-scoring that often happened on their lads' nights out and was relieved when the suggestion that they play 'Rough-Girl Rodeo' – where the loser of a drinking game had to pull the ugliest girl in the club – was roundly rejected. Unfortunately for Simon, who had always felt strongly about the plight of sex workers, the alternative to 'RGR' was a trip to a lap-dancing club in Soho.

As they approached the club, hidden away in a side street, Simon wondered if it was too late to just turn around and go home. He felt horrible entering a place where girls titillated men for a living. He'd heard all the arguments, including the one that 'some of them really enjoy it', but he wasn't so sure. He felt that these must be desperate women and he, by paying to watch them, was an exploiter. But he was here now, and he didn't want to look like a loser in front of Dan, so he'd better get himself a drink and pretend to enjoy it.

Three beers later, Simon was starting to feel less guilty. After all, Sarah had liked making love, most of the time. And since Sarah, he'd done it with tons of girls who'd clearly wanted him. They had obviously enjoyed the sex immensely, so for these girls to be getting paid to turn him on was surely a bonus for them? Downing his fourth pint he nodded his head, absentmindedly confirming his thoughts. Yes, a bonus! Only now did he in fact allow himself a closer look at the girls. The blonde up on stage didn't really do it for him, she was too skinny.

But, wow! That brunette in the corner was something else. Clad in only a skimpy gold thong and high heels, her breasts completely bare, she noticed him looking at her and smiled, setting her tray of empty glasses down at the bar. Then she walked slowly over to him with long, deliberate strides. Simon was mesmerized by her dark hair tumbling down her back, her tiny waist and her astonishing, surgically enhanced breasts, which jutted out invitingly as she bent over him. As she whispered in his ear, her left nipple was just inches from his now watering mouth.

'My name's Cathy, I give private dances.'

She reached for his palm and pulled him towards a booth in the corner of the dingy bar. He followed her unquestioningly.

He sat down and looked up at her, holding his breath. His cock had long ago sprung to attention. She moved rhythmically and sensually – dancing had never been a strong point of Sarah's. She turned round and slowly inched down her golden thong, bending forward so that her round bottom was close enough to his face that he could almost lick it. And then, so cruelly, she shimmied back into her thong and announced she'd finished. Simon was so frustrated and turned on that he wanted to cry, or jump on her, but he could see a great big bouncer eyeing him suspiciously, or was it pitifully? Pulling out a wad of £20 notes, everything he had in his pocket, he gave it to her. Her face lit up at such generosity.

Cathy thanked him and wiggled off, dropping a bit of paper in his lap as she left. '£300 for the night, meet me outside Café Boheme', followed by her phone number.

Simon hurried out of the bar to Café Boheme. He saw her immediately and took her in his arms, kissing her before she had a chance to say anything. The only time he'd seen a prosti-tute was watching *Pretty Woman* with Sarah, and he seemed to remember that they had some rule that they didn't kiss clients. He'd been dying to kiss Cathy all evening. Bundling her into a taxi he breathed his address to the driver, his fingers already inside Cathy's thong. He wasn't sure if she was just a good actress but she seemed to fancy him like mad. He chose to believe it. After all, he had been by far the youngest guy in the bar and right now he had a body like Brad Pitt in *Fight Club*.

Simon soon got Cathy home and into his bed. The sex itself was frantic and short. No sooner had he withdrawn, spent, than he discarded his condom, paid her, and called a taxi. He just wanted her out. After she left he jumped into the shower and let the water rush over him for a long time, until it began to run cold over his body. Climbing into bed he fell into a restless sleep.

Simon had hoped he'd feel better in the morning, but he didn't. He'd never wanted Sarah's comforting body so much, but even if he ever did find a way to make it up to her for being so unreasonable the day they split up, she'd probably never forgive him for what he'd done last night. Oh gorgeous, loving Sarah. He wished he could turn back the clock.

\*\*\*\*

While Sarah's ex thought of her, she thought of Bertrand and Rory. That night on the boat now seemed an extraordinary dream. At the time she'd felt like a sexy, liberated, selfish bitch of a woman. Until then, she'd had only one lover and had not known that she could love like that, without being in love.

From the moment she'd met Bertrand he'd established himself as her elder, her superior and her protector. He'd become her professional mentor, and if the lines between pedagogy and passion had been temporarily blurred, all Sarah now wanted to do was restore the status quo and alleviate her guilt. She felt both ashamed at having drenched herself in the debauchery she and Si had once so vehemently disapproved of – and guilty when her thoughts repeatedly flashed back to the delicious image of Rory's tongue flicking her nipples. But mostly she just felt intensely sad at not having Si in her life any more. He may have behaved like a jealous, narrow-minded prig towards the end, making her choose between her work commitments – so what if 'work' happened to involve a glamorous Christmas party in St Tropez – and him, but she still loved him. She made her way pensively to work.

All eyes were on her when she arrived at Willy Eckhardt Productions that morning. Linda, the receptionist, tittered as she walked through the foyer. Gloria barely looked up at her when Sarah passed her desk, just turned a deep shade of red as she nodded hello before turning sharply away to gather her papers. Finally arriving at her own desk, Sarah saw with surprise that Willy was waiting beside it, looking unusually serious. She felt faint.

Willy must have somehow found out. What a humiliating way to lose one's job. And if she got the sack, how on earth was she going to pay her rent? She forced a smile.

'Morning, Willy, you're in bright and early today!'

'Do you have a minute, Sarah? I'd like to discuss something with you, if you'll pop into my office.'

'Sure. Sounds ominous.' She giggled, frantically.

'I think you can handle it,' was his reply. Not bothering to remove her coat or set her bag down at her desk, Sarah followed her boss to his office. Her notice period was supposed to be three months, but if she were sacked for 'misconduct', where would that leave her legally? Was it really misconduct? Oh goodness, of course it's misconduct; but professional misconduct? She was still weighing up the implications when she was jolted out of her reverie by Willy's outstretched hand.

'Congratulations!' he beamed.

Baffled, she smiled, unaware that she'd done anything worthy of commendation – rather the opposite she thought. It seemed like from the moment she'd bought her first designer dresses with

Tulip she had kick-started an escalating chain of seedy and exhilarating events.

Willy continued, 'Since bringing you on board, my life has been a whole lot easier.'

Sarah thought how she loved his upbeat twang and jaunty enthusiasm. 'Gosh. Thank you!'

'No. Thank *you*. You've been super efficient, super hard-working and have happily worked overtime without a single grumble – always a smile on your face. Come on, say it with me ...'

'Great minds smile alike!' chorused the two of them. Both grinning inanely.

'And people have absolutely *raved* about you. My clients love you, as do the press. Here – take a look at this.' He reached for a press cutting lying on his desk and read it aloud: 'Of course none of this would have been possible if it weren't for Sarah Hunter's hard work and dedication to this charitable cause. Sarah, stunning executive assistant to American actor-turned-music-mogul Willy Eckhardt, has worked tirelessly to ensure that victims of such tragic disasters have access to the financial and social support they need in the aftermath ...'

Sarah blushed and lowered her eyes.

'Sarah, what you've done is you've allowed me to pretty much ignore the day-to-day running of the production company so that I can concentrate on my other businesses and my own music. These other enterprises are now all at a stage where I can take them to the next level. Yes!' He clapped his hands together and pointed at Sarah. 'And to do this I'm going to need to devote even more of my energy and resources to them.'

Sarah still didn't quite see what Willy was getting at.

'So, what I'm saying, Sarah, is that I'd like to formally offer you a promotion to the position of Global Head of Communications for Willy Eckhardt Productions.'

Sarah paused to take in the news before audibly exhaling and resuming normal breathing patterns – she had held her breath for the entirety of Willy's declaration.

'Phew. I … I don't know what to say, I … I'm flattered, and, heavens, I'd love to accept, but won't Gloria feel that I'm stepping on her toes?'

'It was Gloria who put you forward for the job.'

'Oh wonderful!'

'And so I'd like to offer you a salary of £65,000 per annum, with a raise after six months, subject to appraisal. You'll also be getting your own personal assistant, and I'll sadly need to find a new assistant for myself. I think, actually, that overseeing the sourcing of the new staff will be your last project in your current role. The promotion will come into effect as soon as I've confirmed who'll replace me as MD of Willy Eckhardt Productions.'

The first thing Sarah did when she got home that evening was call Si. This new job would mean that she wouldn't have to work so closely with Willy and follow him around everywhere. If Si could only be made to see that he had nothing to be jealous of then maybe they could give their relationship another try. It was too much to hope that Si had used their break to let his hair down a little, be a bit more adventurous himself, but she knew him, he would find it in his heart to understand that she needed a bit more excitement in her life. The phone rang only once before he picked up.

'Hi,' he breathed.

He was met by silence.

'H-hi,' he repeated. 'Sarah is that you?'

'Oh, Si. It's so good to hear your voice.' She hugged the phone to her ear. Everything would be fine.

****

Abena was dreading dumping Bertrand. She'd been hoping to go for the gradual fizzle-out but he simply wouldn't stop calling and texting to tell her how much he wanted her, so, unfortunately, decisive action was called for.

Arriving at Bertrand's house, she saw him through the window, sitting at a table with the *FT* in one hand and a glass of whisky in the other. Mrs Brampton Amis was apparently away again. Did the woman even know what her husband looked like now? Abena made a mental note to 'See Husband' when she got married.

Bertrand rushed out of his house and paid the driver, then ushered Abena in ahead of him.

'Is everything OK, Bertrand? You look stressed.' Maybe now wasn't the right time for her news.

'Sit down, Abena. Drink? I have something to tell you.'

She shook her head. 'No thanks. What's the matter? Are you pregnant with my baby?'

They sat on opposite sides of the table and he held her hands.

'Abena, I'm afraid this has to stop.' And then, when she didn't answer. 'There's too much at stake. My career, my wife, my family, my … my reputation. Abena, I don't think I can leave my wife for you.'

'What?' she spluttered. 'B, you're interviewing me for a job I don't want.'

'Excuse me?' Bertrand sat up, in tense indignation.

'I never expected, nor wanted that.' Abena laughed, and felt relieved. 'You've been so kind to me, and I felt … felt that we sort of connected. But I know your situation, and I've always understood mine.'

Bertrand shook with the galling realization that a player had been played. He'd been a little divertissement for his fascinating mistress who, he guessed, was probably in love with a younger, fitter and quite possibly better-looking man.

'You're too good for the likes of Sebastian Spectre,' he sulked.

'Oh my Spectre days are well and truly over,' Abena said. 'My days of loving men who love themselves too much to have space for me are *finito*!'

She'd blurted that out as she thought it sounded good in a melodramatic, filmic kind of way, but as she said it, she looked at Bertrand and realized it was true. She got up, unburdened, now ready to leave Bertrand to his terrifying-looking wife and his next conquest.

Bertrand sat heavily on a chair, facing his former mistress, but couldn't bring himself to look her in the eye when he asked, 'It's been … fun, though, hasn't it? I mean, I … I really fancy you.'

Abena saw a man who'd once been beautiful but whose waist was starting to spread and whose hair had to be regularly dyed to erase the grey. She saw a man who had once been able to score on the strength of his looks alone, but who now had to call in the reserves – his breeding, his education, and his fortune – to get half the female attention he used to get. And she knew what to say.

'It's been wonderful.'

'Thank you,' Bertrand replied. 'I needed to hear you say that.'

# Chapter 30

'Baby, this came for you earlier.' Claude carried a small parcel into the master bedroom where Natalya was having a back massage, performed by her favourite masseuse, Ingrid. Much to Ingrid's annoyance, Natalya reached for the parcel mid-massage. It must have aroused Claude's suspicion if he was dealing with it personally. After all, they had staff for that.

'Well? Open it!' Claude snapped.

Ingrid cleared her throat before announcing, 'Natalya needs complete silence to fully enjoy the relaxing qualities of Swedish massage.'

A thick-set woman with a fierce demeanour, Ingrid had been a top women's rights campaigner in Stockholm before opting for a slower pace of life and becoming a masseuse. She could feel Natalya flinch every time Claude entered the room and she glared at him with a venom even more fervent than the combined outrage of the six thousand construction-company employees he'd made redundant that morning.

'No, it's OK Ingrid, I think we can finish up early today. Thenk you.'

'As you wish.' Ingrid pursed her lips and packed up her oils. She kissed Natalya goodbye, nodded curtly in Claude's direction and marched out of the room.

Claude immediately turned to Natalya and barked 'What is it?'

With trembling hands Natalya opened the parcel and was at first euphoric that the scrawled, childish handwriting and paper she'd come to dread was absent. But she quickly recognized, to her dismay, a new threat emerging. The parcel was wrapped in the chic Cartier packaging that had once given her such pleasure.

'What!' Claude dropped his voice to a whisper and brought his face close to hers. 'Somebody is sending you jewellery? You impertinent bitch. How many men do you need? One is not enough for you? No? Answer me?'

His face was white and the hand that gripped her chin was as cold as steel. Snatching up the compliment slip accompanying the Cartier box, he read aloud: 'To Natalya, Our favourite and most talented star, Love everybody at Moda Nova Models'.

'You see, it's not from a man, of course not. There is only you, Claude.'

Visibly calmer, and somewhat sheepish, Claude shrugged his shoulders and grudgingly conceded. 'Hmmn. You know what I think of this mindless modelling anyway.'

He turned on his heel and walked out of the house to where his driver was waiting.

'Sure, but that won't stop you boasting about your supermodel girlfriend at parties,' muttered Natalya to nobody in particular. She opened the parcel and pulled out a large special-edition Cartier watch. The very model she had dreamed of owning only a year ago. She contemplated it briefly, and then placed it in her wardrobe beside a similar one in a rare shade, which Claude had bought to match her favourite eye shadow.

The next minute her phone rang. Natalya checked that Claude had left and that there were no spying maids within earshot, then answered.

'Hello, Gaby. Thenk you for the watch. Very nice.'

'Natalya. Thank *you*. Kate's defection hasn't made even a dent in our bottom line thanks to your success. And now, what a coup! You've been chosen for one of the biggest campaigns of the year. Gucci want you for everything! You'll work exclusively for them in Milan for a season and you'll be fronting everything – the perfume, the sunglasses campaign, you'll be opening the shows. And it's a multi-million-pound contract, sweetie. Your first one.'

Natalya closed her eyes.

'Natalya, you still there?'

'It's not the money. It's just … to be wanted. I've never been wanted so much in my life.'

'Everybody wants you, baby. You're the best.'

'When do they need me in Milan?'

Gaby took a deep breath, and just hoped that her trickiest and most valuable girl wouldn't choose this moment to be difficult.

'They want you in Milan next week, but we wouldn't dream of putting you in a model apartment with the other girls, we've booked you into a suite at the Hotel Principe di Savoia for the next few months. Now, we know you wouldn't like to spend so much time away from Claude, so we're also arranging business-class flights back to London for you whenever you have at least two days free without any modelling assignments.'

'I don't think this will be necessary,' Natalya cut in.

'Now, now, honey,' Gaby cooed in the baby voice she used on

the more demanding models who let the attention get to their heads.'Don't tell me you don't want this contract.You know, it'll—'

'No. I will accept this contract. But I don't need the flights to London. I will enjoy a spell in a new city. And I would like to stay with the other models.'

In one moment everything was clear. She loathed her life in London, living in constant fear and repression. She wanted to escape. She felt almost giddy with relief and she wondered why the thought had never occurred to her before.

'Fantastic, darling, I'll have everything booked and forwarded to you in the next hour.'

'Very good. Goodbye.'

The decision was instant, total and unwavering. She knew, just *knew* it was right. Natalya stood and looked at her watch. She didn't have much time – Claude would be back in four hours.

Something had changed inside her over the last few months. She'd come so close to realizing her dream with Claude, only to discover that this dream was in fact a nightmare. What were untold riches compared with freedom? In Tara she'd seen how a person's reality could be altered by a single decision and by the courage to see it through. She had also seen that true happiness was only possible when one learnt to love oneself despite one's flaws. She had once viewed her own success in the modelling industry as an indicator of her worth as a person, and the constant setbacks had destroyed her confidence. Since her success with Blue Whisper, she'd come to understand that the key was in her, not in anything or anyone else. Sure, she wanted to enjoy the high life, and she still would – she was making money herself – but the real success was a new-found sense of worth that came from within.

Just as, at Appletons, Philip had helped to show Tara that she deserved to be loved but that it was up to her to save herself, the fashion industry had, in its warped way, shown Natalya that she too was utterly loveable.

She thought of Tara, out in the countryside, recovering well, she hoped. Although Natalya had considered hooking her up with her agent as a quirky Stella Tennant-style Brit model, she knew it would be better for Tara to stay out of London for the time being. She would miss her. She hoped they'd keep in touch.

Reaching into her jewellery cabinet, she pulled out boxes upon boxes of gifts, mostly from men, and the odd piece she had treated herself to. This was almost seven years' worth of jewels, with Claude's diamonds being the crowning glory. Scooping every-thing into a tote bag, she took a taxi to Hatton Garden and poured the whole lot out in front of a flabbergasted jeweller. After much deliberation he valued the entire collection at £1.2 million. Finger-ing the glimmering stones encrusted in a thin gold bracelet, she suspected the true worth was closer to £2 million, but she needed closure.

'I'll sell it all.'

Next stop was Claridge's, where she charmed a concierge into letting her hire their most sumptuous suite. From the comfort of her temporary dwelling, she called Claude's home and instructed Sylvie, one of the maids, to pack up her things and leave them in cases in the hallway. Lastly she called her mother to tell her of her recent modelling successes and to invite her and the boys to London for the week, before she set off for Milan.

'No, mother dear, do not protest,' Natalya urged into the phone. 'I know you are worried about letting the boys experience such opulence, but I'm going to buy you a nice home now, Mama. I have enough for all of us now.'

And so it was with both elation and fear that Natalya returned home that evening to announce to Claude that she was leaving him. Claude was standing in the hallway when she arrived. His eyes were narrowed, his arms crossed tightly over his chest, and his head hung low.

'What is all this? he asked.'

'I'm leafing you Claude.'

'Ha, ha!' Claude laughed, though his face was thunderous. 'I'll pretend you never said anything so ridiculous. Go and put on a dress – and put on some jewels. We have a dinner in Holland Park at nine.'

Natalya stared down at the shoes Claude had given her; the girlie ballet slippers he thought made her look her like a teenager.

'I'm serious. I'm leaving you. I'm moving to Milan. My flight is booked.'

She didn't look up at him. She couldn't. She bit her lip and waited for something. A cry of outrage. A blow maybe? But nothing came.

Slowly, she raised her head. Claude was surveying her meditatively but without betraying his emotions. This was his negotiating face. In the past he'd squeezed extra millions out of deals with this look, never revealing that while he pretended to contemplate the offer, coolly and at length, he was secretly terrified. It was the same face he'd worn when he'd staked most of his fortune on a particular deal, in a gamble that could have seen him lose his entire empire.

'And how do you suppose you'll support yourself without me?'

'I'll model.' Natalya stood up straight and looked him in the eye.

'Are you seeing somebody else?' Claude blinked slowly, though his expression remained impenetrable. 'You've changed. You are different. Somehow.'

'I hef nobody else, Claude. Thenk you for all you hef done for me, but I hef made my decision.'

'There are no second chances with me, Natalya. I am going to go and have a glass of wine, a good Romanée-Conti red. Then I will ask you again if you mean what you say. If you have managed to come to your senses I am prepared to dismiss what you have just said to me as a childish tantrum. If, however, you repeat what you have just told me, I will want you out of my home and I will not want to see your face again.' Claude turned and walked carefully towards the dining room.

When he returned, five minutes later, Natalya was standing in the same spot.

'Well, have you changed your mind?' he asked.

'I must go.'

'Get out.'

He stood in silence as Natalya ushered in the driver of the large taxi she had waiting outside, and instructed him to carry her things to the vehicle. Although she'd already asked Sylvie to donate twelve suitcases full of her clothes to charity, there was still a lot to move. All the while, Claude stood quietly, waiting until the last bag had been squeezed into the car. Natalya wasn't sure what the etiquette should be in this situation – after all, for all its brevity, she had lived with the man, and at one point had thought they might marry. She decided to kiss him goodbye. As she brushed

359

her mouth against his cheek he closed his eyes but remained silent until Natalya had retreated again and stepped out of the house. Before she could shut the door behind her, he called her name.

'Natalya.'

'Yes?' she whispered. For a second she thought he might say sorry.

Instead, he shook his head and said, 'I will miss you.'

When she left, Claude opened one of his safety deposit boxes and got out a wad of photographs, which he laid out methodically on a table. They were all of Natalya. There were a number of photographs of the girl out shopping. A fair few with that coked-up English whore. Even one of Natalya putting Hugo Bridges to bed. He picked up one of Natalya on the toilet and studied it. Then he held up the picture of her natural father and reached for his phone.

He might not be able to control her any more, but he could still hurt her.

\*\*\*\*

As April rolled over into May, Abena sat alone on Sarah's sofa. She flicked on the television. No, she didn't want to watch people locked in a house together. Gay refugee dating transsexual midget? Check. Bigoted homophobe? Check. Evangelical anti-capitalist freegan? Check. Head of Bank of America? Check. Violent woman-hating psycho? Check. His estranged ex-wife? Check. She turned off the TV. Funnily enough, the nuances of a relationship between, say, a schoolteacher and a nurse would probably be more interesting in the long run.

Sarah's flat was very quiet without the television. She switched it back on to ease the loneliness, got up and logged on to the internet to see if there were any nice apartments available to rent. She'd just found something promising, posted by a friend of a friend, when her mobile rang.

'Carey, hi, how's it going?'

'Hi, Abena. Yeah, good, good. Sorry to have been a bit out of touch but I've been wrapping up the last bits of post-production on the movie.'

The two chatted for a while, and then conversation moved back to film.

'So, are you still at that den of mediocrity?' Carey asked.

'What, Mallinder? Yep, 'fraid so. It's killing me.'

'I've decided to make *Vanity Fair*,' Carey said.

'No way!' Abena was stunned and didn't know what to say.

'Yes way! I spoke to some bigwigs, they love the idea, and much of it will be set, as you suggested, in the South of France. Abena, I'd like you to be involved in its production.'

'Wow! But, how?'

'Well, you could come on the publicity tour with my current film? We're about to head off for six months, starting with Cannes and then on to LA and New York, then Toronto, South Africa, the rest of Europe and finally back in the UK. And in the process we'll be starting to raise the funding for *Vanity Fair* and beginning on pre-production.'

'When are you heading off?' Abena was still utterly astonished. 'It … well, it sounds amazing. Almost too good to be true. So I'd be your sort of assistant? And would I be paid?'

'Well, you'd be working for, and employed by the studio, not me personally. And you wouldn't need to spend any money either

– flights, meals, hotel rooms, everything would be paid for.'

Abena tensed. 'But I'd get my own hotel room and everything, right?'

Carey's laughter reverberated down the phone. 'Of course you would; I'm not asking you as my date for Christ's sake! Look at it as a decently paid internship. I like you, Abena, you're good fun and you don't get star-struck around high-profile people. I'd be quite happy to have a smart girl like you around to help out. As I said, first stop is Cannes, so if you're on board I'll have somebody get in touch with you about it tomorrow.'

Abena was on her feet now and skipping around the room in exhilaration.

'Oh my God!' she screeched. 'I'll hand in my notice tomorrow – I can be in Cannes in two weeks. What have I got to lose?'

'You said it!' laughed Carey.

'I hate my job, I'm in between flats, I'm single and – oh fuck it – I'm just going to do it. How exciting!' Pausing, she added more soberly, 'I only wish Tara had someone to keep an eye on her. Her family situation is shaky to say the least.'

'Oh sure, but you're big girls now. You can't spend your life caring for Tara, it won't do either of you any favours. And besides, we're talking six months. And then who knows what trouble you'll get yourself into …'

'Oh thank you! Thank you! Thank you! I just don't know what to say. You're quite simply amazing.'

'Don't be silly. It's my pleasure and I'll enjoy having you around. I'll have someone call you about it tomorrow.'

'Speak tomorrow!' Abena nearly sang down the phone.

That night in bed Abena was so excited she couldn't sleep, her mind playing over the delicious moment when she would stride into Olympia's office and serve her with her notice. But by the time morning came, the euphoria of yesterday had subsided and a quiet uneasiness had grown in its place.

She couldn't fathom the uneasiness at first. She thought it might be the issue of leaving Tara behind, and yet she knew Carey was right and her friend's over-reliance on her would be bad for everybody. Perhaps it was her family? No, she was used to being away from them, and besides, like Tara, she knew they would always be in her life no matter what she did or where she went. It slowly dawned on her that the feeling she had was brought about by unfinished business.

It was Benedict. She had fallen for him. Plain and simple. She'd tried for months to dismiss him for superficial reasons. First it was his beard, then it was his job, then it was the fact that he'd lied when they first met. Now the prospect of losing touch with him for good forced her to face up to her feelings. How stupid she'd been. She had to tell him how she felt before she left. She knew she'd probably blown it the night of the Mallinder party, but she had to at least try. Maybe, just maybe, he'd still feel the same.

Two hours later Abena was staring at her phone, willing a little envelope icon to appear. She had tried Benedict's phone nine times with no luck – it must be switched off. Dammit! She had to see him! Suddenly she had a brainwave. Booting up her computer she logged on to Mallinder's offsite server and opened the contacts folder. Bingo! There was his address. She could drop by on her way to work – if she caught him unawares and woke him up he might be more likely to respond to her on impulse instead of being guarded or upset because of their last meeting. Thinking of what he must look like sleeping was making Abena melt; probably in his boxers, short hair messed up, those long eyelashes resting on his cheek. She must pull herself together and get going.

She raced out of the flat and jumped into a taxi – there was no time to mess about on the tube. The cab pulled up outside a town-house. She rang the doorbell to the ground-floor flat, adrenaline pulsing through her body. After a few minutes an unfamiliar man opened the front door and scowled in that unfriendly way that people in big cities do so well.

'Er, I'm so sorry to disturb you,' began Abena, 'I was looking for somebody called Benedict Lima.'

'The guy who lived here before has moved out. Sorry. Left a couple of weeks ago and didn't leave a forwarding address, think he moved abroad.'

He gave Abena a sympathetic smile and closed the door. He seemed less angry now, but that was no use to Abena.

Taking a few dejected steps away from Benedict's front door, Abena leaned against his wall and slowly slid down it until she was sitting on the pavement. She stayed there for a minute, slumped against the brickwork, looking straight ahead but seeing nothing. She didn't care that people walking past probably thought she was a beggar. Even the thought of a beggar wearing sample-sale Prada didn't make her laugh.

# Chapter 31

Hugo Wittstanley hung up the phone, his face white.

'Who was it? asked Tina.

'Just some foreigner,' said Hugo. 'Wrong number.' But his forehead was sweating as he left the room. He waited for Tina to start busying herself in her dressing room and checked that her Audi wasn't in the forecourt; Tara must have taken it into the village. The coast was clear. He took a final gulp from the bottle of vodka he had smuggled into the house and staggered to his studio. In a little room to the right his guns nestled in their cases. He walked towards the first case; slowly, as though he were in a dream. Calm now, he stretched out both arms to lift the case off the shelf. Pulling out the gleaming Purdey shotgun, he ran the back of his hand up and down its length, savouring the sensation as though it were the soft, warm skin of a woman's inner thigh. At length, he locked it back in its case and moved further down the shelving to where the handguns lay.

\*\*\*\*

Tara swept up the drive and parked in the huge forecourt. Built to accommodate hundreds of cars around the central fountain, it looked desolate with just her mother's Audi and her father's small classic car. Before climbing out of the driver's seat, Tara checked her reflection in the mirror and was pleased to see that her local hairdresser had done a good job of colouring her hair.

She let herself into the house and headed up to the calm of the library, with its deep, worn sofas, soft lighting and studious atmosphere. Settling into an armchair by the fireplace, with Lamb curled up by her feet, she opened the *Vogue* she had pinched from the salon and flipped through it. She could smell the aroma of the duck roasting in the Aga in the vast kitchen, now the sole domain of old Connie. Her stomach rumbled beneath her slouchy white cotton dress. Looking down, she wondered crossly what the point was of wearing such a cute dress when there was nobody around to see it. Perhaps it was time to start thinking about returning to London. As if on cue, the doorbell rang. Mildly curious, she set aside her *Vogue* and padded over to the window to see if she recognized the car in the forecourt.

Parked beside Tina's Audi was a black, two-seater Porsche, which looked brand new. The top was down and she could just make out a number of books strewn across the passenger seat. Well, she didn't know anyone with a brand-new Porsche. It must be one of her mother's friends.

A breathless Tina burst into the library.

'There's a young man at the door. Says he's come to see you!' she gasped.

'Well who is he?' Tara frowned. If it was Harry or some other ex she'd tried to get rid of then he had a cheek turning up unannounced at her door.

'I don't know, darling, but he claimed to be a friend of yours. He's awfully good-looking!'

'Really?' Tara's tone was indifferent, but a hand shot instinctively to her newly highlighted hair and tousled it a fraction.

When she saw him standing in the huge panelled hallway, deep in conversation with Connie, she stopped dead.

'Philip!' she cried out, jumping into his arms and hugging him. 'What are you doing here? I can't believe it's you! I wouldn't have thought you'd be a Porsche driver!'

'Sorry,' he grinned, 'but they're so well constructed. I'm a bit of an engineering geek! How are you, my angel?'

Tara wrapped her arms around Philip's neck and clung on as if her life depended on it. She could have stayed there forever but Tina was loitering with intent, eager for an introduction.

'Oh, this is my mother,' she told Philip. And then, turning to her mother, 'I met Philip at Appletons.'

'You must invite poor Philip in for a drink, darling. All that driving – he'll be exhausted,' Tina purred, beaming at her daughter's enthralling new friend.

'Why don't we go for a drive?' Tara asked Philip. The last thing she needed was her mother buzzing around while they talked. 'Sure,' he replied. 'Where shall we go? How about I drive and you navigate?'

'That sounds like a perfect partnership.' Tara mussed up her hair again as she waved goodbye to her mother and beckoned Philip towards the door.

Philip gathered up all the books on the passenger seat and threw them into the boot before opening the door for Tara to climb in. Instead of driving off he turned to face her.

'I'm so sorry for just turning up like this, it's just, well, I wanted to surprise you. And I wanted to talk to you, but face to face, and, I was desperate to see you.'

'Oh God, me too! You're the only one who really knows what I'm going through.'

Philip put his arms around her waist and pulled her towards him. 'I know, I know,' he murmured into the top of her head, brushing her hair with his lips.'

'Where's Diane?'

'She met somebody else while I was in the clinic. Said I'd never loved her, that she was just a habit of mine.'

'I'm sorry.' Tara *was* sorry; she didn't want to be just a shoulder to cry on.

'Don't be sorry.'

'Why?'

'Because she was right. I thought I loved her. But then I met you.'

'And how have I changed things?' Her voice quivered and was barely audible.

'It sounds … silly … but now I know what love truly is. I love you.'

Tara said nothing for a while, savouring the sound of those words.

'I love you too. I've loved you from the very beginning, as soon as I heard you speak at group therapy.'

She kissed him and then pulled away. 'But I'm … I'm too silly for you.' She looked sad.

'Teach me to be silly, Tara. I love you. I love everything about you. I love your mind, I love your body, I love your heart and your soul. I love you.'

They kissed again, and this time she didn't pull away.

When she finally tore herself from his arms, Tara glanced up at the enormous house and revelled in the romance of the setting. Then she caught sight of her mother peering out from the library window, sobbing into a handkerchief. Realizing she'd been spotted, Tina lifted the hanky from her face and waved it high above her head, so Tara could see that she was smiling broadly though her tears.

Then she nearly jumped out of her skin with shock as an ear-splitting sound rang through the air.

\*\*\*\*

'Please go faster!' Natalya urged the harassed taxi driver. She squeezed her mother's hand tighter and tried to fight back the terrified tears threatening to reappear.

'I'm so sorry.' Daina's whisper was almost inaudible. This was not the kind of excitement she'd been expecting of her trip to London.

Finally the taxi careered up the winding drive, past some outhouses, and screamed to a halt outside Willowborough Hall. Flinging £300 towards the driver, Natalya jumped out of the back seat followed closely by her mother, breathing hard as she struggled to keep up. Natalya rang the doorbell countless times but nobody emerged to answer it, so she grabbed her mother's arm and ran around the side of the house, where the doors to Hugo's studio were flung open. Both mother and daughter screamed.

Slumped on the floor was Hugo Wittstanley. A small black

handgun lay two metres away from him on the ground. An old lady was kneeling beside him, frantically pumping his chest. In the background Tara held her mother tight, the two silent, stricken, as they watched the pale unmoving figure on the ground. The only noise came from a young man standing with his back to the room, one hand clutching his long and dishevelled dark hair in anguish as he spoke into his telephone:

'Ambulance, please. You must come at once!'

'It's too late!' Natalya wailed.

But no sooner had the words left her mouth than Hugo started to murmur incoherently.

'He's not dead!' Natalya exclaimed, mouth open in disbelief.

'Wh-wh-what are *you* doing here?' Tara was shocked and confused. 'My ... my father was just about to shoot himself when he passed out cold from drinking a whole bottle of vodka.' Tara held up the empty bottle for Natalya and Daina to see. 'He pulled the trigger just as he collapsed and shot a hole right through the wall.'

'Oh my God!' Natalya cried. She turned to her mother and a long look passed between them.

'We need to talk,' she announced to Tara. But this was no time for talking. The ambulance was screeching up the driveway, blue lights flashing, and all hands were needed to tend to Hugo.

It wasn't until that evening that the incongruous gathering was able to reconvene in the library in a calmer state of mind. Hugo was also present, having been considered fit enough to return home from the hospital within the same day.

'OK now, Natalya darling, will you please explain why you and your mother are at Willowborough and why Papa looks like he's

370

seen a ghost?' demanded Tara.

'It's *my* duty to explain,' Hugo said, to Natalya more than anybody else in the room. 'What I'm about to tell you will probably result in your despising me for the rest of your life, and it is the reason I chose to try to end mine. Tara, Tina, I should have told you years ago. Natalya Ozolin is my daughter.'

Tara gasped and made to speak. Tina seemed stunned into silence.

'Please let me finish.' Hugo held up one hand. 'I never thought for a minute, all those years ago, that the woman I spent three blissful days with on an art research trip in the former Soviet Union would end up giving birth to my child. And when Daina wrote to me – her 'darling Stan' – all those years ago, to inform me that I had a daughter, a beautiful baby called Natalya, I hated her for threatening what I had gone on to build at home. By then I had a young wife with whom I was infatuated and a baby girl of our own: Tara. I didn't ever imagine, Natalya, that circumstances would one day cause your path to cross with Tara's. I thought I could deny you. Forget about you. Exorcize you from my life. And so it was that I, in my selfishness and inexcusable deceitfulness, decided to disown my own child.'

Natalya was openly sobbing now, while Tara, seemingly in a daze, patted her shoulder ineffectually. Hugo drew in a deep breath.

'I wrote back to your mother, Natalya, and denied knowing her. I wrote that the child was not mine and would never receive love, money or fathering from me. I told Daina, in no uncertain terms, that neither she nor her baby were ever to contact me again, and that if she did there would be dreadful consequences.'

371

Hugo met Daina's eyes, ashamed. He expected to see hatred etched on her face, but her expression was one of understanding. She nodded, gently, and Hugo went on, turning to Natalya and opening his hands in a gesture of surrender.

'That was the last I heard from Daina. And then you arrived. You arrived in London and your presence threatened to expose the coward that I am. What could I do? I panicked, and I bombarded you with hateful and frightening letters. I wanted you gone – I hoped to frighten you away. But you were so good, and so b-b-brave, that you stood your ground.' Hugo began to weep. 'Not only that, you were also drawn to your half-sister, and through sheer kindness, and with no other agenda, you saved her from herself.'

Hugo took another deep breath and composed his face.

'Natalya, I am so desperately sorry. All I can do is offer my heartfelt apology, but to think that that is enough would be an insult to you, a failure to acknowledge the gravity of what I did.'

'I also must some blame take,' Daina said in her faltering English.

'What!' Natalya cried. 'He tricked you! Bullied you into sleeping with him.'

'He tell me it is love, yes, and that he would make wife from me, to live together here. I was frighten, yes, but also happy, and because I did not know what love, I give him my body.'

'I was out of line,' Hugo shouted. 'A monster. I led you astray, lied to you, pressured you. And then all these years I gave you nothing. Nothing, Daina! Absolutely nothing!'

Daina smiled. 'You give me greatest gift of all. You give me Natalya.'

Natalya wrapped her arms around her mother, crying into her neck. She looked up at Hugo, her father. She remembered the cruelty in Claude's voice when he had called her at the hotel.

'I know who your daddy is,' he'd said, and Natalya had frozen. 'But he won't be your daddy for much longer. I would say that right now he is opening his gun case ... Think of the mess he has made.'

Natalya had screamed down the phone at him until finally he had said, in little more than a whisper: 'His name is Hugo Wittstanley. I believe you know him.' Although Natalya didn't know how she felt about Hugo, what she wanted from him, she realized now that she didn't want him to die.

'Hugo,' she said, 'I understand now thet you sent those letters because you were desperate, because you love Tara, as I do. But I don't believe you would ever actually hef tried to harm me physically.'

'No,' Hugo sobbed. 'As soon as I saw you I knew you were mine, and I felt a deep bond with you.'

'At times I wanted you dead,' Natalya said, 'But I could never hef tried to kill you. Only you did that, twice. In the end you hef punished yourself more than anyone else possibly could.'

Finally Tina shook herself out of her stupor. Taking Natalya's hands in hers, she said, 'This is a shock for all of us. But let us look at the good that has come from the bad. You have been a rock for my daughter through her life-threatening drug dependency. Your generosity saved her life. Hugo's infidelity was so long ago, and perhaps I must take some blame that he was unable to confide in me, so that he went to such terrible lengths to prevent us from knowing.'

'No—'Hugo cried.

'I feel I've gained a daughter in you, Natalya,'Tina sobbed. 'And you have gained a father and a sister.'

Tara was still in a state of numb disbelief, but she too spoke up.

'Papa, I really thought you were dead. To be honest, the news that you and Daina had it away in Latvia is actually a slight improvement. And now I have a sister to gang up on you with.'

Hugo gave a wan smile. Tara and Natalya hugged each other tight, burying their faces in each other's necks. Tara looked up at Philip, who was beaming at her proudly. She felt blessed to have them both in her life. She was determined to shower her new sister with all the affection she'd missed out on from their father.

Tina insisted that Daina send for the rest of her children, who were waiting in London at Claridge's, and that they all spend a few days at Willowborough before flying out to Milan with Natalya. Philip was also invited to stay, and he happily accepted. Tara couldn't believe he was unfazed by the day's lurid events. If he could cope with this, then there was nothing he'd be unable to deal with. Nothing could be worse than this. The thought made Tara incredibly happy.

# Chapter 32

Days later, a small group gathered at Gatwick Airport to see Abena off on her worldwide publicity and pre-production tour for *Vanity Fair*. She'd spent the last few days at home with her family and now it was time to say goodbye to the girls. She'd been in a bit of a daze since she'd learnt that Benedict had moved away, but had resolved that this trip was just what she needed to take her mind off him. Looking relaxed but radiant in cream skinny jeans, chunky burgundy high heels and three tight T-shirts layered over each other, with a classic trench thrown on over the top, she kissed Simon on both cheeks before taking Sarah in her arms and hugging her.

'Good luck with the new role, hon, I'm sure you'll do amazingly. You're a press and production hotshot now.'

Sarah laughed. 'Well, have an unbelievable time, and then, when you come back, let's take over the world together.'

Turning to Philip, Abena told him how happy she was that he and Tara had found each other.

Lastly she turned to Tara – for all her flaws, the best friend she'd ever had – and wrapped her into a long hug. Tara kissed her friend, partner in crime for so long, and they exchanged knowing smirks.

'Have fun,' they said simultaneously.

The sight of the customs officers and x-ray machines soon shook Abena back to reality. As it hit home that she would never have to enter the Mallinder offices again, and that a brand new life experience lay just a few short hours away, she was overcome with an uncontrollable wave of nervous excitement. Exactly this time last year she and Tara had been on their way to St Tropez and she'd had the same intense, expectant feeling – only now it was ten times stronger. She looked up at a gigantic billboard on the airport terminal wall and winked at Natalya's beaming face, peering out from behind a bottle of Blue Whisper. She thought of the extraordinary events at Willowborough, the heartbreak that had accompanied Natalya her whole life, and of the new beginning they could all now look to. Smiling, she exited the gate and boarded the aircraft.

Lolling in her seat near the front of the plane, Abena fiddled with her seatbelt as her fellow passengers filed past – an assortment of slick City types, chic French women and harassed Brits with screeching children. And then, suddenly, a familiar figure emerged. She could see his soulful eyes clearly, and although he looked tired and a little drawn, he was perfect. She'd longed for this moment incessantly, yet now that it was upon her she was at an absolute loss.

As Benedict's gaze finally alighted on Abena she surprised them both by starting to cry. She had rehearsed this moment many times, and tears had certainly never been part of the equation, but she was overwhelmed with relief and happiness. Benedict raced down the aisle towards her, stopping only to help an elderly lady who was struggling with her luggage. Abena laughed through her tears – even at a time like this he was thinking of others. Finally he flung himself into the empty seat beside Abena; his seat.

'Abena!' he cried. 'I can't believe it! You're working on *Vanity Fair* too? Oh don't cry, please don't cry!'

He wanted desperately to hug her, but remembering their last encounter he hesitated. Abena solved the dilemma by throwing herself into his arms.

'I thought you'd gone back to LA or something! I … I went to your flat and they said you'd moved abroad …'

'What were you at my apartment for? I thought you wanted nothing to do with me because, well, because you seemed so shocked when I kissed you and then we had that stupid row which by the way was completely—'

'It doesn't matter,' Abena half sobbed, half laughed. 'You're here now. I'm here now.'

'But then I called you and left you missed calls and … Oh God, your baby nephew must have got hold of your phone again—'

'What?'

'And then I didn't think you wanted to see me, and then Carey asked me to do this thing, and my rental contract was ending on my house anyway … So I spent a couple of weeks in LA before coming back to pick up a couple of things and get my flight out from here.'

Ben cupped her head gently in his two hands and kissed her. She kissed him back. It was the most tender kiss of her life.

'It's amazing,' she said, 'every time I meet you, you reveal another side to you … I just, I can't wait to get to know you … And yet I feel like I know you better than anybody else in the world.'

'Abena, in some ways I don't know you at all, but I know that

I love you.'

'I love you too, Ben. I think I was doomed ever since we listened to Bob Dylan that rainy day in Bristol.'

'Oh, honey! I found you gorgeous the very first time I saw you. But I became your slave the first time we kissed.'

'So what are you saying? That I loved you before you loved me?' They kissed again. The plane took off and soared into the sky, but these two were already high on life and the promise it held for them.

# *Epilogue*

The wrap party for *Vanity Fair* was held in St Tropez. Carey Wallace had employed all the best people to work on his blockbuster and now they were all gathered at *Sin*.

Bertrand Brampton Amis had provided a large chunk of the film's funding, and he was in the mood to party. Scheherazade, the winner of *Britain's Next Musical Megastar*, had recorded much of the film's soundtrack, and as she sang her first hit single, 'Today's the Day', Bertrand started up a dance-off with Benedict Lima and Simon Tamarand. Abena, giggling helplessly as the three men posed and wiggled on the revolving dance-floor, judged the competition and rewarded the victorious Benedict with a kiss. Willy, Sarah and Si and the rest of Willy's team had flown out for the party.

Abena was already in France, where she had been holidaying with Benedict at George Clooney's beach house. She had taken an especially keen interest in the casting of the film and had arranged for Natalya to make a cameo appearance as a mysterious beauty. Abena was thrilled when, during filming, Natalya and Jake Jendar, the hot male lead had fallen for each other; these days, the celeb magazines just couldn't get enough of the gorgeous couple. Tara had also blagged a job on the film, as assistant costume supervisor, and had made a grand entrance to the party in a vintage Valentino cocktail dress that she'd 'borrowed' from the wardrobe department, complementing Philip, handsome in heirloom white tie, as if they were made for each other. Tara had invited her parents to the party too, so they could meet all her new friends in the film world, but Lord and Lady Bridges were too busy enjoying the romance of their Cotswolds home with Lamb and Ferdy, tons of sparkling elderflower cordial, and of course each other.

Reza had left the organization of the wrap party to Henry, who, as usual, had done a superb job. And he had his own reasons to celebrate. Now officially Henry Spectre, he had taken Alex's name following their civil partnership ceremony at Claridge's last month. Sebastian had appointed himself maid of honour and bought his brother an engraved Rolex to show him how sorry he was for his earlier behaviour. Even Reza was in the mood to make amends – he'd been forced to forgive Sebastian for ruining his launch because, in reality, he would do whatever Henry wanted, and Henry wanted his husband's family at the party.

'Two years later, and here we are again!' Abena sat sipping champagne on the deck of *Sin* with Tara, Natalya and Sarah. The sun glinted off the solid gold bar and the four friends couldn't have been happier.

Tara watched as a familiar pale figure pleaded to be let on to the boat. She poked her head over the side and smiled down at the rock star Dan Donahue.

'Hi,' he called up, 'I know you!'

'No,' Tara replied, 'I don't think you do.' She rejoined the girls and took a long sip of champagne.

# ACKNOWLEDGEMENTS

This book was immense fun to write. Thank you to everyone who helped inspire it – rest assured I won't name and shame you all!

Thank you also to my delightful agent, Sallyanne Sweeney, my fantastic editor and now friend, Laura Palmer, and to Rina Gill and all the brilliant people at Corvus.

All of my friends have been wonderfully supportive, so I am sorry for many undoubted omissions. The following people have offered particularly useful advice, jokes, tips, support and encouragement, or just exceptional friendship while I was writing *Sin Tropez*:

Jenny Bacon, Candice Baseden, Paddy Docherty, Roley Finer, Laura Fraser, Mark Kent, Nura Khan, Nicholas Lezard, Ella Lister, Miles Morland, Faridah Nabaale, Amy Nelson, Katie Prescott, Leonie Schneider, David Wildridge, and a dear friend departed, Jessica MacKenzie.

Finally, I'd like to thank my family: my mother, father and two sisters, Enida and Natasha. Your unwavering love and encouragement means more than I can say.